The Promise

John S. Hofmann

© 2017 John S. Hofmann
All rights reserved.

ISBN: 1546558659
ISBN 13: 9781546558651

Dedication

Being able to have this book brought to life could not have been accomplished without the support of my wife, Elaine, and daughter, Michelle. They were very instrumental in helping me to put together this second book in a series of three.

A special thanks goes out to good friends Jeri, and Collette for their input as well. I wish to personally extend to them my sincerest appreciation for the encouragement and kind words they extended to me.

Chapters

The Home Coming	1
Windows Rattled	12
I Think She Likes Tuna	33
A Little Boy's Dream	45
Forgiving Yourself	50
Will Sing for Food	60
This is Going to Sound Dumb	73
Oysters and Crackers	85
A Waste of Skin	93
Very Sensitive Kids	103
I Just Can't Do This	111
Learning The Job	157
Now I Understand	175
Cutting the Ribbon	185
The Words Guy	212
The Yokes on Me	233
The Singing Italian	249
Handshake as Our Bond	262
Now Take a Deep Breath	270
What If	290
Wrapped In Red	303
Heads I Win Tails You Lose	310
I Want to Fire Her	322
Do You Like Ice Cream	337
Grand Opening	354

Field of White	369
For the Love of Mothers	384
Miracle in Song	397
The Bouquet	412
Facing the Bills	416

The Home Coming

Melissa paced back and forth by the front window as Susan, Melissa's mother, and Edith watched her from the kitchen table. Both women looked at each other and smiled.

"She reminds me of when she was a little girl waiting for the ice cream truck to ring its bells," Susan said. "You could see the excitement in her eyes then, too."

"That's how it was when Greg was small. Kids will always be kids, I suppose," Edith said, reminiscing about her son as well. "She'll probably have a path worn in my carpeting if she keeps it up."

Their husbands, Frank and Kenneth, sat on the couch in the front room enjoying a cup of coffee. Every time Melissa walked by them the men would glance at the other, nodding their heads slightly.

"He should have been here by now," Melissa stated impatiently as she looked out the front window again. "I've waited so long for this day."

"So have I," Edith said.

"I think we all have," chimed in Susan.

"You're right," Kenneth said.

Frank nodded his agreement as he looked over at his wife, Edith, and smiled.

"Maybe he got hung up in traffic or is just enjoying the summer weather," suggested Frank.

"Or maybe he forgot you were waiting for him," offered Kenneth with a sly smile on his face.

"That's not even funny, Dad. I've waited so long for this day to come, and now that it's here, it's just dragging."

Greg's car quickly pulled into his usual parking spot making an abrupt stop. This caused a little cloud of dirt to be kicked up by the braking tires. The honking of his car horn sent Melissa scurrying through the front door. Everyone followed her as fast as they could. Melissa ran into Greg's waiting arms giving him a large kiss.

"I've missed you so much," Melissa said, as she held onto him tightly.

"It's so wonderful to finally hold you in my arms again."

Everyone surrounded the young couple as they hugged and kissed Greg, all happy to welcome him home from the army.

"It's so good seeing everyone. I missed you all so much, but Melissa just a little bit more. Sorry Mom and Dad."

"There's no need to explain, we all understand," declared Edith.

"We missed you, too, Greg," Frank said.

"We all did," Susan added.

"Welcome home, Greg," Kenneth said, as he gave him another large hug. "We've all been waiting for this day to arrive."

"Thank you everyone, and it's nice to be home."

The group made their way back into the house, some taking seats in the front room.

"There's so much to tell everyone, I really don't know where to start," Greg said.

"A very wise woman once told me to start at the very beginning, and I found that's the best advice to follow," Kenneth said. He squeezed Susan's hand. She smiled at him knowing that he was referring to her.

Susan thought back to the very first night they met the Wilsons, Edith and Frank. What a horrible set of circumstance brought them to their house. While Kenneth and Susan were welcomed with outstretched arms into the home, the news Kenneth brought was very hurtful and harsh for them to hear... let alone comprehend. Kenneth didn't know exactly where to start with his story to them that night. "Start at the very beginning," Susan had told him. Kenneth remembered those words of mine, she thought. Susan turned and smiled at him as she squeezed his hand once again.

"Well, they really wanted me to extend my military service."

"But you didn't; right?" Melissa inquired quickly.

"You're home for good now, aren't you, Greg?" Edith said, showing a little more than just motherly concern or fear on her face.

"Well, they always say they're looking for good men," Frank offered.

"Hush, Frank," Edith said quickly, wanting to hear his answer.

"The thought did run through my mind, —"

The room fell into complete silence.

"— but then I was tired of missing the three most beautiful women in my life. So I said, 'thank you, but no thank you.' "

Edith reached for her customary box of tissue as she let out a sigh.

"You scared me half to death, Greg," Melissa said.

"And me as well," Edith added.

"Well, Kenneth and I are so glad you're home for good, we both missed you so much," Susan said, as she placed her hand on Greg's shoulder.

"My plane got delayed so I got messed up somewhat, and that's why I'm late. Maybe they forgot to put enough air in the tires, I don't know, but we were delayed a little while on the ground."

"But you got home safely, and that's all that's really important to all of us," Melissa said.

"Would everyone mind waiting here for a minute, I want to get something from my bag in the trunk. I'll be back in just a minute or two."

"Here, let us get it for you," Frank offered.

"I'll give you a hand, Frank," Kenneth said.

"No, that's okay, gentlemen, I'm kind of used to carrying it. I'll be back in just a second. Mom, can I have a cup of coffee, please?"

"Let me get it, I'd like to do that," Melissa said.

"Thank you, Honey," Edith said as she nodded her head.

Greg walked through the front door and out to his car. He opened the trunk pausing for just a moment or two before he lifted his heavy duffle bag from its interior. He stood there for a few seconds, his mind deep in thought. Greg flung it over his shoulder and returned to the inside of the home. He set the bag down beside the front closet door;

then took a seat. Melissa brought him his cup of coffee and placed it on a small table beside him.

"Thank you."

"You're welcome," she answered as she reached down and softly rubbed the back of his neck. She then smiled at him before taking a seat nearby. Every once in a while he took a sip of his coffee, though not engaging in any conversations which were taking place. Everyone couldn't help but notice that Greg seemed to be contemplating something since he sat quietly for some time now.

"Honey," Melissa inquired, "are you a little tired from your trip, you seem a little quiet or distracted?"

Greg didn't offer any reply to her. He sat for another few seconds before standing up and looking around at the group before him.

"Isn't it funny how in your mind you know things are going to present themselves in a certain way, and then when it happens it's completely at odds with what you thought it would be? You make plans, and then in a flash you change them, sometimes for the better, and sometimes they're not. That's how it was for me. I was going down a road in my life quite happily, or at least so I thought... and then I met you, Melissa, and a whole new wonderful world appeared before my very eyes."

Everyone's attention was now on Greg. They all knew he had something important he wanted to convey, at least his voice reflected that fact along with the words he was expressing.

"Melissa, I met you a little over a year and a half ago. You've changed my life completely, and so much for the better. I can't imagine it any differently now. During the time I was home on leave, the days we spent together, they all seemed to rapidly disappear. When I returned to my duties I held those memories of you very close to my heart. I've missed you so much.

Melissa, your daily letters meant the world to me. They gave me the strength I needed to help me through the difficult times I faced without you."

Melissa, Edith, and Susan's eyes all began to water as Greg spoke. Edith handed her tissue box over to Susan. She took a couple just as Edith had done earlier.

"While I was away I made many different plans on how I would ask you the most important question of my life, where we would be, what I should say. Yet, after running those thoughts through my mind over and over, I came to the same conclusion. It really doesn't matter where you ask the question, as long as your love is strong and binding in nature."

Frank and Kenneth knew in their hearts what Greg was trying to say. They also understood neither one of them could have done a better job of it than what Greg was doing now. They looked at each other and smiled.

"I had planned on taking you to the beautiful site beside the creek to ask you this question, a place where we once sat and talked so long together. The skating pond was also a very special place, our first kiss. Then it occurred to me when I just went out to the car, wouldn't it be wonderful to have everyone who loves us so much, our families, to have them present when I asked you to be my wife."

"Oh, Honey, I will," Melissa said, as she jumped to her feet.

"But I'm not done yet," he said.

Everyone but Melissa and Greg chuckled. Melissa quickly put her hands to her face, a little embarrassed at having jumped the gun.

"Well, though you haven't really asked me formally, you always said you wanted me to be your wife. I just thought you — Oh, never mind, I'm sorry. Go ahead."

"Now that we all know she's going to say yes, let's get it done so I can give both of you a big hug and kiss," Edith said.

"I want to hear what else he has to say," Susan stated, "he's doing such a wonderful job of it."

The men looked at each other and nodded their agreement, both wanting to hear what else Greg had to say.

"We do, too," Frank said.

"Yes," Kenneth added.

"Okay," Greg said as he took a deeper breath. "Melissa, my life is so much better with you than I would have ever imagined it could be." Greg knelt down on one knee.

Edith wiped her eyes as she handed Susan some more tissues from her ever-present box on the table. Both women removed tears from their faces.

"Melissa, will you do me the honor of becoming my wife?"

Tears ran down Melissa's cheeks as she looked at Greg kneeling before her. His left hand cradled a small black velvet box. The top was flipped open revealing a beautiful diamond ring.

"It's so beautiful, Greg, I just love it."

Greg's smiled as he looked up.

Melissa pulled the ring from the box and handed it to Greg as he stood up. He then placed it upon her ring finger.

"So now you can answer me," Greg chuckled.

"Yes, I do, I will, of course I will," Melissa said as she hugged and kissed Greg.

Melissa turned and held her hand out with her fingers spread slightly showing it to everyone as she admired it herself.

"Congratulations, Greg... Honey," Kenneth said as he hugged Melissa and shook Greg's hand. He then turned and shook Frank's hand as well. "Now that was well worth the trip here today," he said.

"Congratulations, son," Frank said. "And if I'm not mistaken you're supposed to wish the bride to be — hum," he said, "those words escape me right now so I think I'll just simply say, welcome to our family. Melissa, you've made me a very proud father-in-law to be."

Melissa and Frank embraced as they smiled.

The mothers both grabbed the young couple at the same time squeezing them strongly.

"So, Melissa, what are you thinking of for a date?" Susan inquired.

"Yes, we've got plans to make, Susan," Edith added. "She's going to need all the help she can get."

"And we'll both be there for you, Honey, so don't worry about a thing," Susan said. "Now, Edith, what colors are you thinking of?"

"Mom! I just got the ring," Melissa exclaimed.

"That's okay, Edith and I make a great team." Susan said, "We'll be there for both of you."

Those few words alone said more about the relationship between the two mothers than anyone could have ever imagined. Since their first meeting in Frank and Edith's home, the friendship the families shared grew stronger with each passing day. Though it began under extremely rocky circumstances the two families were able to make peace with each other. It was the beginning of an enduring friendship between the parents. Greg's mother and father loved Melissa as if she were their very own. Susan would joke how Edith and her must have been separated when they were little babies in the hospital. Their minds ran like two sets of railroad tracks placed side by side. It was as if they knew what the other was thinking.

Though the two women were like night and day in appearance they possessed an unmistakable kinship that was obvious for all to see. Susan looked very much the part of a successful businessman's wife while Edith's appearance was that of the housewife and homemaker. This contrast, though only one in many between the women, made absolutely no difference to either one of them. They loved each other.

Kenneth, Melissa's father, relished the time he spent with Frank as well. As the two men got to know each other, both were amazed at how close some of their interests were. If you met either one separately, you never would have imagined their close relationship was even possible. Coming from such diverse backgrounds, the harmony they enjoyed and shared was quite evident.

Whether it was simply looking through an automobile magazine, discussing engine sizes, or even the quality of a car's interior, it didn't matter. They both enjoyed expressing their thoughts to one another, and hearing the other's point of view. It was, nevertheless, vintage automobiles that stimulated their conversations frequently. To both, however, this was just one facet of interests they had in common.

With the arrival of warmer weather one year, Frank casually mentioned to Kenneth that fishing season would soon be arriving. Much to Frank's astonishment Kenneth presented him with a smile as big and wide as an old Buick's grill. He loved fly fishing, too, whether for bass or trout, it didn't matter at all to him what the species was. Both men agreed that catch and release was their favorite way of fishing, after all, it was just for the fun of the sport. The two spent hours talking about dry flies, wet flies, feather streamers, each learning from the other. On more than one occasion Kenneth would sneak off from the store to catch up with Frank along the shoreline of a creek.

"So Greg, what were you thinking about as far as a time table?" Susan asked.

"Well, I was planning on leaving that entirely up to Melissa. I kind of thought that was the bride's choice to make. I personally wouldn't care if we did it this afternoon with a Justice of the Peace."

"You're joking now; aren't you?" inquired Melissa in a serious voice.

"Of course," was Greg's quick response after seeing the looks on all the women's faces. "Yeah, I was just joking."

"Smart answer, son," Frank said.

Kenneth chuckled to himself.

"Well, Honey," Susan said, "Edith and I won't be intrusive, but we would enjoy it very much if we can play a part in any plans you'll be making. Am I right, Edith?"

"Yes, you are."

"Well," Melissa said, "I can't imagine making any plans without both of you being a very important part of it."

"So who do you think will be your best man?" asked Kenneth.

"Well, I haven't given it any thought but I can only think of one person that would fit the bill, and that would be my best friend, Dan," Greg said. "I would also want Stanley to be included as a groomsman."

"Oh, Greg, do you think you can talk him into letting us have Karen as a flower girl, she's just so adorable," suggested Melissa.

"And what about your Maid of Honor?" inquired Susan.

"It's got to be Kate without question," Melissa said in excitement. "And you know what, I just have to have Kim as a bridesmaid. I wouldn't want to get married without Kate and Kim being a part of it, they mean so much to me." Melissa paused as she nodded her head affirming her thinking. "Without either one of them playing a very important part in our wedding, I just wouldn't feel right."

"And Kate will be so happy," Susan said.

"And Kim as well," added Edith.

The remainder of the morning was spent with three women huddled around a kitchen table laughing and smiling. On the table a large pad of paper laid before them with various lists started on it. Each woman made suggestions to the other. There was a large variety of topics discussed, dates, colors, flowers, possible reception halls, just to start with.

The men sat in the living room chatting. The question came up between them as to when they were going to be fed. Viewing the busy ladies in the kitchen they finally concluded it would be a good idea if they simply placed an order for some pizza. With the doorbell ringing, announcing the pizza's arrival, the women looked up. The men informed the ladies they had, "made lunch" and that it was ready to eat. However, the women asked them to fix a plate for each of them as they had their hands full and couldn't be disturbed now. The three men sat once again alone in the front room talking as they ate their lunch.

"Gentlemen," Kenneth announced, "this is one of the happiest days I've ever seen Susan and Melissa experience, it's just so obvious by their faces."

"And Edith as well," Frank added.

"Say Dad, —" Greg said.

"What?" both men answered in stereo.

Greg laughed along with the men.

"It is so nice to have two dads. I know I've used that description for a long time now, but it means all the world to me. I just wanted both of you to know what's in my heart."

"We're both very lucky; aren't we, Frank?" Kenneth said. "I'm so glad you let me address you as son even before the two of you became engaged. I feel very honored by your words, Greg."

Frank nodded his head.

"You're very welcome. Say, do you think I'll have any say as far as the wedding goes?" Greg inquired.

"You got to pick the best man; didn't you, be happy with that," laughed Frank.

Overhearing Frank mention the best man, Melissa thought of Kate as her Maid of Honor once again.

"I have a wonderful idea," she said in a somewhat excited loud voice. "Honey, if Kate's my Maid of Honor, do you think Henry would sing at our wedding?"

"Personally I can't think of anyone better," Greg answered.

"Who's Henry?" asked Susan.

"Melissa," Greg quickly said, "let her wait and see."

"Good idea, Honey, they can all wait and see. I'll give Kate a call in a minute. Oh, heck, I'll do it right now. I'm just so excited about everything. Can I use your phone, Mom?"

"You don't need to ask, we're all family here," Edith replied.

Melissa picked up the phone and called Kate. Susan and Edith sat looking at the lists the three women had started to compile. They could overhear Melissa as she talked to Kate on the other end of the line. They looked at each other smiling as Melissa said, "I'm just so excited. I've got both of my moms here and everything is falling into place beautifully. Thank you, I knew you would be so happy for me." She hung up the phone.

Susan reached over to Edith's shoulder and placed her hand on it to get her attention.

"What would you think if we all went dress shopping together one day. I value your opinion so much."

"Oh, I'd be happy to," Edith answered.

"So we're all set," Melissa stated smiling. "Kate is my Maid of Honor, and Henry will sing."

"Oh, was he there at her house?" asked Edith.

"No, but Kate said she would see to it he did. She figures he and Doc can sit together during the reception."

With the mention of a singer being brought to the women's attention, it opened up a whole new line of discussion. What songs should be sung at the wedding, DJ or band, and then there was the food.

"I just love doing this," expressed Edith.

"We all do," Susan said.

"And Moms," Melissa said emphasizing the word, 'Moms' with a little laugh, "I want both of you to know how thankful I am for your help. I just know it's going to be a wonderful wedding for all of us."

Both women reached across the table taking Melissa's hands in theirs and gave them a squeeze.

Windows Rattled

Henry put the finishing touches on his car. He thought to himself, she's a little older every year but boy she's dependable. Just look at the way she gleams in the sunshine. He began to roll the water hose up to be returned to its regular position by the basement window. A car pulled into Henry's driveway as he picked up a plastic bucket and started walking to the garage. Oh, it's Kate, he thought.

"How are you, Honey?" she asked.

"Fine. I was over earlier this morning to see Emma. Did you happen to call while I was gone? I've been out here washing the car, too."

"No, but I got a call from Melissa."

"Oh, is she in town?"

"Not only her, but her mother and father. They came to see Greg, he got home today."

"That's great news. I've always liked him, he's just such a likeable guy. I can't say as I felt that way about Melissa when I first met her, but she's sure changed my mind about her. They sure do make a nice couple."

"I'm going to be her Maid of Honor," announced Kate proudly, a large smile written across her face.

"Maid of what?"

"Honor, silly."

"Oh, for who?"

"Melissa."

"So they're getting married? I wondered when that was going to happen. Wait a minute, if you're the Maid of Honor, who am I going to sit with?"

"How about alone on a piano or organ bench by yourself."

"What!"

"Melissa wants to know if you'll play the piano and sing at their wedding. I told her you would. Now, I know you're probably mad at me for telling her that, but she's my best friend and Henry... please."

Henry slowly shook his head back and forth as he thought to himself, she knows I can never say no to her.

"Honey?" Kate said in a timid voice.

"I'll be happy to," he said in a somewhat mild disgusting voice.

"Thank you. I knew you'd do that for me... I just knew it. That's another reason I love you so much."

"Because I do what you want?"

"No," Kate said emphatically, "it's because I know you're always there for me, and I love that so much about you."

Henry smiled.

"Henry, what are your plans for dinner tonight, if any?"

"Well, I was actually thinking about a little honey and —"

"You're kidding; right?" Kate said. Not really expecting an answer, she continued, "I put a nice roast beef in the oven earlier and Grandpa and I need your help doing a magic trick with it."

"And what magic trick would that be?" he asked.

"The three of us are going to make it disappear. I also put your favorite red skins in along with some carrots. I'm going to head home now and set the table."

"Well, let me finish up here, clean up a little, and I'll meet you at Doc's."

"Okay, that sounds great." Kate gave Henry a little kiss on the cheek. "You know, Sweetheart, it still takes me back a little bit when I kiss you and there's no beard. You'd think I'd be used to it by now."

Henry nodded, a small smile on his lips.

Kate returned to her car and headed home, waving as she pulled away. Henry finished putting his cleaning materials away and went into the house. After a quick shower he got dressed. He grabbed his wallet and keys as he walked to his car to head over to Doc's home.

Henry reached down and pushed a button on the unit setting the CD player into motion. The background music started playing. He cleared his throat and began singing. Henry had quite a large selection of music to choose from. Buying different background arrangements on CDs to accompany his voice was something he enjoyed spending his money on. For the sake of a few dollars his car carried the equivalent of his own private orchestra, which fulfilled his every musical request.

As Henry drove towards Doc's house, the sound of a horrific explosion shook him, as well as his vehicle to the core. Heavy smoke filled the air just under a block ahead of him, and slightly off to his right. Henry pressed down on the accelerator as he headed in the direction of the smoke. Pulling up to what once was a large two-story home he looked at a large pile of smoking debris and rubbish scattered about. Sections of the building still standing appeared to be nothing more than a skeleton of itself. Small and large fires were burning everywhere. Getting quickly out of his car he ran toward the home looking for survivors. The area was so thick with smoke, he began choking from the contaminated air. Henry took his shirt off. He wrapped it over his mouth using the sleeves to tie it around the back of his head. Henry made his way closer to the home searching for injured individuals, listening intently for any hint of cries for help as he did. Henry's skin began to take on a darkness as soot and airborne dirt started to cling to his sweaty body.

A crying child's voice could be heard from what had been the back of the house. Henry carefully made his way over the tangled remains of the building, trying to get to the child as quickly as possible. He faintly heard the sound of sirens. Off to his left side, splintered boards, piping and roofing were twisted and piled. Henry thought to himself, that's where the child's voice is coming from.

Getting to the area, he bent down and grabbed a large chunk of rubbish, throwing it to the side. Nails ripped his hands, some digging in deeply as he sought to find the little child. Splinters from wood dug at his hands and legs as he adjusted his stance. Pain and nausea began to take over Henry's body, but still he persisted in his quest. Pulling up a heavy portion of roofing, he spotted a woman's arm wrapped over what appeared to be a small child's body. In Henry's mind the woman was either dead or just unconscious. Either way, she was definitely in need of immediate medical attention. Henry could observe blood on the woman's arm. He carefully removed the final portion of trash and attempted to free the woman from her prison of rubble. Finally he succeeded. He lifted the woman up with one arm, and the small child with his other. The child's voice could no longer be heard. He staggered back and forth from the uneven load in his arms. Henry pressed forward towards the street, the woman's legs dragging on the ground as they moved together. Just a few more feet, he thought, and I can get them to the edge of the lot.

Henry heard a voice from beside him. "We'll take it from here, buddy, thank you." Henry turned to see various firemen and emergency individuals coming to his aid. He released his grip on the two victims as they were taken from him by several rescue personnel who began caring for them immediately. Henry could observe them attempting to get the youngster breathing again, as others worked on the woman. Turning he made his way out to the sidewalk stumbling as he walked, coughing and choking as he did. It was the last thing he remembered.

Kate stood fussing over the roast she had just removed from the oven. The potatoes were placed in a glass covered bowl to keep them warm. She smiled to herself as she thought over the wonderful news she had received earlier from Melissa. It's going to be a beautiful wedding, she thought, I just know it.

"Grandpa, are you coming downstairs pretty soon? I've got the food just about ready, and Henry should be here shortly."

"I'll be down in a just a second," he answered.

Doc came walking down the steps just as the sound of a large explosion caused the windows on the home to rattle. Kate and Doc looked at each other stunned.

"What on earth was that?" Kate asked.

"I don't know," Doc answered, "but I wouldn't be surprised to get a call pretty soon."

They both quickly made their way over to the front windows and peered out, but neither saw anything out of the ordinary. Doc shook his head as he looked over at Kate. She looked back at him shaking her head as well. Doc shrugged his shoulders. What had happened, what it could or couldn't be, neither one really had any clue to offer the other. Not very long afterwards the phone rang at Doc's house. Kate walked over and picked up the phone.

"Hello," answered Kate. "It's for you, Grandpa, it's the hospital."

"That comes as no surprise," he said as he took the phone from Kate. "Hello. I'll be right there," he said as he hung the phone up. "Kate grab your purse, we need to go to the hospital right away, it's Henry."

"Oh, Grandpa!" Kate said as she held her breath. "Is he all right?"

"That's what we're going to find out."

Doc and Kate got into the car and drove quickly to the hospital with Doc pulling into a physician's parking spot. Kate followed him into the hospital. Going into the emergency section Doc saw the on-call physician coming towards him.

"Doc," he said, "we've got two casualties coming in right now, a woman and a small child. They weren't breathing when EMS got to them, but they're breathing now. They radioed they're within a block or so from arriving. There's another victim, Henry. We expect him to be here shortly. I could sure use your help on this."

Doc instructed a nurse, "Call Dr. Peters in, we can use his expertise as a pediatrician, and tell him to kick it in the butt on his way over here!"

"You bet I will," the nurse said nodding her head. As she reached for the phone, two casually dressed doctors rushed into the emergency room.

"We heard the explosion and saw the smoke from the restaurant, we thought you might need some help."

"Great!" Doc was quick to state. "Thanks guys."

The men nodded their heads as they quickly went to change.

"Kate, take a seat in the waiting room and I'll get back to you as quickly as I can. I need to get ready to help Dr. Ellis and the others right now."

Kate nodded her head as she turned and headed to the waiting room. The last time she had been there was when Emma suffered her mild heart attack. The room brought back vivid memories of that day. Kate's emotions were in a complete and utter shamble. She sat down and began to sob.

Everything was in place awaiting the first victim's arrival, which occurred within the span of a few seconds. Their care was immediately addressed. The breathing concerns were checked first. With Henry arriving shortly thereafter, Doc could only give an occasional glance over to see Dr. Ellis attending to him. Doc, however, mainly kept his attention focused on the mother's injuries. Fortunately for her, broken bones were the main issues of contention, her left arm and leg especially. Cuts and abrasions covered various portions of the woman and child alike. After the little girl and mother's injuries were addressed, both were moved from the emergency room and admitted to the hospital.

"Just so you know, Doc," Dr. Ellis said as he looked up, "his breathing is a concern, and he seems to be going in and out of consciousness, but it appears Henry is going to be okay. I'll get some tests setup to run on him, then I'll give you a fuller evaluation. I can't find anything else wrong with him other than cuts, puncture wounds and such."

"Thanks, Jack," Doc said, as he nodded his head.

Once Doc was free he went immediately to the waiting room to confer with Kate.

"Grandpa, is Henry going to be okay?" she said, as she wiped her eyes.

"Let's go see him together."

"Grandpa, is he okay!"

"I think he's going to be fine... eventually. He's in and out of consciousness, I want you to understand that. What he needs from you the most is just be with him. Talk to him, let him know you're here. Even if he doesn't respond, continue to talk to him, he needs to hear your voice."

Kate nodded her head as Doc gave her a half-hearted smile.

Doc reached down and took Kate's hand as they walked down the hall to one of the rooms. A nurse and Dr. Ellis looked up as they walked in. Kate and Doc observed Henry laying on a gurney, a plastic mask covering his mouth and nose. An IV had been placed in his arm. He had a monitor attached as well. His upper body was dark in color. It was obvious he was having difficulty breathing. Henry's eyes were closed. Doc once again conferred with Dr. Ellis. Once done, Dr. Ellis left the room as Doc walked over to speak with Kate.

"It's not as bad as it could have been, but Henry is going to need some time to recover. He doesn't require an operation to fix anything, we can be very thankful about that. Henry has been through quite an experience. He's suffering from shock, of course. We're going to run some additional tests, but it's his breathing we have to watch."

Kate and Doc walked the short distance to where Henry was laying. Doc bent over Henry.

"Henry, it's Doc."

Henry tried to comprehend what was going on as he laid there, where he was, who was talking to him, it was all surrounded in a dense fog. His mind could not make simple decisions, nothing made sense. His eyes were closed and he couldn't seem to open them.

"Henry, can you answer me? Henry, it's Doc, I'm here with Kate. I'm going to check your eyes. You may see a flash of light. Don't worry about it, everything will be fine. When I'm done, I'll be sending you to get a series of tests."

Doc lifted one of Henry's eyelids and then the other as he ran a small flashlight in front of them. Henry thought he saw a flash of white, then darkness, then white again.

A nurse walked into the room to take Henry for his tests. Kate squeezed his hand before he left. As he was being wheeled down the hallway Kate yelled out, "I'll be here waiting for you, Honey!" Doc followed behind the nurse and Henry. He was too concerned to leave him now, though he knew that time was coming. Kate walked over to a chair in the corner of the room by a window and sat down. She buried her face into her hands and began to sob once again.

Just before beginning some tests, Doc spoke again to Henry. "Listen to me, Henry, it's Doc again. You're going to be all right, though your hands have taken a real beating. You have cuts on your legs, but we'll have all of that taken care of shortly. Your breathing is going to take a little while to clear up, too. That's what the mask is for, to help you breathe. I'll check on you later, but now you need to rest. As I said, we'll address your cuts, punctures wounds and so forth in just a bit. You're in the hospital. Kate is here to watch over you. You're in good hands with her, and our nurses are excellent."

Henry's mind still remained cluttered, though he could understand that Kate and Doc were there with him. That much he could comprehend. Yes, he knew that much, and that was all he needed to know, they were there with him.

Doc sat down on a bench in the hallway to take a well-deserved break.

"Say, Doc, how's the little girl and mother doing?" asked an EMT, with a couple of firemen standing beside him.

"Unbelievable as this is going to sound, since we're talking about an explosion, it's a miracle no one was killed. Mind you, I never saw the house, but only the mother's arm was broken and her leg. She, however, has a fair amount of cuts and bruises on her back. I'm sure she must have taken a large portion of the blast, from what I could observe from her injuries. Fortunately her body protected the child. It was their breathing problems that gave us the most concern. They were very lucky, to say the least. They're going to make it, thanks to you guys getting them here as quickly as you did. You know how you hear every second counts, in their case it really did matter. You gentlemen did a great job getting them oxygen right away. From what I could see on their faces and mouths, they needed that immediately. You obviously saw how dirty their faces were. If it had taken any longer, especially with the baby, who knows."

"I wish we could take credit for that, Doc, but some guy got there well before we did. If he hadn't found them right away, I don't know how long it would have taken us to find them. He's the real hero in all this. Once we took the little child and woman from his arms he dropped like a lead balloon. We worked on the females first since they weren't breathing, and fortunately for us he was. It was obvious to see he was completely spent. We're all concerned about him as well. How is he doing?"

"Henry's going to be all right, but he won't be doing any handyman jobs very soon."

"Henry Lewis!"

"Yes."

"I didn't know that. I didn't even recognize him with all the dirt and grime on his face."

"Well, someone recognized him because when I got the phone call to come here they used his name."

"Oh man, I know him personally. He's the type of guy who's there when you need him to be, and not afraid to dig in and help people out."

"Just like you fellows."

"Well, you thank him for us, all of us."

The other emergency workers nodded their heads as they turned and began to leave.

"That I will," Doc said nodding his head as well. "That I will," he repeated softly.

Doc got up and walked over to be with Kate who was sitting next to Henry, her hand wrapped in his.

"I just found out you're dating a real hero," Doc said.

"For as long as I've known him, he's always been my hero, Grandpa."

"And mine as well."

"Grandpa, should I call Emma, or just wait?"

"Why don't we wait until he's feeling better, and then we'll have him call her. I think it might be easier on her heart, if you know what I mean. There's no sense in getting her all upset when she can't do anything about it anyway."

"That's a wonderful way to handle it, we can do that."

When Kate felt she could spare the time from Henry, she found the phone number she needed and placed a call.

"Hello," came the voice on the other end.

"Jackie, this is Kate."

"How are you?"

"I'm doing fine, but Henry is doing so-so." Kate paused as she swallowed hard before going on.

"What is it, Kate?"

"Henry is in the hospital," her quivering voice said.

"Oh, no."

"He's going to be all right according to Grandpa, or Doc I should say. There was a home explosion and —"

"Was that what that was? Was he working there?"

"No, but he stopped to help."

"That sounds like our Henry."

"He's got injuries to his legs, hands, and he's having some difficulty breathing. They have him on oxygen. He's unconscious, but Grandpa and the doctors feel that's temporary."

"What can I do for you, Kate, just ask."

"Well, you know how Henry is, his first thoughts are going to be about Emma, her being taken care."

"She'll be taken care of, Sid and I will see to that. Don't you give her another thought, we'll see to everything."

"Thank you. I'm wondering… Emma is going to be asking where he is."

"Well, I'll have Sid say that Henry told him that something came up and he had to leave town for a little while. Heck, it can be some job he has to give an appraisal on. If she asks where or for what, Sid can just say he wasn't paying a lot of attention. Emma will believe that."

"Good idea. Thank you."

"Think nothing of it. We'll handle it from this end."

"Thank you."

"And Kate, keep us advised on Henry's condition, will you, please?"

"Of course."

"He'll be in our prayers."

"Thank you. Good-bye."

"Good-bye."

Kate thought for a moment as her mind seemed to be racing. She picked up the phone once again and made another call.

"Hello?"

"Can I speak to Melissa, please, is she there?" inquired Kate, her voice breaking up as she spoke.

"Sure," came a male's voice. "Melissa, I think it's for you, I couldn't understand her very well."

Melissa picked up the phone just in time to hear the voice of a woman starting to cry.

"Hello?" There was no audible response she could hear. "Who is this? Hello? Are you all right?"

With those few words uttered by her, everyone turned their immediate attention in Melissa's direction.

A shaky voice began to speak to her, heavily laden with what sounded like more crying.

"Melissa, it's me, Kate," her quivering voice said. "Henry is in the hospital. Can you come and be with me... please?"

"I'll be right there."

"Thank you," came the teary voice on the other end.

Melissa immediately hung up the phone as she turned to Greg. She moved quickly towards the door.

"We need to get to the hospital right now!" she stated in a frantic voice. "Henry is hurt and Kate needs me to be with her."

Greg didn't say a word as he jumped up from his position in the chair and headed to the front door, Melissa's hand already on the door handle. The four parents looked at each other stunned. Greg and Melissa disappeared quickly from the house. The sound of rubber squealing came from his car as they left the driveway.

"Is that the man we just talked about singing at the wedding?" asked Susan.

"The very one," Edith answered. "Kate and Henry are dating, and from what I hear, they're very much in love."

The Promise

"Well, Kate and Melissa are wonderful friends, and we know Kate very well obviously. Kenneth, we need to go immediately to the hospital and support our daughter and Kate, let them both know we're there for them."

Turning in Frank's direction Susan asked, "Can you tell us the fastest way to get to the hospital?"

"Yes, by getting in our car," Frank said.

Upon arriving at the hospital Greg and Melissa made their way quickly to the front desk.

"Can you tell me where I can find Henry?"

"What's his last name?" the receptionist inquired.

"I don't know, I've never heard Kate or him use it," Melissa said, a great deal of amazement showing on her face.

"Neither have I, come to think of it," Greg said.

"He's the one that's dating Kate, Doc's granddaughter, they just brought him in. He's probably in emergency, I guess," Melissa said.

"Oh," replied the woman behind the desk. "Let me page Doc McDonald for you."

"Thank you."

It wasn't but a minute or two before Doc came walking through a set of folding doors that opened automatically.

"I'm so happy to see you here, Melissa. I know that Kate will be, too. Let me just give you a quick heads up about what's taking place before I take you back to see Kate and Henry."

"Oh, Mom, Dad, I'm so glad you're here," Melissa stated, as the four parents walked up. "Doc was just beginning to give us his assessment on Henry."

"Good," Kenneth said.

"Doc, this is my mother and father, Susan and Kenneth Summers. Of course, you know Greg's mom and dad, I'm sure."

"Yes, we've met," Doc said nodding his head. "Apparently there was a house explosion and Henry just happened to be the first one on the scene. He started looking for survivors and came across a woman and a young child."

Edith put her hand over her mouth as she listened to Doc. She was very much concerned with what he had to say to the group. The word "child", frightened Edith the most. She never could stand to listen to any news involving a child being hurt.

"Because of all of the soot, smoke, and what have you in the air, he's having some difficulty breathing. He was in and out of consciousness when he got here. We've run some further tests to check that out. From what I've seen so far, he'll be okay, but we want to keep a very watchful eye on him."

Melissa began to cry. Susan stepped closer to her as she placed her hand on her daughter. Melissa turned into her mother's shoulder.

"Henry's suffered some damage to his hands, cuts, nail punctures, and an array of different injuries to his legs as well. He apparently suffered these injuries from digging through the rubble while looking for victims. I am happy, however, to tell you that he saved the woman's life along with her little child, but he's paid a price for doing that. I truly believe they wouldn't have made it here alive had he not gotten to them soon enough... especially the child. He found them even before the emergency personnel got there. They weren't breathing, the two females, but because of the quick action, theirs as well as Henry's, they were able to get them breathing again."

Now Susan and Edith started to reflect watery eyes as well.

"So now I'm going to take Melissa back to be with Kate. We can only allow a limited amount of people back there, but I think Kate needs Melissa to be with her right now."

"Yes, please," Susan stated.

"Of course," Edith said.

The men simply agreed with his statement as both nodded their heads.

"When we know more about how Henry's doing, I'll have Melissa come back here and she can give you an update. Okay?"

"Thank you, Doc," Greg said.

"Now, Melissa, you come with me, I'll take you to see Kate."

"Thank you, Doc," Melissa said.

Melissa followed Doc through the double set of doors and down a hallway to the right. On their left-hand side was a room with a bed in it. Henry lay unconscious, still on the gurney. Kate stood at his side.

"Thank you for coming," Kate said as the two women embraced. Doc simply turned and left the room.

"I would ask how you're holding up, but it's pretty obvious this has been very hard on you," Melissa stated, as she squeezed Kate a little harder.

"We were supposed to have a quiet dinner together, just Henry, Grandpa and me. And now look at what's happened. I could have lost him today," she said as she sobbed.

"He's in good hands, Kate, and you've got your Grandpa here as his guardian angel."

Kate gave Melissa a small smile, her eyes still heavily filled with dampness.

"Kate, I want you to know that Greg and his mother and father are out in the main lobby along with my mom and dad. They're all so concerned about Henry's wellbeing, along with yours."

"I'm glad they all came, it means a lot to me." Kate wiped her eyes with a tissue in her hand.

"Doc said there was some type of an explosion, and that's how Henry got hurt," Melissa uttered softly.

"Well, he was on his way to eat with us when everything happened." Kate sniffled a little as she reached for another tissue from the small box on the table beside the bed. "Apparently Henry stopped to lend a hand and that's how he got hurt. Grandpa and I even heard the explosion, but didn't know what it was."

"Doc told us he saved some people, a child or something. I didn't really hear everything he was saying, I was so concerned with getting back here to be with you."

The sound of a man groaning alerted the women that Henry might be coming to. Together they moved over closer to him as Henry began to roll slightly back and forth.

"Henry, can you hear me?" asked Kate taking his hand in hers. "Henry, it's Kate, I'm here with Melissa. Can you hear me?" she asked again.

Henry's eyes remained closed as Kate tried to get him to respond to her. He simply laid there restlessly. Kate held his hand as he moaned every once in a while. After a period of about five minutes, as Kate looked over at Melissa shaking her head back and forth slowly, Kate felt her hand being squeezed.

"He squeezed my hand, Melissa, he squeezed my hand!"

"Wonderful," was all Melissa could say. "I'll be back in just a second, and you keep squeezing his hand."

"I will," she answered, as she squeezed it once again.

Melissa left the room quickly looking for a nurse or anyone who could help. "I think he's starting to wake up a little bit, does someone need to look at him?" she asked a nurse in a concerned voice.

"I'll inform Doc McDonald, he wanted to know of any changes at all."

Within a matter of a few seconds Doc came walking into the room.

"So our hero is starting to wake up? Good." Once again Doc looked him over, checking all of his vitals. "Well, he won't be going anywhere for a little while, but his vitals are good." Henry slowly began to open his eyes, blinking them as he did.

"Honey, you scared me so much," Kate said softly in his ear as she stroked the top of his head. "I love you much."

Henry merely squeezed Kate's hand producing a smile from her face. She reached over and took some tissue to wipe his face.

Melissa stood watching Henry and Kate together. She was so happy he was able to acknowledge Kate.

"I love you, Henry," Kate said once again.

Melissa looked down at Henry noticing a tear making its way down the side of his face from the corner of his eye. She reached over taking a tissue from the box and wiped his eye. He slowly turned his head to look at her, his eyes blinking as he did. Melissa looked down upon his face giving him a smile. He returned a very small smile from behind the mask. Melissa reached down and took his hand in hers. She placed a small kiss on his fingers.

"Kate, I don't want to leave you right now, but I would like to let everyone else know Henry has regained consciousness. I don't even know if they know that much." Looking at Henry, Melissa said, "I'll be back as soon as I can."

Henry moved his head slightly up and down. Kate nodded her head in approval as Melissa turned and left the room.

As Melissa came walking through the folding doors everyone who wasn't standing already stood up immediately. Melissa took a deep breath.

"Henry is now awake, though he can't talk because of the mask they have on him to help him breath. He did, however, give Kate's hand a squeeze, so we know he's hearing her and understanding what's being said to him."

"Oh good," Susan stated as she sighed.

"That's a good sign, isn't it?" Edith said, "I mean being conscious."

"Well, it sure beats the alternative," Frank said.

"Frank, you know what I mean, and that's not funny at all."

"It wasn't meant to be, I mean, I'm glad he's awake and appears he's going to be okay. Was anything said about residual effects?"

"Not while I was there," Melissa answered. "I'm wondering if it's okay with everyone if I just stay here with Kate."

"Of course," Susan said.

"Mom, Dad," Melissa pausing as she looked over at Frank and Edith, "and Mom and Dad, is that okay with you?"

"You know it is," Frank said.

"Sure," Edith stated, nodding her head.

"This mom and dad thing confuses me, too, sometimes," Greg said." but I wouldn't want to change it for the world."

Kenneth smiled as well as Frank.

"Okay, so we're set," Melissa said. "Every one of you go back to the house and I'll have Greg come and get me when things have settled down with Kate and Henry."

"And what about me?" Greg asked, "I don't get to stay and see you?"

"No, you get to babysit the parents," Melissa said. "I'll give you a call if anything changes in the meantime. Now, I'll see everyone later." Melissa paused, "And thank you all for being here for Kate and Henry. I know they both appreciate it, she even told me so."

"You be sure to call us if you need anything at all, anything," Kenneth was quick to say.

"I will, Dad," she answered.

Melissa watched as Greg and their parents left the hospital and headed out the front door to their cars. She turned and headed back through the folding doors. They quietly closed behind her.

The following day Melissa sat talking to Kate in Henry's assigned hospital room. By now he had been placed in a hospital bed which was more comfortable. It had been hours since Henry first arrived at the hospital. Kate couldn't believe how long ago it felt. Henry stirred a little as he laid there.

"Henry, do you want something to drink?" Kate asked as she walked over to be at his side. He slowly shook his head gently up and down. The mask had now been removed and Henry's throat was dry once again. Giving him a drink from a straw stuck into a cup filled with crushed ice, Henry quenched his thirst as best he could. Melissa got up from her chair and walked over to him.

"Henry, are you able to talk?" Melissa asked.

"Yes," he said in almost a whisper.

"I don't want you to do any harm to yourself in talking to me, so if you'd rather wait until you feel better, that's okay."

"No, that's alright," he softly said.

"Let me do the talking, Henry, and if you can answer in just a yes or no, that's fine with me. I'll try to ask you my questions so they can be answered in that way. Maybe you can just answer with a simple nod."

Henry shook his head affirmatively.

Kate looked at Melissa with a questioning expression on her face. She wondered what questions could she possibly have for Henry. The last time Kate had heard Melissa ask Henry a personal question it concerned his facial scar. This must be important to her, she thought.

"Henry, when I came here to check on you and Kate yesterday, I stopped at the front desk. When they asked me for your last name, I had no answer for them. I don't even know your last name. What is it?"

"When I was adopted, their last name was Lewis." Henry took a slow deep breath. Melissa moved a little closer so she could better hear Henry's quiet voice. "I didn't take their name, or use it other than when I had to for school, a driver's license, stuff like that." Henry coughed a little. "I didn't want anything to tie their family name into my life."

"Oh, Henry, were they that bad or what?"

Henry didn't respond. It was then that Kate stepped in and tried to answer Melissa's questions for Henry.

"Maybe I can help you out on this," Kate stated.

Henry nodded his agreement with Kate's suggestion.

"Henry had a very rough upbringing. He was a small child when he moved in with them. The people who adopted him basically wanted someone to do work for them. As Henry got older he started doing more work around the house, though still being of a very young age. He told me it wasn't a relationship of love, just work, even some abuse. How people such as that can be given children is beyond me."

"Unfortunately there are people in this world like that," Melissa stated. "So what is his last name?"

"The people who adopted him burned the paperwork. When he asked them for any information they would never talk to him about it. Other times they simply ignored his request. They told him, 'It's Lewis, and you better get used to it.' The fact of the matter is, Melissa, he doesn't know his real last name, what day he was born on, or even where."

"Unbelievable. That's so sad, Henry. I'm so sorry for you," Melissa said. She could feel tears forming in the corners of her eyes.

Henry knew Melissa cared by the look on her face, her eyes saying everything to him. He lifted his hand up and waved it back and forth in an apparent attempt to tell her it didn't matter.

"Yes, it does matter, Henry, and it means something to me. I'm sure it does to Kate as well."

"She's right, Henry," Kate said nodding her head.

"Henry, you deserve so very much more in life than what has been given you."

Melissa reached over the side bar to the bed and gave Henry a kiss on his forehead.

"Well," Henry said in a whisper, "I do have a lot, I've got Kate. There's nothing more I need."

Kate gently squeezed his hand as she half smiled. Melissa turned her head away from Henry as she wiped tears from her face.

As the late evening hours approached Kate informed Melissa she thought it best if she headed home. Over Melissa's objections, Kate called Greg. It was a short time thereafter when he arrived. Getting into the car Melissa expressed to him how sad it was that Henry didn't know his real name, let alone the other items one takes for granted. As she told Greg what Henry had said, he shook his head slowly as he absorbed her every word.

"There's got to be something we can do about this, there's just got to be," she said.

"I don't know, things like that are pretty well hidden behind a thick curtain of secrecy."

"Well, it shouldn't be, especially in a case like this."

"And I agree with you wholeheartedly," he said.

"I'm going to do some checking into this and see what I can come up with. This just makes me so mad."

"I'll help you in any way I can, Honey."

"I knew you would."

Greg looked over at her. He had seen that look in her eyes before, and it was one of total determination.

One morning while a nurse was changing some of his dressings, she commented that his condition seemed to have improved immensely. His breathing was much better, which she knew was the main concern of the doctors. Henry discovered he couldn't hold his breath nearly as long as he used to. He was told it would get better with the passage of time.

Henry had received a tetanus shot when he first arrived at the hospital. This necessary experience was one he never liked at all, shots. He expressed to Kate that being unconscious at the time it was given was really a blessing to him. As far as the punctures on his hands, they showed signs of healing as well. He would flex his hands in pain, though the aching began to dissipate. He was able to be released on just the third day. Doc indicated to Kate that Henry's fitness was what he partly attributed to his quick recovery.

Melissa kept in close touch with Kate, calling often to ask how Henry was doing. When the phone would ring, Kate knew automatically who was on the other end. She appreciated Melissa's concern. It was but one of the things that kept the fabric of their friendship so tightly woven together as one.

While Henry knew he couldn't return to work right away, he began to suffer the effects of cabin fever. Though he was happy to be home and sleeping in his own bed, he grew restless, wanting to get out and about. Henry sat at the kitchen table eating cereal from a bowl he had made, his horizons concerning breakfast now expanding. A cup of freshly brewed coffee sat off to his right. As he got up to put the bowl in the sink he heard a firm knock on the door. Setting the bowl down, he walked over to answer the door. He opened the door to find Emma standing before him. He was shocked.

"Are you going to invite me in or stand there with your mouth wide open waiting for a bird to build a nest in it?"

"Come in, Mom."

"Henry, whatever gave you the idea you could end up in the hospital and I wouldn't find out about it?"

Henry didn't respond.

As Emma stepped through the doorway she turned and gestured with her hand, waving it slightly. "Get in here, Sid," she said in a demanding voice. Sid stepped through the doorway, his head hanging down slightly. His appearance could be likened to a child caught in a lie. Emma saw the cup of coffee steaming on the kitchen table.

"Now before you sit down again and finish that cup of coffee, you're going to explain to me what happened, and don't leave anything out. And I want you to talk real slow so I don't miss a single word of what you have to say. How could you not see to it that I was notified right away? Well,... well!" Emma stated.

"Mom, I'm fine."

"When I was in the hospital I was told I'd be okay when you said I was. Now that the shoe was on the other foot — You weren't considerate enough to give me the same pleasure of doing that with you, watching over you. Explain yourself."

"Well, Mom, Kate didn't want you to worry."

"Don't you go blaming that wonderful woman for me not being informed about this, don't you dare."

"Okay." Henry took a deep breath. "There was an explosion in a house, I helped find a couple of victims, and after being checked out, they sent me home."

"After three days they let you go home. I'm just glad Sid isn't any good at fibbing, or who knows when I would have found out the truth. Well, I'm going home to take a little nap now, but don't you ever think you can get away with stuff like this again. I'm no fool, and I don't like to be treated like one."

"I won't. Mom... I'm sorry."

"As well you should be. Sid, get the door, we're going home now."

"Yes, Emma," Sid said as he opened the door.

"Henry, come over here," Emma instructed strongly.

Henry stepped over to Emma.

"Now you let this old lady give you a kiss on your cheek."

Henry bent over to her.

"I'm so glad you're okay," she whispered in his ear. "I love you, Henry. I don't know what I'd do without you."

She then placed a soft kiss on his cheek.

"And I love you, too, Mom."

"Okay. Sid, I'm ready to go."

"Yes, Emma."

Henry smiled as he closed the door behind them.

I Think She Likes Tuna

"A December wedding, it's such a wonderful and magical time of the year to have one," Melissa excitedly exclaimed to Edith.

"But what about the timeframe, there would be so much to do, let alone get a hall, church, photographer?" asked Edith. "How did December come into the picture all of a sudden, I thought we were going to talk it over?"

"Edith, promise me you won't get mad at me or Melissa... please," Susan stated, "We know it's a big step forward."

"And why would I be mad?"

"One night not very long ago Melissa came into our bedroom and woke me up. She put her finger over her mouth, so I knew she wanted to talk to me alone and not wake Kenneth. We went downstairs so we could talk. I think it was somewhere around 1:00 a.m. We sat there and talked and talked until five-thirty in the morning."

Melissa smiled as she listened to her mother telling Edith the story.

"Melissa wondered what I would think about having her wedding this December, if it was a dumb idea. She realized there was practically no time to get everything put together, yet it was something she really desired in her heart. She said it was that important to her. Melissa is willing to even cut the wedding back to just our families. She told me she was so determined to do it, that no matter what it took to make it happen, she was willing to take those very steps. Our daughter even suggested skipping the reception. No matter what had to be done, her desire for a Christmas wedding meant the world to her."

Edith put her hand on Melissa's and began patting it slowly as she continued listening to Susan. She turned and looked over at Melissa, her face wearing a smile. Edith smiled back at her.

"December?" Edith said.

"Yes," Melissa answered.

"This December?"

"Yes."

"Edith, I have done some checking already, made a lot of calls," Susan said. "It is workable. What do you think, what are your thoughts on all of this?"

"Well, it's really up to you and Greg in the end. I remember him telling us he wouldn't even care if it was a Justice of the Peace who performed the wedding."

Susan and Melissa both chuckled with those few words having been said. They both recalled the circumstances of that very day, the day Greg proposed to Melissa.

"I think I know the answer to this question already," Edith said, "but just the same I want to hear it from you, Honey. Why December?" she asked Melissa.

"It's the month I met Greg. It's the month we fell in love. How could I ever come up with any other time of the year to get married. December is more precious to me than anything I can think of. Yes, to me it represents everything about Greg and our relationship together. I can't conceive of any time in my life when I've been happier. December represents the month of love, in more than one way.

If you really think about it, it's a wonder we even met at all. It all started with Kate inviting me to the Christmas Program. That really bought us two together at the cast party.

Edith... Mom, it's really a miracle that we even met that night at all. If I hadn't come in to town the day before to talk with Kate, Greg being home on leave, Sharon deciding to go through with her part in the Christmas program, who knows? To meet him and then fall in love in such a short time still makes me shake my head in amazement."

"Melissa, I hope you don't mind me for asking you that question, it's just I love so much hearing how you and Greg found each other, and how much you're both in love with one another. Maybe it's the mother in me, but I never get tired of hearing it."

"And neither do I," Susan confessed.

"And I don't mind telling it either," Melissa added.

"So a December wedding, huh?" Edith said as she looked at Melissa's smiling.

"Yes," answered Melissa again.

"Well, I once saw a cooking show on television, and what the chef said to the audience then is very much an appropriate statement to say now."

"And what's that, Edith?" asked Susan.

"All he said was, 'So let's get cooking, baby.'"

Susan and Melissa just couldn't stop laughing along with Edith. Finally the women were able to collectively get their composure together. Susan pulled the writing pad over in front of her and picked up the pen.

"So let's get cooking, baby," Melissa stated loudly, bringing forth a second series of laughter.

"So what items can we cross off our to-do-list?" inquired Edith as she reached up and wiped her eyes. "That was so funny, Melissa."

"Oh," Susan said, "that really was."

Susan once again looked over the large yellow pad of paper as she began to study it over carefully.

"Well, we can have the hall over on Sheppard Road, it's available, if you think that's okay, Edith?"

"That's in our hometown, or is there another Sheppard Road here?"

"Edith," Susan stated, "Melissa and I have talked it over. If you and Frank have no objections, we'd like to have the wedding in your church with Pastor Phil officiating. Pastor Phil has been kind enough to agree to do the wedding."

"What dates are you thinking of?" Edith asked.

"Probably the early part of the month since the Christmas Program date is booked and an array of other parties and such are going on. It's a very busy time of year for everyone. If we want people to attend, early in the month is our best bet."

"There isn't going to be too much left for me to do, is there?" Edith said, a little disappointed at being left out on the plans.

"And who is going to help my mother pick out that special wedding dress for me to look beautiful in for your son, figure out the food selection, the caterers, the invitations, the music, photographer, florist, and the table arrangements? I can go on and on. Mom, we absolutely need your input." Melissa's voice was strong, wanting Edith to realize how much she was needed. "So please don't be mad at either one of us for stepping on your toes, neither one of us meant to do that."

"How can I be mad at two people I love so much?" Edith said as she smiled. She then took a deep breath and announced, "So, ladies, —"

"Let's get cooking, baby," Susan and Melissa stated in unison as everyone once again laughed.

The front door opened with Kenneth walking into the house. In his hands he held a fairly large box in size with the flaps on top closed.

"Well, you ladies look awfully happy, is it because I'm here?"

"You're home early, it's not quite noon," Susan stated.

"That's because I'm on a mission. I knew Edith would be here, of course, and the three of you would be busy working on the wedding plans. I took it upon myself to bring a lunch for each one of you. I've got some salads, sandwiches, and desserts. I didn't bring you any drinks, I thought we'd have something in the refrigerator."

"That's so considerate," Edith said.

"Yes, it is," added Susan. "Thank you, Honey."

"You're welcome. Hanging around Frank and Greg, even when Greg was home on leave, has taught me a few things in the last year and a half."

Melissa got up and hugged her dad.

"Thank you, Daddy. Now, let me fix a plate for you and the ladies. You can join us for lunch."

"No thank you, Melissa, I don't want to be the fourth wheel on a three-wheeled tricycle. I'm going to run back to work and do a few little odds and ends that need to be addressed. The fact of the matter is I don't plan on working very long today, just a few minutes. Then I'm meeting up with Frank later and we're going fishing together."

"Good for you," Edith said.

"Well, I'm going to run upstairs, change my clothes, and then I'm out of here."

"Have a good time fishing with Frank," Susan said.

"We always do," he answered as he left the room and headed up the stairs to change into his fishing clothes.

After Kenneth disappeared into the bedroom and shut the door, Susan turned to the women. "Who would have ever thought we all would be sitting here planning a wedding today, your father would bring us lunch, and then taking time off to go fishing with Frank. I just can't fathom the difference in our lives since you, Greg, and Frank have become such an important part of it."

Melissa nodded her head.

"I think a real strong part of it has to do with something you didn't mention," suggested Edith.

"And what's that, Edith?" Susan asked.

"That your husband really loves both of you very much."

"I think that's very true," Melissa said thoughtfully nodding her head in agreement.

"Yes, you're right," Susan said.

"I think I found that out the night dad held me tightly and I felt his tears on my cheeks and face. I've never seen or known him to cry before."

"I have, unfortunately."

"When was that, Mom?"

"It had to do with his parents and grandparents, but let's not get into that now, okay?"

Melissa nodded her head. She then continued on with her thoughts.

"Well, I knew that night he was truly sorry for everything he had said to Greg and me earlier that day. It became obvious to me he was truly sorry for how he treated both of us," Melissa said.

"Melissa, I don't want you to repeat what I'm going to tell you now," Susan stated.

"I won't."

"One evening your father —"

"Do you want me to leave the room so you can speak together?" inquired Edith.

"No, of course not, but this is something you should hear, too, it affects you as well indirectly. I should say you were kind of a part of it from the very beginning, or at least a part of what happened. I want you to hear what I have to say."

"Okay," Edith said nodding her head.

"One evening not so long ago, this being well after the confrontation we had at your home, Edith, almost a couple of years ago now, I thought I heard some quiet sounds coming from Kenneth's office. I walked over to the door and I could hear Kenneth crying softly inside. As I entered the room I found him sitting behind his desk with his head in his hands. I asked him if he was okay. He just shook his head back and forth, he wasn't. 'What is so wrong with me?' he asked.

I walked behind him and placed my arms around him as he sat there, his face still buried somewhat in his hands. Kenneth has suffered a great deal in his lifetime. I really didn't know what to expect from him on that day. He continued quietly crying as his head moved slowly back and forth. 'I don't know what to think about myself anymore,' he told me, 'it's in my thoughts every day now, every day and how I've hurt everyone.'

As I've said, Kenneth has had a great deal of tragedy to deal with throughout his life. Now I understood what he was referring to. It wasn't about what I thought it involved. It was concerning what had happened with Greg and you, between all of us some time ago."

She looked in Edith's direction. Edith nodded her head slowly back and forth but said nary a word.

"I told him everything that had transpired was for the better. We had just met you and Frank, Greg is a wonderful young man, we had our daughter back, and besides that, our family is stronger because of it all. I told him again that everyone had forgiven him. He said he understood that, that he was grateful we forgave him, but that wasn't the problem. He said he couldn't do the same for himself. His exact words were, 'I'll never forgive myself for what I did as long as I live, for what I put everyone through. I just can't get it out of my mind. It haunts my thoughts almost every day. What kind of person acts like that?' "

Melissa looked at her mother as she wiped her eye with her finger.

"When dad held me in his arms that night and I was fighting to get away, those were some of his strongest words that struck me the most in my heart, the fact that he said he would never forgive himself for putting us all through that turmoil. I remember those words so clearly, almost as if he said them today. I guess what that really tells us is just how sorry dad is for what he did. It makes me feel horrible to know that even after all this time he still feels that way, has that much pain lingering inside of him."

Edith reached over and took both Susan and Melissa's hands in hers. "I wish I could tell you what to do, but I can't. Perhaps Kenneth will just have to find his own way down that dark pathway by himself. I just wish I knew how all of us could help him through this difficult time of his."

Edith squeezed both of their hands as she spoke to them.

"Well," Susan said, "he knows everyone has forgiven him, so we'll just have to wait and see how he does at forgiving himself."

With the last sentence being spoken by Susan the bedroom door opened. Kenneth walked down the steps.

"Well, I'm off to work, then over to catch some fish with Frank, we hope."

"Have a good time, Honey," Susan said.

"Tell Frank there's always cans of tuna in the cupboard we can eat," joked Edith.

"We always catch and release, so you might want to keep the can opener handy," Kenneth said in a chuckling voice.

"Dad, wait!"

Melissa got up from her seat and walked up to her father. She placed her arms around him and hugged him hard. Kenneth, following her lead, returned the hug.

"Daddy, I want you to know I love you so much and I'm sorry for not telling you that often enough."

"Well, I love you, too, Sweetheart," he answered smiling.

"Daddy, I really mean it," she said as she hugged him again laying her head on his chest.

Kenneth bent down and kissed Melissa on the top of her head.

"Now, what brought all of this on?" he asked.

"I think she likes tuna fish," Edith said, "So if I were you, I would stop at the store on the way home and buy some, and several cans by the size of those hugs."

"Well, if I do as well at fishing as I just did in getting hugs, those fish don't have a prayer." Kenneth once again bent over to Melissa and kissed her on her forehead. "I do love you Honey," he said.

"I know."

Melissa released her grip on her father.

"And thanks for buying us all lunch," Edith stated.

"It was my pleasure."

Kenneth turned and walked over to the front door.

"I'll see everyone later," he said as he closed the door behind him on his way to his vehicle.

"Honey, it's the little things like that, what you just did, that will live forever in his heart. I know that for a fact," Susan said.

"Your mother is a very wise woman, I'd listen to her," suggested Edith.

"I'm so fortunate to have two mothers that are so wise. Now, before we do anything more, I want both of you to sit where you're at and let your daughter, and future daughter-in-law, serve you both lunch. As you can see by this big box, I've been cooking all morning," she said chuckling. She placed the box of food on the kitchen table.

"This is kind of like when the guys cooked us that delivered pizza lunch," joked Edith.

"And it didn't taste too bad either, but probably better than if they had done it themselves," Susan added.

"Well, let's see what treasures dad brought us," Melissa said as she lifted the flaps open and peaked into the cardboard box.

The rest of the day was spent doing what they had planned on in the first place, making wedding plans. Each woman had her own ideas on different things, but like a good recipe, everything blended together in the end.

"Susan, why did you and Melissa decide on having the wedding in our little town rather than yours? There's so much more to be offered here," inquired Edith.

"Well, to tell you the truth, Edith," Susan started out, "it's because there are so many people that know and love Greg, Frank, and you. We don't have the same connection you do with friends, family, and what have you. Some of our friends are — and I hate to say this, but they're superficial in nature. I don't know if you've ever heard of the term, 'plastic people,' but that's what a lot of them are. People invite us to various events, weddings and such just because of our business relationship, who we are in the community. They're not anywhere near the people you know and associate with, warm and loving. I don't want to celebrate our daughter's wedding surrounded by people that feel they're compelled to be there."

"Our town would take that as a compliment," declared Edith.

"I would, too, if I were in their shoes. Besides, our side of the church would be rather sparse, I'm sad to say."

"Well, I think at the wedding there shouldn't be any side selection, groom or bride. We can have the ushers simply say, 'Melissa and Greg are very happy to have you here to celebrate their wedding day with them, please take a seat of your choice.'"

"I like that," Melissa, said.

"And so do I," Susan exclaimed.

"It's like two things rolled up into one. We can let people know we're happy they came, and it also takes care of our seating problem. Thanks, Mom," Melissa said as she smiled at Edith.

"Well," Edith said nodding her head, "I don't want this to sound like I'm pushing his business or anything, but Frank's brother Norm is a florist by trade, and I was thinking —"

"If the roses I got from Greg are any indication of the flowers he carries, I would love to have him do the arrangements for the wedding party, or anything else he wants to do," Melissa said excitedly.

"And I know he'd do them as his wedding gift for both of you."

"Mom, the roses I got from Greg were simply gorgeous."

"So that takes care of another item on our to-do-list," Susan said as she wrote a note on the pad.

"I know this is premature, but have you and Greg given any thoughts to writing your own vows?" Edith asked. "That, of course, is entirely up to the both of you. I was just thinking, if you are going to do that, you may want to start thinking about it now. That, at least, would give you more time to work on it."

"Gee, I don't know about that," Melissa said, "I hadn't thought that far ahead. Speaking in front of people is something I have a great fear of doing."

"She sure does, and I don't think she should do it," Susan said, "or even attempt it."

"Well, it doesn't have to be anything elaborate, but as I say, that's entirely up to you," Edith said.

"And Greg has a beautiful way of expressing his thoughts," added Susan. "The words he used when he asked you to marry him brought tears to my eyes."

"And mine, too," Edith agreed. "I know he didn't get that from Frank," she chuckled.

"They were beautiful, weren't they?" Melissa said. "I just wish I hadn't interrupted him like I did."

"Well, you were excited," Susan said.

"We all were," Edith expressed with a smile.

"I think I'll mull that over in my mind for a while, what words I should use, or if I should every try. It is something to think about," Melissa said as she nodded her head.

"Well, you know my feelings on the subject," Susan said. "Just because he does it, doesn't mean you have to."

"It'll be fine, Mom."

As the clock ticked away more and more items were covered in their discussions. The women decided who would call whom, what other contacts needed to be made.

"You know, I better get going," Edith said. "I still have to fix the men supper when I get home."

"Wait a minute," Melissa stated.

Melissa got up and went into the front room returning with her purse in hand. She opened it, did a quick search of the interior and then removed a small plastic card from it.

"Do you have one of these restaurants in your hometown?" she asked as she handed the card to Edith.

"Yes, we do, just outside of the city limits at the other end of town. It's a very nice restaurant."

"I've had this gift card for quite some time and have never had the opportunity to use it. Would you do me a favor and take everyone out for dinner with it? It can be a cook free night for you."

"Oh, I couldn't, but thank you just the same, Melissa."

"Please."

"Well, —"

"Then take the love of my life out for a steak dinner, we all know he just loves steak. I'll bet Frank would even tag along, but I would suggest you go also so they don't get into any trouble."

"Thank you, future daughter-in-law of mine," joked Edith, "I will."

"So I'll give you a call, Edith, and let you know when we can get together and work on this again," Susan suggested. "If it's okay with you we'll make it at your house next time and save you the drive."

"Whatever works best for either of you is fine with me."

"Bye, Mom," Melissa stated.

"Bye, Melissa," Edith answered, "and thank you for the card."

Edith got up and went to the front room to get her purse as Melissa and Susan accompanied her. Once Edith had left Susan turned to Melissa.

"That was a good idea giving her that gift certificate. I'm sure they'll enjoy themselves with it. Besides, Edith doesn't need to be cooking food when she gets home. I'm sure she's tired."

"I bought that gift card a few weeks ago when I went to visit Greg. I knew, of course, the restaurant was there. I kept it in my purse for just such an occasion as this. I was hoping they would make use of it."

"That was very thoughtful of you."

"Thanks, Mom."

A Little Boy's Dream

Taking the mail from the mailbox Henry began to sort through it as he walked to the house. He quickly noticed there was an envelope that bore the return address of the local fire department. He slid his finger into a slight opening in the back and began to open it. However, he destroyed about half of the envelope in doing so. He pulled a sheet of paper from its remaining portion. There was mention of some type of plaque or award. The letter also informed Henry that the fire department and local authorities wanted to acknowledge the fact that he had saved two individuals that were involved in a home explosion. As he read it he wondered why they wanted to honor him for something he felt anyone would have done. Opening the door to the house he stepped in and walked to the kitchen area. He tossed the mail onto the counter.

A couple of weeks had now passed. Henry was doing a little storm clean up around the house. A few small branches had fallen from some trees in his front yard. As he placed them into a black garbage bag a red pickup truck pulled into his driveway. Henry glanced up and read the sign on the side of the vehicle, "Creek Side Fire Department." The individual behind the wheel opened the door and got out. Henry knew him, though not very well. It was Kevin Wolfe, the local volunteer fire department chief.

"Hello, Henry."

"How you doing, Kevin?" he answered.

"Fine. Say Henry, did you happen to get a letter from me a few weeks ago?"

"Yes, I did."

"I didn't hear back from you, that's why I'm here."

"You guys don't need to honor me for something you fellows do normally."

"I think you're missing the point."

"And what point would that be, Kevin?" Henry said as he reached for another small group of branches.

"If you hadn't been there to begin with they'd both be dead, no matter how many of us showed up too late."

Henry knew he couldn't argue with that, being anywhere too late is still too late.

"Tomorrow night we plan to honor you. We would appreciate it if you'd do us the honor of being there with us. Will you do that for me... for us?"

"I don't know."

"Please, some of our guys would like to say thank you for your help."

"I don't have to dress up or anything?"

"Just stand there and smile."

"Okay, Kevin, I'll be there."

"Thanks, Henry. I'll see you at the fire department at seven-thirty sharp."

Henry nodded his head before he reached down and picked up another small group of branches.

Kevin turned and walked back to the pickup truck. As he sat behind the wheel he momentarily looked at Henry working. He thought to himself, I wish this community had a hundred Henrys.

Henry never said anything to anyone about his upcoming meeting at the fire department. To him it was very simple, have a few people thank him and go home. I wonder if there will be any refreshments, he thought.

Unbeknownst to Henry, Chief Wolfe contacted Emma, knowing her to be his mother, or at least so he thought. He surmised she would want to be there. Emma got on the phone and called Kate. Kate informed Doc of Henry's pending award as well. They all wanted to be with Henry on this important night, even if Henry didn't think enough of it to let them know.

Henry pulled up to the fire department. Cars were everywhere. Oh man, I should have walked, he thought. They must be having another program going on at the elementary school across the street. He looked over at the school. Lights were on in a few rooms. Finally finding a parking spot he made his way to the fire station. As he walked in the door he was surprised at how quiet it was. One lone fireman sat over in the corner drinking a cup of coffee. He got up and walked over to Henry.

"Am I at the right place, or should I say the right night?" Henry asked.

"Are you at the right place," the fireman stated, "yes, you are." In a loud voice he shouted out, "It's nice to see you, Henry."

Henry was stunned with the man's loud statement, but not as much as what was about to take place before his eyes. Like a swarm of locust descending upon a farmer's field the room filled almost immediately. People were everywhere. Though Henry knew almost everyone there, he still was surprised to see some he didn't recognize. Many patted him on the back as they greeted him. Over in the corner he saw Emma. She reached up with her hand and waved to him. Henry smiled back at her. Kate stood beside her, along with Doc. Dan and Kim stood with their parents. Henry was astounded. Greg, Melissa, and their parents were also in attendance. He saw Sid and Jackie back in the corner, both of them smiling. Sid raised his hand in a little wave.

"Can I have everyone's attention, please?" stated Chief Wolfe. "Thank you. Tonight we celebrate not only the fact that two individuals in our community are alive today because of the heroics of the man before me, but we are also grateful and proud that he lives in our very own community. I would like to have Mrs. Cain come forward, please."

A woman Henry didn't recognize stepped forward with a young child at her side. Her left arm and leg were both casted.

"Henry," she began, "not only did you save my life that day, but more importantly to me, you saved my child." Now the woman began to cry softly. "I am so thankful you were there for us," her shaky voice stated. "Thank you." She reached up and placed a kiss on Henry's cheek.

The people in attendance applauded. Chief Wolfe stepped forward once again.

"Henry, I have in my hand a check in the amount of $2,000.00. This money is donated by various people in our state to show their appreciation to citizens who unselfishly put their own lives on the line to help save people in their community. He held his hand out to Henry with the check.

"I'm sorry, I can't accept this," Henry said.

The room became very quiet.

"I don't understand."

"Simply put, I wouldn't feel right accepting a monetary gift for someone else's pain, I just wouldn't feel right doing it. Thank you just the same."

"Well, you all heard our 'Gentle Giant,' " the chief stated, "he won't accept the money."

Some of the people clapped their hands.

"I didn't say someone else couldn't have the check," Henry said with a small smile.

"Pardon me?"

"If it's okay I'd like to give the check to Mrs. Cain. She can use is for any medical bills, maybe some new furniture, anything she needs. Is that okay with you?"

"Thank you again, Henry," she said as Chief Wolfe handed her the check.

Once again the people applauded, only a lot louder now.

"And if it needs to be endorsed or whatever, let me know," Henry whispered softly to Mrs. Cain.

"Henry, is there anything we can do to show you our appreciation for what you've done, anything?" the Chief asked.

"Well,... there is one thing, but it's kind of an odd thing to ask for by someone my age."

"And what would that be?"

"Ever since I was a little boy I've always wanted to ride on a fire truck."

Some of the people immediately around him laughed, thinking of things they always wanted to do as a kid.

"Well," Chief Wolfe announced loudly, "Henry always wanted a ride on a fire truck, and I can't see any reason he shouldn't get one now. The parade begins in five minutes. Get into your cars and jump in line wherever you can. We'll be going from the fire station here, through town, circle through the park, and just in case they didn't hear all of us the first time, we'll all go through town again. Then it's back here for refreshments for everyone. Has everybody got that?"

The noise the individuals made going to their vehicles was actually quite loud with all the excited voices and so forth. People in general love a parade, and to even play a small part in one is something everyone enjoys. People got into their cars turning their emergency hazards lights on. Soon they all began honking their horns. It was as if everyone in town was joining in, or at least wondering what was going on. The fire truck's siren sounded out loudly as it slowly led the large group of vehicles through town. A water truck, an ambulance, and two police cars also joined in the procession. Some people in the downtown area joined in quickly. Henry stood waving to everyone as they drove by. He wore Chief Wolfe's helmet on his head, a large smile across his face. The town had never experienced such an impromptu spectacle before, and probably wouldn't ever again. People laughed and cheered. They waved and yelled at people. It was a time to be remembered.

Once back at the fire station the rest of the evening was filled with a variety of different desserts being served, soft drinks, and coffee. The refreshments also included a plate filled with fruitcake, which didn't last too long. Yes, the people loved Henry, and the big heart he seemed to demonstrate so freely to every one of them daily. This night would be no different, one that would not be forgotten soon by anyone, especially Henry.

And so a little boy's dream to ride on a fire truck was at last fulfilled in the body of his adulthood, and joined in by people who loved and admired him.

Forgiving Yourself

It was Sunday afternoon, and as was the tradition, the families shared their dinner together. One week it was at the Wilsons' home, the next weekend the Summers if the family schedules warranted it. Even when Greg was away in the service, that fact didn't stop them from sharing their mealtime experiences together. It gave both families time to get to know each other better and spend time with Melissa, which Frank and Edith both loved.

Melissa stood by the stove as she watched Edith and Susan. They began setting the table for dinner. Greg and Frank were in the living room visiting. Her father sat at the kitchen table alone drinking a cup of coffee. Melissa walked over to him. She felt the time was right as she placed her hand upon his shoulder. He turned slightly as he looked up at her.

"Dad, can I talk to you for a minute?"

"Sure, Honey."

"Can we go outside, it's such a nice day?"

"Of course."

Kenneth looked at the expression on Melissa's face and knew immediately this was going to be more than just a casual conversation they would be having. He got up and followed her through the sliding glass door out onto a very large wooden deck. The sun felt warm on their faces as they walked over by the railing. While Kenneth didn't know what the subject matter would entail, Melissa had her plan well worked out before she even asked him to step outside with her.

Melissa knew from the earlier statements of her mother how much pain her father still harbored in his heart for what he had done to her, her mother,

Greg, and the Wilsons as well. She understood he couldn't forgive himself, and that was now her mission, to help him forgive himself. Her idea was a simple one, based on how Greg handled different situations. How would Greg deal with this, she thought many times, what would he say? After thinking it over, Melissa found the answer was really quite easy. Yes, she said to herself, that's what Greg would do, that would be his solution to all of this. It was now time for her to put her plan into place.

"Dad, there's something I've never told you or Mom."

"What is it, Honey?"

"Do you remember the day when I went to visit Kate and I came back home right away, that same day?"

"Yes. I was somewhat surprised to see you back so quickly."

"Well, I had a fight with Kate."

"Oh."

"We've, of course, made up obviously since then. I was always thankful in my heart for her doing that, forgiving me."

Kenneth nodded his head. He knew, however, she had something more she wanted to convey to him other than the story of a simple fight between friends. He didn't want to interrupt her from her thoughts, so he simply waited for her to continue.

"I said some awful things to Kate, terrible words that I've strongly regretted since that meeting with her, but I still find it hard to forgive myself for what I said. Kate forgave me for what I did, but I'm still having trouble trying to deal with it all. It's in my thoughts every day. What do I do to make myself feel better about what happened? Dad, how do I ever forgive myself?"

Kenneth stood there perplexed at the question Melissa asked him. The two looked at each other as Kenneth reached down and took her hand. He didn't answer. In his mind he thought to himself, how do I answer the very question I've asked myself almost daily, how do you forgive yourself. What do I say to help her figure this out?

Melissa could see her father was in deep thought. She expected this reaction to her question. Melissa said not a word. Kenneth reached up after releasing her hand and put his arm around her shoulder. Melissa put her arm around his waist as she cuddled into him.

"Melissa, I guess nobody really knows the answer to that one. Every one of us carries emotional baggage in some way or another. I know I have for years. Perhaps it's how we deal with it that sets us all apart. You know Kate has forgiven you, and that should be enough for you to let it go, to forgive yourself. I'm sure it can be very relieving to do that. Maybe it is as simple as that, just let it go."

"So is that how you would handle it, just let it go and move on?"

Kenneth didn't respond, he just ran his lower lip under his upper teeth.

"Well, I think you're right, Dad, just let it go and move on."

It was then that Kenneth came to the realization that Melissa knew much more than she had let on. He smiled at her as he squeezed her shoulder.

"You're a very wise young lady," he said as he kissed the top of her head.

"So we're in agreement then, we can both let it go?"

"Yes, we can both let it go."

"Thank you, Daddy."

"No, thank you, Sweetheart."

"I love you."

"And I love you, too," he replied.

The relief Kenneth felt within himself was immediate, it was unmistakable. He knew the burden was gone, and he had his daughter to thank for that.

Kenneth and Melissa didn't join the group in the house right away, they simply talked and enjoyed the company of each other, a father and his daughter sharing quality time together.

The glass sliding door slid to one side as Susan stepped through the door partially.

"Okay you two, we're ready to eat."

"We're coming, Mom."

"Susan," Kenneth stated —"

"Yes."

"— you've raised a very intelligent daughter."

"Of course I have," she replied as she turned and stepped back into the house.

"After you, Honey," Kenneth said as he stretched his arm out indicating for Melissa to go first.

The families sat enjoying a homemade Italian dinner cooked by Susan. Fresh rolls in a couple of large bowls only added to the feast.

"This is absolutely wonderful," exclaimed Edith.

"Thank you. It's an old family recipe handed down from my grandmother to my mother, and then to me," Susan said with pride.

"So you're Italian?"

"Yes, I am. My mother lives in California now while my grandmother is in Italy. She's quite frail at times and stronger on other days. Of course she's very old and doesn't get around a lot."

"So you speak the language, I assume?" continued Edith.

"Yes, I do. My mother said that she's an American now, she would learn to speak English. From what she told me, when I was born she stopped speaking Italian outside of the house entirely, though inside was an entirely different matter."

"So Melissa, can I gather by that you do also?" Edith asked.

"Yes, when I need to," Melissa answered.

"Will you teach me?" inquired Greg quickly.

"It will take a while but, yes, I'd love to."

"Do you see them very often?" Edith inquired.

"Not nearly enough. We went to Italy to visit my grandmother some years ago. She was simply taken in by Melissa, she just loved her. I was so thrilled with her response."

"I can understand that," Greg was quick to say, "she's hard not to love."

Melissa smiled.

"And what about your father?" Edith asked.

"He passed sometime ago as well as my grandfather, I'm sad to say."

"Oh, I'm so sorry to hear that, Susan."

"Thank you."

"And what about you, Kenneth," Edith said, do you have any grandparents, a mother and father who will be attending the wedding? I haven't heard you mention them at all, now that I think about it."

"They're all gone, both of my grandparents... my mom... and my dad as well," he replied slowly in a very depressed tone of voice.

Susan reached over and placed her hand on Kenneth's. Edith felt horrible inside after listening to his words, and then seeing Susan's response to her question by placing her hand on his. Edith's heart ached within. She didn't know what to say next as she gazed upon Kenneth's face, a saddened appearance exhibited in his expression. Finally she spoke the words that came naturally to anyone in her position.

"It's just so sad to hear that," Edith said softly.

Kenneth slowly nodded his head up and down.

"Thank you for your concern."

He bit down on his lip for a second or two.

"I'm so sorry, Kenneth," Edith repeated. "I didn't mean to upset you with that question."

Edith kept her curiosity to herself, afraid to ask another question for fear of what she may uncover. His few words were all she needed to hear, and really hoped to hear no more concerning his misery. He had said enough as far as she was concerned. The room carried a somber theme to it.

Kenneth looked at everyone around the table and then took a deeper breath. He felt it necessary to continue with his answer, though it tore at his heart to do so.

"It was a terrible car accident," he began. "The four of them went out together for dinner and then to take in a show. My mother and father... my grandmother and grandfather, we lost all four of them that night. A drunk driver took them from us in literally the snap of a finger, my parents instantaneously, my grandparents shortly thereafter... within a matter of an hour or so."

Greg reached over and took Melissa's hand. The room remained completely silent, even the air seemed to carry a deep heaviness to it. No one else spoke. The silence was disturbed only by the occasional sound of birds chirping outside a window.

"The thing is," Kenneth said in a soft voice, "the driver fought with the emergency personnel and police, even as they extracted her from the vehicle. They say she screamed for them to keep their filthy hands off of her. She just bore cuts and bruises, some facial bleeding, a broken arm, a few broken ribs. I also understand from what I've been told she was supposed to be on her way home. Funny thing is she was five miles from there and going in the opposite direction. She had no concept of what she was doing or what damage she had inflicted. We found out later she had been charged twice before with drunk driving. Little good that did our family.

At least it was over quickly for our loved ones. It took Susan and me quite some time to recover emotionally, me especially. There are days I am still trying to cope with it all, though they are fewer in number now. I suppose that's probably due to the passage of time. Thank goodness Melissa was very small at the time. We were very thankful for that fact alone. I don't know if either of us could have bared her going through it with us."

"That's so sad, Kenneth," Edith said as she reached for her own husband's hand; squeezing it as she took it in hers.

"Every morning I woke cursing God and the world for what we had been put through. In my heart I knew I was wrong, but I needed something or someone to blame, not just her, the driver. I wanted an answer for what had happened to me... to us. The woman, I knew she would be dealt with, her freedom finally taken from her. In my heart I wished for closure, but none readily came to me.

When I was home alone I would sometimes stare at their pictures. There were days when Susan had a hard time dealing with my sorrow, the bitterness I felt inside. I know I wasn't the best person to be around. Susan was always there for me with more understanding than I deserved. I finally came to the realization that if our family had any chance at all of surviving this tragedy, we had to survive as a family first. So daily I channeled my thoughts into making Melissa and Susan my first priority.

Sometimes I'm still quick to anger, an item I never carried before that day, and it's cost me dearly at times. Greg knows what I'm talking about, he's felt it firsthand unfortunately. I'm sorry for that Greg."

Melissa squeezed Greg's hand as he nodded his head. She looked at her father, her eyes glazed over as she listened to his words. This was the most she had ever heard her father speak of what transpired that day. He and Susan had always kept their feelings to themselves along that line. Kenneth especially had taken great care to build an emotional wall between his daughter and his pain. As he spoke Melissa watched him dealing with his inner feelings. She felt tears running down her cheeks. She could see her mother's sorrow in her eyes as well. She wished she could help him deal with this agony, just as she had helped him not so very long ago.

"Throughout the years I've had some counseling, talked with different people, but Susan was the one that helped me the most. She spoke to me, she listened, she comforted me through each new day. Her shoulder was always there to lay my head on, to catch my tears when necessary.

Not very long ago I observed that very same trait play itself out in my daughter. In fact, it was only moments ago. She showed me how to just let things go, and that's what I'm going to do with both of the heartaches I've carried for so long."

"Just let it go," Melissa half smiled as tears continued to run down her cheeks.

Kenneth nodded his head.

"The caring and love she possesses for my wellbeing, helping me to deal with issues is... Maybe it's something in their genes, but the two most important women in my life have supported me beyond belief. They've both found a way to comfort me in dealing with the inner conflicts I've suffered through."

Kenneth looked at Melissa. He reached over and took her hand in his. He placed it to his lips giving her fingers a gentle kiss. He then turned and did the same to Susan. Kenneth smiled slightly.

"Both of you have been there when I needed you the most. I love you both so very much. I want to thank you Susan... Melissa, for everything you've done for me."

Kenneth reached up and wiped his eyes. No one said a word, they all held hands tightly with the love of their lives. Kenneth took another deep breath.

"When people look at us, our family, see the store, this home, I'm sure they think we've got it made. It's what they don't see behind our facade, the hard work we've put into our business, the hours of sweat. They don't see our tragedies, the tears we've shed together. There are days when it just amazes me we've survived and done as well as we have.

I think because of what we've gone through is why Susan loves her charity work so much. It allows her the opportunity to return something to our community, perhaps even take her mind off of some of our own problems. It's a chance, if you will, to help others who suffer, whether it's feeding them, clothing them, whatever. When she sees the smiles on people's faces she's helped, I think that means the world to her. Susan just loves helping people. She never misses an occasion to do something for someone, no matter who they are."

Susan squeezed his hand lightly. Kenneth rubbed his thumb gently over the back of her hand.

"Today we turn a new page in our lives and move on together. I know I feel much better inside since I talked to Melissa, and Susan many times throughout the years."

Edith and Frank smiled slightly as well as Melissa. Greg nodded his head slowly.

"So we can agree to let it all go," Melissa said in a soft voice.

"Yes, we can let it all go," Kenneth said in a voice that slightly quivered.

Susan looked at her husband, knowing in her soul Kenneth was at last free of the burden that so long had haunted his heart.

" If I may just say one last thing. Edith, thank you. You bringing this subject up has done me a world of good. I know that wasn't your intent, but still, it's brought a clear sky to where there once were many dark clouds."

Edith nodded her head as she reached up and wiped her eyes.

"You know," Kenneth continued as he wiped his eyes lightly with his napkin, "enough of these sad memories, let's move on and enjoy our meal together. Pass me some of those rolls, Frank, before you eat them all," he half jokingly said "they'll go great with this Italian meal Susan's made us."

"And Melissa helped me cook it," Susan acknowledged quickly.

Melissa's lips curled in a semi-smile. Frank smiled at Kenneth as he reached for the rolls. Kenneth halfheartedly smiled back at him.

Edith wanted to quickly change the subject matter as well. The only thing she could think of was along the lines of Italy. Perhaps it had to do with the fact that the aroma from her Italian meal sat silently beckoning to her.

"I would love to someday go to Italy," Edith said, "but there is, of course, the language barrier."

"Maybe we can go together and I can translate for you," Susan suggested, trying to help Edith to change the conversation's direction.

"Wouldn't that be wonderful," Edith said, a large excited smile written across her face.

"Yes, it would."

"Will your mother be coming to the wedding?" inquired Edith.

"We plan on it. I still have to give her a call but I wanted to wait until things are more in place so she can make her plans. I did talk to her a couple of days ago. She's so thrilled for both of you kids."

"That's great, Mom. I can hardly wait to see her," Melissa said. "I only wish Great Grandma could be here, but I know she's very old and frail."

"She would love to see you getting married I'm sure," Susan said.

"Well, unfortunately you can't have everything you want in life," Kenneth stated. "I do know it's going to be a beautiful wedding just the same with the three of you planning it. I took a peek at your list, but didn't see anything on it about making sure the father of the bride and groom were invited."

"Frank, are you going to say anything or just sit there filling your face?" inquired Edith.

"Please, I'm eating. By the way, will you hand me back the rolls?"

Edith shook her head back and forth.

Kenneth chuckled.

"Boy this is good," Frank said in somewhat of a louder voice.

"We can always send some home with you," Susan suggested.

"That would be great."

"Frank!" Edith stated.

"I would take a plate home, too, if it's okay," Greg offered.

"I'll fix you one when you're ready to leave," Melissa said.

"Don't worry, Frank, when Edith isn't looking I'll sneak some on a plate for you also," Kenneth added.

"Kenneth," Edith said, "please, you're not helping matters."

"Thanks, Kenneth," Frank said.

Susan smiled as she watched Frank eat. She loved having him come over on Sundays to taste the meals she prepared. Kenneth, on the other hand, was used to her tasty Italian meals so compliments were slow in coming, and very infrequent. Ah, but Frank, he was a horse of a different color. He would give you an ovation if the water in the glass was cold. Susan loved that about him.

When meals were being served at Edith's home, Susan savored the difference in the two cooking styles as well. Yes, Edith knew her way around the kitchen, there was no doubt about that. However, it was the men who relished the Sunday meals the most. Yes, there were many good discussions to take part in. In the end, it was the food that called out to both of their palates. They were all sure to give it their full attention on Sunday afternoons.

"I'll bet in Italy it's even an insult if you don't finish your plate and ask for some to go home with you," suggested Greg.

"I don't know about that," Susan said laughing, "but there's more than enough for you to hit the road with."

"Good," Frank said.

"So how was your day of fishing last week, I forgot to ask," Susan inquired.

"Well, " Kenneth said, "we do catch and release, but Frank was having a little trouble doing the catching part."

"Heck," Frank stated, "I actually let them go before I even caught them. I was just cutting out the middle man in the catch and release part.

"Good answer," chuckled Kenneth.

"I thought so," smiled Frank.

Will Sing for Food

The afternoon sun shinned brightly onto leaves in the trees causing leafy shadows below them on the ground. A warm breeze set some leaves into motion as if giving the trees a lazy life. Henry and Emma sat on the front porch of her home. Emma gently rocked in an old wooden rocker as she watched the quiet activities of the neighborhood about her. Henry sat propped up against a porch support, his legs resting on one of the steps. The creaking sound of her rocker was the only noise that broke the silence that embraced the two of them.

"Oh Henry, Henry, Henry," Emma said, "I do so love warm summer days. Spring brings forth the beauty in flowers, autumn fills us with colors, winter blankets the earth with its purity, but I'll take a warm summer breeze anytime." Henry looked over at her. Emma's eyes were closed as if soaking in every warm ray the sun it had to offer. She continued to slowly rock to and fro. Henry smiled as he watched her. After a moment he closed his eyes as well, as he turned his head to capture a little more of the sunshine's warmth on his face.

"Henry, will you do something for me?" Emma asked, her eyes closed as she continued to rock slowly.

"Sure, Mom."

"Would you sing a song for me?"

"What would you like to hear?"

"Something slow and peaceful to go along with today's weather." Her eyes remained closed as she spoke.

Henry thought for a few seconds, his back still resting up against the wide wooden support. He placed both of his hands behind his head interlocking his fingers. Resting his head in his hands he began to softly sing to Emma the song, "Danny Boy."

As Henry sang Emma continued to rock, her eyes still shut.

"That was so beautiful, son."

"Thank you, Mom."

"Will you do something else for me, please?" Emma said as she looked over at Henry.

"You know if I can I will."

"When I die, in many, many, years from now, will you sing that song at my funeral, son?"

"Oh, Mom, please let's not talk that way."

"Please."

"If it will stop you from talking that way, yes, I will."

Emma nodded her head happily.

"You know the words in that song, 'I love you so.'"

"Yes."

"That's how I feel about you, and how I felt about my Paul. It's days like this when I miss him the most. Now, Henry, every time you hear or sing that song I want you to remember me, our peaceful day together and the fact that I love you so."

"That's a wonderful thought for me to cherish. I'll keep those words tucked deeply in my heart, along with the love I have for you."

Emma continued rocking, a gentle smile on her face. She was a picture of complete contentment.

A half hour or so passed without either one of them saying a word to the other, too absorbed in the serenity of their surroundings.

"Paul and I used to do this when he was alive."

"What's that, Mom?"

"Sit together on the porch enjoying the weather together. Sometimes we'd have a sandwich or even a piece of cake, maybe just a cold glass of lemonade. These are the times I miss him the most," she said nodding her head.

"You know what, Mom, what would you say if we took a drive over to the cemetery and put some fresh flowers on his grave tomorrow."

"Oh, Henry, I would very much like to do that," she expressed excitedly.

"Then I'll pick you up say around —"

"How about one o'clock?" she suggested.

"You know what, let's make it eleven-thirty."

"Okay."

"That will give me a chance to have lunch with my favorite girl."

"What about Kate, won't she be jealous?"

"What would you say if I asked her to come along with us?"

"Do you think she can, I would really enjoy seeing her."

"I'll give her a call right now. Now, don't go running off with anyone while I'm gone."

"I won't," she said as she watched Henry get to his feet and go into the house to use the phone. Emma began to hum the song Henry had just sung as she slowly rocked. Henry returned shortly.

"Well, she's looking forward to it. Now, here's my idea. I'll first get Kate and then come over here to get you. I'll be here to pick you up at about eleven-thirty. We can then head to the restaurant and have a nice lunch together. After that, we can go to the florist and pick out some fresh flowers for your Paul."

"Wonderful."

"We can then go to the cemetery and visit Paul's grave. Mom, I don't want you to feel rushed in any way tomorrow; okay?"

"Thank you, I appreciate that. It's been some time since I've been to his grave."

"I know. We're going to take whatever amount of time you feel you need while we're there."

"Thank you, Henry."

The next morning Henry pulled his car into a parking spot in front of Doc's home. He got out and walked to the front door. As he reached for the handle on the door it quickly opened before him, somewhat startling him.

"I heard your car and saw you coming up the walk," Kate said. "You should see the look on your face, you actually looked shocked."

"I almost felt like that guy in the movies where he says, 'open sesame,' and the door opens before him, but I didn't even have a chance to say that. I really wasn't expecting that to happen."

"I could see that by the expression on your face," laughed Kate.

"So are you ready?"

"Uh-huh. I'm looking forward to seeing Emma. It's been a little while since we've seen each other. After what you told me over the phone, I'm glad we can do this for her, take her to the cemetery and have lunch together."

"I should have done this long ago."

"Well, you're doing it now, so that's what's really important."

The drive to Emma's house didn't take the couple very long. Once there, they went into the house and sat talking at the kitchen table. Emma served them hot drinks as they visited.

"Well, Mom, what do you say we go and have a little lunch now?"

"Only under one condition," Emma announced.

Henry was taken somewhat back by her statement.

"And what would that be, Emma?" asked Kate, noticing Henry didn't say anything at first.

"That it's my treat," Emma said.

"No, no, no, I'll pay the bill," Henry said, thinking to himself about the fact that Emma surely had plenty to handle with her own medical expenses.

"Well, then I guess I can't go."

"Henry," came the strong voice of Kate, "if she wants to pay that's entirely up to her."

"Thank you, Kate," nodded Emma.

"Well, okay," Henry said.

The three made their way to Henry's car with Emma being helped down the stairs by Henry and into the car.

"So how is it going with your marriage plans?" Emma asked.

Oh, here we go again, thought Henry. Every time these two women get together Emma wants to know the answer to that question.

"Emma, I'm going to be the Maid of Honor in Melissa's wedding."

"Isn't that wonderful. That will give you practice for your own wedding."

"Hmmm," thought Kate, as she absorbed Emma's statement.

"When are they getting married?"

"I don't know, she hasn't told me yet. Melissa and I are such good friends. When I get married I want her as my Maid of Honor as well."

"I wonder if she'd even think of inviting me. I would just love to go to her wedding."

"Maybe a little bird will talk to her," smiled Kate.

"Do you think that could happen?" Emma asked excitedly.

"Chirp, chirp," laughed Kate.

Emma chuckled.

"I suppose I'll never make it to your wedding, at Henry's rate of speed. You may just have to start looking elsewhere for a husband."

"Emma, don't give her any ideas," Henry quickly interjected.

"Well, I'm just saying."

Henry nodded his head back and forth as he grumbled to himself the rest of the way to the restaurant.

Henry pulled into Richard's Steak House. Getting out of the vehicle the three of them made their way inside taking a seat at a table.

"This restaurant has very good food," Kate said, "I've been here a few times with Grandpa. It really hasn't been open very long though."

"Well, I'm a little hungry, so that's good to hear," Emma said.

"And, Emma, do you see the electronic piano over in the corner by the dance floor. I was hoping to get Henry here one night so we could dance, but he's just not interested in it. They have a small group of musicians that play on the weekends. Henry, I would love to dance with you at Melissa's wedding some day."

"But I don't dance," he said.

"Oh, Henry, really," was all Emma could say.

"So what kind of food do you like," Kate asked her.

"Anything that's tasty, I guess. I don't have a very fussy palate."

"Good morning," came the voice of the waitress, "or maybe I should say good afternoon. My name is Judy and I'll be your server today."

"Good morning," Emma responded.

"Hello," Kate said.

"So what would you like to drink?"

"Hot tea, please," was Emma's answer which didn't come as any surprise to Henry.

"I'll have the same," he said.

"Coffee, please," Kate said. "And, Judy, could I get a glass of water with a slice of lemon, please."

"Of course."

It was just a matter of a few minutes when the waitress returned with their drinks.

"I'll give you a moment to look over the menu," she stated before leaving them.

As the three individuals sat talking, the subject of Melissa's upcoming marriage was brought up again.

"Melissa has asked Henry to sing at her wedding," Kate said.

"How wonderful, Henry," replied Emma. "It's really quite an honor to be asked to do something like that, don't you think?"

"Well, I think Kate volunteered me."

"No, I didn't, she asked me to ask you," Kate was quick to say.

"Kate, Henry did a wonderful thing for me yesterday," Emma stated as she returned her cup back to the saucer on the table.

"What was that, Emma?"

"He sang a song for me."

"I wish he'd do that for me once in a while."

"He's never done that?" Emma said, somewhat surprised with her statement. "You should be ashamed of yourself, Henry, not regaling Kate with songs of love."

"Well, she never asked me to," he said, not knowing what else to say.

"Well, ask him," Emma said in a demanding voice.

Kate didn't know quite what to say. She didn't want to put Henry on the spot but still, she thought, if he loves me he would sing a song to me, just as he had done for Emma. Kate looked over at Emma. She could see in her eyes Emma was waiting for her to make the request.

"I want a song, too," Kate stated in a somewhat demanding voice, "just like Emma got."

"Okay," chuckled Henry as he nodded his head, "When we get back home I'll sing a song for you, I promise."

"Now, Henry!" Emma said.

"Mother!"

"I didn't have to wait for my song to be sung, and neither should Kate."

"Please don't make me embarrass myself or look foolish," Henry said shaking his head.

"Please," Kate said as she fluttered her eyes up and down quickly.

Emma laughed.

"Really," he said.

"Please, Honey."

"All right, but this is under protest. I never want either one of you to ask me to do anything like this again."

Emma could see Kate cross her fingers as she nudged her. Emma winked at Kate.

Henry got up and walked over to the dance floor. He pulled a chair out from the electric piano and sat down. A few people took notice of what Henry had done. They watched to see what would happen next. There was a large feedback from the sound system as he turned on the electronic piano, which he adjusted quickly. More people looked over in his direction to see what had caused the noise. Background chatter still filled the air from patrons.

Slow heartfelt love songs were Henry's favorite, though his repertoire extended well beyond that. Henry began playing the introduction to an old favorite song he enjoyed. He started singing the lyrics to the song, "Somewhere over the Rainbow." Customers who hadn't seen Henry go over by the dance floor area turned their heads as he sang. Within seconds the restaurant became completely silent as individuals froze in their positions. Even the waitresses stood motionless as they listened to Henry's voice. A couple of cooks moved to the food serving window to see what was going on. As the last notes to the song drifted off into the still air, people began applauding. Henry simply nodded his head, as he gave a slight wave with his hand.

A man in a black suit came walking up to Henry as he was about to step from behind the piano.

"Sir, I'm here with my wife. We will be celebrating our 35th wedding anniversary with our family tonight. Your voice is so beautiful. We were wondering if you would be kind enough to sing a song we danced to at our wedding reception. It's very dear to the both of us, so if you can, we'd appreciate it very much. Can you do that for us? I know you probably can't. I doubt if you would even have the music to do it with."

"I'll do my best," Henry responded. "So what song would you like to hear?"

"I think he's going to sing another song," Emma exclaimed.

"You could be right," Kate said in surprise.

Henry once again stepped back behind the electronic keyboard. Now everyone in the place watched. You could literally hear a pin drop.

"This young couple," Henry said as he gestured with his hand in their direction, "is celebrating their 35th wedding anniversary today. I have been requested to play the song they danced to at their wedding reception."

The people in the restaurant applauded the couple.

"And so it gives me great pleasure to sing for them their song, a song they have cherished through the years."

Once again Henry played the introduction and then began singing.

Emma slid her hand in Kate's direction as she took it in hers. They looked at each other smiling.

"He is such a wonderful man," Emma said.

"Emma," Kate said as she squeezed her hand, "I wish he'd ask me to marry him."

Emma looked at her and nodded, her heart wishing the same thing for Kate as well.

"Waiting for something like that to happen can seem like forever, and when it does occur, the time you've waited will disappear like that of a flash of lighting, gone before you even realize it's there. My Paul was not in any hurry, even though we married at a very young age. We had many wonderful years together, and that's the time that really counts. He'll ask you when he's ready, and probably when you expect it the least."

Approximately a quarter of the way through the song Henry held a note a little longer as he looked over to the couple and motioned with his hand in the direction of the dance floor. The man held his hand out to his wife, she taking it immediately as they then walked out onto the floor. Together they began dancing, smiles upon both of their faces as they made their way around the dance floor. The people applauded. With the end of the song the sound of applause was even louder. The gentleman gently kissed his wife. Henry looked over at the couple and smiled. The man nodded his appreciation. His wife threw a gentle kiss to Henry with her hand.

Henry walked back to the table to rejoin the women.

"That was wonderful. Thank you so much," Kate said as she placed her hand on his shoulder once he sat down.

"That was something I never expected to happen when I came in this morning," the waitress stated. "You have such a beautiful voice, sir, and what you did for that couple was wonderful."

"Thank you," Henry answered.

"Your food will be right up. I just wanted to mention to you how much I enjoyed your singing."

The sound of a small bell rang out announcing an order of food was ready to be picked up. The waitress immediately turned and made her way toward the food counter. As the three individuals sat eating their lunch Henry noticed the gentleman and his wife making their way up to the cash register to pay their bill. The gentleman and his wife turned and waved to Henry as they made their way out of the restaurant.

"Henry, thank you again for doing that for me. I know you don't like singing in public. I really expected you to turn me down," Kate said, a soft smile reflected on her face.

"And that's what makes it such a special gift for you, Kate," Emma offered.

"As I once told you, Kate," Henry said, "I'm not as inhibited as I was before, especially over my scar."

"And thank God for that," Emma stated.

"When that couple asked you to play the song for them, I was so very proud of you," Kate added.

Henry smiled.

"That was a very good meal," Emma said as she set her napkin to the side.

"It sure was," Kate nodded.

"Now we can head over to the florist, and then to the cemetery," Emma said.

"Okay," Henry responded. "Miss," Henry said trying to get the waitress's attention.

"Henry, it's my treat," Emma said in a firm voice, "so no arguments."

"Okay."

"Can I have our bill please?" Emma asked the waitress.

"There's no bill, I'm happy to say," she replied.

"Pardon me?" Emma said.

"The gentleman and his wife paid your bill. He told me to thank you so much, it meant an awful lot to both of them."

"Doesn't that beat all?" Emma said.

Henry put his cup of tea down as he looked at the women. It was then that Henry offered the following.

"I've heard of people holding signs up that said, 'will work for food,' but I've never seen one saying, 'will sing for food.' Whoever would have thought that would happen to us today. Well, Miss," Henry continued, "at least let me leave you a tip."

"That's been taken care of, too," the waitress said nodding her head smiling. "The couple wanted your meals to be completely free and clear."

"Well, thank you."

"When we get home maybe I'll make up a sign for you," joked Kate, "will sing for food."

"And dessert," smiled Emma.

Henry, Kate, and Emma went out to Henry's car. Once inside they drove to the florist.

"You know, Henry, Norm's Florist has such a wonderful selection of fresh flowers and arrangements. I always get anything I need from here," Emma said, as they walked into the building.

"My grandpa does, too," Kate added.

"Emma," Henry said, "while we're here I'd like to get some flowers for Sam's plot also, if you don't mind."

"Of course not, Henry."

After the parties made their selections they once again got back into Henry's car and headed over to the cemetery. Henry drove the car through a large metal entrance gate and headed right for Paul's gravesite. He parked fairly close to the grave. Getting out of the vehicle Emma walked the short distance to the headstone.

"Emma, I'm going to take these flowers over to Sam's grave. I'll be back in just a little while or so, but you take your time. Take all the time you need."

"Thank you, Henry," she replied.

"I've never been to Sam's grave, so I'll go with you, Honey," Kate said.

"Thank you," he said as he reached out and took her hand in his. Together they made their way to Sam's grave.

Henry stood at the grave deep in thought for a little while. He then placed his flowers in a metal receptacle near the headstone.

"Sam was very important to you; wasn't he?" Kate said.

"No one will ever know how much," he expressed softly. "He was the father I never had, the friend you always hope for."

"In some ways you're a very lucky man. Even with all of the sorrows you've had to endure in your life, you still had Sam."

"That I did," Henry said as he nodded his head slowly... "That I did."

Henry and Kate stood there for some time. Finally he turned to Kate taking her hand again.

"Well, let's walk over and see Emma."

"Okay."

Kate and Henry stood back a short distance from Emma wanting to give her time alone. They watched as she placed her hand on the top of the tombstone, then gently rubbed her hand slowly back and forth on its top. She still held the flowers in her left hand. Kate thought she saw her wipe a tear from her face, but wasn't quite sure. Slowly Emma bent down placing the flowers in the container beside the headstone. She stood up with a single rose still in her hand. Emma kissed the rose and then placed it on top of the gravestone. She turned noticing Henry and Kate standing behind her.

"I think I'm ready now, Henry."

"We're in no hurry, Mom, take your time."

"Yes, take all the time you need," added Kate.

"No, that's okay. Thank you both for bringing me here today."

"You're welcome," Kate said.

"It's so comforting to come here and talk to Paul. It only seems like yesterday when he was alive."

Henry simply nodded his head.

"I think it's time to go home now," Emma said.

"Whatever you say, Mom."

Kate reached over and took Emma's hand as together they made their way back to the car. Henry opened the door as Emma slid in the front seat.

After taking Kate home, Henry drove down the street leading to Emma's home.

"Henry, what are your plans for tomorrow?"

"Nothing special. I have to finish up a little plumbing job at the Smith's home, but other than that, not much."

"Well, can you come over after you're done?"

"Sure, Mom. What do you need?" Henry asked.

"Tomorrow I thought we'd start on your dance lessons."

"Oh, Mom, really?"

"Just imagine the look on Kate's face when you step onto the dance floor at Melissa's wedding with Kate on your arm. I might even be there to see it."

The thought of taking dance lessons was truly Emma's. Henry thought, however, it would really be something to dance with Kate. He didn't say anything more on the subject as he continued driving her home. Once at Emma's home he helped her from the car and up to the front door.

"So I'll see you tomorrow, Mr. Astaire," Emma joked.

"Astaire?"

"Oh come on, Henry, Fred Astaire. He was a great dancer who used to dance in movies with Ginger Rogers."

"It sounds familiar. I think I watched them in an old black and white movie one time."

"Well, beginning tomorrow we start our lessons. Bring a comfortable pair of shoes, and not your work ones, I don't want you breaking any of my toes."

Henry just shook his head as he walked off the porch and down the stairs. He looked back at Emma standing at the window waving. Henry returned a gentle wave to her.

This is Going to Sound Dumb

Greg and Melissa continued to make their wedding plans, although Greg's portion of it was somewhat limited and at a distance. He would sit at the table watching the three women deeply involved with every aspect of it. Melissa wanted him to be a part of the plans, therefore, she wanted him beside her as items were discussed. Whenever he was asked a question he was quick to answer, but he really didn't care what they decided on. He had his best man selected, a groomsman, and that's all he needed to know. As long as he was there on time, everything else was really immaterial.

Greg didn't find it necessary to opine information on dress colors, flower selections or even table arrangements. If the food tasted good and the band was adequate, he would be happy. Yes, he knew everything would be perfect, the three women would surely see to that. There was no need to worry. Though he didn't say it out loud he was looking forward to seeing Melissa in her wedding gown. She's going to be a beautiful bride, he knew that in his heart.

"So now we move onto the guest list," Susan stated.

Those words immediately peaked Greg's attention. There were certain people he wanted to make sure were invited.

"Is there anyone whom you want invited, Greg?" Edith asked.

"Well, what would you and dad think about inviting Mr. and Mrs. Cash?"

"Who is that?" inquired Melissa.

"He's been my hockey coach for many years. When I was young he started coaching and we've been together ever since, even when he took on the high school coaching position."

"I'll bet they'd love to come," Edith agreed.

"Neither one of our kids know this person very well," Susan said, "but Greg, do you remember the clerk at our store, the woman from the shoe department?"

"Yes."

"I know her, too. She's very nice," Melissa said.

"I would ask you, as a favor to Kenneth and me, that we be allowed to invite her. Her name is Jean Parker. If she's available, I'd like to have her there."

"Susan, why would you even ask that? Anyone you want is fine with us; right Greg, Melissa?" Edith declared.

"Of course," Melissa said.

Greg nodded his head agreeing with her statement.

"Thank you. Greg, I met a young man at the gas station by the name of Dwight a couple of years ago," Susan said. "He drew us the map to your mother and father's house when we were trying to find it. He's also the one who requested me to be sure to wish your family a Merry Christmas. Do you know who he is, Greg?" Susan said.

"Yes. His name is Dwight Shutter. We went to school together. He played goalie on our team."

"I'll need to get his address."

"I'll get it for you. Of course we'll be inviting Kim and Dan's parents?" inquired Greg, not really sure of what they would say.

"As far as I'm concerned the door is wide open when it comes to invitations," Susan said. "We won't really be having but a few individuals coming from our side."

"So the sky's the limit," Greg joked.

"Oh, oh," Melissa stated excitedly. "I talked to Kate, and she was wondering if we would be kind enough, and that's the way she stated it, to invite Emma to come."

"That would be fine," Susan stated.

"Will your mother be making it?" Edith asked.

"I talked to her a few days ago, and she's very excited about Melissa's marriage," Susan said. "She wouldn't miss it for the world. She's having some health problems, but I'm planning on her being here."

"Mom, you didn't mention that to me," Melissa quickly added.

"Well, I wanted to wait to make sure, and then we've been just so busy with everything. I'm sorry, Honey, it slipped my mind."

"I'm just so excited she's coming."

"You don't really think she'd miss your wedding, do you?"

"Not really, it's just that I wanted so much for her to be here."

"I understand, Melissa."

"I wish great grandma could make it here from Italy," Melissa stated with a sigh.

"Well, it's an awfully long trip, and she's not that young," Susan said. "Frankly, I think it would do her more harm than good."

"I understand," Melissa said as she nodded her head.

Suggestions of who else should be invited was discussed.

Kenneth and Frank came through the front door of the house. Heading to the kitchen area, Kenneth turned to Frank.

"Want anything to drink?"

"Yeah, I'll take a bottle of soda, please. Thank you."

"You're back already?" Susan said.

"Well, the game finished a lot quicker than we expected," Frank said.

"So how is it going with the 'to-do-list'?" asked Kenneth.

"Very well," Susan stated.

"We've got a lot of it done," added Melissa.

"And I've been the most help of all," joked Greg.

"Greg, really!" Edith said.

"I stayed out of the way; didn't I?"

The women simply smiled to themselves.

"Greg, did you drive here by yourself?" asked Kenneth.

"No, I rode with my mom and dad."

"I see."

"Is there something you need a hand with?"

"Well, Susan and I wanted to talk to you about something, ask you a question or two."

"Oh, Kenneth, stop being so secretive, we're all family here," Susan stated.

Greg and the remainder of the individuals looked at Kenneth wondering to themselves what was going on. Melissa got up and walked over to a vacant chair next to Greg and sat down beside him. Inside she felt it necessary to be by him now, though she didn't know why.

"What are your plans for the future, if I may ask?" Kenneth said.

"Well, once we save enough money I want to finish my education."

"Greg," Kenneth started out, "Susan and I have talked this over and we would be very proud if you would join us in our family business."

Edith put her hands to her face, not expecting at all what she had just heard. What a wonderful offer to make him, she thought. Melissa reached over and took Greg's hand in hers.

"We both know you would do a wonderful job for us," Kenneth said. "after all, anyone who can sell two pairs of shoes to a man who has one foot, make absolutely no profit at all, and then pay for the shoes himself is the type of person we know we can trust to do a good job for us."

Greg smiled while Susan and Melissa actually chuckled.

"Can I think about it?" asked Greg, shocking everyone in the room.

"Honey, you heard what he said, it's a wonderful opportunity for both of us," Melissa said as she looked at him somewhat shocked.

"Can I ask you a couple of questions then?" Greg asked.

"Of course," Kenneth said shaking his head back and forth, somewhat in shock himself.

"Where would I start at?"

"How about in an office just down the hallway from mine?"

"Can I have just a minute with Melissa alone?"

"Sure. You can use my office if you'd like."

Greg stood up as Melissa followed him into Kenneth's home office. He reached behind her and closed the door.

"I don't understand, Honey. As I just said, it's a wonderful opportunity for us."

"You're absolutely right," he replied.

"So what's the problem?"

"I know this is going to sound dumb to you, but still I would want to do this on my own terms, make my own way if you will... I always have."

"You really don't have to explain anything to me, Honey, I trust you completely, but you're going to have to do some explaining to my parents about what you mean. Whatever you decide we'll both live with it, good or bad."

"Thank you for supporting me in this, it's really very important to me."

This, Melissa thought, I wonder what this really is going to end up to be.

Greg pulled Melissa close to him kissing her.

"Oh, Greg, I want to show you something while we're in here," Melissa said excitedly as she spoke.

"Okay."

Melissa walked around the desk and pointed to a large calendar sitting on top of the desk. Dates leading up to the present were crossed off in a large red "X." A lot of dates had a variety of things written on them, call on cake, do this, do that. Greg smiled as he looked at it. Melissa lifted a calendar sheet revealing the next month's events. A large red heart had been drawn denoting their wedding date. Two rings were also drawn in the box with a red pen containing the date.

"You're quite the artist, Honey," he said, "and I see you used your very favorite color, red."

Melissa smiled at him as he pulled her into his arms kissing her once again.

"Well, let's go face the music," he said.

Melissa and Greg stepped from the office door.

"So where are we at on all of this, Greg? Susan and I thought you would be thrilled with our offer. Is it about money, what, we don't understand?"

Frank and Edith sat waiting for Greg's answer as well.

"The offer you've made to me, for us, is more than just generous, it's absolutely wonderful. The problem I have with it is —"

"Problem," Kenneth said in a somewhat disgusted voice, "did you say problem?"

"Give Greg a chance to talk," Susan quickly stated, realizing Kenneth was getting upset with Greg's failure to jump at their offer.

"Well, we're talking business, so let's deal with it in that way, if that's okay with you," Greg said.

"Whatever you say," Kenneth answered, nodding his head.

"Mr. Summers, this offer by you and your wife is almost beyond comprehension. It is extremely generous, to say the very least. The problem I have with it is that you and your wife are getting the raw end of the deal. You're starting someone in a position who has way too much to learn."

"But we would teach you," Susan quickly stated.

Kenneth put his hand up to her indicating for her to stop.

"If you can see fit to allow me to start out in, say, the stock room, work there, do some sale jobs, get to know the business, that's what I'm thinking of. Both of you deserve to get an employee who knows the ins and outs of the retail business before he moves upstairs so to speak."

Frank and Edith smiled their agreement with Greg's words. Both of them were proud in their hearts as they listened to their son discussing the offer. Kenneth nodded his head. He liked what he was hearing from Greg. The fact of the matter was, he once again realized how very smart his daughter's fiancé was, and honest. When will I ever learn, Kenneth thought as he smiled to himself.

Frank and Edith sat taking everything in. Edith felt it was almost like watching a soap opera playing itself out before her eyes. She couldn't wait to see what happened next.

"Now let's talk about your salary, Mr. Prospective Employee," Kenneth said, going along with Greg's suggestion of dealing with everything in a businesslike manner.

Melissa and Susan smiled at each other; they were enjoying this friendly feud.

"Well, whatever the position's pay is, that's what I'll get, simple as that," Greg said nodding his head.

"Well, we both want our daughter to be comfortable. She makes a good salary, but still and all —"

"You once told me you do the payroll; right, Mrs. Summers?"

"Yes, I do."

"Well, pay me for my job description, and if you feel more comfortable you can give Melissa anything over that you want to. That's entirely up to you two ladies. My dad brought me up to believe you live on what the man makes, whatever your wife brings in is all bonus."

Frank smiled at Greg, Edith nodding her head.

"So we're in agreement, you can start right after things have settled down from the wedding," Kenneth stated.

"I do have another condition."

"He's got another condition," Kenneth said shaking his head, almost laughing out loud.

"Kenneth," Susan said in a laughing manner.

"Okay, what other condition do you have, Mr. Prospective Employee?" he asked.

"Just one, that no one knows that I'm your son-in-law unless it just happens to come out. I don't want any doors shut before I get the chance to walk through them and learn the job. I know people would treat me differently, and I don't want that to happen. Is that okay with you?"

"Fair enough. Anything else?"

"No, sir."

"Good. Well, welcome to Summers' Department Store," Kenneth said as he held his hand out to Greg which he shook immediately.

"Thank you, Mr. Summers. I'm sure I'll enjoy working for both of you."

Melissa laughed.

Susan chucked.

"Oh, I'll have to talk to Jean Parker," Susan stated. "She's sure to remember you from when you spoke to her two years ago. I know it was a fairly long time ago, but I also know I'd remember anyone who did what you did for that family. I'll talk to her at work tomorrow, and besides, I want to invite her to your wedding. She's a wonderful woman.

Kenneth, is it all right with you if we give Melissa and Greg that special gift we've been working on?"

"I guess now is as good a time as any," he answered.

"What gift is that, Mom?" inquired Melissa.

"It's something your dad and I wanted to give the two of you," Susan stated as she got up and walked towards the office. She soon returned carrying a package wrapped in wedding paper. A card was tucked in behind some of the ribbon on the gift. Susan handed the gift to Melissa as she winked at Kenneth. From simply observing its size and shape it appeared to be a picture of some kind. It was about the size of an 8x10. As Melissa held it in her hands she could feel the framing through the paper.

"Well, open it," suggested Greg.

"I will, but first the card," Melissa stated.

"Oh, I'm sorry."

Melissa placed her finger in a slight opening in the back of the card pulling it open. She then removed the card from the envelope. The front of the card had a picture of a wedding bouquet made of red roses with long streamers coming from it. When she opened the card, it was obvious the inside had originally possessed a blank interior. Hand written were the words:

"May this remind the both of you when you look at it, that we love you very much." It was signed by both Susan and Kenneth.

Greg continued watching Melissa from her side as she slowly began opening the gift. As she had thought, it was a framed item. The gold frame had small hearts and flowers embedded in the wood as well as some that protruded slightly from it, giving it somewhat of a 3-D effect as well. The item the frame held was matted. It was a yellow piece of notepaper with a hand drawn map on it. On the matted portion below the drawing, engraved in a lovely handwriting font were the words:

"Through Love Anything Can Be Accomplished"

"This is so beautiful, Mom."

"Can I see that, for a second, Melissa?" asked Greg. "This is a map to my mom and dad's house from over by —"

"From the gas station Dwight works at," smiled Susan. "He drew this map for us the night we searched for your mom and dad's house."

"You've had this since then?" Melissa asked.

"Well, Honey," she said, "Edith found it on a table of theirs and held onto it for us. One day she showed it to me and asked if I had any use for it. She didn't want to just throw it away. She suggested that I may want to do something special with it."

"And so this is the result?" Melissa said smiling.

Susan nodded her head.

"I want to hang this somewhere very special in our home. I want it hung where I'll see it every day. Thank you, Dad and Mom, and thank you, too, Mama Edith."

"Thank you," Greg said. "That's a very thoughtful gift you've given us."

The announcement was heard throughout the store over the sound system. "Would Jean Parker please report to the main office?" Jean looked up at the clock. It read eleven o'clock. I wonder what they need me for, she thought. Turning to her right she made her way to the main office section on the fourth floor. Walking into the office portion she was greeted by Susan.

"You need me for something?"

"Yes, Jean. It's nice to see you... come on in."

Jean stepped into the room somewhat apprehensive. While she had been to Susan's office before, this time there was something that just didn't feel right to her. Why, she had no idea.

"Have a seat."

"Thank you, Mrs. Summers."

"Jean, the reason I asked you here is really two-fold. I'm sure you remember coming to my home a couple of years ago last December."

"Yes, I do. You called me on the phone and asked me to tell your husband what had transpired in my shoe department concerning your future son-in-law. I assume that's what you're referring to?"

"Yes, it is. So you do remember meeting with my daughter's fiancé earlier that day?"

"Yes, one doesn't really forget someone who did what he did for that woman and her kids."

"Now here's the first part of my request. Our daughter and Greg — oh, that's his name. I don't know if you knew that."

"No, I didn't," Jean said, shaking her head back and forth.

"Well, their wedding is being planned for this December, literally just around the corner."

"Oh, how wonderful, you must all be so excited."

"Yes, we are. Kenneth and I would like to have someone there to be a representative at her wedding from our store."

"Oh."

"Now let me explain a few things to you. First of all, the wedding is on a day you are scheduled to work, therefore, I would request that you take the day before and after off, plus the day of the wedding obviously. Also you'll have to stay in a motel for a few nights."

Susan could see Jean's mind working as she spoke. She knew Jean's face reflected her thoughts on what this was going to cost her financially.

"I can see by the look your face you have some questions, so let me answer what I think you're wondering and then we can go from there. Is that okay?"

Jean nodded her head.

"I've already made arrangements for you to stay in a newly built motel in the area that will be paid for by us. This motel has a restaurant attached to it. Your meals will simply be added to the bill, which we will take care of also. In addition, the three days you spend doing this favor for our family are paid days off. Now, there are a few more items I want to discuss with you."

"Mrs. Summers, this is very generous on the part of you and your husband."

"Miss Parker... Jean, you're doing us the favor, remember that. Now, I'm a woman just as you are and I know a new dress or two can come in handy, especially if you're attending a wedding. Here is a check so you can get any additional accessories you may need to have."

"Mrs. Summers, it's for $600.00."

"Well, don't you want to look good?" Susan said smiling at Jean.

Jean nodded her head, overwhelmed with what was taking place.

"Now, if you're anything like the person I think you to be, you're going to feel obligated to bring a wedding gift. Don't you dare, and I mean this strongly. You representing our store is enough of a gift to give. Oh, and one last thing, I almost forgot. Take this, you'll need it also."

Susan handed Jean a plastic card.

"It's a gas card," Jean said as she held it in her hand.

"We don't want this costing you a single penny."

"It's obviously too much, Mrs. Summers."

"Well, I never was very good at figuring out miles per gallon and so forth, so you just keep any overage. Also, you'll be getting an invitation in the mail from us. Is there anything you think Kenneth and I have forgotten?"

Jean shook her head back and forth.

"Okay. Now, the second portion of my favor of you, and to tell you the truth I feel a little guilty asking you to do this, but I need you to keep a little secret for us. After our daughter is married, her husband will be coming to work here."

"So all of you will be together here on the fourth floor, kind of a family section in the store," Jean speculated.

"That's what Kenneth and I thought, actually hoped for, but that wasn't Greg's view of it at all."

"Oh?"

"He told us if he was going to work in the store, he wanted to start at the bottom and work his way up. It's his thinking that this would be the best way to learn our business."

Jean couldn't help herself, she started to chuckle.

"Am I missing something?" Susan asked.

"I've only met your future son-in-law for a few minutes, twice for that length of time, but you know something, I really like him. This isn't my place to say, but I'm going to say it anyway just the same. Do you two realize how fortunate you are to have him? There's quite a few women that work here, and I'll bet a lot of them don't have a husband or boyfriend that's anywhere near his level of consideration."

"Oh, we know what you're saying, Jean, and you're absolutely right. Every day he surprises us. Well, as I say, he wants to learn the business from the bottom up, so when you see him in the store, will you please keep his secret to yourself?"

"I'll be glad to."

"And if he comes to work in your section, can you help him, keep an eye on him?"

"Of course, but I would do that anyway, no matter who they are."

"I know, I'm just saying. And Jean, I want you to know that Kenneth and I both feel privileged to have you as an employee."

"Thank you, Mrs. Summers, I appreciate that."

"If you think of anything I've missed, or anything you need, just let me know."

"I will. Well, I better get back to work."

"Thank you, Jean. Oh, Jean," Susan said shaking her head back and forth, "it never dawned on me to ask you if this was alright with you. Please forgive me for that, but is it? We wouldn't want to force you into doing something you'd rather not do."

"I understand. You have a lot on your mind. And just so you know, I really am very pleased that you've asked me to attend."

Jean stood up and walked to the door of the office. She placed her hand on the door handle and paused.

"Mrs. Summers, for some reason I feel... is there really more to this than what you've just told me?"

"Well, actually there is. I wanted you to be invited to Melissa's wedding because I like you."

"And I like you, too, and your whole family," Jean said smiling.

She opened the door and nodded one last time to Susan as she closed the door behind her. Jean took a deep breath, excited from both the words and gifts she had just received. As the door closed behind Jean, Susan took a deep breath as well, happy that everything worked out so well for everyone.

Oysters and Crackers

Everything was in place. Edith, Susan, and Melissa sat looking over their now famous, "to-do-list" with nothing more to write on it.

"So that does it," Susan stated as she took the pen and crossed off the last item remaining. All the "T's" were crossed, as well as all of the "I's" dotted. Everything was in place and ready to go.

"I feel kind of sad," Edith offered, "it was so much fun working on this together, and now it's all over."

"Yes," Susan agreed.

"I'm not going to shed any tears over this," Melissa said, "I'm kind of glad it's done. Still, it is a little sad. I loved the fact that we were altogether and could visit as well."

"You three look like you've all lost your best friend," stated Kenneth as he walked into the room.

"We've got everything crossed off on our list, Dad," Melissa uttered, "there's nothing more to do."

"Great, now it's all downhill from here, unless you've forgotten something on your 'to-do-list,'" Kenneth suggested.

"No, we covered everything twice, and then twice again," offered Susan.

"Okay. Well, let's give it a run through. You three ready?" he said.

The three women looked at each other wondering what the run through would consist of, but they didn't want to miss anything either.

"I'll mention an item, you just shake your heads yes or no and we'll see if I can throw a wrench into the mix."

The women shook their heads in agreement.

"Church, minister, limo, photographer, reception hall, cake, dress, food, hair dresser appointment, tuxedos."

"That's the men's responsibility, the tuxedos," Susan said, "and yes on the rest of those items."

"Well, just the same I'd check into it," Kenneth suggested. "Moving on. The invitations, usher and bridal party gifts, hall decorations, table decorations, band, rehearsal dinner, restaurant reservations."

The women kept nodding their heads very content that every item was covered.

"Well, I can't think of anything else," Kenneth said. "Oh, organist, singer, programs."

"Yes, yes, and yes," Susan said proudly.

"How about a card to put some money in for the pastor?"

The women looked at each other, faces blank.

"And the flower girl's basket and petals, is that taken care of?" he asked.

"Ladies, we've got a little more work to do," Edith stated. "You've been very helpful, Kenneth, thank you."

Kenneth nodded his head as he reached in the refrigerator to get a cold drink. He turned to face the ladies.

"And, by the way, did you get stamps for doing your mailings?" he asked.

Susan rolled her eyes as she wrote a little note on the pad of paper.

"Oh, and what are we doing as far as food when we all decorate the hall the day before?" he inquired.

"And where were you when we were making this list up?" joked Susan, "We could have used your help then, too."

"Where was I, with Frank making our own list of food for the pre-meal and snacks we'll have waiting for the people after the wedding service is over. And ladies, Frank and I were wondering what your thoughts would be concerning serving oysters out of the can they come in?" Kenneth face reflected a gleam in his eye, a small smirk resting on his lips.

"Not at my wedding you don't," Melissa was quick to say, her face looking like she had just tasted something bitter to her tongue as she thought about what he had just said.

"Oh, come on, Frank and I were even going to have crackers to go with them."

"You better not, Dad."

"I'm just saying," he said smiling.

Susan, and especially Edith, both made faces when they thought of his suggestion as well. Observing their faces somewhat distorted with the thought of eating snacks out of a can made him chuckle inside. He had accomplished his job, made them thankful for what Frank and he had already decided on, and still giving them a little tease in the form of a joke.

The phone rang in the kitchen. Kenneth walked over and picked it up. He offered the customary greeting.

"I see. And when will you find out? Okay. Do you want to speak with Susan? All right, I'll let her know."

"Who was that?" Susan asked.

"Your mother. Apparently she may need to have an operation, but they wanted to check out some things before they decide."

"What kind of operation?"

"Bunion."

"Oh," Susan said, "she could be tied up for weeks."

"You mean she may miss my wedding?" Melissa asked.

"Well, we'll have to wait and see. Who knows, maybe she can postpone it.

"Oh, Mom."

"I know, Honey, I wanted to see my mother, too."

"Look at it this way, Melissa," Edith stated, "you can only control certain things in your life, so let's take control of what we can, and work on our newly added 'to-do-list'."

"You sound just like Greg," smiled Melissa.

"And maybe that's where he learned it from," suggested Susan.

"Maybe so," commented Edith.

Another Sunday and another two-family dinner would be served and enjoyed as usual. Frank found himself doing what he usually did on these occasions, hanging around the kitchen soaking in the smells. Every once in a while his hand would meander to a dish full of waxed beans, pickles or olives to steal a small morsel. Everyone always saw him do it, he simply wasn't very careful at camouflaging his intentions.

"Well, dinner's on," came the announcement by Susan.

"Good, I'm really hungry," Kenneth stated.

"Don't forget to save me some," Greg said. "I see dad is on the prowl again."

"He's always on the prowl when it comes to eating," Edith added.

"I'm not on the prowl, I'm just studying over my options," Frank stated.

"So, Melissa, how are your vows coming?" asked Susan.

"Oh, they're coming."

"If you need some help, I'll help you," volunteered Greg.

"Really, Greg," Melissa said nodding her head back and forth.

"You can always use my office, if you need somewhere to have a little quiet time to yourself," Kenneth said.

"To tell you the truth, Honey," Susan said, "I wish you would forget doing that altogether."

"Mom, it will be okay."

"You know how you are at speaking in public, and a wedding is a lot of pressure."

"Mom, it's going to okay."

"And how are you doing on yours, Mister, I'll help you if you need it?" asked Edith.

"Actually I've got it all done. I'm working on the memorization part of it now," Greg said smiling.

"You're kidding me," Edith stated.

"No, not really."

"And how am I supposed to stand up and give mine by memory, I can't do that," Melissa said.

"I'll tell you what, I'll go first, and then when everyone is bored and sleeping, you can read yours."

"I thought ladies got to go first?" Melissa expressed.

"Okay, you go first and then I'll follow you."

"Not so fast, I think I will let you go first. You're in a little too much of a hurry to let me go first. No, you better go first."

"Okay, whatever you want. My vows basically just say I love you over and over and over," smiled Greg, "that's how I could memorize them so easily."

"And they better say just that," joked Susan.

"They will, I promise you that much ladies," he answered.

Sitting around the family table discussing events and plans for the wedding was truly a time to be savored by all. No one enjoyed this more than the women. As they finished up the meal, Greg asked Melissa if she'd like to go for a walk.

"I'm sorry, kids," Kenneth said, "but we would like to address a few things with you both."

"Can't it wait until we get back, Dad?" asked Melissa.

Taking long walks on Sundays with Greg was her favorite past time, and she didn't want to miss out on it. Sometimes the parents tagged along, especially when days were warm or mild. The weather never bothered Melissa, she just put on a heavier coat. Holding Greg's hand always seemed to keep her warm enough, even when the breeze carried a bitter bite to it.

"Well, I suppose we can wait," Kenneth stated, "but I think you might be interested in what we have to say."

"We can go after," Greg suggested.

"Okay, Honey."

"Let me make us a fresh pot of coffee before we start," Susan stated. "We can all discuss this while we have dessert."

"I'll serve the dessert," Edith declared as she got up and walked over to the refrigerator, opening the freezer portion. "A little ice cream to go along with my homemade apple pie will help hit the spot, I'm sure. Now, who wants their pie heated?" Edith put the ice cream on the table along with the scoop.

A few hands went up in the air.

With everyone seated, their desserts in front of them, Kenneth took a drink from his coffee cup and then set it down. He looked over in Frank and Edith's direction and winked.

"So what are your plans for your honeymoon, we were all wondering?" Kenneth asked.

Greg and Melissa were stunned. The last thing either one of them thought they'd hear about was their honeymoon.

"Dad," Melissa said as she looked at him, "we haven't really even discussed that, it's kind of the last thing on our minds; right, Honey?"

"We just thought we would talk about it when..." Greg stopped in mid-sentence. "We just haven't really talked about it. The fact of the matter is we just never brought it up to each other. Well, once we discussed it for a minute."

"So you haven't really broached the subject, I guess," Kenneth stated in a matter of fact voice. Kenneth looked over in Frank and Edith's direction again. "Frank," he said as he nodded his head.

"Well," Frank started out in his one word reply, then stopped immediately. He looked at Edith and Susan. "This all began as Edith's idea, and then Susan and her ran with it, so I'm going to defer to Edith, if that's okay."

Melissa and Greg looked at each other, both faces dazed. They felt they were at a tennis match watching the subject of their honeymoon being bounced back and forth. Neither one of them knew what anyone was talking about. Greg took a drink from his coffee cup, as if it would clear up his confusion, which, of course, it didn't. Melissa reached over and took his free hand in hers. Edith cleared her throat as she looked in Susan's direction.

"Your parents, all four of us," she began, "love both of you very much, but you already know that. Melissa, you are not going to be just our daughter-in-law, in our eyes you are much more than that. You're as much a part of our family as Greg is to us. To Frank and me you are like our daughter, just as Greg is thought of as a son by Susan and Kenneth. Susan has indicated that to me on many occasions. How truly fortunate we all are to have two kids such as you."

Melissa and Greg squeezed each other's hands at the same time.

"The excitement we all feel over your pending marriage is unbelievable. As we've gotten to know each other, the four parents that is, we've come to realize that the two of you have given us a wonderful gift. You introduced us to each other, and a beautiful friendship between us has materialized from that. Gifts of true friendship are a very precious thing to possess. All of us thank you for that.

Now, to get to the point. The four of us would like to treat you both to a honeymoon, which we believe you'll never forget, at least that's what we want it to be. Susan has done a lot of leg work putting this together, and we all hope you'll accept this gift from our hearts." Edith took a deep breath and then wiped her eyes.

"Well, Kenneth, you spoke, then Frank and now me. I think it's time you take over, Susan, my voice is starting to act up a little bit."

Edith wiped the corner of her eye with her finger once again.

"Do you need your tissue?" asked Susan.

"Not yet, but I know where they're at."

"Melissa, Greg, this was Edith and Frank's idea," Susan said. "They've been kind enough to include Kenneth and me in it. When we heard about it, we wanted to be a part of it. We were so excited with their idea. We've checked into airline tickets, accommodations, schedules and so forth. We know where you go on your honeymoon is entirely yours to make, but we would... all four of us would like to know if you would consider going to Hawaii on our dime, so to speak."

"Oh, man," uttered Greg as he placed his hand upon the brow of his head.

Melissa put her hands up to her lips in amazement.

"Well, you don't have to make up your minds right away," Susan suggested. "As I say, it's your decision to make. All of us just wanted to do something special for both of you."

The young couple sat there stunned, not knowing what to say. Finally Greg broke the ice.

"We kind of talked a little bit about maybe camping or something to save money, we never dreamt of anything like this. So what do you think, Honey?" asked Greg. He turned and looked at Melissa, her eyes sparkling in excitement. She just nodded her head up and down, unable to speak.

"Well, I don't know," Greg stated, "that means I'd have to pack a pair of swimming trunks, and we all know how much room that can take up in luggage."

Melissa reached over and punched Greg on the arm.

"Ouch, that hurt," he laughed.

She then grabbed him in her arms hugging him around the neck.

"I guess that means we're going to Hawaii," he said.

Once again Melissa shook her head, slight tears in her eyes.

"Don't worry, Melissa," Edith stated, "I have plenty of tissue to go around."

"Well, pass them over here first." Susan said.

Greg and Melissa got up and walked around the table embracing each one of the parents. With the final hug completed, they all sat down in their chairs.

"Now it's time for dessert," Frank exclaimed happily.

"There he goes with the food again," Edith said shaking her head.

"Your ice cream is really starting to melt, Greg," Susan said.

"Kind of like what your daughter did to my heart," Greg declared.

"Now that statement is sweeter than my pie," laughed Edith.

"This is more than wonderful, what you've done for us. Thank you," Melissa expressed.

"It sure is. Thank you, everyone, thank you so very much," Greg said, a large smile filling his face.

"Maybe we can return the favor someday," Melissa laughed.

Melissa then smiled as she laid her head down on Greg's shoulder. He reached over and put his arm on her other shoulder, then squeezed it with his hand.

A Waste of Skin

The morning sun shining through the window awoke Kate. A sprinkling of curtain shadows lay across her comforter announcing the beginning to the new day as well. She got out of bed and went into her private powder room, as she liked to refer to it as. She began to run water into the sink to brush her teeth. She took a few seconds to look around. Numerous fond thoughts of working on the project with Henry rushed through her mind as she glanced about the room. Whenever she had an occasion to go into the powder room, those memories came alive to her as well as her heart.

Over on the shelf sat the plant Henry had gotten her, the dark blue ribbon and bow still attached to it. Her thoughts next went to the day when she first heard Henry singing. She chuckled to herself remembering how she had cautiously sneaked up to the room and heard him singing from behind the closed bathroom door. Kate smiled as she shook her head slightly.

She placed some toothpaste on her toothbrush and began brushing her teeth. As she did, Kate recalled the day Melissa came to visit her, how she had made many hurtful statements to Kate concerning Henry. She recalled asking Melissa to leave, and the torment of a lost friendship that lingered in her heart that awful day. She quickly relived how a few days later Melissa came back to see her and asked for Kate's forgiveness. That day they hugged, Melissa offering an apology, Kate happy to accept it. It seemed almost like decades ago she thought, and now she was going to be Melissa's Maid of Honor. A smile reflected back to her from the mirror she stood in front of. Kate got dressed, combed her hair, then started down the stairway. As she reached the bottom steps, the phone rang. Kate reached for the phone and answered it.

"Hello?"

"Kate, it's me, Melissa. I'm in town and wondered if we can get together for breakfast."

"Boy, you sure got an early start today."

"Well, I needed to. Can you do that, meet me for breakfast?"

"Sure. Mom's Country Kitchen, is that okay?"

"Perfect. I'll meet you there in a little while."

Kate wondered why Melissa needed to have gotten up so early, and then to make the drive to the town of Creek Side. I'm sure it has to do with some last minute wedding projects, she thought to herself.

"Grandpa, I'm going to go meet Melissa for breakfast. Do you want me to cook something for you before I leave?"

"No, Kate, I'll get something at the hospital."

"Okay, Grandpa. I'll see you later."

"Have a nice day with Melissa."

"I will."

Once at the restaurant Kate joined Melissa in a booth. Kate couldn't help but notice that Melissa was, "dressed down" so to speak. She wasn't wearing the usual beautiful attire that frequently adorned her. Instead, she wore jeans and a plain nondescript blouse. Even her jacket was black, vague in description, with nothing fancy about it whatsoever. Her hair was combed, but not every hair was perfectly set into place.

"Just coffee, please," Kate said to the waitress.

Melissa sat with a plate of eggs and potatoes before her. She held a piece of toast in her hand with grape jam spread on it.

"So what's new?" Kate inquired.

"Kate, I did something I don't know if I should have."

"What's that? It can't be all that bad."

"It depends on how you look at it, that's why I wanted to talk to you." Melissa took a bite from the bread.

"Okay."

"My mom and dad have a retired detective that works for them at the store, he handles security and such."

"Yes."

"Well, he's a wonderful man and I've known him for years. I asked him to check something out for me that concerns Henry."

Now Kate's interest peaked.

"You checked up on Henry?"

"Kind of."

"Why in the world would you do that?" Kate asked, a little tone to her voice.

"Remember when Henry was in the hospital?"

"How could I ever forget that."

"We talked about Henry not having a last name, or I should say he didn't know it."

"Uh-huh."

"Well, I had Mr. Sheppard, that's the security guy's name, look into it. Oh, I shouldn't have mentioned his name. Well, anyway he did a little checking for me and I know where the Lewis family now lives. I wanted to go and talk to them about Henry, but that is not my decision to make. I was hoping, if it was okay with you that I even do that, that you would go with me."

"Oh," was all Kate could say.

The waitress brought Kate her coffee and set it down in front of her. Melissa sat slowly eating her breakfast waiting for Kate to respond. She understood Kate's reluctance to go there, but she also knew Kate would want to solve Henry's dilemma of not knowing his real name, when he was born, and where. This was a door Melissa would walk through with Kate, but would Kate be willing to take that same journey? Melissa could see a battle being fought in Kate's mind, her face revealing that fact. Melissa sat silently.

"How far do they live away?" Kate asked timidly.

"We could be there in a little over a half an hour."

Kate nodded her head. Melissa offered nothing more to Kate, no questions, no statements. She just waited for her next words to be spoken.

"Let's do it, let's go and talk to them, after all, what do we have to lose?" Kate said in a strong voice that surprised Melissa.

"Once you finish your coffee, we'll go."

"No, now, while I still have the nerve."

"Okay, let's do it, and we'll do it together." Melissa reached in her purse and placed some money on the table as she and Kate got up.

As Melissa and Kate rode together on their way to the Lewis home, Kate thought they should work on some type of plan. What should we say, and what if Mr. Lewis looks a little nuts. They discussed many possibilities between themselves. Kate didn't know what to really expect, though Melissa had a plan already worked out in her mind just in case. Their apprehension, however, was abundantly clear to each of them.

The women pulled up to an old two-story home very much in need of paint. The front yard was just as unkempt as the house appeared to be. Patchy grassy areas attempted to grow but were choked out by weeds, some over a foot high. The women looked at papers nestled up against a fence, having been blown there by the wind. Melissa looked at a sheet of paper in her hand.

"Well, this is the address," she said.

Kate and Melissa got out of the car and began their walk up to the front door. They both took a deep breath as Melissa pushed the button to the doorbell. Nothing happened. There was no sound from the doorbell button. Melissa next reached for the storm door, pulling it open and began knocking on the main front door loudly. A heavy set gray haired woman who obviously hadn't seen a comb in quite some time answered the door. Her mouth was badly in need of a dentist's attention. She wore a dress that showed two rips on the shoulder. It appeared to have been slept in.

"What do you want?" came her gruff voice.

"Are you Mrs. Lewis?" inquired Melissa, in a loud harsh voice.

"You with the police or court?" came her reply.

"No, we're not," Melissa said.

"Well, what do you want?" she asked again.

"We want to speak to you about Henry."

"He doesn't live here, he's gone."

"Well," Melissa stated, "we were wondering if you could answer a couple of questions for us?"

"Look, lady, he doesn't live here anymore, just get the hell off of my property. Get out of here and leave me alone. I don't have to answer any of your questions."

As she spoke she began to close the door in the women's faces.

"Well, maybe the police will have some questions for you then," Melissa said loudly as she put her foot in the door. "You can jerk my chain all you want to, but remember this, I can jerk yours a lot longer and harder."

Kate thought she'd actually faint. Never in her wildest dreams had she expected this from Melissa, or observed her act this way before.

"You can answer a few questions for me now and I'll be on my way," Melissa said in a demanding voice, "but don't, and I'll have some uniforms here in no time. Now, cooperate or you can face the consequences. I can have you served with a subpoena, and we'll drag your butt downtown, it makes no difference to me. Now, what's it going to be?"

"Okay, okay, but be quick about it."

"That depends entirely on you, now move over so we can come in."

The women entered the house, Kate's heart beating wildly.

"What exactly do you want?" asked the woman.

"So where's Mr. Lewis, is he here?"

"Ah, he died a couple of years ago last month, good riddance."

Kate's legs felt very weak. She looked at Melissa, completely awestruck with what she was doing. Her complete command of the situation was amazing for her to watch.

Kate looked around the front room. A dirty striped couch sat up against a wall. The walls appeared to have various sizes of holes in them. It was as if something had been thrown at them, or even the sign of a fist having hit them. A few old pictures hung on the walls. Up and down brown stains appeared from ceiling to floor giving the impression of jagged mountains. Blotches in odd shapes covered the ceiling along with areas of peeling paint. In one spot a portion of the ceiling hung down slightly. Over by the corner sat an old television. Kate thought she could actually write her name in the dust that had gathered on its top.

"Listen, I don't have all day so let's get down to the nitty-gritty," Melissa said in a louder than normal voice. "I know for a fact you know things about Henry, facts about him I'm trying to uncover. Now, what paperwork do you still have, and where is it? I'm not going to wait all day, get moving."

"My husband burnt it all," she stated.

"Don't give me that bull-crap, I've heard it all before. Now, where's the rest of it?"

"Okay, okay. Henry didn't mean that much to me anyway. He's lucky we even took him in to begin with, after all, who wants something that looks like him to begin with, especially after he got that ugly scar. That kid was kind of a waste of skin to begin with," she responded. "He was always gone, you could never count on him for anything."

When Kate heard those words about Henry, she had the greatest desire to plant one across the woman's face. Of course she knew better than to do that, and besides, who knows what you might catch by even touching her. The old lady walked from the darkened living room, the drapes pulled almost completely shut.

Melissa and Kate followed her as she went down a short hallway into a bedroom on her left. The repulsive smell of an unflushed toilet seemed to be coming from a half closed door on their right.

In the room was an unmade double bed with a single wrinkled sheet laying partially across a nasty appearing mattress. An almost unbearable stench was emanating from it. A gray flat pillow lay across the front portion of the bed, stains covering it as well. The appearance of a half eaten sandwich sat on a small table next to the bed, a fly or two feasting on the remainder of it.

Up against one wall was an old wooden dresser, watermarks and stains covering the top of it along with burn marks from cigarettes on its edge. What appeared to be some type of droppings dotted the one end, almost as if something had left a trail. On its back was a large mirror with a big crack running from one side to the other. The woman reached down to the bottom drawer, pulled it open, and retrieved an envelope from the very back of it.

"This is what you want, now get out of here," she stated angrily as she handed the envelope to Melissa.

Kate wanted to run for the door. Simply grab the envelope, she thought, and let's get out of here. Kate, however, held her ground, as well as her breath much to her own surprise.

"I'll be the judge of that," Melissa stated as she opened the envelope. She studied it over for a few minutes.

Kate thought to herself, let's just get out of here, I think I'm going to throw up.

"Okay, I think this is what I need. Is there anything else concerning this subject?" Melissa demanded.

"No, that's all. My husband burned the rest of it. You're lucky I even kept that much."

"I better not find out there's more to it than just this, or I'll be back."

"You won't, that's everything that's left."

Melissa nodded her head.

"Let's get out of here, I'm done with her," Melissa said as she turned and started for the bedroom door.

Kate amazed herself on how fast she exited the room, let alone the house. Each woman took several deep breaths once they were outside of the building. With the sound of the car door closing, Kate once again took a deep breath and let it out. As she did, she started laughing, unable to control herself. Melissa let out another deep breath as well, as she started laughing also.

"I hated to even take a breath in there," Kate said, "the air was so foul. Every time I took a breath, it actually burned my lungs."

"Well I also could feel a heavy stench in the air, it was unbelievable. It was almost like the air was weighted with odors as you walked through it."

"I can't imagine living in that day after day. Can you, Melissa?"

"Ugh," Melissa said as she shook her shoulders.

"I'll bet we looked like a couple of women practicing our Lamaze breathing techniques when we stepped out of that house, attempting to get fresh clean air back into our lungs," laughed Kate.

Melissa nodded her head as she started the car engine, then pulled out onto the roadway.

"Now I can actually breathe in comfort," Kate said, "and it's all fresh air."

"Boy that place stunk," Melissa said agreeing. "I've never been in a place like that in my whole life, and I hope never to be in one again. How does anyone live in that filth? It's almost sub-human!"

"Melissa," Kate shaking her head back and forth as she spoke, "Henry grew up in that atmosphere, how did he ever survive?"

Melissa shook her head back and forth as well, unable to answer her question.

"Melissa, what you did was simply amazing. You had her actually afraid of you. How did you do that?"

"Well, remember me telling you about Mr. Sheppard this morning, the security guy?"

"Yes, at the restaurant."

"I sat down with him one day and told him what my feelings were concerning Henry, and what I wanted to do. He did some research and then got back to me. Anyway, he took the time to tutor me on what to do and say. We even practiced together. He told me to take complete command of the situation and speak in a harsh unforgiving voice. Mr. Sheppard instructed me to dress down, don't look too good or fancy. I actually had a hard time trying to figure out what to wear. We even went shopping one day in the store.

He also told me the type of people I'd be dealing with always have something to hide, every one of them do. Mr. Sheppard also conveyed to me, 'Don't be afraid to mention getting the police involved.' He even suggested that I call them uniforms instead of police officers. He told me about using the word 'subpoena' to make her think we'd have her dragged off to the courthouse, or even jail. Heck, Mr. Sheppard even mentioned that people like this aren't really that smart, that's the reason most of them get caught doing things wrong in the first place. He's a very smart and kind man to have helped me as he did. He even offered to go with me, but I felt I needed your permission."

Kate shook her head back and forth in amazement, yet chuckling loudly enough for Melissa to hear her.

"Mr. Sheppard also said that even though some of the papers were probably destroyed, these type of people seem to hang on to some items for whatever reason, maybe even keeping it like a souvenir. He said it was a gamble, but one he'd try. So that's why I asked her for any additional paperwork. After all, he said, 'it's like gambling with someone else's money, what have you got to lose.' "

"I'm just so thrilled everything worked out," Kate said. "Melissa, I was so scared."

"And so was I. Well, the only part that really worried me was... truly scared me was what if Mr. Lewis was there. We were very fortunate we didn't have to deal with him."

"Amen," Kate said.

"Kate, take the envelope and look through it. I didn't take a long time looking at it, but I think what you need is in there."

Kate reached over and picked up the envelope laying next to Melissa. She opened the flap and removed the paperwork from inside. As she studied it over Melissa could see a smile growing across her face.

"Melissa, it's all here, everything we need, everything Henry wanted to know about himself."

Kate held the papers in her hand waving them back and forth while laughing.

"Why, Melissa? Why did you do this for Henry, I have to know?"

"The day in the hospital when Henry told me he didn't want to take the Lewis family name, that broke my heart hearing those words. I made a promise to myself that I would do whatever I could to help Henry find closure. He needed to have those questions answered. I didn't know what I could do, but I knew I had to do something."

"Thank you, Melissa. Those words seem hardly enough to say for what you've done for Henry. What a wonderful thing this is going to be for him."

"Kate, how you came into possession of this information is something Henry doesn't need to know. He doesn't have to know we saw what he grew up in, that's not really important here. I personally don't think he would want us to know that, how bad it was for him. What you decide to do with this information is entirely between you and him. It'll be our little secret as friends."

"But Melissa, he should know you got it for him."

"What he needs to know is in your hands, let's keep it that way, please."

"Thank you, Melissa. Henry will be so happy. Just think, he'll know his real name, when he was born, and how old he is. How wonderful is that."

"You know what the worst thing about today was for me?" Melissa said.

"What was that?"

"When I heard that terrible woman refer to Henry as a waste of skin, I just wanted to reach over and take her by the —"

"I felt the same way, too, Melissa. For someone like her to say that about Henry really makes my skin crawl."

"It's like look who's calling the kettle black."

"Exactly," Kate stated nodding her head.

Very Sensitive Kids

It was a little over a week before the wedding and nerves were on edge. Edith required more than her usual amount of tissues to get through the day. The women ran each and every detail through their minds, time after time. The phone calls between Edith and Susan mounted with every day that came closer to the weekend celebration. The men, however, took everything in stride. Susan and Edith checked and rechecked everything. Melissa found it comforting to know the two mothers were so engaged in this project, and she appreciated it deeply.

It was Monday morning as Melissa sat working on her vows at the dining room table. Susan walked up behind Melissa and placed her hands on her shoulders.
"So how is it going?"
"Mom, I just know that Greg will have such wonderful words to say, and I'm just not very good at this. I don't want to embarrass him by making a fool out of myself. This is such an important part of the wedding ceremony."
"Can I make a suggestion to you, Honey?"
"Please, Mom."
"What made you fall in love with Greg in the first place?"
"It was a lot of things, big things, little things."
"Give me an example."
"Well, this is kind of silly, but when he kissed me the very first time, after he did, he apologized to me for doing it. It was like he didn't want to take advantage of me, if you know what I mean. It was right after he did that kiss, that's when I kissed him. It was then I knew I was in love with him. Silly, isn't it?"

"Not at all, Melissa."

Melissa looked down at the sheet of paper before her. A large amount of eraser marks were evident on its face.

"Melissa, write just a word or two about each item. With your father it was his smile that first caught my eye. Now, where did you meet, was there anything special about that? When did you know he loved you? Put down what you just said to me. How about that first kiss, it sounds like that was very important from what you've told me. Melissa, you fell in love with a man who your father and I are so thrilled with. We've learned to love him just as you do, but you did that in just two days. Write down what it was that caused you to feel that way. Put down your dreams for your life together. Do that, and your vows will be wonderful, and the reason for that is very simple, they'll be from your heart to the man you love."

"Thank you, Mom, I'll do just that."

Susan reached down and gave Melissa a kiss on the top of her head. She then turned and left the room wanting Melissa to have some quiet time to work on her project. Melissa took the pencil in hand as she then began to write her vows, the words now coming quickly to her.

The next day Kenneth and Melissa sat at the table as Susan took a dish from the oven and placed it on the table.

"Supper looks good as usual," Kenneth commented.

"Mom, your idea on the vows worked, I'm almost done. Thank you for your suggestions, it really helped."

"You're welcome, Honey. I can hardly wait to hear them."

"So why don't you read them to me," suggested Kenneth. "I can play the part of Greg, and your mother can be the audience."

"Not on your life, Dad, you can wait like everyone else."

Susan chuckled.

"I understand," he said with a smile.

Melissa looked at her father as he smiled broadly.

"You're right, Mom, it's his smile. I never really looked at him in that way, but you're right."

"I know, Honey," Susan said as she placed another bowl on the table.

"Looked at who in what way?" asked Kenneth.

"Oh, it's not important, " Susan said as she took her seat.

Just as Kenneth reached for his coffee, the telephone rang.

"I'll get it," volunteered Kenneth. As he conversed on the phone, both women listened intensely to his every word.

"I understand. Well, you do what's best for you, she'll understand, they both will."

"It sounds like he's talking to Grandma," Melissa offered.

"And it doesn't sound good either," Susan stated. "I was looking forward to visiting with my mother."

"Oh, mother, I wanted her to be here so much. It's not like we see her as much as we would like to, but I wanted her to be here, especially for my wedding."

"I understand, but we can't always have what we want."

"But my wedding, and Greg," she said, tears forming in her eyes.

"Honey, let's wait and see."

Once Kenneth hung up the phone he looked over at both women. Melissa sat before him wiping her eyes with a napkin. She knew in her heart what she was about to hear.

"I'm so sorry, Melissa."

Melissa got up and ran from the room in tears, going directly to her bedroom. Both Kenneth and Susan could hear her door closing behind her.

"It broke my heart to tell her that," Kenneth said as he shook his head.

"I know. She's going to need some time alone. Well, let's eat and then I'll go and have a talk with her. I just wish I knew what to say."

"I'd go with you, but I think this is a time when a daughter needs her mother the most, and dads just stand off to the side for moral support."

Susan reached over and patted Kenneth's hand. Each sat staring at their food, toying with it, their appetites completely vanished from sight. Kenneth and Susan sat quietly, each lost in their own thoughts. They sat there for some time.

"Well, I'll put this all away and then go and talk to Melissa. We can eat something later."

"You go now, I'll take care of this."

Kenneth never clears the table, she thought. She smiled at him and then reached up kissing him lightly.

"Thank you, Honey," she expressed verbally, as well as in her heart.

He nodded his head. By the look on his face, she knew this all weighed heavily on him as well.

Walking up the steps and across the landing leading to Melissa's room she contemplated what to say, but words weren't coming to her. Susan stood outside Melissa's door. She could hear the sounds of crying coming from within. Susan softly knocked on the door as she asked for permission to come in.

"Come in. You don't have to ask, Mom," Melissa said in a quivering voice.

Melissa lay sideways across her bed, the napkin still in her hand. Susan walked over to her and sat down on the bed. Melissa sat up placing her arms around her mother, her head upon Susan's shoulder. Susan looked at her as she half-heartedly smiled.

"Mom, I wanted grandma here so much."

"I understand, Melissa. I'm sorry she won't be."

"Mom, it's more than just that."

"What do you mean, Melissa, I don't understand?"

"Greg told me one day that he wished his grandparents were alive to see our wedding. He told me how he was going to have grandparents back in his life, that I'd have to share mine with him, like it or not… and now she won't be able to make it to our wedding."

"So that's what this is all about."

Susan held Melissa a little tighter in her arms, fighting back her own tears as she did. Holding your tearful child, Susan thought, no matter how old they are is a very emotional experience for anyone to go through. Susan's heart was deeply saddened. The mother and daughter held each other for a long time, Susan trying to comfort her little girl, Melissa wanting to be comforted like one.

Kenneth meandered aimlessly around the house. His eyes occasionally looked up in the direction of Melissa's room. Eventually he found himself pouring another cup of coffee. He walked out onto the deck placing his cup on the railing. Hearing the sliding glass door opening and closing behind him, Kenneth turned around as Susan walked up to him.

"Well," he said.

"She actually fell asleep in my arms. I laid her down and covered her with a blanket. Our daughter is completely spent, this news took an awful lot out of her."

"I mean," Kenneth stated, "this shouldn't have that strong of an effect on her. I realize she's unhappy about it, but still, there are a lot worse things in life than this."

"Not in our daughter's life. It's because of Greg, the fact that his grandparents have all passed and she wanted to share her grandmother with him at their wedding, and now she can't."

"Ah, now it all makes sense to me. No one knows that feeling better than you and me," Kenneth said as he nodded his head back and forth. "We have very sensitive kids getting married," he expressed, "each thinks of the other one first."

"I guess what we should do is keep her very busy," Susan said, "and that won't be a problem now that the wedding is getting so close. We'll just have to work at keeping her mind off of it."

"Oh, well," Kenneth said, "Que Sera, Sera."

Susan nodded her head in agreement with the words of her husband. She reached over to the rail taking Kenneth's coffee in her hand. She placed it to her lips taking a sip from the cup.

"That sure tastes good on a cold day like this," she said.

"That's why I made it."

"Well, I better get busy," Susan said as she handed the cup to Kenneth.

"And speaking of busy, I've got some work to do in my office as well."

The day of the wedding rehearsal had at long last arrived. The church was completely decorated in a theme entirely commensurate with Christmas.

Everyone gathered in the sanctuary. Even Henry tagged along to be with Kate. Besides, he thought, he had to see where his part took place in the ceremony. Pastor Phil instructed where each person was to stand, when and what order different events were going to take place.

"I understand, Henry, you will be singing a song at this juncture in the ceremony. At least the program says, 'Greg's song to Melissa.'"

"Yes, I will," Henry said."

"Would you like to do a quick run-through, check the sound system equipment, the organ?"

"I sure would."

"Henry," Greg's voice quickly said somewhat loudly, "aren't you going to wait and do it tomorrow?"

"Oh, don't worry about it, I can use the practice," Henry said as he sat down by the sound system next to the organ. Henry was well aware Greg didn't want Melissa to know what song he would be singing at the wedding. Greg had made that abundantly clear to him on numerous occasions.

"Let's see, how do those words go again?" Henry said, jerking somewhat on Greg's chain. "Oh, yes," he said, "I remember now."

He placed his hands on the organ keyboard as he began to sing and play "Jingle Bells."

As Henry lifted his fingers from the keyboard, everyone started laughing, enjoying Henry's teasing of Greg. Yes, everyone thought it was funny, including Greg.

"Tomorrow we'll be hearing a different sound in bells," Henry said as he smiled. "Yes, I may have to use a different song altogether, if that's okay with you, Greg?"

Greg nodded his approval.

"It is at this point where you'll express your vows to one another," Pastor Phil stated. "I'll have you turn to each other and that's when you take over. Who is going to go first?"

"I will be," Greg said. "I'll be doing mine from memory," he smiled.

"Well, I'll be reading mine, if that's okay, Pastor?" Melissa asked.

"Of course, Melissa."

"Can I do a quick run-through like Henry just did?" asked Greg.

"If you'd like to," Pastor Phil said.

Greg smiled at Melissa as he took her hands in his. He looked over at the parents and winked.

"I love you, I love you, I love you, I —"

The parents started laughing, though Pastor Phil didn't.

"I'm sorry, I just couldn't resist myself, Pastor. It's an inside joke."

"Good, I thought that's all you were going to do, say that over, and over, and over."

"I'm really sorry, Pastor Phil."

"Well, let's move on, if we may. Even I enjoy a joke or two," he said smiling.

The rest of the evening took on a more serious tone, no more jokes, just listening to the pastor's instructions and following his every word. One could tell, even though it was just a rehearsal, everyone was a bit nervous. No one wanted to mess anything up in the performance they were about to give the following day.

"Well, that should about do it," Pastor Phil said. "Does anyone have any questions they need answered?" Hearing no response, he continued with his thoughts.

"We'll see you all here tomorrow, and please bring your largest smiles. It's going to be a wonderful day for every one of you to remember the rest of your lives. Can I speak with both of you for just a moment or two?" Pastor Phil said to Melissa and Greg.

Melissa and Greg stepped forward onto the altar following Pastor Phil as he moved back slightly.

"I just want to say something to the both of you. Over the years I've known you, Greg, I've watched you mature into a wonderful young man. I know you better than you realize. And, Melissa, I've gotten to know you as well, though obviously not nearly as long as Greg. The fact that the two of you have chosen each other to become husband and wife tomorrow makes me happy to no end. I believe this to be one of the happiest weddings I'll ever have the privilege to perform."

"Thank you, Pastor Phil," Greg said as he shook his hand.

Melissa reached up and kissed Pastor Phil on the cheek.

"Thank you, Pastor Phil," Melissa said. "Oh, my goodness, I don't think I've ever kissed a minister before," Melissa said, a little shocked at what she had just done. "In fact, I know I haven't."

"Well, I forgive you," joked the Pastor Phil. "Even my wife does that on occasion," he chuckled.

As they moved back Kenneth walked up to the group.

"Sir, Pastor Phil, I spoke with your wife, Marsha, and she said if it was okay with you, you both would join us for the rehearsal dinner. Please, all of us would enjoy that very much. You can even say grace for us if you'd like to," Kenneth joked.

"I think we'd both like that very much, so yes, we will join you."

"I don't know what this really means, Pastor, but your wife told me to tell you there was no singing allowed at dinner."

Pastor Phil laughed.

"If you heard my voice, you'd understand that statement."

I Just Can't Do This

A large beautifully decorated Christmas tree stood on the left side of the sanctuary in the front section of the church. Numerous poinsettias in various colors lined the edge of the steps to the altar. Additional poinsettias surrounded the organ area framing it in delightful holiday colors. The lights from the tree illuminated the slightly darkened church along with some tall green and red candles. Green garland with red bows were draped from the windows as well as on the ends of each pew. Melissa and her father stood together at the end of the church slightly off to one side. Their position hid them from the view of people attending the wedding. They could see just enough to know that the church was completely filled. Kate, Kim, and Karen also stood out of sight across the aisle in the back of the church as well. Their position was on the opposite side from Melissa and Kenneth.

"The Wilson family have a lot of friends that obviously love them with this many people here," observed Kenneth.

"Greg and I can't go anywhere without people saying hi to him," Melissa said.

"I noticed that about Frank also. I'm sure Susan finds the same thing with Edith."

Melissa nodded her head.

"This is such a perfect day for your wedding," he said.

Melissa and Kenneth looked at each other smiling. She lifted her heavily laden red rose bouquet and took a deep breath from it.

"These smell just like the ones Greg gave me the day I fell in love with him."

Kenneth simply nodded to her.

"You look beautiful, Honey, every bit as stunning as your mother did on our wedding day."

"Thank you, Daddy."

Kenneth held his arm out slightly to Melissa as she slid her hand in behind it.

"Are you ready, Honey?"

"Yes, Dad... Daddy?"

"Yes."

"I know I've said this to you before, but I just want you to know how much I love you and mom. I wanted to thank both of you for the wonderful wedding you've given the both of us today."

Kenneth nodded his head slightly, not able to answer her verbally as a slight pooling began to form in his eyes. Melissa looked up at him and smiled, her eyes also beginning to reflect a watery glaze to them as well.

The two watched as little Karen walked slowly down the aisle dropping red rose petals on the white runner leading up to the altar. Kate and Kim followed shortly behind her. With the beginning of the wedding march being played on the church organ by Henry, Kenneth nodded to his daughter. The people stood as the music began playing. Father and daughter stepped into the middle of the aisle and began their journey together to the front of the church. How handsome Greg is, Melissa thought, with each step she took closer to him.

Melissa looked every bit the part of a wedding magazine's presentation. The ball gown style accentuated her slim waistline. Her china doll complexion was smooth and creamy in appearance. The "V" shaped neckline revealed a gold necklace hanging around her neck as well as a charm of golden skates. It was the very item Greg had given her that represented his love for her. Her long sleeves were embellished with rose patterned lace. A chapel length veil gently swung with every movement of her head. It bore a lacey edge of roses as well. As Melissa walked beside her father down the aisle, the train from her dress softly swayed with each and every step she took towards Greg. Chiffon and beaded sequins melted into one bringing the beauty of the dress together.

The people standing were but a blur to her as she walked with her father, her attention solely fixated on Greg at the front of the church waiting for her. She thought to herself, after all this planning, after everything that's taken place, she would now be united in marriage to her true love. She smiled as tears began to steadily flow down her cheeks.

"And who gives this woman in holy matrimony?" asked Pastor Phil.

"Her mother and I do," Kenneth responded, as he reached over to Melissa giving her a kiss on her cheek. "Your mother and I love you so very much, Melissa."

Kenneth then reached over and took Greg's hand in his. Their hands shook lightly. To Greg's utter surprise Kenneth placed his arms around Greg hugging him, his hand patting him on the back. Kenneth then placed a small kiss on Greg's cheek.

"We all love you, Greg," he stated.

"And I love both of you as well," he answered.

As Kenneth sat down beside Susan she reached over and took his hand in hers, interlocking their fingers together. She smiled at him nodding her head slightly. The young couple stepped up onto the altar.

Pastor Phil asked everyone to be seated as he began to follow the wedding format. Edith and Frank looked over at Susan and Kenneth. They exchanged smiles. Sitting near the front Emma watched the group of seven in the wedding party. She thought to herself as she looked at them, let's see, there's Kate, of course, and little Karen. There's Stanley and Dan, so that must be Kim. I don't think I've met her. She must be Dan's girlfriend.

Some of the audience members looked at the program wondering what was to transpire next. The words, "Greg's song to Melissa" was listed. Melissa didn't know what the song was, Greg kept that secret to himself and Henry alone. Henry reached over and turned on the church's musical sound system. He next pushed the button on the CD player. An orchestra background from the CD started playing. Henry cleared his throat quietly to himself as he started to sing the song, "Some Enchanted Evening." Melissa listened as Henry sang. Some people in the audience thought it very unusual for such an old song to be sung at a wedding. Melissa took in each word as she gazed into Greg's eyes knowing full well what every one of the words meant to the two of them. With the conclusion of the song, Pastor Phil asked the couple to face each other.

"It is my understanding the couple have chosen to express their very own vows to each other. Greg will go first."

Greg stepped slightly forward taking Melissa's hands in his.

"The words to the song just sung describes how we first met. We were at the Christmas cast party two years ago. I was home on leave visiting with my family. You were here from out of town. I watched you sitting with Kate laughing, smiling, and I knew in my heart I had to meet you."

As Greg spoke his words pulled gently on Melissa's memories of that wonderful night. They rekindled every single moment of the evening inside her, bringing them back to life in her heart. She began to tear up once again.

"As I made my way to your table I knew with every step I took I was falling in love with you. To me it was love at first sight. It was my dream to make you my wife, however, my greatest fear was that you were already married, engaged or perhaps seeing someone. Imagine my joy when I learned you weren't."

Some people in the audience laughed.

"There are so many different things that transpired on the evening we met, the night that brought us together, unbelievable events that all fell into place. Melissa, I don't believe for one second they just happened that way. I know in my heart you are the miracle I was supposed to discover that evening, an evening filled with many other miracles as well.

On the following day I gave you a bouquet of red roses. Secretly I wished them to express to you how I felt, and what you were doing to my heart. That very evening we went skating together. It began snowing very large flakes. I looked down into your sparkling eyes, snowflakes nestled in your hair and couldn't resist myself as I kissed you. I actually felt some fear as I thought to myself, what would you think of me, would you be mad at me. I didn't want to lose you. I quickly apologized to you. Then you kissed me back... and I knew then and there we would someday marry. It was that very moment when I believe our hearts became inseparable, and now together as one.

When I went back to continue my tour of duty, the time I spent apart from you was as if I was going through a very dark tunnel. I could feel your love calling out to me through the darkness that surrounded me. You were the beacon of light at the end of the tunnel that I so very much needed. The darkness was my loneliness for you. You beckoned to me daily through your letters. I was so happy when I finally reached the end of my journey. I wanted to be with you, to love you, to have you love me. I desired us to begin a new adventure together with you in my life, a partnership surrounded and nurtured with love.

Today, that's why I am so happy. You will become as much a part of me as my heart, as my very soul. I never want to be without you. I will cherish you with every part of my being forever. You mean everything to me, just as our families do to both of us."

The sound of Edith crying softly was just audible to some of the people around her. She looked in Susan's direction realizing she was doing the same.

"Today I welcome you into my heart forever as my wife, my soul mate, and ask that you allow me to be a part of yours forever as well. I love you so very much, Melissa."

Melissa's body softly started to quiver. Greg could feel it in her hands. Her eyes were now laden heavily with tears.

"And now Melissa," Pastor Phil stated knowing Greg had finished.

Melissa reached up to her necklace with her right hand taking the gold ice skates hanging from around her neck. As she held the skates in her fingers she placed them to her lips giving them a soft kiss. She smiled at Greg. Melissa had never taken it off since that day. Greg told her he would someday give her a wedding ring. The charm and necklace represented that promise by him to her. Today that promise would be full filled. Upon gently releasing the charm Melissa turned slightly in Kate's direction. Kate handed her a folded sheet of paper.

"I made notes," Melissa softly stated.

Everyone chuckled. Melissa looked into Greg's eyes. He smiled at her. His eyes bore the signs of dampness.

"Greg," Melissa's said, her voice being very shaky, "I love you so much."

It was now that she began to strongly tear up, tears running down her cheeks. She swallowed hard, it didn't help. Her voice was empty and still, unable to speak the words she had so carefully written on the paper she held in her hand. Her body started to shake. The more she tried, the less she could accomplish as she attempted to speak. Emotionally she felt overwhelmed. Melissa's face told that fact to Greg immediately. He could see her inner feelings were getting the best of her. He had seen this expression on her before, and he knew exactly what to do. As Greg looked at her he simply stepped forward taking her in his arms. He lightly kissed her on the forehead as he pulled her closely into his body. Greg then held her tightly as she rested her head sideways on his chest sobbing. The sheet of paper Melissa was holding slipped from her grasp and fluttered to the floor as she reached up taking Greg in her arms as well. The two melted together as one. Melissa looked up to Greg.

"I'm sorry," she softly said to him.

"It's okay, Melissa. I love you, Honey."

"I'm messing everything up," she responded as she tightened her grip on him.

"No you're not. This just tells me how much you love me, how lucky I am to have you in my life."

"Do you need to sit down?" inquired the pastor quietly.

"No, I want to go forward," she said tearfully. "Please, Pastor," she said softly, "I want to marry Greg so much. I'm sorry, I just can't do this."

"That's okay," Pastor Phil said, "let's just take our time. We'll take all the time you need."

"Thank you," she said.

"Now take a few deep breaths, Melissa," Pastor Phil suggested in a soft assuring voice.

Pastor Phil shook his head slightly, understanding what was going on. He had been through this before with other couples. Nerves are always a great part of any wedding, or even a funeral, he thought. Being very happy or very upset has only a thin line that sometimes separates the two.

Now it was obvious to everyone that Melissa was having a great amount of difficulty. People felt sorry for her, while others simply waited to see what would happen next. Greg continued holding her in his arms, Melissa not wanting him to let go of her. He whispered his thoughts of love for her. He knew she needed to hear those very words, especially now.

Dan looked at the sheet of paper on the floor. He reached down and picked it up. Kim motioned with her hand for him to hand it to her. She stepped slightly behind the couple taking the paper from Dan's hand. Kim wanted to give the sheet of paper to Kate, but Kate's eyes were filled with her own heavy tears.

"Melissa," Kim said in a whisper, "shall I?"

Melissa nodded her head slowly in approval, holding ever so tightly onto Greg as she did.

Kim stepped slightly forward, the sheet of paper in her hand.

"Melissa has requested me to read for her the vows she has written for today. She is having a little problem speaking right now. I am very proud and honored to do this on her behalf, knowing her as I do, and having personally observed the tremendous love she possesses for Greg. So here I go. I only hope I can do the words justice."

With those words having been conveyed, Kim looked over at the audience and then began reading Melissa's words.

"My love for you Greg began in a very simple way. It all started with us meeting in the church gym after the Christmas Program. I want to especially thank Kate for inviting me to attend the program that night, otherwise. I probably never would have met you. I would like to also thank you for being my Maid of Honor, and very good friend.

Greg, you walked over to where we were sitting at the table and into my life. As I listened to you talk that evening I got to know you. It became quite clear to me you were someone very special. We talked, and talked some more. I can't remember ever in my life being so attracted to someone by simply listening to them. You spoke in such a warm and kind voice. You carried a gentle laughter I loved hearing.

We decided to go the next day with a couple of your friends and see some of the beauty this area has to offer. When you came to pick me up in the morning you presented me with a dozen long stem red roses. How thoughtful was all I could think, red roses, my favorite. We then met up with your friends, Dan and Kim. They are such a wonderful couple. Thank you Kim and Dan for being a part of that wonderful day, and this one as well. I shall forever carry that day, and this, in a special part of my memories."

It was now Kim who was having difficulty in speaking. Pastor Phil handed her a couple of tissues from a box he had handy for certain necessary occasions. As Greg listened to each word being said, his thoughts relived every moment over in his mind. He smiled as he gently began to rub his thumb on Melissa's back.

"That evening you and I went to the skating pond. I told you I thought the place was enchanted, almost like a fairy tale. Little did I know how true those words would become to me. It began snowing large flakes. I called them, 'Big fluffy pillow feathers.' "

Some of the audience chuckled while others just smiled.

"As the snowflakes came down from the sky I looked into your eyes. I realized then you were filling my heart with love for you. I also knew that I wanted to reach up and kiss you. I didn't, even though it was the wish I carried in my heart. You asked me to say those words as quickly as I could three times, big fluffy pillow feathers. And so I did, stumbling over each and every one of my attempts as I did it. You took me in your arms and held me tightly as you kissed me. And then you apologized to me for doing so. It was then I knew without any doubt in my heart that I was head over heels in love with you."

Feeling the emotions Melissa's vows invoked in them, many of the women sitting in the audience wiped their eyes.

"That evening we met with your mother and father at your parents' home. That's when I came to the realization that we possessed something very important for every couple to have, a deep love for each other, and the strong love and support of our families. How fortunate we are to have that as we start our lives together."

Frank looked at Edith and smiled. Susan squeezed Kenneth's hand.

"Greg, I will love you forever. I look forward to every sunrise we will share together, as well as all of the sunsets that await us. I am so grateful to have you as a part of my life. I love you with all of my heart."

Kim took the sheet of paper and slowly folded it. She wiped her eyes again as she then turned and handed it to Kate. Kate nodded to Kim as she took the folded paper.

"That was done beautifully, Kim," Pastor Phil stated, "thank you. It isn't my habit to say anything when people do their own vows, but in this case I just want to say how heartfelt I believe both of these young people's words are to each other. They both took the time to mention how they met each other, the love they possess for one another, and very importantly the support of their families. How wonderful.

I would like to digress for just another minute, if I may. These two young people standing before me referred to their meeting at the church Christmas Program. I remember that night very well. It was filled with numerous miracles.

That evening our groom played the part of a soldier, which he was at the time. Stanley, his groomsman here today, was overseas, or so we all thought. He switched places with Greg on stage to surprise his wife and daughter, Karen, after returning home unbeknownst to them. Stanley's daughter is Karen, the little flower girl up here with us. All three of them are part and parcel to this wedding. I just felt the urge to share that information with you today."

Pastor Phil stepped closer to Greg and Melissa as he whispered, "Do you feel strong enough to go on?" Melissa nodded her head with a small smile.

The rest of the wedding went forward without incident. Frank and Edith, along with Susan and Kenneth lit their portion of the unity candle. Greg and Melissa soon followed their parents as they did the same, though Greg was sure to keep his arm around Melissa's waist as much as possible. Everything was a daze to Melissa, as she just followed Pastor Phil's lead. With the rings being exchanged, Pastor Phil turned to the audience and proudly announced the two as a newly married couple. Greg and Melissa kissed as people applauded. Greg reached over and took Melissa's hand in his. He gripped it somewhat tightly, wanting to make sure she was strong enough to walk.

As they finished the last steps from the altar and started down the aisle, Greg's hand was jerked somewhat backwards stopping him immediately. He turned to find Melissa frozen in place. She stared at the people seated in the pew beside her.

"Nonna, Nonna" came Melissa's loud words. Everyone stretched to see what had taken place to cause her to make such an unexpected intense exclamation. Melissa's bouquet dropped to the floor as she put both of her hands to her face. She started crying loudly. Melissa then quickly stretched her arms open as she bent down embracing two people sitting in a pew next to her. The three of them held each other crying for some time. Some people even stood up to see what was going on, their curiosity having gotten the best of them. Greg watched from the aisle. He smiled as he observed Melissa shedding tears of joy. While he didn't quite understand what was transpiring, he was happy for her. Noticing her bouquet at his feet, he reached down and picked it up.

Kenneth and Susan stood up. They turned slightly to better face the audience.

"Ladies and gentlemen," Kenneth said in a fairly loud voice, "for those of you who don't speak Italian, Nonna means grandma or grandmother. Apparently Melissa has just realized her grandmother from California, along with her great grandmother who lives in Florence, Italy are here. They both wanted to share in the celebration of Melissa's wedding."

Melissa reached up wiping her eyes with her fingers as her father spoke. "I would say she's a very happy young lady by the look on her face."

The amount of applause was loud and prolonged. Perhaps it was because Melissa demonstrated such a warm heart to everyone, and they loved her for that, or just simply because she had survived her wedding. Be whichever it may, everyone was happy for her.

The reception line would take place at the hall immediately following the wedding with photographs being taken at the church. Music from a sound system playing could be heard throughout the hall as the musician's instruments lay at the ready. People sat at various tables talking, looking around at others to see if they recognized anyone. The hall began to fill rapidly.

Some individuals made their way to a food table, which held quite an array of everything from cheeses, vegetables and dip, chips, cocktail sausages, and smoked salmon. The list of items went on and on. The women didn't want anyone waiting for dinner to go hungry or get light-headed from not eating.

Frank and Kenneth had been put in charge of this particular project, and the table reflected a job well done on their part. This was one undertaking the men enjoyed. They would sit with pen in hand making their list out, laughing as they did. When Frank and Kenneth suggested they could put some fish on the table they caught while fishing, the women put their foot down quickly. Yes, the men were having fun participating.

In the back of the hall on the left-hand side in a corner all to itself, sat a large table covered with a white linen cloth. On top of the table stood an impressive three-tiered wedding cake. Positioned on either side of it sat four smaller cakes, if needed, making sure everyone had a piece of dessert. The smaller cakes were neither round nor square. They were, however, very unique in shape. Per Melissa's instructions, they were in the design of very large white snowflakes. This, in part, also represented to Melissa the evening of her first kiss from Greg.

The larger cake was decorated with small red roses encircling each level. The top of the cake presented itself with a huge single red rose made of frosting. Three large fondant red ribbons of icing came from underneath it draping over the cake's edge leading one's eyes downward. On each ribbon little white snowflakes were periodically placed. At the bottom of the cake, and leaning up against it, was a set of six inch gold ceramic ice skates.

To the left of the cakes was a wishing well covered with red ribbon and small red bows for guests to place their wedding cards in.

Unbeknownst to anyone except the hall owner, Dan and Greg were given permission to place something beside the empty cake table while the business was closed. Greg was furnished with a key to the hall. Sneaking out of the house in the early morning hours the day of the wedding, Greg met up with his best man, Dan. In the back of Greg's car was a very large box with the words, "Norm's Florist" printed on the top of it. As Greg pulled up to Dan's house, Dan smiled as he gave him a big thumbs up. Dan got into his car and followed Greg to the reception hall. Together they laughed and joked as they accomplished their task. Once they got back near the cars, Greg expressed his thanks for Dan's help. Dan nodded his head as he chuckled.

"I can hardly wait to see Melissa's face," Dan said.

"Neither can I," Greg laughed.

"It will look better when the cake is put into place, too."

"It doesn't look all that bad now."

Dan nodded his head in agreement.

"See you in the morning," Greg said.

"Or in a few hours, whichever comes first," laughed Dan.

As the people entered the reception hall, many walked over to the cake to view it. Some placed cards into the wishing well, while others laughed at what sat next to the table. Just off to the side of the cake stood three white artificially lit deer from the front of Dan's house. Their necks moved slightly up and down bringing attention to the area with their lights. A large hand-printed sign before them read, "Melissa's Christmas Deer." Greg knew in his heart of Melissa's fond love for deer at this time of year. Perhaps it was just because of the holidays, but deer was something she adored. They were, in her mind, all Christmas deer, whether they were artificial in nature or not. All over the deer, numerous red roses had been tucked in place between the wires. The lights seemed to bring the roses to life. An especially large red rose had been placed where the nose would be on the largest of the three deer. Greg wanted to surprise his wife with yet another item he knew she loved. It was Greg's hope they would bring a smile to her face, and another memory to be cherished by her. He could hardly wait for her to see them.

With the announcement of the wedding party coming into the hall, an evening of celebration commenced with its first steps being taken. People eagerly approached the reception line wanting to offer their congratulations to the couple. As the individuals made their way through the line, Susan and Kenneth were happy to see some familiar faces. Susan recognized Dwight almost immediately, though he wore his hair much shorter now. A young lady held his arm. When Jean Parker stepped up to Susan, the women looked at each other and found themselves embracing.

"So now I know what it's like to attend the best wedding I've ever been to," Jean said as she stepped back from Susan. "I will definitely have a wonderful story to tell everyone when I get back home."

"Don't forget to keep Greg's secret when you talk about it."

"Oh, that goes without saying," Jean said in a whisper.

"I was so concerned for Melissa's wellbeing, during the wedding. I wanted to rush up to the altar, grab her and hold on tight, just like I did when she was a little girl."

"And that's what I think Greg saw in Melissa's eyes, that she needed to be held and comforted by someone that loved her."

"Yes, he did, didn't he?"

"As I've said before, you have such a wonderful family."

"Thank you, we're very lucky."

Henry was the last individual to go down the receiving line. He put his hand out to Greg shaking it, and then gave Melissa a kiss on the cheek.

"Thank you so much, Henry, you helped to make our wedding beautiful," Melissa said. Henry nodded his head as he smiled. He slowly worked his way down the group shaking hands, kissing Edith, Susan, and Kate, of course.

Finally he came to the grandparents. He reached down taking Melissa's great grandmother's hand as he stated, "Piacere di conoscerti."

Melissa and Susan's mouths dropped with the mention of those words. Greg quickly looked at Melissa.

"What does that mean?" he asked.

"Nice to meet you," she responded. Melissa bent over a little bit looking down the line at Kate, confusion written across her face. She mouthed the words, "Does Henry speak —"

Kate's nodded her head affirmatively.

Unbelievable, Melissa thought to herself as she straightened up smiling.

"Melissa, you're going to teach me Italian; okay?" Greg said.

"As I told you before, Honey, I'd love to."

"Great."

Henry and the two grandmothers stood talking Italian for a short time. At one point Henry promised to meet with them later so they could visit longer. With that agreement being made the wedding party and parents began taking their seats as the musicians started playing. Henry felt a hand on his arm. Turning he saw Susan.

"Henry, would you do something for me?"

"I'd be glad to."

"I have a friend here from work and she's sitting by herself, would you mind if she sat with you?"

"Sure, there's just Emma, Doc and myself, we'd be glad to have her join us."

"Thank you. I'll go and get her."

Susan made her way over to Jean. After a short conversation the two of them joined Henry's group.

"This is Miss Parker," Susan said introducing her.

"It's nice to meet you," Henry stated. "This is my mother, Emma, and Doc, my girlfriend's grandfather."

"Hello," she said acknowledging everyone.

"Please, have a seat and join us."

"Thank you, Henry, if I may call you that."

"Sure. Of course."

"I enjoyed your singing so much during the wedding. I must say this has been the most unusual wedding I've ever attended along with everything else that's occurred. This was the most emotionally filled exchanging of vows I have ever experienced."

"You can say that again," Emma said agreeing. "I've never enjoyed attending a wedding more than today's, other than my own, of course."

"It sure was," agreed Doc.

"Well, everyone," Emma stated, "I can personally attest to the fact that some people here are in for more surprises than you would think."

"Mom, please don't say anything more on that subject," Henry said.

"Fiddlesticks. You see, Jean, Henry and Kate are quite the item, it's just that he hasn't wised up enough to ask her to marry him, but I'm working on it daily."

"Who is Kate?" inquired Jean.

"She's the one sitting next to Melissa right now."

"She's a beautiful young woman, and the Maid of Honor; right?" Jean said.

"Yes, she is. Anyway I taught Henry to dance so he can dance with her tonight. I can hardly wait for that to happen. Kate will be so surprised."

"That's got to be exciting for you, Henry." Jean expressed.

Henry merely nodded his head.

"You know what," Henry declared, "I'm going to go over and talk a little bit with Melissa's grandmothers. I promised them I would, and besides, I could use a break from the marriage and dance talk. Jean, I'll see you a little later. It was very nice to meet you."

"See you later, Henry," Doc added.

"So," Emma began, "tell us a little bit about yourself. You aren't married obviously, or otherwise you wouldn't have been introduced as Miss Parker."

"Please excuse Emma, Miss Parker," Doc quickly stated, "she has a way of going for the throat of a question rather than simply —"

"Working her way into it, I understand," Jean said nodding her head with a small smile reflected on it. "My mother possessed that same quality, so I understand quite well."

"So is there an answer to my question?" Emma asked.

"There is, Emma, but it's kind of a sad story that's a big part of my life," Jean said.

"Miss Parker, this is nothing that Emma and I would want you to delve into, it's none of our business," Doc said turning and looking Emma directly into her face, "None of our business at all."

"Let her answer if she wants to," Emma said as she looked at Doc with a somewhat scolding expression.

Doc just shook his head.

"It's really quite simple. I never dated very much, if at all, as I grew up. When I was in my early forties, I met someone who I felt I wanted to share my life with. We dated for a long time, years actually. Neither one of us had outgoing personalities. We were both shy, bashful, introverts, whatever you want to call it. But after about five years or so we decided to marry. A week before our marriage was to take place he literally broke my heart with his, you might say."

"He left you?" Emma asked.

"No, he had a massive heart attack at work. They say he was dead before he hit the floor."

"How sad," Emma said, as she placed her hand upon Jean's.

"So that day two hearts were broken, one that didn't know it was broken to begin with, and one that was broken by it."

"I'm so sorry," Doc said.

"Yes, so am I," Emma added.

As the three of them continued visiting, enjoying each other's company, Jean realized how much she liked talking to Emma. It brought back to her memories of her late mother. Emma carried all of the same characteristics and mannerisms as her own mother. Simple expressions on Emma's face awoke greater thoughts to Jean of her own mother. Even the way Emma reached over and placed her hand upon hers, it was exactly the way her mother had done to her before.

"Jean, another question for you, one you may not want to answer with a man sitting here at the table with us," smiled Emma.

Doc rolled his eyes, but said nothing.

"And what is that?"

"So how old are you?"

"Well," she said with a chuckle. "I'm younger than you, and younger than Doc by about I'd say—" there being a twinkle in her eyes as she looked at him, "— say — oh, five or so years, probably less... yes, probably a little less. That's about as far as I can go on that question," she said as she smiled at both of them.

"Fair enough," Emma said with a smile of her own.

Doc smiled with Jean's answer to Emma. He thought she had done a very credible job of answering Emma's question without answering her question. He got a kick out of it.

"Another question, if I might?"

"Oh, Emma, give the young lady a break," Doc said quickly.

"I think you'd like to hear the answer to this one also, Doc," Emma said shaking her head.

"Okay," Jean said, "I think I'm ready for it," a little chuckle in her voice once again.

"You stated earlier you were very shy and bashful, what made that all change for you, if I may be so bold as to ask?"

"And that never stopped you before," Doc said.

"Well, it started for me the day I went to work for the Summers. We all like to eat, and I needed a job. I had to talk to people and deal with them every day at work. When I first started, and I doubt that Mrs. Summers remembers this, but she came up to me in the first week I was there. I think she knew I was bashful. Anyway, she walked up to me on that day and put her hand on my shoulder. 'Do the best you can, that's all we're going to ask of you. You understand?' I nodded my head. 'Good, enough said.' She walked away.

I would see her on occasion, once in a while after that. She always took the time to wave to me, and I think that's what changed my life as far as being shy. I knew I had her support, not to worry if things went wrong, just do my very best."

"And here you are at her daughter's wedding, many years later," Emma offered.

"Yes, here I am, and grateful to be here."

Henry pulled a chair out from the table as he inquired in Italian, "May I?"

"Please," Melissa's grandmother stated.

Melissa's grandmother, great grandmother, and Henry began conversing solely in Italian.

Henry relished this opportunity to test his knowledge of the language, to immerse himself in it wholeheartedly. What an opportunity he thought.

"I think we all got caught up with the language and forgot our proper etiquette," Henry said. "My name is Henry. My girlfriend is Kate, your granddaughter's Maid of Honor."

"Oh, my name is, Maria," answered the great grandmother.

"And mine is Cameo. Susanna is my daughter and, of course, Melissa is my granddaughter."

"So Susanna, that's her name, not Susan?" Henry said. "And what a lovely name it is," he added as he nodded his head.

"This has been just a memorable day for my mother and me," Cameo said, "although it's been a long trip for Maria."

"Let me see, you're from Florence, Italy as I understand it?" stated Henry as he nodded his head slightly to her.

"Yes, I am," Maria said.

"It's truly a beautiful area. And at night when the lights from the stone bridge over the River Arno, shows its reflection, such beauty to be observed and treasured by all," Henry said in a matter of fact voice.

"So you have been to my Italy?" Maria asked.

"No, I'm sorry to say, but I have read and studied your country through the years. I was introduced to it and the language by a very close friend of mine named Sam."

"We have much to offer, the statute of David, the Uffizi Gallery, many things," Maria added. "I've missed some of those things when I came to this country."

"I think the music, especially the opera, is something that pulls at my heartstrings the most," Henry declared.

"Yes, the music," Maria said. "Have you ever heard the song, *Nessun Dorma*, it's my very favorite song. It's from the opera *Turandot*."

"The final act," Henry said, nodding his head. "It's probably one of the best known tenor arias in all of opera, a favorite of mine also."

"You impress me, Henry," Maria stated. "You're a very knowledgeable man."

"Thank you," Henry said. "Well, it looks like they're getting ready to serve the food. I better go. Perhaps we can visit again later."

"I hope so," responded Cameo.

"I would enjoy that very much," Maria said nodding her head.

With the announcement that food was going to be served shortly Pastor Phil stepped to the microphone and gave the blessing. The wedding party made their way to the food tables followed immediately by the family members. Greg and Melissa looked at the wedding guests sitting, chatting together, and smiling as they ate their meals. The meal was interrupted occasionally by the sound of people tapping their silverware on their glasses requesting the young couple to kiss.

Once the wedding party completed their meals, Dan made a short announcement that he was about to make a toast to the couple. He reached down and took a glass from the table in front of him and held it up slightly. A silence quickly filled the large room. Dan stepped to the microphone that had been placed just off to the side of him. He looked down at Kim sitting just to his right. He smiled at her. Turning his head he gazed slowly around the room.

"You would think this would be a very easy toast to give, say a few nice words about Greg and Melissa, wish them well, sit down and enjoy the remainder of the evening. Yet, would anyone of us really want to know someone who did just that, I don't think so, and I'm not that type of person either.

Many words have passed through my thoughts over what I wanted to say this evening. I've written and rewritten sentence after sentence in my planning for this toast. I spoke with my parents who have known Greg for many years, and who have come to know and love Melissa as well. I told them of the difficulty I was having expressing my true feelings for both Greg and Melissa, of putting it into words. They suggested that I do what they thought I did best, just shoot from the hip. Still I took pen to paper, and after attempt after attempt of trying to put my thoughts down, the words failed me once again, and so I've decided to follow their advice. So what I'm going to say now, I have no idea."

Dan took a deep breath in and exhaled out slowly. It was overheard loudly on the sound system. Some of the audience chuckled to themselves when they heard him do it.

"As I stand here looking at everyone before me, friends, acquaintances, family members, I wonder how many of us are as fortunate as this young couple here, to have someone in their own lives that they can share their love with, a love filled relationship like these two carry in their hearts for one another. What a remarkable gift these two possess, something much more precious than silver and gold, something to be cherished the rest of their lives together, a love that's pure and simple.

Because of the relationship I have with these two, close friends as we are, I was able to observe them when Greg was able to come home from the service on leave and visit. It was on one of these very occasions that I discovered Melissa wrote Greg daily, though he couldn't do the same to her... obviously. Even while Greg and Melissa were apart, it was quite evident from what we all knew that their day-to-day thoughts were filled with love for one another. I believe in my own heart the love they carried for each other were as frequent as waves breaking upon a shoreline. Greg, Melissa, I know when I look at the love of my own heart, Kim, sitting here beside me, —" Dan placing his hand upon Kim's shoulder as he spoke, "— I can only pray our love will be as timeless and strong as what both of you have demonstrated to all of us here today."

Dan took another deep breath.

"I could stand here and wish both of you all of the happiness in the world but frankly, I believe those words would be a waste of my breath. You see, it's clear to those who know and love you both that you already possess that happiness, something I don't believe you'll ever lose. It's locked deeply within your very souls, and the key to that lock is the love you possess for each other.

And so I'm not going to wish for both of you to have a happy marriage, instead I believe I'll just simply say this... continue with the deep love you have for each other, hold one another in your arms daily, and know that you are loved by everyone of us here. Greg, Melissa, I love both of you with all my heart."

With those words spoken, Dan lifted his glass high and said, "Cheers." The guests followed his lead as they did the same. When Dan placed his glass down Greg stood up and embraced him for some time as they patted each other on the back. Greg then gave Dan a slight kiss on his cheek.

"Well," Greg said, "that was wonderful, Dan, and we both love you also."

Melissa stood behind the men waiting for her turn to do the same.

"Thank you, Dan, that was so beautiful," Melissa said. She stepped towards him, Dan taking her in his arms hugging her.

"I do love both of you," he said.

"And we love you as well," she replied.

Once again the musicians began playing, people moving about, others simply sat visiting together.

"Well," Emma stated, "I think I'll find the lady's powder room. Do you think I should get Henry to sit here and protect you from Doctor McDonald?" joked Emma.

"Oh, I think I can handle the situation, Emma, but just the same, keep an eye out." Jean chuckled as she winked at Emma.

Emma got up, took her purse in hand and headed to the back of the hall.

"You know, Dr. McDonald," Jean started out —

"Please, Doc is fine."

"Well, everyone knows quite a bit about me, so now it's your turn. Are you married?"

"You and I have a lot in common on that subject. My wife died at a fairly young age. It was an icy road guarded by a group of trees that — needless to say it was the worst day of my life."

"Oh, I'm so sorry," Jean said as she took his hand in hers.

"I was working at the hospital that night. Betty had gone over to help a friend who was having a baby. They were decorating a room together, getting it ready. She was on her way home when the accident occurred." Doc swallowed hard. "I think the thing that bothers me the most about it happening is not for the loss that I suffered, I found a way to deal with my pain, it's what Betty's friend went through that haunts me the most. I know she believes that if she hadn't asked her to help, she'd be alive today."

Jean squeezed Doc's hand slightly.

"And that's so unfair, it's not her fault." Jean voice reflected a deep sorrow to it.

"You know, Jean, I've talked to you more about this than I have to anyone, including my own family. It's something I just don't bring up, and neither do they."

"Well, you and I have had to deal with a significant tragedy in our lives and we've both survived."

Doc nodded his head in agreement. Neither one of them offered to release the other's hand.

As Emma walked towards the table she saw the two sitting in what appeared to be a deep discussion. The fact that they were holding hands caught her eye as well. She thought to herself, let them be, I'll find Henry and see what he's up to.

The wedding reception followed the usual course of events. When it came to cutting the wedding cake Melissa grabbed Greg and gave him a huge kiss and hug. She absolutely loved her, "Christmas Deer" being in attendance.

"This is so special, Honey."

"Well, Dan helped a lot."

"And why doesn't that surprise me, you two working together. Thank you for doing this, it's so very special to me. I just love the roses on them."

"You're welcome, Honey."

"When I see Dan I'll have to give him a thank you hug as well."

"I'm sure he'd enjoy that," smiled Greg.

The introduction of the wedding party received the customary applause. Greg and Melissa danced together, Dan and Kim, Kate and Stanley. Karen danced around them all with her own imaginary dance partner. The sparkles from a large mirrored ball in the middle of the room flickered lightly through the air. It changed as a small spotlight shined different shades of colored lights on it.

Once the dance was completed, it was announced there would now be the father/daughter dance. Kenneth and Melissa walked to the center of the floor and waited for the music. As the selected music played, the father and daughter glided over the dance floor effortlessly. One would think they had practiced their dance before, they were that graceful. But did it matter that they practiced, not to anyone who watched them.

When they finished it was announced that the dancing would now be open for all to enjoy. Henry stood up, took a deep breath, and walked over to where Kate was seated at the front table. Greg and Melissa stood behind her. Kate looked up at Henry. He placed his left finger over his lips indicating for her to not say a word. With the palm of his right hand facing downward he slowly rotated it upward as he brought it towards her in a beckoning fashion for her to take it. Melissa and Greg looked at each other smiling as Henry took her hand as she rose from her seat. Together they walked to the dance floor. Taking Kate in his arms she smiled at him, thrilled by this unforeseen turn of events. Together their bodies acted as one as they seemed to float across the floor. Kate was thrilled in her heart to know that Henry had taken the time to learn to dance. It's just another wondrous secret he carries within, she thought to herself.

"Oh, thank you, Honey, that was so amazing," Kate exclaimed as the dance came to an end..

"I had a wonderful teacher."

"And I bet I know who that teacher was."

"I bet you do," he replied smiling.

Greg and Melissa made a tour of each table, sure not to miss anyone as they did. They laughed, they smiled, they hugged friends. The joy on both of their faces was almost radiant in nature. They were thankful their friends were attending their wedding, and they made that clear to everyone they spoke to. As they came to the table where Doc and Jean sat, Melissa bent over and kissed Doc on the cheek.

"Hi, my name is Jean Parker, you don't know me but —"

"Oh, yes, I do," Melissa exclaimed, "we met at the store two years ago. I've also seen you in the store from time to time."

"That's right."

"And we also met then," Greg said.

"This is the most unforgettable wedding I've ever attended," Jean said with a smile.

"I kind of messed up a bit; didn't I?" Melissa stated as she nodded her head.

"Melissa, when someone's heart is so filled with love that their words get caught in their throat, or they need to be held by the love of their life, I can't think of anything more wonderful than that. You not being able to speak, and then your friend, Kim, reading your vows, that's my most precious memory of this wedding."

"Thank you," Melissa said, happy to realize how much it meant to Jean.

"Well, have a good time tonight," Greg said. It's nice to see the both of you here."

Doc nodded as Greg and Melissa moved onto the next table.

"That was a marvelous thought to leave them with, Jean," Doc said. "You have quite a way with words, I've noticed that about you."

Jean tilted her head slightly towards her shoulder as she shrugged her shoulders.

"Would you do me the honor of dancing with me?" Doc asked. "It's really been quite some time since I've done that, so perhaps you may want to pass on it. I'm not really very good at it."

"And neither am I," she answered.

"Perhaps we ought to flip a coin to see who leads," smiled Doc as he got up. What a marvelous sense of humor she has, he thought to himself. It was very apparent that Jean and Doc were having a good time together, their faces bore that fact out often.

Henry walked over to Emma who was sitting with a few acquaintances of hers. He repeated his hand gesture to her, the one he had used with Kate.

"And doesn't that movement with your hand work well?" Emma expressed, as she got up taking his hand.

"Just as you taught me it would, Mother."

The three women at the table smiled as well as Emma.

Together they made their way to the edge of the dance floor. Once the music stopped Henry looked over to the musicians and nodded his head. The recorded music of a Viennese waltz began to play. Henry and Emma walked to the center of the floor to begin their dance together. They were the only couple there. Henry slowly placed his arms in the proper position as Emma did the same. Emma slightly tilted her head, much as a ballroom dance contestant would have occasion to do. As the music played they started to dance. Making long flowing movements Emma and Henry were elegant. People stopped and watched them as the couple smoothly moved around the floor. Emma's dress slightly flowed in the air. With the final notes being played, Henry held his arm up as Emma made a small circle extending her arm out gracefully as the dance came to an end. Emma and Henry were offered a large hand of applause as they walked off the dance floor.

"Wasn't that remarkable," Jean said to Doc. "Henry is such a — he's a —

"Very talented man," Doc suggested.

"Yes, very talented. When I first heard I was coming here, —

"What do you mean you heard?"

"Mrs. Summers asked me to attend. I feel very honored they asked me."

"So you don't really know anybody here, I take it?"

"Other than you, Emma, Henry, the bride and groom, and I hardly know them, you're right. Of course there's Mr. and Mrs. Summers."

"Jean, when I came here tonight I didn't know who I would be sitting with. Kate is in the wedding party, of course, and that kind of left me on the outside looking in. There are acquaintances here, of course, but it's not the same thing."

"I know just what you mean," she said nodding her head as she spoke. "Thank goodness Mrs. Summers brought me over here to sit with Henry, Emma, and you, otherwise I'd be all alone."

"Jean, I just wanted to say how much I've enjoyed sharing your company tonight. I hadn't really looked forward to this part of the evening, the fact that I would basically be all alone, but you've made it a highlight of my day. I just wanted to let you know that for what it's worth."

"Thank you, Doc, it's been a very pleasant experience for me, too."

At their table the four parents sat resting.

"I am so tuckered out," Susan said.

"Oh," Edith said, "just let me slip these shoes off under the table for a minute."

"Edith, I already have," laughed Susan.

"Hello everyone," came the statement from Norm, Frank's brother.

"I don't know if you know Norm and his wife, Marylou," Edith said to Kenneth. "Susan knows Norm, of course."

"I met Norm at his place of business," Susan stated, "but I haven't had the pleasure of meeting you, Marylou. This is my husband, Kenneth."

"Nice to meet you both," Marylou said.

"Norm, the work you do with flowers arrangements is magical, to say the very least," Susan expressed.

"Well, I take the bows because I'm out front, but Marylou is the artist," he said. "I'm very lucky to have her working beside me every day."

"Don't let him kid you, he's a very talented florist," Marylou was quick to state.

"Actually you're both right," Edith said.

"Well, it was nice meeting the both of you," Norm said, "but we do have to say hello to a few more people. I'm sure that's keeping the four of you busy tonight as well."

"Yes, it has," Edith said.

"Well, maybe we'll see you a little later," Marylou said as they turned and left the group.

Frank toyed with a piece of cake on his plate. He cut a small section with his fork and placed it in his mouth.

"And how many pieces does that make?" Edith asked.

"Look it's not my fault my stomach is like a cement mixer, it just grinds it all together and off it goes," Frank said.

"Oh, did you have to put it that way?" Edith expressed while making a funny face.

" Frank, I envy you," Kenneth said.

"Really?" Edith said.

"So when did you discover you had a cast iron stomach?" Kenneth asked.

"Well, let's see." Frank acted as though he was pondering the question over deeply in his mind. "I think it was when we first got married and Edith was learning to cook."

"Really!" Edith said.

"I'm just kidding, Honey."

"I'd be careful of any sandwiches she prepares for you in the near future," Kenneth joked.

"Look up there at the bridal table, there's Henry talking to Melissa. I wonder where Greg is?" Susan asked.

"He's over there," Kenneth indicated, pointing in the direction of a small group of men.

"Henry is kind of a jack of all trades; isn't he?" Susan said. "He sings, he speaks Italian, and now he's Gene Kelly and Fred Astaire all rolled into one. Kate will be getting a marvelous man when she marries him."

"And I wonder when that will be?" inquired Edith.

"I don't know, but I hope they do soon. They are such a nice couple," Susan said.

The women watched as Melissa signaled for Greg to join her with Henry near the bridal table. Once he arrived, Melissa took his hand in hers.

"What's this all about?" whispered Greg.

"I just need you to be here with me. Henry and I have worked out something for him to do special for me."

Greg didn't respond to her, if she wanted him by her, that was all he needed to know. As the musicians played the final notes to a song, Henry stepped up to the microphone stand.

"Can I have everyone's attention for just a minute," he stated. "Please take a seat now. Thank you very much."

The people on the dance floor walked over to their seats and sat down. Others sat down where they were visiting people. As the room became quiet, even the small amount of chatter in the very back drifted off into total silence.

"I wonder what this is all about?" Susan asked Edith.

Edith merely shook her head as she shrugged her shoulders slightly.

"From now on I will be speaking to you entirely in Italian, therefore," Henry declared, "Melissa will be translating for me."

Melissa moved over to the microphone as she released Greg's hand. She waited for Henry to speak again. People looked at each other with questioning faces. Why in the world would someone who spoke perfectly good English decide to talk in a foreign language no one understood? It made no sense to them at all.

"I do this to honor Melissa's grandmothers who are seated to my right."

Melissa quickly repeated Henry's words in English.

"Melissa and Greg are so thrilled that her grandmother and great grandmother are able to attend their wedding today," Henry stated in Italian.

Melissa repeated his every word in English once again. As he continued speaking, Melissa translated for him verbatim. The people began to enjoy listening to Henry as he spoke, then trying to figure out what he was saying before Melissa translated it.

"The gift of you both being here means the world to them."

He could see the grandmothers holding hands, smiling at Melissa and him as he talked.

"When I spoke to Melissa earlier, I told her that the women both loved Italian opera, —" Henry paused giving Melissa time to catch up with him, "— she asked me if I could sing a song as a gift from her to them. I told her I would be more than happy to." Henry paused again. "And so as a wedding present from Melissa to her lovely grandmothers," Henry paused. "I wish to sing a favorite song of theirs and mine as well."

He looked over at Melissa and winked once she had finished translating his last sentence. Stepping back from Henry, Melissa again took Greg's hand in hers. Henry moved over closer to the band as he smiled at the audience. He knew his voice was strong enough to not need the assistance of a microphone. Henry nodded to a musician who pushed a green button on the CD player.

The background introduction to the song "Nessun Dorma" began playing through the sound system. In a rich operatic tenor voice Henry began to sing the words in Italian. Edith and Susan almost mirrored each other as they sat listening to him sing, their heads slowly nodding as they absorbed his every word. Kate and Emma sat together listening as Henry sang. The quality of his voice was no surprise to either one of them, having been privy to it on several occasions. However, they had never heard him sing a song of this nature. While the people who attended the wedding at the church had enjoyed a taste of Henry's voice already, no one could have prepared any of them for what they now heard.

"Isn't his voice magnificent?" the two women overheard someone say from their left. Emma and Kate smiled at each other after hearing the comment.

Maria and Cameo were extremely impressed. They sat almost in shock, not expecting what their minds were telling them. Henry's voice was spectacular and truly impressive, they thought. Such a marvelous gift to receive from their granddaughter, not only a song they loved, but one sung in their own language. Maria reached up wiping her eyes as she listened to Henry. Cameo soon followed suit.

As the final notes hung in the air the applause began, and it was astounding. Many individuals stood as others rose to their feet as well. Henry just nodded his head as Melissa walked over to him and kissed him on the cheek. Once again the applause encompassed the room, although not really stopping in the first place. Melissa then reached up with her fingers and wiped the corners of her eyes.

"I think they loved you, Henry," Melissa said in a somewhat shaky voice. Melissa took her hand and placed it to her mouth, throwing a kiss to her grandmothers. They returned it to her as they wiped their eyes. Greg walked up and placed his hand on Henry's shoulder. They nodded to each other.

"That was glorious, Henry," Greg said.

"Thank you so much, Henry," Melissa said. "Your voice is such a wonderful gift to share with our family. Thank you for doing that."

"You're welcome, Melissa."

As Henry stepped away from Melissa he saw Maria and Cameo waving for him to come to them. The second he got close to them they both placed their arms around his neck and body.

"Grazie, grazie," Maria said.

"Yes," Cameo stated, "Thank you, thank you."

Once again the people showed their approval by clapping their hands loudly.

"Oh my goodness, how would you ever go about topping this day?" asked Edith.

"This is when I'm happy I have only one daughter," stated Susan.

"And one son," Edith said shaking her head in agreement.

"I know how you could top this," suggested Frank.

"And how would you do that?" Edith asked.

"When they renew their vows."

"Oh, please, I don't think I could take it," Susan said, a slight laughter expressed in her voice.

"What do you think we could serve as food, Kenneth?" Frank said with a wink.

"How does oysters out of a can sound?" Kenneth chuckled.

"Well, Edith," Susan stated, "we've got more important things to talk about than oysters. You and I better hit the visitation trail again, there's still lots of people we need to talk to."

"Only if I can find my shoes," Edith joked.

As the evening wore on Henry danced once again with Kate, and then Emma. He was actually enjoying himself on the dance floor, which seemed a little odd since he fought with Emma so much in the beginning over the dance lessons. The musicians did a very credible job playing a large variety of music throughout the evening. Greg and Melissa laughed with friends as they went from table to table.

"Could everyone please take their seats?" came the announcement from the band area. "We're now going to have the garter and bouquet tossing." The people took their seats. A chair was placed in the middle of the dance floor where Melissa took a seat. Greg stepped before Melissa and kneeled down in front of her. He mockingly rubbed his hands together as Melissa laughed. He winked at her. He slowly reached up slightly under her dress taking her hidden garter off. Greg stood up holding the garter in his hand. People applauded the chivalry he had demonstrated in accomplishing his task. As Melissa stood up, Greg sat down in her place. He reached down pulling his pant leg up revealing a garter of his own. Melissa laughed along with many others. She kneeled down, rubbing her hands together just as Greg had done and slowly retrieved the garter from his leg. Everyone showered them with applause as they laughed. Soon a group of young men assembled behind Greg as he prepared to throw the garter in their direction. Flipping it over his shoulder he turned quickly and observed Dwight holding it in his hand.

Next Melissa took her bouquet and prepared to do the same thing. As the young women gathered into place a man at the microphone gave her a verbal count down. "Three, two, one," he said as the bouquet flew high into the air. Melissa quickly turned around to see who had captured it. She started laughing immediately. Two women held the prize, neither one of them attempting to take it from the other, both sharing their flowery trophy. Each one possessed a portion of the flowers, both laughing as they held it high in the air. Melissa shook her head as she looked at Kate and Kim, their hands grasping the bouquet together, both victorious in their quest.

People gradually drifted out from the hall's interior, a person here, a couple there. Many didn't want to leave wondering what, if anything, the next surprise held in store for them to enjoy. Doc and Jean sat alone at the table now. Kate looked over at her grandfather. He was smiling as he sat engaged in a discussion with the woman. She took Henry's hand in hers and walked over to them.

"Grandpa, who is this lovely woman?" she asked.

"This is Jean Parker," he answered. "She's been keeping me from spending a very lonely evening by myself while my granddaughter dances the night away, partying every minute of the evening."

"Grandpa!"

"It's nice to finally meet you," Jean said. "I know you've been very busy this evening. I have, however, met your Henry already." Turning her head in Henry's direction she asked him, "Henry, how is it you happened to have in your possession the orchestra accompaniment for 'Nessun Dorma', it's not something one simply pulls out of the air."

Kate laughed a little. Before Henry could answer, Kate responded to her question.

"If you knew Henry, you'd understand why. He literally has hundreds of CDs containing background music, and he keeps a lot of them in his car and at home. So," Kate pausing, "when the urge hits him, he has a full orchestra at his fingertips. And another thing, 'Nessun Dorma' is a favorite of his, though tonight is the first time I've heard him sing it."

"Well, that explains a lot for me," Jean said nodding her head slightly.

"Jean, would you mind if I dance with my grandfather, I want to do that before the band leaves tonight."

"Oh, I'm not holding him captive, he can do whatever he wants."

Henry sat down beside Jean as Doc and Kate walked over to the dance floor. Doc took Kate in his arms as they began dancing to a slow musical arrangement.

"So Grandpa, is Jean someone I should know about?"

"No, we just met tonight," he chuckled, "and we're keeping each other company, it's as simple as that."

"If you say so. You know, Grandpa, it would do you some good to get to know the woman better, I mean have a woman back in your life again."

"Maybe so."

"Grandpa, will you do something for me?"

"What's that, Honey?"

"Ask Jean if she'll go out for lunch with you tomorrow. You can take her to the Old Mill, it's such a beautiful area. I'm sure she'd like to see it."

"Well, frankly I'd be surprised if she'd accept a lunch date, I mean we've just met."

"And I'd be surprised if she didn't accept. I saw you two laughing together. Will you ask her, please?"

Doc's mind contemplated Kate's suggestion. She wondered what his answer would be.

"Well, I'll ask her, but I won't be surprised if no is her reply."

"Thanks, Grandpa."

Once the music stopped Doc and Kate walked over to the table to join Henry and Jean.

"I'm sorry, Jean," Kate said, "but Henry and I have to go meet with the bride and groom's parents. I know we've just met and now we're leaving. I'm sorry for that. It was very nice to meet you."

"But we just sat down," protested Henry.

"We'll see you later," Kate said as she reached down taking Henry's hand and pulling slightly on it. Together they walked over to join Greg and Melissa's parents sitting at a table.

"You have a beautiful and wonderful granddaughter, Doc." Jean said.

"Yes, she is. I see her mother's likeness in her face, even her mother's personality. I'm so happy she came to live with me."

"Are her parents here?"

"Kate lost her mother through illness sometime back, and her father, well, he couldn't deal with it and so he just left."

"How horrible for her to have to go through that."

"Yes, but she's stronger than she looks. Henry was the best thing that came into her life, and Kate for him as well."

Now Doc remembered Kate's words to him on the dance floor. He was somewhat afraid to fulfill Kate's request of him, but finally he got up the nerve.

"Miss Parker..."

"Jean, please."

"Jean, I was wondering if you would consider... I was thinking that perhaps tomorrow you and I could... If you don't have anything that..."

"Now look who's bashful," Jean joked. "Doc, are you asking me out?"

"Well, yes, I guess I am. Is that okay?"

"It certainly is."

"I thought if it was okay we could have lunch together. There's this Old Mill —"

"I'd love to go." she said as her right hand reached over taking Doc's hand in hers. Jean gently squeezed it as a small smile reflected on her face.

"Thank you."

"You're welcome."

They looked at each other and chuckled.

"It's been a long time since I've had lunch with a woman, I mean, other than Kate and the nurses at the hospital cafeteria... but I don't think that counts."

"No, I don't think so," Jean said.

The two sets of parents sat quietly enjoying the break they finally were able to take. They all felt they deserved it.

"We've visited with everyone," Edith stated, "if anyone else wants to visit with me, they can come over here and do it."

Susan laughed.

"Kate said we had to come over here and visit, so here I am," Henry stated as he sat down in a chair. "I am whipped," he declared.

"Henry," Susan said, "you are a bundle of surprises today. I just want to personally thank you for singing to my mother and grandmother. I could see on their faces they loved being serenaded by you. Your words about it being a gift from Melissa were wonderful. Thank you so much for doing that for them."

"You're welcome, Susanna."

Edith's ears perked up a little when she heard Henry refer to Susan in that way. She thought he must have simply misspoken.

The Promise

Henry looked at Susan, he could see her genuine thanks reflected on her face.

"I was wondering, if it's okay with you and Kenneth, "Henry said, "if we might stop by your home and visit with your mother and grandmother before they leave. They are staying with the both of you, I presume?"

"Yes, they are as of tonight," Susan said. "We had to keep them under wraps before the wedding."

"What are you doing Monday?" suggested Kenneth.

"You both won't be too tired after tonight?" Henry said.

"Not in the least," Susan said, "I'm just too excited."

"Monday it is."

"Why don't you and Kate come for lunch, if that's alright?" Kenneth asked.

Henry looked over at Kate. She nodded her head approvingly.

"Monday it is, Susanna," he said smiling.

"Susanna, I thought I heard that right," exclaimed Edith, her face showing a touch of amazement on it.

"It's a beautiful name my wife has, and I wish she would use it," Kenneth said.

"Oh, Susan,... I mean Susanna, it is a beautiful name, and if you aren't going to use it then we are! Right, Frank?" exclaimed Edith.

"Whatever you say, Edith," Frank said as he took a sip from his cup.

Edith held her hand out as she said, "It's very nice to meet you, Susanna."

"And it is for me, too," Susan said, as she took Edith's hand. "And by the way, what's your name, if I may ask," she laughed.

"Why it's Edith. I think the meaning of my name is —"

"Please pass the tissues," Frank quickly said.

The people all laughed.

"When we were sitting at the table with Doc, why couldn't I just sit there and relax, Kate?" Henry asked, "You made me come all the way over here. It's a good thing I like these people or you'd be in real trouble."

"Oh, come on, Henry, it was only a few feet and besides, I wanted to give Doc and Jean sometime alone."

"Did you say Doc and Jean, you mean Jean Parker and your grandfather?" inquired Susan.

"Uh-huh," Kate said.

"Unbelievable," Susan said smiling. "You know Jean is such a wonderful woman, wouldn't it be something if —"

"I told Grandpa to ask her out for lunch tomorrow."

"Do you think he will?"

"Well, he didn't think she'd go, but I feel otherwise."

"Here we go with the match making again," Henry proclaimed.

Kate nodding her head strongly said, "It worked on Greg and Melissa, didn't it, and look how that turned out. I'm one for one on the score sheet of dating, then marriage."

"Say, where are the kids anyhow?" Edith asked.

"I think they're over there by the wall sitting with the grandmothers," Frank said.

"Well, we need to spend some time with them," Edith stated. "I think we should all go over together and visit the grandmothers now. That will give me a chance to work on my Italian."

"You speak Italian, too?" Susan asked stunned.

"Of course. Pass-au da pizza," joked Edith.

Susan smiled as she looked over at Edith.

"Got ya!" Edith said.

"That you did," Susan said laughing.

"You realize pizza is an American dish?" Frank said with a chuckle.

"You understood me, right?" Edith said. "Obviously my Italian worked."

"Yes, it did," Susan said.

"Now I speak two languages, Italian and English," Edith expressed.

"Henry," Kate said, "I'm going to ask Emma to join us. I noticed she was sitting with that group of women earlier, but I think I saw them leave a few minutes ago."

"You sit down and relax, I'll get her," Henry said.

As Henry got up and walked over to Emma, the parents and Kate headed to where the grandmothers were sitting with Greg and Melissa. Susan introduced everyone to her mother and grandmother. Within a short time Henry walked up with Emma on his arm. Susan immediately introduced Emma as well.

Melissa looked over at her grandmother and great grandmother as she addressed them both in Italian.

"You could have knocked me over with a feather," Melissa said, "when I saw both of you in church today. I was in total shock. I was so thrilled to see both of you here. Greg and I are so appreciative you were able to make it to our wedding. You'll never know how very happy and thankful we are to have you here. I never dreamt I'd have both of you here, and now my husband has a set of grandparents we can share together."

Melissa reached down taking both grandmothers' hands in hers. She bent down slightly as she slowly pulled them up to her. Melissa placed a delicate kiss on each one of them. Both grandmothers smiled as they nodded their heads.

"You have your father to thank for that," Cameo stated in English. "When I called and told him I wasn't able to make it, he called me back within an hour or so, probably less. I told him I just couldn't sit in a plane seat with the condition of my foot, it being what it is. I told him the seats were just too cramped and it's such a long flight to begin with. He said first class seating would solve part of the problem, more leg room, and I should expect the tickets waiting for me when I went to the airport, round trip.

Melissa,... Honey, when your father told me about how you had... how much it meant to you for me to be here, I knew in my heart I could bear any pain I had to, and be here no matter what... first class or coach, it didn't matter to me then. The one thing I feel sorry about today is I wish I could have danced at your wedding, but with my foot being what it is —"

Melissa wiped a tear from the corner of her eye.

"Kenneth asked me to call my mother in Italy and ask her if it was at all possible that she make the wedding. I explained to Kenneth that she is very fragile. However, I called my mother right away, as I said I would. I was amazed to hear her say she would come, she actually wanted to come. She felt she needed to attend your wedding at all cost, even if it affected her health. That's how much you mean to her. I informed her that Kenneth would make all of the arrangements for her, just pack her clothes and any medications she needed to have with her. The rest is history."

"Daddy," was all Melissa said as she took him in her arms, "you knew how important this was to me." Tears ran heavily down Melissa's cheeks.

"Well, you blame your mother. She told me how you reacted that day in your bedroom, crying yourself to sleep. She also told me what it meant to you concerning Greg. What's a father to do for his little girl?"

Now, all the women began wiping their eyes as they watched Melissa hugging her father. Henry looked over at Greg. He knew he was feeling the same physical problem he was suffering from himself — a choking up inside oneself.

"Thank you, Daddy."

"You're welcome."

"Mom, when did you hear about this, or were you a part of it all along?"

"Actually not for quite some time," Susan stated. "This was all your father's doing. I found out shortly after that. When you were getting dressed in the church, we were able to sneak them in. They wanted you to be surprised as well."

"And I almost dropped dead from shock on my wedding day," laughed Melissa.

"So the surprise obviously worked from the response you gave in the church," Susan expressed.

"It sure did, Mom."

Greg smiled to himself as he walked away from the group, a mission in his heart to fulfill, or at least an attempt to accomplish it.

Emma stood observing all that had taken place. She missed nary a word as she quietly listened. Emma was having a wonderful day, the wedding, the food, which she thought could have been seasoned a little better, and now the reception. She had danced, heard Henry regale the two women, and now she was learning the secrets hidden behind each little story that was presented.

Greg returned shortly to the group. He stood in silence simply listening to everyone.

"Greg," Emma said, "I thought your vows to be very unique. I know that song well, 'Some Enchanted Evening.' Your vows dovetailed into it beautifully."

Greg looked in Emma's direction as she spoke.

"How did you come to use that as part of your vows," inquired Emma, "it's an old song. I was just wondering."

"It was my Mom's idea, she just didn't know it at the time."

"What!" exclaimed Edith.

"When I was home on leave, one day I went into the living room to be with you. I sat down next to you and put my arm around your shoulder."

"I remember that," Edith said, "I enjoyed that so much."

"Well, you were watching an old musical on television. At one point a man sang that song to a woman. As I sat there with thoughts of Melissa, those words crept into my heart. It could very well have been me singing the words to her. The simple words were so strong and true, how I met her, that I wanted to marry her, just everything about the song. It was then and there I knew what I wanted to say to Melissa on our wedding day, and the last words I wanted her to hear from me were... I love you."

"That's a beautiful sentiment," Emma said.

"Tissue alert," Frank stated loudly.

"Oh, be quiet, Frank," Edith said.

"I'll take a tissue," Susan said laughingly.

"And me, too," Edith said.

"Well, we have to get going, I'm sorry to say," Sharon said as Stanley and Karen walked up to the group with her. "It's been a big night for all of us, and especially for our daughter."

Karen smiled at the group.

"Hi everyone." She looked at Emma as she said in her little voice, "My name is Karen and I was in the wedding."

"I saw you," Emma said, "you did a beautiful job today."

"Thank you."

Greg knelt down on one knee so he could make eye contact with her.

"What was the best part of the wedding for you?" he asked.

Karen thought for a moment. "The cake."

"It was so beautiful," Emma agreed.

"No, it tasted good."

"You did such a wonderful job for us," Greg said.

"Thank you both for allowing her to be an important part of our wedding," Melissa said. "She is so adorable."

"She takes after her mother," Stanley said with a smile.

"It was lots of fun today," Karen said as she began to rock back and forth on her shiny black shoes.

"And, Karen, you and I got to dance; didn't we?" Greg said.

"I had fun dancing with you, Mr. Greg."

Everyone chuckled with those words by Karen.

"So dancing with me was a lot of fun?" Greg said smiling.

"And my daddy. I liked dropping the flowers in the church. I didn't have to pick them up. I liked that."

"Is it okay if I get a little hug from you, Honey?" asked Greg.

"Okay," Karen answered as she reached her arms up to Greg.

The two hugged as those around them smiled. Greg then stood up and faced Stanley.

"Thank you for everything," Greg said as he shook Stanley's hand.

"You're welcome," he replied.

"And thank you again for letting her be a part of our wedding today, it meant a lot to both of us," Melissa said again.

Sharon nodded her head. As the couple turned with their daughter holding onto her mother's hand, Karen looked back and waved good-bye as they left.

Doc and Jean hadn't moved from their original spot at the table. Other than a dance every once in a while, they spent the majority of their evening together visiting. The crowd at the reception had now dwindled somewhat more.

"Would you mind if we went over and sat with the bride and groom's family for a little while?" Doc asked.

"Actually I'd love to," Jean answered.

"I see Kate is over there as well," Doc said, "and I forgot to tell her how lovely she looked tonight."

"Every woman likes to hear those words, but she does look beautiful in her dress."

Doc and Jean stood up, Jean picking up her purse as she did. They walked the short distance to the table everyone was sitting at.

"Hello, Jean," Susan said.

"Hello, Mrs. Summers," she responded.

"Jean, would you mind calling me, Susan, I'd like that better, if you don't mind."

"I'd be glad to," Jean said with a smile.

"Well, Jean, —"

"It's really Susanna," Edith instructed her.

"Susan is just fine with me," Susan stated.

Susan turned to the group and introduced every one of them to Doc and Jean.

"I must say all of you ladies look beautiful tonight, everyone of your eyes sparkling in the light," Doc said.

"Well, actually I think the sparkles are from the rotating glass ball over the dance floor," smiled Frank.

"Frank, it wouldn't hurt you to say a compliment every once in a while," Edith said, "that didn't always concern food."

"You're absolutely right, Dear. Edith's cooking is really good... now."

"Oh, Frank," Susan said, as she laughed, "I don't think she means it in quite that way."

"A compliment is still a compliment," stated Kenneth, sticking up for Frank.

"So where have the two of you been hiding all night?" asked Susan.

"Well," Doc said, "we were just over at the table talking. We've been here, it's just that we didn't make the rounds like you had to do tonight."

Kate couldn't resist herself as she asked, "So what are your plans for tomorrow, Grandpa, I thought we could —"

"Actually Miss Parker... Jean and I are having lunch together at the Old Mill. I told her it was a beautiful drive up there."

Now it was Greg who couldn't resist himself.

"A very wise individual who resembles a certain doctor standing here once told me something about that area, and I never forgot his words."

"What's that?" Edith asked as she looked over at Greg.

"He said, when I told him I was taking Melissa there for the first time, his exact words were, 'that's where I'd take a young lady if I wanted to be alone.'"

Doc blushed a little as everyone laughed.

"Well, Jean, it is a beautiful drive, and the food is excellent," Edith said. "You can see Dan's picture hanging above the fireplace. Exactly where is Dan and Kim?" Edith asked.

Greg began surveying the hall, looking for them.

"There they are, they're sitting with both of their parents." Greg then waved over in their direction trying to get the couple's attention.

"They're coming over," Melissa said.

"Aren't they a lovely couple?" Edith said. "I love Dan like my own."

"And I think he feels the same way about you, mom, though I don't know if he'd say that outright to you."

As was Susan's custom now, she turned and introduced everyone once they arrived.

"Daniel, —" Emma said.

"That's my dad's name," he interrupted, "just call me Dan if you don't mind, it's easier for people to keep track of us that way."

"But of course. You and Kim make a beautiful couple," she said.

Kim looked over at Dan and started to chuckle.

"Go ahead," Dan said, "I think it will be alright."

"Mr. Greg Wilson," Kim said as she put her arm around Greg's waist, "your very good friend and best man, Dan, listens to you more than you realize."

Everyone was curious to hear where she was going with this subject matter.

"You told Dan how you asked Melissa to marry you with your family members present, not at the skating park, not even on the way to the Old Mill."

Dan and Greg both smiled.

"Dan told me how you said that having family around was so very important to you. Tonight as we sat with our own family members —"

Kim held her left hand out, a brilliant marquis diamond ring sparkling in the light on her ring finger.

Melissa grabbed Kim, Kate grabbing both of them, forming a small circle. They began jumping up and down, squealing loudly, laughing, and hugging.

"Oh my," Emma said.

"Oh yes, oh my indeed," Edith agreed.

The grandmothers smiled as they watched everything unfolding before them. "What an unexpected surprise," Cameo said to Maria in Italian.

Edith stood smiling broadly.

"Come here, Dan," she said, her eyes showing a great deal of dampness to them. She gave him a large hug, not letting go. They embraced for some time together. Edith placed a kiss on his cheek. "I'm so happy for the both of you."

"Thank you, Mama Edith," he said smiling. "I hoped you would approve."

"With all my heart. Now, Kim, come here, please." Once again Edith reached out as she took Kim in her arms as well. "You're getting a wonderful man who's a little raw on the edges, but still a treasure of a man," she said as she continually smiled.

"You're not telling me anything I don't know already," laughed Kim.

"And he's getting a wonderful young lady. I'm so happy for both of you."

"Thank you," Kim said.

There were hugs exchanged, handshakes, congratulatory words spoken, but most importantly words of love offered to each of them. It was yet another unexpected revelation in a joy-filled evening.

"We didn't know if we should tell you," Kim said, a large smile still upon her face. "We didn't want to take anything away from this wonderful day of yours."

"And spoil the best wedding gift we'll get tonight?" Melissa said, "I don't think so. We're both so happy for the two of you, all of us here are."

"Yes, we all are," Edith said nodding her head.

"I want to say something important now," Melissa stated, "and I want everyone to hear what I have to say." Melissa took Kim's hand in hers. "Some time ago Kim stepped in and helped me though a very difficult time in my life." Melissa paused, as she looked at everyone before her. "That makes two times she's done that for me, and I'm very thankful for her friendship."

Greg looked at Melissa as she spoke. He understood exactly what she was talking about. Greg remembered well the evening when the two of them stopped at Dan's house to get Melissa's mind off of the extremely hurtful words her father had said to both of them. Taking her to Dan's home was his effort to give Melissa's mind a chance to escape from having to deal with the worst day of her life. When Melissa began crying in the front room and then went into the bathroom, Kim followed behind her. Kim found a way to get Melissa to Greg's car, and out of Dan's parents' home. Melissa's heart was truly breaking that day. Kim understood that fact very well. She wanted to protect Melissa from Dan and his parents finding that fact out. They had no idea of the turmoil Melissa was dealing with concerning her family, and Kim did everything she could to shield her from embarrassing herself in front of them. Yes, Greg knew Melissa appreciated Kim's efforts. He also understood Melissa discovered that Kim was a true friend to have. Greg knew no one other than the three of them really understood what Melissa was talking about.

"Kim, on the happiest day of my life I couldn't even hope to speak my vows to Greg. You stepped forward and did that for me. I don't know how I can ever thank you for doing that for me... for us," Melissa said.

"I knew I was useless to you," Kate stated, "and I'm very sorry for that."

"You shouldn't be, Kate. Just having you there beside us meant the world to me."

Kate nodded her head in a silent thank you.

"Well, I know how you can thank me," Kim said smiling.

"And what's that?" Melissa asked.

"By being my Matron of Honor," she said taking Melissa in her arms.

"Oh my," Emma said, "oh, my."

Greg smiled as he looked at the two women embracing, everyone there smiling.

"And I think I'm supposed to get a best man, Greg," Dan said as he stretched his hand out to Greg.

Greg, however, replied with a large hug while patting him on the back.

"So you will, I take it?" Dan asked.

"Without a doubt," he replied. "I would be so honored to."

"Isn't love wonderful," Emma said. "It seems like everyone is getting married or already is, Greg and Melissa, Dan and Kim, but no Henry and Kate. How sad is that?" she said as she shook her head back and forth. "Isn't that right, Henry?"

"Mom, please," Henry responded, as he put his hand to his forehead and slowly rubbed his hand back and forth.

"And if he doesn't ask you pretty soon, Kate, you may just have to ask him, that is unless someone else special comes along."

"Mom, please."

"Well, I'm just saying."

Emma knew Kate loved Henry, and he loved her as well. How will I ever get these two together, she thought, it may just take a miracle.

"Now it's time for us to try a little something I thought of," Greg said, "and see if it works." Greg's voice was fairly loud, wanting to make sure everyone heard him. "Melissa, stand between your grandmothers. Susan, next to your mother. Kenneth, next to Grandma Maria." Everyone followed Greg's instructions, wondering as they did what his plan entailed. "Now, let's have the rest of you fill in next to the person beside you." Jean stepped beside Susan, Doc next to her. The wedding party and others began putting their arms around each other's shoulders forming a large circle, everyone laughing as they did. Kate stood on one side of Emma, Henry on the other. As the music being played came to an end, Greg looked up to the leader of the musicians and waved to him. The leader of the musical ensemble stepped to the microphone.

"Ladies and gentlemen, if I could have your attention, please. Tonight we are going to do something a little different. The family members are going to enjoy a dance together, just them, and do it from where they are now. Since some are unable to move about the dance floor for various reasons, they're just going to flow with our music. So let's have a large round of applause for them."

The people, of course, responded in the expected way, their hands brought together clapping. The music began as the musicians played their instruments to a very slow song. The wedding party and relatives in their somewhat huge circle began slowly swaying back and forth, smiling and laughing as they did. Melissa didn't know the words to the song, but sang in her usual way of handling that situation. She began singing "la, la, la" for the missing words. Soon the entire group was singing the same words as Melissa. When the music finished and applause had subsided, Greg walked over to Cameo, and took her hands in his.

"Now, I hope this fulfills your wish, you danced at your granddaughter's wedding."

Cameo smiled as she reached up and placed a kiss on his cheek.

"Thank you for being so thoughtful," she vocalized loud enough for most to hear.

Learning The Job

With Melissa and Greg on their honeymoon the parents both suffered withdrawal from their kids. The fact was, they missed them greatly. For Edith, though, it was different than when Greg was away in the army. She slept better at night, her slumber was without fear for her son's welfare. Edith was very thankful for that. It was, however, the postcards that brought the two sets of parents laughter, while keeping them informed of their kids' whereabouts. An occasional phone call also kept them all in touch.

Susan went to the mailbox and returned with yet another card. The postcard depicted Diamond Head on its front. Susan turned the card over and read the short note to Kenneth.

"Today we swam in the ocean. Greg watched for sharks — didn't see any. Tonight we're going to a luau. Hope to make pigs of ourselves, Ha Ha." It was signed Love, Melissa and Greg.

"I can't believe how much I miss them already," Kenneth stated.

"I'm going to give Edith a call and read her our card. You know something, —"

"What's that, Honey?"

"— each time Melissa and Greg write, they put different messages on each card they send to Edith and Frank, or you and me."

"I think they do that on purpose so we'll call each other," Kenneth suggested.

"That could be."

"Stop and think about this," Kenneth added, "in another week or so our son-in-law is going to be working for us. I still can't get over that fact. I hope it all works out, after all it's a big step for him, and us as well."

"Well, I have lots of faith in his ability to do a good job," she said.

"It won't take long to find out one way or the other, that's for sure."

"What's your gut feeling, Kenneth, I mean what's the strongest feeling you have about Greg's success?"

Kenneth shrugged his shoulders.

"If I've learned nothing else about that boy it's one thing, never underestimate him," he said nodding his head.

"I know Melissa has all the faith in the world he'll do a good job for us," she stated.

"As I said, time will tell. But if he doesn't work out, that's the part that worries me the most."

Susan nodded her agreement.

Before anyone could have imaged it, the honeymoon was over. The parents were happy to hold their children in their arms again. The joy they all felt was understandable. It was time in their life, however, to move on. Greg would start to carry the weight of being a new husband and support his wife. He knew everyone would stand behind him, but still —

Kenneth and Susan sat at one side of a large wooden table, Melissa and Greg seated across from them.

"Well, Greg," Kenneth stated, "are you ready to begin your first day of work?"

"As ready as I'll ever be, I guess."

"Well, just do your best," Susan said.

"Thank you, Mr. and Mrs. Summers," Greg joked, "and thank you both for this wonderful opportunity."

Melissa smiled.

"Son, both Susan and I commend you for doing this. We just want you to know that before you start, we're behind you one hundred percent," Kenneth said.

Melissa reached over and put her hand on Greg's.

"Don't take any wooden nickels, Honey," she joked to him.

The Promise

How long ago it seemed to Greg when he was asked by Melissa's parents to join in their family store. Now he was about to begin his adventure in learning the business, something he wanted to do a very credible job on. Well, he thought to himself, every journey begins with its first step. Greg stood up, bent down and gave Melissa a light kiss.

"Wish me luck," he said as he walked out of the conference room.

"Good luck!" both Susan and Melissa said in harmony.

Greg left the room and walked over to the elevator. He reached over and pushed the down button. Once it arrived, he entered it along with questions in his mind of what to expect on his first day as their employee. As the door to the elevator closed Greg looked at the series of buttons before him. He pushed the bottom one marked with a big "B" on it. As the elevator made its descending motion downward, it stopped at the second floor. The door opened. An older gentleman wearing a suit stepped in to share a ride.

"Hello, Mr. Wilson, I'm Ted Sheppard," he said as the door guided shut. "Welcome to the Summers' family business. " He stretched out his hand to Greg.

"Thank you, sir," Greg acknowledged as they shook hands. "So I take it you obviously work here, too?"

"First of all, let's get a few things straight. I'm in charge of store security, number one. Number two, my loyalty lies strictly with the Summers family, they've treated me very well through the years. Number three, until I get to know you better, you're strictly just another employee to me. Mrs. Summers explained to me about your desire to start out at the bottom of the food chain, so to speak, and I admire you for that. I believe the only reason she told me that is because she also knows I check into every new employee's background, even when I'm not asked to."

"Well, now that that's out in the open," Greg said, "you should know some things about me, also. Number one, I love Melissa with all my heart, and the fact that I'm married to the boss's daughter shouldn't affect our relationship at all. Number two, if you observe me messing something up, let me know. And you can use any method you wish to employ, though a swift kick in the butt always gets my attention. And number three, I think I like you already," Greg said smiling as he nodded his head. "An open and honest man is a treasure for anyone to behold." He then stretched his hand out to Mr. Sheppard. "As I said, it's really nice to meet you, Mr. Sheppard."

"You can call me, Ted."

"And you can call me, Greg."

The men shook hands hardily, both wearing a small smile on their faces. It was obvious to both men, the ground rules were established, and they already liked each other.

"You know, Greg, I think I'm going to enjoy getting to know you."

"I hope so."

Once the elevator stopped, Ted turned to Greg. "Let me take a few minutes and show you where you'll be working."

"Thank you, I'd appreciate that."

The two men walked down several aisles and then through a maze of different boxes containing merchandise. Large lights brightly lit their path on their way to the back. As they turned the corner, a young man holding a clipboard in his hand stood looking over a large stack of boxed inventory. As Greg and Ted walked up to the man he turned in their direction.

"Hi, Mr. Sheppard," he stated.

"Greg, this is Jack Whiting, you've been assigned to work with him."

"Nice to meet you," Greg said reaching out his hand.

"Same here," he said as he lowered his clipboard and shook Greg's hand.

"Listen, I've got to be going," Ted said. "If you have any questions, Jack will be glad to answer any of them for you. He's a very smart man, listen to him, and he'll teach you well."

"See you later, Mr. Sheppard," Jack said as Ted walked away. Though he didn't look back, he raised his arm and waved it back and forth slightly as he continued down an aisle.

"Well, I'm glad you're here. I can sure use the help, that is, unless you cause me more work," Jack stated. "If you're lazy, you might as well start looking for another job because I don't have time to waste on you."

"I don't think you'll find that in me, I'm not afraid of hard work."

"Good. Let's get started."

The hours flew by for Greg. Jack was very knowledgeable in his job. Even an amateur such as Greg could quickly see that. He was also extremely well versed in all of the products carried by the store. Jack could tell volumes about a box's interior just by glancing at the outside of it, the numbers revealing everything to him. When it came time for lunch, Greg asked him when their lunch break was to start.

"Not until that large pile of inventory is taken care of," he was instructed. "Lunch is sometimes a privilege we don't get around here," Jack told Greg.

"And why is that?"

"Well, we're overworked."

"So why don't you say something about it?"

"It's simple, because I owe them too much."

"You mean you're in debt, I don't understand?"

"No, I owe Mr. Sheppard and the Summers."

"I still don't understand."

"When I was younger I used to get into a lot of trouble. Mr. Sheppard helped me out, he was there for me. Anyway, he went to the Summers and asked them, as a personal favor to him if they would give me a chance. He got me this job, so I owe him. I owe them as well for giving me the opportunity also, the Summers that is. If it means skipping lunch to show them I can do a good job, it's a small price to pay. Let me tell you one thing, Greg, I better not hear you complaining to anyone while you're here with me, or you'll have to answer to me personally. You just do your job; okay?"

Greg nodded his head.

"Well, let's get back to work," Jack stated as he handed Greg a cardboard box that was sitting next to him.

It was well past three o'clock in the afternoon before the two of them sat down to eat their lunch.

"You know, Greg, they sure could save some money around here," Jack stated as he took a bite from his sandwich.

"Like what?" Greg said, being all ears.

"Look at those lights up there, way too big of bulbs. We need light, yes, but not a tan. And the shipping schedule, it's all wrong. If they'd move it around a little, make some adjustments, deliveries would flow a lot smoother."

"Anything else?" Greg asked while making mental notes in his mind.

"How the trucks are parked waiting to be unloaded. If they switched the schedule around there, like I said, the trucks could get in and out a lot faster. It would save us time, people could move onto different areas, and the parking would open up. It's like a win-win situation."

When the workday finally came to an end Jack bid Greg a good night. Greg walked over to a makeshift desk, it being more like a shelf supported by wooden boards attached to a wall on either side. A phone sat on it at an angle. Two nails had been driven in beside it to make sure it didn't fall or slide to the floor. He took a pad of paper from the top and wrote down Jack's suggestions, things he wanted to keep track of for himself.

Melissa could hardly contain herself as Greg walked through the front door of their newly rented home. She grabbed him quickly giving him a kiss.

"So how is my new working husband doing?" she asked.

"Much more knowledgeable than I was this morning," he answered.

"So tell me about it."

"You know something, Honey, would you care if I waited on that. I'd just like to have a cup of coffee and spend some quiet time with you."

"That sounds good to me. I'll make the coffee for you."

"Thanks."

As Greg sat on the couch with Melissa cuddled into his arm he looked down at her smiling. Her legs were pulled up onto the couch. Every so often he reached down and kissed her forehead. She would then move back into her favorite position, his arm wrapped over her shoulder as she nestled into it.

"Do you think we can get some suggestion boxes put around the store?" he asked.

"I suppose."

"I wonder what your parents would think about suggestion pay or merit pay?"

"What do you mean?"

"Well, just suppose someone could save the store money with an idea, wouldn't it be nice if you could reward them with some money, maybe a paid day off? What do you think of that idea, Honey?"

"I like it, especially if you get the day off and we can spend it together," she chuckled.

"I'm serious."

"I know you are. Well, I think it's a good idea, one worthy of pursuing."

Greg just nodded his head, various ideas running through his mind as he sat beside Melissa. He started rubbing his hand slightly up and down on her arm as he thought.

Each day ran into another with Greg learning much from Jack. He not only was a good teacher, he was patient with Greg as well. A friendship began to flourish between the two. Greg liked the fact that Jack made his job the number one priority, with breaks taking second place to him. Greg, however, knew some things had to change, one way or another. Soon days turned into a few weeks.

"What's this?" inquired Jack looking at an object hanging on the wall.

"They apparently put it up when we were upstairs," Greg answered.

"We don't need any suggestion box, nobody's going to listen to us."

"You might be surprised. Say, why don't you put down your ideas on the delivery schedule, the lights, the truck parking, after all, what's it going to hurt?"

"You want to put it in under your name Greg, go ahead, I don't care."

"Like I can write it down correctly."

"I'll tell you what," Jack said, "I'll write it down for you, and you can put your name on it, get all the credit for it, if any."

"Okay, I will."

"Good."

Jack walked over to the desk and jotted some of his ideas on a sheet of paper. He looked at it for a minute, then handed it to Greg.

"Now, put your John Hancock on it, and good luck hearing back."

"Thanks, Jack, I will."

As more time passed, Greg was really getting the hang of his new job. His proficiency at it had grown quite a bit under Jack's tutorage.

"If we can get those televisions upstairs by noon, that should give us more time to work on the kitchen merchandise," suggested Jack to Greg.

"Would Jack Whiting please report to the office as soon as possible," came Susan's voice on the sound system.

"Just what I need now," Jack stated shaking his head.

"Go on, I can handle this," Greg said.

"No, they said as soon as possible, and it's not possible for me now. You need the help, I'll get there when I can."

"But shouldn't you get up there now, I mean they called you?"

"If it's that important, they'll call me again, otherwise they can wait until we're done. Now, let's move this pile over here next."

Greg smiled to himself. He knew in Jack's mind getting his work done first meant more to him than someone requesting his attention. He's right, Greg thought, if they need him that badly they'll announce it again.

About a half an hour went by when another announcement for Jack's appearance was requested over the speaker system.

"Now they have my attention," he stated. "I'll be back as soon as I can."

"Okay," Greg said.

Jack stepped from the elevator and walked through the doors into the office. He looked at Mrs. Summers sitting behind her desk.

"Oh, good to see you, Mr. Whiting, please come this way."

Jack followed Susan as she left her office heading for the conference room. Walking through the door behind her he immediately saw Mr. Summers and their daughter, Melissa, standing in the room. This can't be good, he thought to himself.

The Promise

"Please have a seat, Mr. Whiting," Kenneth said as he gestured with his hand.

Jack took a seat, a pit in his stomach beginning to form.

"I have here some suggestions made by you on how you think we can best make use of our delivery schedule, improve it, and a number of other items as well."

"Oh, Mr. Summers, that's not my idea, it's a mistake. The new guy, Greg, it's his ideas, he should get any credit, and if it's not correct, it's all my fault for not explaining things to him in a better way."

"So what do you think of his ideas?" Kenneth asked.

"Well, I think they'd be worth trying. After all, what's it going to hurt? He's a smart kid, you were wise to hire him."

"Mr. Whiting," Susan pausing. "Jack," Susan starting again, "are you trying to tell us that a man who just started here came up with these ideas on merchandise deliveries, and all by himself?"

"As I said, he's a smart kid. You should also know that if anything is wrong, it's my fault, I should be blamed entirely, not him."

"Well," Kenneth stated, "be that as it may, I frankly think these are all your ideas, I'd bet money on it. And speaking about money, Susan, would you take it from here?"

"I'd be happy to," she said as she turned to face Jack. "Jack, all of us are very happy you work for us, and we would like to reward those who work so hard for us, and possess good ideas as well. So to begin with, this is for you."

Susan handed Jack an envelope.

"Thank you," he said taking it from her, though he didn't open it.

"We are going to institute your ideas," she went onto say, "and we want you to be in charge of setting it up for us. You should also know you'll be getting a proper desk and chair. We will be hiring more employees to help alleviate the stress we're sure you'll be dealing with because of your new position. You will be in charge of the hiring. These new employees will be under your personal supervision, of course, and your pay will be raised commensurate with your new duties. Oh, and just so you know, the check in that envelope is strictly for your ideas, it has nothing to do with your raise. You'll see that raise reflected on your next check. As I said, we appreciate you."

Susan ended her words with a smile.

Melissa said nothing, she just smiled knowing her husband's ideas were appreciated as well by her parents. A simple suggestion box, she thought, who would ever have guessed it could make this much of a difference in someone's life like Jack.

"Do you have any questions?" Susan asked.

"No, ma'am."

"Now, you better get back to work," Kenneth said, "and thank you."

"Thank you, and I appreciate this," he said as he waved the envelope up and down slightly.

Susan nodded her head at Jack.

"And Mr. and Mrs. Summers, —"

"Yes," Kenneth said.

"— it's nice to know when you're appreciated."

Kenneth nodded his head as well as Susan.

Jack left the room and went immediately to the elevator. Once the door closed and he was by himself he quickly looked inside the envelope. A check in the amount of a thousand dollars stared him in the face. He was stunned. On the check memo line were the words, "Thank you, Jack, we appreciate you." Jack shook his head as he replaced the check in the envelope. He next folded the envelope in half and put it in his back pocket. He couldn't, however, help himself as he removed it and looked at it once again. Jack shook his head back and forth in disbelief as he returned it to his back pocket.

Hearing Jack coming down the aisle Greg turned to him.

"I've got most of this done, but what do you want me to do with the other boxes?"

"Nothing," came Jack's response. "Let's take a break and have a cup of coffee."

"Okay."

Each man took a moment and filled their coffee cups from their thermoses.

The Promise

"So when did you get the idea of putting my name on the suggestion paper, I'd kind of would like to know that?"

"Oh, I don't know. I hope you're not mad at me. I really shouldn't have done it without your permission, I'm sorry. But you have to admit, your ideas are good."

"How would you like $500.00?"

"Who wouldn't?" Greg chuckled.

"They gave me a thousand dollars for my ideas, they're hiring more people for down here which, of course, I will train. They're giving me a raise, I get a decent desk and chair since I'm being made a supervisor. How neat is that?"

"Congratulations, Jack," Greg said extending his hand out to him.

As they shook hands Jack smiled. "Half of this is yours, you put my name on it, it's only fair."

"Jack, just the fact they're using your ideas is enough for me, besides it would hurt my feelings taking money for something I didn't think of."

"Well, okay," Jack said, "but just the same, if you ever need some money for something, anything, let me know."

"I will," smiled Greg.

After enjoying a short break, the two men got back to work. It wasn't very long after that when Mr. Sheppard came walking up to Greg and Jack.

"I understand congratulations are in order, Jack," he stated, holding his hand out.

"I just heard about it myself, how do you know already?" questioned Jack as he shook Ted's hand.

"I have listening devices hidden everywhere, spy cameras," he joked. "I just wanted to tell you how proud of you I am," he said as he nodded his head.

"Thank you, and I mean thank you for everything," Jack stated.

"Don't kid yourself, Jack, you had this coming for quite some time."

Once the new employees were trained sufficiently, Greg asked if it was okay for him to move onto another position, learn something new.

"Of course," was Susan's quick response.

And so it went, Greg moving from area to area, making friends easily as he made his way around the store. People couldn't help but like him, they opened themselves up to him. He learned of their desires, hopes, dreams and most importantly their problems. Greg never judged anyone, his motive was simply to learn the new position, help those he could, and make it a better place to work. He also wanted, if possible, to save the Summers family some money. This last fact didn't come easily for them at times, it sometimes reached deeply into their financial pockets.

One evening while having dinner at the in-law's home, Greg brought up some observations of his he thought should be addressed.

"Mom, Dad, there's some things I'd like to suggest to you, if it's okay."

Kenneth thought to himself, here we go again.

"Why don't you wait until after dinner?" suggested Melissa.

"No, that's okay," Susan said.

"And how much is this going to cost us?" Kenneth asked.

"I'm sorry, it can wait," Greg said, "Melissa's right."

"No, you opened the door, go ahead," Kenneth said as he placed his fork onto the table. He then reached for his coffee cup, figuring this may take a little while.

"Well, I really have a few things I wanted to talk over with you two."

Melissa took a deep breath. She knew Greg's heart was on her parent's side in everything, but Greg was one who said what he thought. She thought to herself, I wonder what he's going to talk about first tonight?

"First, it's the break room," Greg declared.

"Go ahead," Kenneth stated.

"I looked under the sink, behind the doors and it's dirty, filthy, from water leaking. Some of it is actually rotting."

"You looked under the sink?" inquired Susan.

"Yes. Also the tables wobble, the chairs have cracks in them and they've seen a better day. Oh, and the refrigerator needs to be cleaned."

"Anything else?" inquired Kenneth.

"Well, as far as the fridge being cleaned, we could set up a schedule for each section of the store to take turns."

"That sounds logical," Kenneth said nodding his head.

"Besides that, it's not working properly, you can hardly keep anything cool in it."

"So what do you suggest we do about this?"

"Well, Kenneth," Susan stated, "I wouldn't want my own daughter to put up with that if she was working there for us."

"She already is." Kenneth laughed slightly, nodding his head as he spoke.

"Just the same, our employees deserve better."

"Okay. Both of you are obviously right, and I know I wouldn't want to have to put up with that either," Kenneth said as he reached for his coffee cup again. "What do you suggest, we hire a construction crew?"

"I hope you don't mind," Greg said, "but I've kind of thought all of this over and I have come up with what I think is a good idea."

"Well, let's hear it."

"It's Henry. We'll have Henry do the work. You'll get a first class job at an extremely good price, and besides that, Kate can come and help him. They can stay with us. Henry can sleep on the couch, and Kate can have the other bedroom."

"And I can visit with Kate," added Melissa excitedly. "Please, Daddy, say it's okay," she pleaded.

"Like I had any choice in this from the very beginning. Let's do this instead, if it's okay with you," Kenneth said in a somewhat sarcastic voice. "Kate and Melissa can stay with us for a few days, a week, whatever it takes. Henry can use your spare room, that way he'll be more comfortable. How does that sound to you? Henry can ride to work with you, and Kate with Melissa or us."

"Thanks, Dad," Melissa expressed.

"Anything else?"

"Well," Greg said, "I do have an idea about what I refer to as, 'The Summers' Summer Picnic,' if you want to hear about it."

"The Summers' Summer Picnic," that sounds so special, I like it," Susan said. "The Summers' Summer Picnic," she repeated smiling. "And how would that work?"

"By costing us lots of money," Kenneth stated, "at least it sounds expensive."

"Yes and no, mom and dad," came Melissa's voice. "When Greg first told me about his idea, all I saw were dollar signs dancing in my head. We talked quite a bit about it, and here's our idea, or Greg's I should say. One day in the summer we'd close the store."

"Hmm," came the sound from Kenneth's mouth.

"Give her a chance, Kenneth," Susan said.

Melissa continued on with her thoughts, her voice reflecting excitement in it.

"The day would be set aside for our employees, that day obviously to be determined by you two. It could be an employee appreciation day, so to speak. I found out you can actually rent a large portion of the city park, and it's not that expensive," Melissa stated. "They will even cordon off a large section of it, with the ballpark as part of it. I think they use snow fence to accomplish that."

"Okay," Kenneth said nodding his head.

Greg looked at Kenneth as he thought to himself, Kenneth is nodding his head, that's a good sign. At least he hadn't said, "No," to this point.

"All our employees and their families would be invited to come," Melissa continued.

"Not just employees?" Kenneth said.

"No Dad, their families could go, too."

"Hmmm."

"We'd have hotdogs, burgers, chips, lots of things," a large amount of enthusiasm very much evident in her voice as she spoke. "There would be games for the kids, a baseball game, the women against the men or half and half. We even talked about having clowns and balloons, a treasure hunt for the children, just all kinds of things. It's just a way for our family to show our appreciation to our employees."

"Well," Susan stated, "it does sound really expensive let alone giving everyone a day off. I assume that's a paid day off to boot, am I right?"

"Yes, Mom," Melissa said softly looking downward. She knew full well that was a huge expense for her parents to bear.

"I see."

"Mom, can I say something else... please?"

"Of course, Honey," Susan said as she nodded her head.

"The money you've given me, the difference in the pay for Greg's jobs, —"

"Yes."

"— I've been putting that away, saving every cent of it, plus what we could add to it ourselves."

"We were hoping you would do that so someday you and Greg can buy a house," Susan said.

"Well, mom, dad, we'll give you that money towards this party. We'll pay for the party as much as we can, but you'd have to foot the day off. We know that would cost you a lot, we both understand that. Maybe down the road we can give you some more money, too. This way, we can help with the expenses. Would you both at least think about it?"

"Well, I'm not going to waste any time thinking about it," Kenneth stated abruptly.

"Kenneth!" Susan said in a strong voice.

"As far as I'm concerned" Kenneth stated, "it's a done deal. Melissa, you're in charge. I expect a proposed flyer for our employees' party on my desk within the next week or so. But I do have a question for the both of you. Why do you two feel so strongly about this, that you would give up your own savings to help pay for this?"

"Mom, Dad, Greg told me how hard the people work for us, for you, how wonderful they are. Did you know that not one employee has ever said a single negative word about either one of you. They love you. Greg would know all about that, he's with them every day. He told me he wanted to do something to show them how much they're appreciated, each and every one of them."

"Well, Greg," Kenneth said, "I learned about employees being appreciated from a guy named Jack. He told me it was so nice to know he was appreciated. I think that's one reason I like your idea so well."

Greg nodded his head as he agreed with Kenneth.

"And besides," Kenneth stated, "I like your Summers' Summer Picnic name, it's really a cute theme title."

"Then thank your daughter for that, she came up with it," Greg proclaimed proudly.

Susan and Kenneth smiled.

"Is it okay if I help out on this, too, I would love to help put on the party," Susan inquired smiling.

"I was hoping you both would," Melissa said.

"We all will," added Kenneth. As he looked at the smile on his daughter's face, it warmed his heart. He reached over placing his hand on Melissa's.

"So it's settled," he stated. "Melissa will work out the plans with Susan. Greg, you and I will support them in any way we can."

"Great," Greg exclaimed.

"And Mom, I'll give you the money after I get it from the bank," Melissa said, "we can start building up the fund for the picnic."

"The store will pay for everything, you two keep your money," Kenneth said sternly. "Susan, do you think our store can handle the financing of this big of a party?" he said in a half smile.

"I'll see that it does," she answered.

"Good. Is there anything else we need to discuss," inquired Kenneth.

"Well, I'll give Henry a call and see what he has to say about the break room project," Greg stated.

"Can I call Kate and ask her?" asked Melissa excitedly.

"That's fine," Susan said.

"I haven't talked to her in two days, so I'm going to enjoy telling her the news about us visiting, and the job for Henry to do with her."

"So when can I expect the estimate, Greg?" Kenneth asked.

"Is never too soon?"

"Pardon me?"

"Dad, Henry never gives an estimate, but if you feel it's too expensive when he's done, or you don't like his job, he'll either fix it to your liking or not charge you at all, that's how he operates."

"Unbelievable," was all Kenneth could say.

"And just so you're aware, I don't know of anyone who does a better job than he does."

"Greg, I'm sure you have other suggestions on how we can better run our store, but would you mind giving me a break from those ideas for a little while?"

"I understand entirely," Greg answered nodding his head.

The women smiled at hearing Kenneth's suggestion.

"Greg, don't forget you said we'd go for a walk after we ate," Melissa said reminding Greg of his previous promise.

"I didn't forget, Honey."

Once the meal was finished, Melissa helped her mother clear the table, with Greg joining in.

"Mom, would you and dad like to come along with us?" Melissa suggested.

"Yes, I would. Let's just leave this for now, it won't go anywhere."

"Good. Dad, how about it?"

"Why not."

The four left the home and started walking down the road together. It was a time to be spent together with no thoughts of work, just good tasting conversation.

"Look, Mom, there's a cardinal, isn't it beautiful in the light."

"It sure is, Honey. I think the color red is your favorite one of all," Susan said nodding her head.

"I suppose you're right, Mom, after all, I had red roses at my wedding and Greg gave me red roses. It's just a color that keeps coming into my life, and I love it."

Melissa stepped between her parents, taking each one of their hands in hers. Greg walked beside Kenneth. Kenneth reached up and put his arm on Greg's shoulder. Together they headed down the roadway as a group of one.

Unbeknownst to either Greg or Melissa, Susan and Kenneth went into the store a little early the next day. They walked down to the break room, turned on the lights and looked around. Everything was just as Greg had described it to them.

"I think it's worse than Greg said, to tell you the truth," Kenneth stated as he glanced under the sink.

"It appears you're right," Susan answered as she took a peek under the sink with him. "We can't have our employees putting up with this, it's just not acceptable," she said nodding her head back and forth as she spoke.

As Kenneth continued to look around, he turned to Susan. "I'm going to call and get an estimate on this."

"But Greg said Henry would do a real good job, and you've got to admit Greg is usually right."

"Just the same, it makes good business sense to do it."

"Okay, Kenneth, whatever you say."

Susan shut off the lights as they turned and began walking to their offices.

"I think I'll give him a call now, get the estimate part moving," Kenneth said.

"So you're not giving Henry a chance at doing the job at all?"

"He can do the job, that's not the problem I have, I'd just feel more comfortable getting a second quote."

"Okay, Kenneth," Susan said nodding her head.

Now I Understand

A knock on her front door turned Emma's head. She walked over to it, twisted the handle and opened it. As she expected, it was Henry.

"Good morning, Mom," came the usual first sentence from his mouth.

"Good morning, Henry," she replied as she reached up placing her customary kiss on his cheek.

"I didn't want to come over too early this morning, I thought you may want to sleep in a little."

"Oh, I've been up quite a little while now. Come in," she gestured. "I was just about to start a breakfast for you."

Henry reached over and pulled a chair out from the table.

"I see you're wearing the robe the neighbors gave you for Christmas a few of years ago."

"Oh, Henry, that was so unexpected," Emma said as she ran her hand over the sleeve admiring it.

"So what's on your agenda today, Mom?"

"Well, I thought I'd make some fruitcake up, of course, I'm starting to run low. Jackie and Sid are coming over to help and visit with me a little later."

"They're wonderful neighbors for you to have."

"Yes, they are. And besides, I want to make up my gifts that I hand out each year."

"Oh, you mean your fruitcake packages?"

"Yes. Sid and Jackie are going to deliver them for me. It was Jackie's idea, and that will help me out tremendously."

"You know, I would have been happy to do that for you."

"I know, but just the same, they enjoy doing it for me. Oh, I better get the bacon going," Emma said as she walked towards the kitchen area.

"Just have a seat, Mom, that can wait. Let's just sit and enjoy each other's company for a little while."

Emma sat down at the table across from Henry. She picked up her cup and took a sip from it.

"Would you like something to drink?" she asked.

"Yes, I would, but you just sit there, I'll get it myself."

"I don't mind."

"I know."

Once Henry had prepared his tea he sat down across from Emma once again.

"Henry," Emma stated in what Henry recognized as her firm inquisitive voice, "I want to talk to you about something very important. Now, of course, it's none of my business," she started out, "but I need to know something."

"What is it, Mom?"

There was a gentle rapping sound on the front door.

"Oh, Sid and Jackie must be here," Henry said.

"No, they're not coming until much, much later."

"Well, I'll get it," he said as he stood up and walked to the front door. Opening it, he was astonished to see Kate standing there.

"Kate, come in," he said as he opened the door further for her. "So what brings you here today?" he asked.

"Emma, called me."

Henry shook his head, wondering why she would do that.

"Here, let me take your coat."

"Okay, Honey."

Henry laid the coat over a chair as Kate placed her purse next to it.

"Now, the both of you come here and join me. Kate, you have a seat here," indicated Emma with her hand, "and Henry there." The couple sat on the opposite side of the table from Emma.

"Would you like something to drink, Kate?" inquired Emma.

"No, thank you, I just had a cup of coffee a little while ago."

"And Henry, you still okay?"

"Yes, Mom."

"Good," Emma stated. "It's nice and quiet in here, and there's nothing either one of you need to drink. Does anyone have to use the bathroom?"

Henry shook his head slightly back and forth, Kate stating, "No."

"Wonderful, just wonderful, now we can talk without any interruptions to worry about," she smiled.

Henry and Kate simply sat there, perplexed at what was happening. They both knew that Emma had obviously planned this out, giving Kate a call and knowing Henry was expected to stop by her house anyway. As the three sat there quietly Emma reached over to Henry with her left hand taking his in hers. She did the same with her right hand, this time taking Kate's hand in hers as well.

"Henry, Kate, I want to say a couple of things to you. I also have a couple of questions for the both of you, and if you would just answer me honestly and —"

"Mom, neither one of us would lie to you."

"I understand, it was a poor way of posing the statement. I didn't mean it to sound the way it came out. Remember I'm an old lady and sometimes my words don't run as true as they should."

"We understand, Mom."

"Good," she said as she squeezed his hand.

"Henry, do you love Kate, this wonderful woman sitting next to you, yes or no?"

Henry turned his head and looked at Kate.

"More than she could ever imagine, yes, I do love her," he said as he looked into Kate's eyes. His face bore a small smile.

"Good. And Kate, the same question, do you love Henry?" inquired Emma.

"With all my heart," was her quick reply.

"Good, very good. Now, Son, I want you to tell both of us why you won't ask Kate to be your wife, and don't use any of those big fancy words of yours to hide your answer. I want to know why you won't ask her to marry you?"

Kate sat there in shock, as well as Henry. However, Kate wanted to hear Henry's answer to Emma's question. She knew he loved her. The fact that he played the piano and sang a song for her a few days previously at the restaurant demonstrated that to her, it being just one of many little things he did for her to show his love. But why wouldn't he ask her, the supposed love of his life to marry him, she wanted that answered more than Emma did.

Henry sat quietly, not a single word coming forth from his voice, his throat dry. The women looked at each other, wanting to say something, but neither spoke. Henry took a deep breath. He knew they both deserved his answer, especially Kate.

"Kate, I love you with all my heart, I think you know that. There is nothing more important in the world to me than to possess the love of you two women. Now as far as what you need to hear from me, the answer to that question is that I'm ashamed to have you take my last name. Every time I use that name, Lewis, it tears at my heart. You can't imagine what my life was like to live in that atmosphere. Those people were so… every time I hear someone utter that name, it brings back horrible memories to me. I just couldn't have that name become a part of you, your married name."

Kate shook her head back and forth with Henry's words to her. She understood what he meant more than he could have ever known or imagined. Her mind immediately went back to the filth filled rooms, the smells that had tortured her lungs with every breath she took. She knew what Henry had gone through. Yes, Kate had experienced all of it when she and Melissa had gone to the Lewis home. His statements were very clear to her, and now everything made sense.

"Now, I understand," she stated to him, "your name is everything to you."

Kate stood up, walked over to her coat laying across the back of a chair. She put it on, picked up her purse, and walked out of the house.

"Oh, I never would have expected that reaction out of her," Emma said.

"I don't understand it either. I didn't mean for her to feel my last name was more important to me than her."

Henry and Emma could hear Kate's car leaving the area.

"I'm so sorry, Henry, I didn't mean this to happen. Still, now I understand why you didn't ask her. Son, you've never really talked to me about your childhood. Maybe now is a good time to get it off your chest."

"Mom," Henry staring at his hand in hers, "maybe another time if it's okay. I really don't feel up to it now."

"I understand."

Henry nodded his head slowly back and forth.

"Let me make both of us a cup of fresh tea," Emma suggested, "everything goes better with a hot cup of tea."

"Thank you, Mom."

Once Emma made them both fresh tea, she returned to sit across from Henry. Henry turned and looked across the table at Emma.

"Mom, you had to deal with the loss of your husband, Paul, and now I know how you felt to a certain extent. I just lost the love of my life over a name. Even when I was growing up, I never experienced this amount of pain, this much misery." Henry swallowed hard. He looked over at Emma again. She nodded her head, but offered no reply. The memories she carried for Paul were written across her face as she sat there. Henry placed his folded arms on the table before him, laying his head onto them as he did. Emma could see his shoulders moving up and down slightly. He appeared to be softly crying. There were no words exchanged between them, neither one had anything to say. The silence in the room simply embraced both of them. Perhaps a half hour went by, maybe more, maybe less, time was irrelevant to them now.

The sound of the front door opening awakened both of them from the daze they were surrounded by. They both looked in the direction of the door to see Kate standing there. She placed her purse down, her coat next to it.

"I thought I lost you forever," Henry said, "but you came back."

She walked over and put her arms around Henry.

"I love you, Mr. Henry Lewis," she said.

"And I love you, too, Kate," he replied as he reached up and hugged her.

Henry's eyes appeared somewhat watery to Kate as she looked down at him.

"I thought I lost you forever, my heart was breaking inside of me."

Emma smiled, as she reached for a tissue from a box on the corner of the table.

"I'm sorry I walked out a few minutes ago, but I needed to."

"I understand," he said, "you needed some time to think everything over. You were upset with me."

"No, that's not it at all, I needed to get something, and that's all I could think of at the time. I didn't want to tell you what it was, I just needed to get it."

Kate walked over to her coat. She reached into a pocket of the coat, an envelope showing in part from its position. She pulled it out and handed it to Henry.

"What's this?"

"I got this with the help of a very dear friend of mine. You don't need to know who it is, that's not important. In fact, the person would rather you not know who they are. Henry, just read this, please."

Henry carefully opened the envelope. He pulled the papers from its interior, unfolded them and began to read them to himself. It became quite evident to both Kate and Emma there was moisture present on his cheeks. He shook his head back and forth slowly as he held the pages in his hand. Emma knew whatever it was that he was reading was very significant to him. Henry laid the papers down on the table before him. He next wiped both of his eyes with the palms of his hands. Kate smiled as she watched him. She knew what this meant to him, as well as to her.

"Kate, this is more than wonderful, what you and Melissa did for me getting these documents. How can I ever thank you both, and how did you ever get them?"

"I never said it was Melissa who helped me," Kate stated quickly.

Once again Henry wiped his eyes. Emma sat watching the two of them, still not quite sure what the papers represented.

"Will you answer a couple of questions for me?" Henry said with a small smile reflected on his flush face.

"If I can," she replied.

"Who was in the hospital room besides you and me when the question of my last name was brought up?"

"Melissa," she answered.

"And who asked that question?"

"Melissa."

"And a second ago you said a dear friend of yours helped you to get these papers. Who is your best friend?"

"Melissa."

"And who is the type of person who wouldn't want people to know she helped you?"

"Melissa."

"Well, then it's obvious to me it had to be someone other than Melissa," he jokingly said.

"Emma... Mom, I should say, these papers answer the questions I've carried inside me for years. They possess information about my real name, where I was born, and when."

Emma put both of her hands to her mouth, a surprised expression showing on her face. That was not something she expected to hear, but good news is still good news no matter what, she thought to herself.

"What do they say?" she softly inquired as she removed her hands.

"I'm two years younger than I thought I was. I was born in the small town of Decker, not all that far away from here, maybe a couple of hundred miles. But most importantly, I now know my name." Henry took a deep breath. "It's Henry P. Morgan."

"Oh, my," was Emma's response. "I'm so happy for you, Son."

"Kate, did you notice this fact?" Henry stated as he lifted the paperwork up and placed his finger on the sheet.

"Oh, no, I didn't even... I can't believe it," she said as she looked over in Emma's direction smiling.

"What is it, Henry?" Emma said.

"Mom, my middle initial is "P" and it stands for Paul. My middle name is Paul, just like your late husband's name."

"Oh my, oh my," Emma said as she reached for the tissue box again. "Oh my," she repeated as she wiped her eyes.

"Isn't life filled with surprises sometimes," Henry said as he shook his head back and forth.

"It sure is, Henry, it sure is," she repeated. "And what a wonderful surprise it is for me," she said wiping her eyes.

"Henry," Kate said, "I love you. I would have taken any name you had. That didn't mean anything to me, your last name, your first name. Your love is all I ever wanted from you."

"I know, Kate, it's just that that name... I... my life was so horrible. I didn't want to hear people call you Mrs. Lewis."

"Listen you two, we can — you can get your name changed at the courthouse. I think that can be done, if I'm not mistaken," Emma stated in an excited voice. "And when you tell them why you want it changed, I'll bet they'll be glad to do it."

"I think there's a lot more to it than just that," Henry said.

"It's worth a try," Kate said smiling.

"Well, we can always call my lawyer," suggested Emma.

Kate reached over and put her arms around Henry. She smiled and then placed a huge kiss upon his lips. Henry didn't fight her forwardness whatsoever, he just kissed her back harder.

"Henry," Kate stated, "will you marry me?"

"Oh my," Emma stated.

"I wanted to ask you that question so many times myself, Honey," he said.

"Well, I'm tired of waiting, and besides, I do love you so much," she declared.

"Why yes, I will," he exclaimed as they kissed once again.

Emma got up and left the room. Neither one of the young couple noticed her departure. She soon returned and retook her seat at the table. Emma reached over and took a sip of her tea, still listening and enjoying the actions that were taking place before her.

"Kate, Henry, if I may," she said.

Henry and Kate immediately turned their attention to Emma. Emma placed her right hand upon the plain gold wedding band on her other hand.

She rolled it around and around as she looked back and forth between them and the ring.

"When my Paul and I were first married we didn't have much money. This is the ring he gave me to represent his love for me. I've worn it for many years now... it's never been off."

Emma took a deep breath, then smiled at Kate and Henry.

"After some years Paul wanted me to have something much larger to represent the love he held for me. He purchased another ring, a beautiful ring with a very impressive heart shaped diamond with smaller diamonds running down each side of it. I expressed to him that my simple band was all I really wanted, that it was my favorite treasure from him. I suggested that he should take the ring back to the jewelers. He told me he wanted me to keep it just the same, to remind me that his love for me had grown more and more through the years.

Kate, Henry, would the two of you consider taking that ring and making it as part of your family? I understand you might not want to do that. You may wish to pick out your own design, and I understand that fact. You won't hurt my feelings if you decide not to take it, but would you at least think it over?"

Henry looked over at Kate. She nodded her head indicating her approval with Emma's suggestion.

"Mom, that's a wonderful offer you're making us."

"It sure is," Kate added.

"If you see it and don't like the design, that's okay, I'll understand. After all, everyone has a difference in taste when it comes to jewelry."

Emma reached into the pocket of her robe. She pulled a tightly wadded piece of tissue paper from her pocket. She held her hand out to Kate. Kate smiled as she took it from Emma's hand. Slowly she started to unwrap the paper. There were several layers to it. With the final piece of paper unfolded, Kate was completely stunned. She held in her hand a gold ring that appeared to carry at least a five-carat heart shaped main diamond. On each side of the band were seven smaller stones running down each side of it, a total of 15 diamonds altogether. Kate shook her head slowly from side to side, simply amazed with what she held in her hand.

"It's so gorgeous, Emma," she said as she looked at it. "I don't think I can take this, Emma, it's much too expensive, it's too..."

"Beautiful?" Emma said.

"It's just too much, Emma, I couldn't, it wouldn't be right. I just wouldn't feel right about it." As Kate looked at the ring, its sparkle was impressive. Even under the darkened kitchen light, its brilliance was astounding.

Henry looked at the two women as he thought to himself. How did Paul ever afford such an extravagant ring, it was simply magnificent. Then he remembered what Doc once told him when Kate, Emma, and he had shared a Thanksgiving dinner together. Doc had mentioned how smart Paul was, what a great investment counselor he was. He also invested in and sold real estate.

"Kate, I love your Henry like my own son. He has been there for me whenever I've needed him. You have played a very important part in my life also. Whenever I needed something from the store, whatever I needed anything, you were there for me, too. I love both of you as if you are a part of my own family.

I knew on the day we went and saw Paul's grave that I wanted to do this for you and Henry. Even though Henry hadn't asked you yet, I knew in my heart you would be together as one someday... like Paul and me. I even talked it over with Paul, if you know what I mean."

Kate nodded her head, she understood that part of Emma's statement very well. Many a day she had stood at her own mother's grave talking things over with her. Yes, she understood where Emma was coming from, how comforting it was for her to share simple talks with her own mother as well.

"Kate, this ring carries many memories of my Paul for me. With you taking it and having it, his memory and mine someday will be carried on in your heart. Kate, by doing this also for Paul and me, you will be keeping it in our family. Paul and I want you to do that for us. Please take it and wear it."

Kate nodded her head. She stood up and embraced Emma.

"Thank you, Emma. I'll forever keep those memories close to my heart."

"Thank you, Kate," she whispered.

Cutting the Ribbon

Kate and Henry pulled into the driveway of Melissa and Greg's home. Before they could even get out of the car, Melissa came running out of the door and over to Kate. As she got out of the car, Melissa gave her a welcoming embrace. She then went immediately to Henry, doing the same.

"Did you have any trouble finding our place?" she asked them.

"No, we just followed your instructions, it was very easy to find," Kate said.

Greg walked up to Henry and shook his hand. Kate walked over to Greg giving him a hug.

"So did you bring your tools?" inquired Greg.

"I've got mine," Kate laughed.

"The last thing I thought I'd be doing is remodeling the inside of a department store break room," Henry said with a chuckle.

"I can't wait to show it to you. It's a fairly big job, sinks, flooring, walls, and if it doesn't cost too much, I'd like to sneak a few other things into the remodeling project," Greg stated.

The two couples visited for a short time. They took Henry's clothes into the house as they talked, placing them in the spare bedroom. Kate's clothes, however, were moved to Melissa's car since Kate would be staying with Melissa's parents.

"My mom and dad are looking forward to seeing you both," Melissa said in her ever-excited voice.

"I can't wait to see them either," Kate said.

"Well, we're off to the store so the two of you can take a look at your project, get an idea what you're getting into," Greg said.

"Greg, can Kate ride with me to keep me company, and we'll all meet at the store?" suggested Melissa.

"That sounds good to me. Oh, both of you should know something before we go. The employees at the store don't know Melissa and I are married, in fact, they think I'm just another employee, so keep that in mind when we're there; okay?"

"Uh-huh," Kate stated. "It's like a mystery book, 'The Man Nobody Knew Who He Really Was,' " she uttered in a deep mysterious sounding voice.

"Well, I'm just trying to find out how everything works in the store, and I thought this would be the best way of handling it, learning the jobs."

"Actually that sounds like a good idea to me," Henry said nodding his head.

"Just so you know," Greg said as he nodded his head slightly.

"Well, let's get moving," Melissa said. "We'll meet you over at the store."

"Okay," he answered.

Everyone piled into the two cars and headed over towards the store.

"So how is married life treating you?" Henry asked.

"I've never been happier," Greg answered.

"Are you ready to be shocked?"

"I don't know, it depends on what you're about to say."

Henry didn't say anything. He then turned his head towards Greg.

"Kate asked me to marry her, and I said I would," he smiled. "Is that enough of a shock for you?"

"Just that, I mean we all knew you two were going to get married as soon as you got up the nerve to ask her. In fact, Melissa told me one time she thought Kate would do the actual asking. And Henry, I could see and hear that Emma was in Kate's corner, so you really had no chance at all," he laughed.

Henry shook his head back and forth, he being the one who was now shocked.

"So did you give her a ring yet, or does she have to buy one for herself since she asked you?"

The Promise

"I never thought of it in that way," Henry said, a small smile reflecting on his lips.

"Well, there's some beautiful rings sold at Melissa's parent's store."

"Actually Emma gave Kate a ring her husband bought for her some time ago. Emma wanted to keep it, the ring that is, in the family so to speak. She thinks the world of Kate. I don't know how comfortable Kate feels taking Emma's ring though."

"Henry, you've done a wonderful job taking care of that woman, you and Kate together. You should take the ring and make Emma happy."

"Well, Kate did take it, but only after Emma kind of forced her into it. Kate didn't feel she should take it. She's a little uncomfortable having it, it's just so extravagant and expensive. It has to be worth a mint, not that that really matters to us."

"I know what I would do under those circumstances."

"And what's that?" Henry asked.

"I would thank Emma for her gift, let her know that every time you look upon Kate's finger and see the ring, it will bring fond memories to you of her love. And I would also do something else."

"And what would that be?"

"Thank Emma for allowing you to be her son. I think that would mean the world for her to hear those words from you. It's just a suggestion though."

"Thank her for allowing me to be her son," Henry said thoughtfully. "I never would have thought of that. Thank you, Greg, that's a great idea. I'll do that when I get back home, whenever that may be."

"Well, I guess that depends on how long the project takes."

Henry nodded his head.

"There's one thing that's for sure," Henry said.

"And what's that?"

"That I have a beautiful assistant to work with, and she's good at her job."

Greg smiled.

The women drove down the road following the men as they also made their way to the store.

"So how do you like being married?" came Kate's question.

"I'm so happy, Kate, Melissa said. When we went on our honeymoon, it was everything I could have imagined it to be and more. When we got home, that's when Greg started working for my parents. Some things are good about that, some not so good."

"What do you mean?"

"Well, Greg says what he thinks, and means what he says. Sometimes I wish he would step back and let my mom and dad take a breath, but on the same token he's come up with some remarkable ideas, I will say that. My mother and father are still trying to get used to him, but I can see in their eyes they love having him as their son-in-law. What a change that is from what seems like a million years ago with my dad."

"Well, I'm sure everything will work itself out."

"Oh, don't get the impression Greg's failing, I mean, he's always just full speed ahead. Actually I think my dad's getting used to that somewhat."

"That's good."

"So what's new with you?"

"Well, I asked Henry to marry me."

"Finally!" exclaimed Melissa.

"Pardon me?"

"Oh come on, Kate, I knew you'd have to do it eventually. Henry is Henry. There's no doubt he loves you, his face says that every time you're together. The real question was not when the question was going to be asked, it was who was going to do the asking first," Melissa said chuckling.

"Melissa, I did it," Kate said abruptly.

"You did what?"

"I decided to give the paperwork to Henry."

"Wonderful."

"He, ah — he knows you helped me to get it."

"What!"

"Listen, Melissa, I don't know how we thought we could hide it from him. He's a very intelligent man, and when he put two and two together, it sure didn't come out five," Kate said shaking her head.

"You know, you're right. I think Greg or Dan could have figured that one out, also."

"Well, it sure didn't take him anytime at all to do it. He's going to see if he can get his last name changed."

"I hope he can do that."

"He's going to talk to Emma's lawyer, so let's hope for the best."

"Just so you know, we have a very good selection of wedding rings on the third floor, if you're interested."

"Actually Emma gave me a ring her husband bought for her sometime ago before he died. She wanted me to have it."

"Well, you and Henry are the only family I know she has, if I'm not mistaken. She always refers to Henry as her son, and he calls her mother."

"Emma said that way we could keep it in the family, the ring that is."

"What a wonderful idea for both you and Emma. Do you have it with you?"

"Yes," she responded as she held her lower lip with her upper teeth.

"Can I see it?"

"Melissa, would you pull over for a minute?"

"Aren't you feeling good?"

"No, it's not that."

"Sure."

Melissa looked to her right and spotted a business parking lot ahead. She quickly pulled into it, parking in the nearest spot. Her concern now was that of Kate as she turned to face her, wanting to know what the problem was.

"Melissa, this ring from Emma isn't really me. It's absolutely beautiful and I love it. I would have been happy with any ring Henry was to get me, even a simple band that showed his love for me. That was what Emma got from her husband when they got married, a simple wedding band. He bought her another ring to show how much more he loved her. All Emma really wanted was the band from him, and that's all I ever wanted from Henry, too, his love."

"Can I see it just the same?"

Kate reached into her purse. She handed Melissa the same piece of tissue paper she had gotten from Emma. Melissa started to open it. Kate placed her hands over Melissa's hands, stopping her from opening the tissue any further.

"Melissa, what Emma gave me is unbelievable. The fact is I'm having a little difficulty in dealing with it. As I said it's breathtaking, but I'm uncomfortable taking it from her. Suppose she needs money for her medical bills, she could sell it. I really don't know what to do about it."

"If she wanted you to have it, you take it. If she needs money, you can still sell it, and Henry will be glad to get you your band or anything you want. Now, is it okay if I look at it?"

Kate nodded her head as she released her hands from Melissa.

Melissa unwrapped the last of the tissue paper. Her jaw literally dropped.

"This is not a diamond, Kate, it's a boulder."

Kate just shook her head as she tilted it slightly.

"Okay," Melissa said, trying to give herself time to think. She knew now why it was that Kate still had questions in her mind on how to handle this gift of hers. Melissa's eyes never expected to behold a ring of this magnitude.

"So this ring is yours, it's final, Emma gave it to you and it's yours?"

"Yes."

"Well, did you thank her for it? Of course you did, that's a silly question on my part." Melissa slowly shook her head back and forth. She also knew she was talking in circles, but it wasn't everyday one sees a ring like this. Her mind was obviously distracted by it.

"What does Henry think?"

"He thinks I should keep it."

"Well, there you go. You keep the ring and wear it, no ifs, ands, or buts about it. Make Emma proud she did the right thing, and I think you'll be very happy in the end."

Melissa started laughing.

"Why are you laughing?" inquired Kate.

"Because I can just hear Emma's voice now." She laughed again. Lowering her voice she stated to Kate, "What do you want to do, make an old lady unhappy and hurt her feelings?"

Kate started laughing uncontrollably, joining in with Melissa.

"Yes, Kate, make that wonderful woman happy and keep the ring."

"Thanks for your opinion. I wanted to hear what you had to say about it. So I'm not being silly about it?"

"No, you're just being the good woman you are, not wanting to take advantage of anyone, including Emma."

"Thank you, Melissa."

"Well, let's catch up with the boys, they'll be wondering if we had car trouble or something... and keep this ring." Melissa handed the ring back to Kate.

"I will."

After parking the car, the men got out and stood by the vehicle. They looked around wondering where the women were.

"They must have caught a few lights," Greg stated.

"I'm sure they'll be right here. Oh, there they are."

The women pulled into the parking lot, taking a parking spot close to the men. Getting out Melissa went up to the men.

"I'll take Kate with me," offered Melissa, "and you and Henry can look over the project. I want to give her a chance to say hello to my mom and dad."

"Okay, Honey. We'll see you later," Greg said.

Walking into the store the men made their way up some stairs and then over to the break room. Henry looked at the room studying it over in his mind. He walked over and pulled a few drawers open and inspected them. A quick look was given under the sink as well. He tapped on some drywall, and then looked at some windows at the one end.

"What's behind this wall?" Henry asked.

"I think there's a fairly large storage room they don't really use."

As he looked everything over a few employees walked into the room.

"So what's going on, Greg?" one of them asked.

"Mr. and Mrs. Summers wanted this gentleman to take a look at the break room and see what needs to be done."

"Do you think it's possible to add a couple of extra outlets to the wall over there?" one of the men asked.

"I'll see what I can do about that," Henry replied as he looked at the wall.

"Well, I'll tell you what I'd like is a candy machine in here," the younger man added.

"I don't think I can promise you anything like that," Henry said, "it's above my pay grade."

"And do you think we can get more storage space?" a woman asked as she walked into the room after hearing what was being discussed.

"Now that's something I can do. What would work out best for you?"

"The problem is that some of the shelves don't have enough space between them for taller items, if you know what I mean."

"I certainly do. I'll see what I can do about that," Henry said as he opened one of the cupboard doors and peered into it.

"Thank you," she said.

"I know what I'd like," offered the man by the refrigerator, "one of them union-sex bathrooms."

"You mean unisex bathrooms, one for either gender," Henry quickly declared.

"Yeah, that's what I mean.

"Well, you'd have to incorporate some type of hallway or something to keep it away from the break room. Nobody would want people going in and out while you're eating. Yeah, I think you'd want to remove it somewhat from the room."

The next day the project started in earnest. Every employee's eyes were drawn to it. It consumed much of their free discussion time. There were the usual words spoken, how big would it be, what would the color combination consist of, at least that's what some women talked about. The women got a kick out of watching Kate as she carried items to the work site, her work belt wrapped around her waist. The women were quick to notice her name on the back of the belt. Even some of the men enjoyed watching her as she would stroll by carrying a 2x4 or two.

Any loud hammering, sawing sounds that would disturb customers was kept to a minimum or accomplished after the store had closed. It was Henry's hope to have the project completed as quickly as possible. He understood the employees were doing without the sanctuary their lunchroom afforded them. It was, after all, a place for them to escape their jobs, eat their lunch quietly, and simply relax for a few minutes. It also gave them a place to catch up on the lives of each other.

One day Henry and Kate found themselves outside on some back steps eating their lunch together. A woman from the store walked up and stopped in front of them.

"Sir, can I ask you a question?" she said.

"Sure."

"I see you have a large scar on your brow. I don't mean to be nosy, but just the same I couldn't help but wonder. Did you suffer some type of construction accident? I know I shouldn't be asking you this, and I also know it's none of my business, but it's been bugging me to get the answer to that question."

"So you want to know how he got that scar?" Kate said as she looked up at her.

"If it's okay," she timidly said.

"Well, if the truth be told," Kate stated, "the next time I tell him I want to be kissed, I know he'll listen to me."

Henry started choking on his sandwich.

"Oh," was all the woman could say.

Kate looked up at the woman and winked.

The woman turned and walked away, laughing as she did.

Henry always kept the door closed when they were working within the room. First, it helped to hold the noise down, and secondly it kept people from coming in and asking him questions, thereby holding up his work. Keeping the room ventilated was his real concern, but it all worked out in the end. The work progressed steadily, and before either one of them knew it, it was completed. Susan happened to walk up to Kate and Henry as they stood outside of the break room.

"Susanna," came Henry's voice, "do you have a minute?"

Susan enjoyed it when Henry would call her by that name, no one else really doing the same.

"Of course, Henry."

"I would like you and Melissa to be the first to see the break room before it's put into use, if that's okay?"

"I'd love to see it," she responded.

"There's one thing you should know, we haven't picked out any pictures for the walls. I thought maybe you'd enjoy doing that part of it."

"Oh, I'd love to do that," she replied. "Let me get Melissa. I'll be right back."

Standing outside the break room Kate and Henry waited for Susan to open the door and walk in with Melissa. As the two women stepped through the door, Susan just shook her head in amazement.

"Mom, this is beautiful," came Melissa's excited voice.

"It sure is, Honey."

"So it meets with your approval?" Henry said, as he reached over taking Kate's hand in his.

"Beyond what I thought a simple lunch room could look like," smiled Susan.

"I could move in here," joked Melissa.

The room was well lit from above. Where the ceiling met the drywall oak crown molding had been put into place. There was wide matching trim molding running around the floor's edge as well. Under rich oak cabinets, recessed lighting brightly lit the marble counter top. The edges to the marble were beveled. There was also an inordinate number of electrical outlets. A double stainless steel sink with a copper faucet at the back stood ready for use. A garbage disposal sat in position under the sink. The amount of storage offered from the various cupboards was considerable. There were numerous drawers for storage below them as well. A large microwave hung from one of the cabinets. Over near the corner, fitted into the counter stood a large brand new oversized stainless steel refrigerator.

On the other side of the room a pop and candy machine stood waiting for money to be deposited into them. New tables and chairs beckoned to be used. The new tile floor appeared clean and shiny.

At the end of the room to one side was a hallway. Walking over to it Susan looked down to the end and observed a door on a sidewall. It was closed.

"What's that, I don't remember seeing a door there before or a hallway," Susan inquired.

"Kate and I actually knocked down a small wall opening up that portion of the room, making it larger than what it originally was. I hope you don't mind." Susan followed Henry down the short hallway. He opened the door for inspection by Susan and Melissa. The room was bigger than they expected as they stepped into it. Two marble sinks, with large mirrors over them illuminated the area. If anyone wanted to make any adjustment with their makeup, they could see very well. A beautiful plant sat between the sinks. Two soap dispensers, as well as a paper towel receptacle was in place and ready for use. A toilet, and wastebasket completed the room.

"It's a union-sex bathroom," laughed Henry, "but I like to refer to as a unisex bathroom."

"I think that's more appropriate," chuckled Susan.

"The sign for the door is coming this afternoon and will be in place shortly thereafter," he said. "Susanna, all we need are some decorations, pictures, and it's ready to go. If you and Melissa would like to get some, we'll be glad to hang them for you."

"Kate, will you come with us," Susan suggested, "we can use your help picking out those pictures."

"I'd be happy to."

The three women left the break room area and returned shortly with three framed pictures from the living room section of the store. Melissa smiled as she handed Henry a large picture she had picked out personally. It was a framed painting of a black baby grand piano with a long stem red rose laying across the piano keys. A few rose petals were sprinkled across a portion of the keys as well.

"This painting reminds me of you and myself, Henry," Melissa stated smiling. "It recalls to me the night of the Christmas Program when you played that evening on the baby grand, and of the roses I received from Greg the next day."

"Thank you, Melissa, this is very thoughtful of you," Henry expressed as he nodded his head in approval.

He quickly hung the pictures with Kate's help. When finished everyone of them looked around smiling their approval.

"So it's ready for business," Henry said.

"Not quite," Susan stated. "I'm going to get a big bow and ribbon to place across the door and tomorrow I'll have one of our employees cut it with some scissors. We're going to make this a big deal. I can't wait to see their faces when they see what the two of you have accomplished for them. Thank you, Henry, and thank you, Kate. Our people deserved this, and you both made us proud."

"You're welcome," they said.

"Mom, make it a red ribbon, okay?" Melissa said.

"I sure will, Honey."

The next morning, approximately ten minutes before the store was to open Susan announced to everyone that the break room was completed and that after the cutting of the ribbon it would be open for business. To everyone's surprise, especially Kenneth, a large group of employees gathered to see the ribbon cutting. Susan smiled as she addressed the people there.

"I just want to say we're sorry you had to do without your break room, but we hope this room will make up for your inconvenience. Kenneth and I wanted to get this break room done for all of you. We appreciate all of the hard work you do for us every day. Thank you."

Susan handed a pair of scissors with red ribbons hanging from them to an older female employee by the door.

"Would do us the honor?" she stated.

The woman smiled as she took the scissors and cut the large red ribbon across the doorway. The applause of the people actually surprised Kenneth somewhat. As the people went in and looked around, they were obviously pleased. Some of the employees actually walked up to Susan and Kenneth and shook their hands. "We appreciate this," one person said, or "thank you" spoke out another individual. Kenneth smiled broadly. He was taken back a little bit by their reactions. Yes, he was proud he had followed his son-in-law's suggestion, and he felt good inside for having done so.

"What you and Kenneth did for these people was very generous on your part. It's easy to look the other way, turn a blind eye when spending your own money is involved," stated Jean.

"Well," Susan bending over close to Jean's ear, "it was really Greg's idea."

Jean chuckled as she shook her head.

"And why doesn't that surprise me."

"So how are things going for you, I haven't seen you since the wedding," inquired Susan.

"Actually very well. I've been seeing someone, so that's changed my life considerably."

"Anyone I know?"

"You may know him, he was at your daughter's wedding."

"And did you happen to sit with him?" Susan joked.

"Yes, I did," smiled Jean.

"And how often are you seeing this person, if you don't mind me asking."

"Oh, maybe three or four times a week."

"Whoa, did you say three to four times a week?"

"It's not my fault, he just keeps pestering me to go out with him, and I just can't seem to say no. Susan, he's a wonderful man, and I just love Kate to no end. I've even taken some vacation time so we can spend more time together. Going to the wedding turned into something I never expected."

Both women looked at each other and laughed lightly.

"Oh," Susan said, "did you see Kate, she was here with Henry. They redid the break room together. I heard they'll be heading home today."

"I saw her earlier and we talked."

"Have you seen the job they did on it?"

"Not yet, but by the look on the people's faces coming out of there, I'm looking forward to seeing it."

"Well, I'll tell you one thing, they did an absolutely beautiful job on it for us."

"I'm sure they did."

"Well, I've got to get upstairs with Kenneth. I see he left a few minutes ago. I'll see you later, Jean."

"You can count on it."

Once upstairs Kenneth looked over the completed flier Melissa and Susan had come up with for the picnic announcement to their employees. Not only was it cleverly designed with various graphics, the different fonts they chose were fancy, and easy to read. Everything was covered in the unique notice. He thought to himself, they really did a good job. As he perused it, his mind checked over everything that needed to be put on it, the time, location, date, that employees and their family members were all invited. It mentioned the free food, games, prizes, and most importantly of all, that it was a paid day off by the Summers family to show their appreciation to every one of their employees. Kenneth smiled as he read the very top of the notice. It made him chuckle to himself. "The Summers' Summer Picnic." He simply loved it.

Susan walked into the room taking a seat across from Kenneth.

"Well, I see that you received the final flier from Melissa. So what do you think about it?"

Kenneth didn't respond.

"You did get a chance to look it over, didn't you?"

"Both of you did a beautiful job on it. I think I'll stop paying our advertising people and hire you two. I'm really happy with it. You know, I get such a kick out of the name Melissa came up with, it's just so unusual."

"You should mention that to her," Susan said.

"You're absolutely right."

Kenneth picked up the phone and gave Melissa a call at home.

"Hello," she answered.

"Honey, your mother and I are so proud of the job you did on the announcement for the picnic. I really like the name you came up with."

"Thanks, Daddy, but don't forget mom did a big share on it also."

"I know. Are Kate and Henry still there?"

"Yes, we're just visiting. I think they're going to leave right after lunch."

"Can you put Henry on the phone for a minute?"

"Sure. Henry, my dad would like to speak with you."

Melissa handed Henry the phone.

"Hello, Mr. Summers."

"I was wondering if you would mind bringing me your bill for the break room work, I want to make everything square with you."

"What would you say if Kate and I stop by after lunch on our way home."

"Perfect. I'll see you then."

"Great."

After lunch Kate and Henry bid Melissa goodbye as Melissa followed them out to the car. Once at the vehicle Henry thought to himself, this usually takes a good ten minutes for the good-byes to be accomplished. Kate and Melissa gave each other their usual long hug, then talked about when they would see each other again. This action, which Henry was accustomed to from being around them was not unforeseen, or unexpected for him in the least. He always allowed sufficient time for their, "good-bye, farewell, can't wait to get back together time." It was just something he planned for. He thought to himself once again, here it comes, almost there, and then the women said the words he was waiting for from their lips, "I'll call you." He chuckled to himself once more as he sat behind the wheel. As he backed out of the driveway and entered the street, Henry knew there was but one thing left for the women to do, wave as he drove down the street. He was not disappointed.

Kate and Henry took the elevator to Kenneth's office. Once there they knocked on his office door.

"Come in," beckoned a voice from within. Henry held the door for Kate as they walked into the room. Kenneth was sitting behind his desk.

"I will say one thing to both of you, the job is simply beautiful, very impressive. I'm still getting little thank you notes from our employees in the inner office mail."

"I'm glad to hear that, Mr. Summers."

Kate smiled.

Susan walked into the room. She stepped behind Kenneth as he sat in his chair. She placed her hands on his shoulders.

"Henry," Susan said, "I want to thank you again for what you did for my mother and my grandmother."

"Well, you're welcome. I enjoyed singing to them at the reception."

"That's not what I'm referring to. I'm talking about when you were kind enough to come to our house on the following Monday to visit with them before they had to return home. They just loved visiting with you. And Kate, thank you for coming along."

"You're welcome," she said. "Both of us enjoyed the homemade meal you prepared for us as well."

"That was wonderful for me, too. I got to enjoy cooking with my grandmother and mother. It was a real treat for all of us."

Walking around to the front of the desk she turned her head and looked back at Kenneth.

"I never thought I would ever hear anyone play the baby grand in our home. You know something Henry, it actually came with the house. No one has touched the keyboard since we've lived there. It's a shame, but none of us play an instrument whatsoever. My mom and grandmother enjoyed so much listening to you playing the piano and singing to them. None of us could believe how you could play any request we made, and do it without music. I think my grandmother loved hearing you sing to her in Italian the most. They talked on and on about you after you left. Thank you for doing that for us. It was another precious memory for them to take home with them, and for me personally to treasure."

Kenneth nodded his head.

"Well, let's get down to business, have you got our bill?" Kenneth asked.

"Right here."

Henry handed Kenneth a handwritten bill.

"Everything is on there. I denoted each and every item so you know exactly what you're paying for. I got an exceptionally good price on the marble. I know you didn't ask for it, but as you can see I passed that savings onto you. The new flooring was a little more than I anticipated, I feel badly about that. Of course you furnished the microwave, garbage disposal, faucet and refrigerator, so even though it's listed on there. You can see I put a "0" by the price.

And as far as the bathroom goes, you didn't ask for that so I didn't charge you. I purchased the toilet and sink from a store here at my own expense. I had to get some items from a local hardware store also. I just didn't feel right charging you for those things. Greg thought the employees would enjoy having a room so readily available to them that customers wouldn't have access to. If you have any questions, I'll be more than happy to answer them for you."

Kenneth studied over the bill very carefully. Susan peered over his shoulder at the invoice.

"Henry, is this everything?"

"Yes, it is, Mr. Summers.

"Henry, as a businessman, I deal in many different fields with numerous individuals in our business community. To tell you the truth, I got an estimate on the job ahead of time, it just makes good business sense to do that."

"I see," Henry said nodding his head.

"Henry, this bill is frankly outrageous to say the least. I can tell you I've never been more insulted in my life by this figure. And to think Greg recommended you to us, I'll have a talk to him about that. Look at his bill, Susan, what do you have to say?"

Kate had never been privy to presenting bills, negotiations, any of that whatsoever. She just stood there stunned by Kenneth's words, feeling very uneasy.

"It looks fair to me," Susan stated.

"No, it's not, not even close to a fair amount! Henry, the estimate I was furnished with was well double this amount, and they didn't even list any marble. In fact, there was no mention of a bathroom being included by them to me. We are not going to accept this from you, and I want it corrected now, or we'll take it upon ourselves to correct it for you. Do you understand that?"

"Yes, sir," smiled Henry.

Kate smiled at Kenneth and Susan. Kate was proud of her Henry. She thought to herself, it's just one more reason people wanted him to do work for them. He was an honest person to deal with, and they trusted him implicitly. But then, she already knew that.

"Now, what's a more realistic figure, double this?"

"Well, Melissa is Kate's best friend, and I wanted to give you two a break. And besides that, Greg set this job up for us, and I stayed at his home. Melissa even had to move in with both of you so Kate had a place to stay."

"And I loved having the both of them there," Susan quickly stated as she looked in Kate's direction. "Frankly, it was like old times, wasn't it, Kate?"

Kate smiled as she nodded her head.

"I'm going to miss that so much, having you at our home, laughing around the kitchen table," Susan said.

"That fact shouldn't enter into this either, Henry," exclaimed Kenneth, "her staying at our house. It wouldn't surprise me if Susan even offered to pay Kate to visit us, the three of them having so much fun together. She absolutely loved having you there, Kate, and Susan told me about it every night."

Now both Susan and Kate wore big smiles.

"Susan, would you get the store check book, please?"

Susan left the room and went to her office. While she was gone Kenneth wrote something down on a piece of paper. When she returned, Kenneth instructed her to write Henry's check in the amount of what he had written on the piece of paper. Susan looked at the figure and then complied with his request. After removing the check from the ledger she reached out attempting to hand the check to Henry. Henry, however, didn't make any motions to take it. He could see the amount reflected on the check's face.

"Mr. and Mrs. Summers, this is well over double what my invoice says. I can't accept this."

"Fine," Kenneth said. "Susan, give the check to Kate, I'm sure she'll be glad to accept it. You're his partner, am I right?" he asked.

"Yes," she responded.

"Well..."

"I don't have any problem with that," Kate stated smiling.

Susan walked over to Kate. She handed the check to Kate, Susan smiling broadly as she did.

"Kenneth, would you mind if I told Henry and Kate about our idea?" Susan said.

"I don't see why not," he answered.

Susan now walked over to be by Henry.

"Henry, you're such a wonderful musician, singer, builder and —"

"And soon to be my husband," Kate blurted out interrupting Susan. She just couldn't keep that information hidden from them any longer, her words quickly escaping through her lips without any warning.

Susan walked over to Kate taking her in her arms.

"I'm so thrilled and happy for the both of you," Susan said excitedly.

"Thank you," Kate said.

"Does Melissa know?"

"Yes."

"Wonderful."

Kenneth made his way around the desk and over to Henry, extending his hand as he did.

"Congratulations, Henry."

"Thank you, sir."

As Susan looked in Henry's direction nodding her head she said, "And you're getting my second daughter."

"Thank you," Kate said as she squeezed Susan once again.

"I would say part of that check might help to pay for a wedding, I imagine," Kenneth exclaimed.

"I think so," Kate said.

After all the hugging was completed, and further congrats spoken, Susan looked over at Kenneth once again.

"Now can I say what I wanted to earlier?"

"Go ahead, Honey."

"Henry, as I said, you're a very gifted person. We were wondering, Kenneth and I that is, whether you would do us the honor of accepting a gift from us?"

Henry looked over to Kate, she at him as well. They both wondered what gift they could possibly be talking about.

"Henry, simply put, we would like to know if you would accept the baby grand in our front room as a gift from us to you. No one plays it in our family as I said earlier, and we both feel it's such a waste to have it just sitting there. Would you do that for us?"

Henry didn't say a word, he couldn't, the lump in his throat blocked his words. He was too overwhelmed, too stunned, and in shock. It was every one of those emotions all rolled into one for him. He simply couldn't speak, however, his smile was very prevalent for all to see.

"We'll take it," Kate stated. She looked over at Henry as she said, "And he wants to thank you for it."

Henry nodded his head.

Susan continued. "Kenneth has made the arrangements to have it delivered, he just needed your permission and a timeframe on when they can do that for us. It's also been tuned, though it did sound pretty good when you played it at our home. I understand it may have to be rechecked again once it's moved."

Kenneth and Susan looked at each other and smiled.

Henry thought to himself as he sat in the chair, a baby grand, a baby grand for me, unbelievable, and a diamond ring for Kate. These last few weeks have just been incredible for the both of us. Henry knew in his heart though, that the best thing that had happened to him over the past few weeks had to do with Kate. He was afforded the time to work hand-in-hand with the love of his life. That was the one thing he savored more than anything else.

"Thank you both," he was finally able to mumble.

"Well," Susan said, "it's because we love you both that we want to do this for you. You can consider it a pre-wedding gift, if you like."

"Thank you, thank you both," Kate said as she gave Susan a hug again.

Henry just sat there thinking to himself, a baby grand, how wonderful a gift is that.

The drive home took only a matter of minutes in both Henry and Kate's minds. The miles literally flew by. Their emotions were wrapped tighter than a mummy in a museum. The two of them would look at each other and laugh.

"Henry, a baby grand, how unusual of a gift is that?"

"I never would have dreamt it possible. When I played the one at the Christmas Program a couple of years ago I was taken back so much by its sound quality. The piano Sam left me doesn't really compare."

"So what are you going to do with the piano Sam left you?"

"I can't get rid of it, it means too much to me."

"Don't worry about it, there will always be a place for it in our home, —"

Henry nodded his head as she spoke.

"— it's far too much of a memory of Sam for us not to keep it."

"Thank you, Honey."

"So I guess the next thing we should discuss is the check," Kate stated as she looked down at her purse, their payment having been safely tucked in it.

"Well, we have to pay for all of our materials, although most of it has already been taken care of."

"Henry, what about the remainder of the money?"

"Well, I've been thinking about that. Why don't you take the rest of it and put it away for our wedding expenses, if that's okay with you."

Kate reached over as best as she could, her seatbelt tugging at her, and gave Henry a quick kiss on his cheek.

"I was hoping you'd say that," she said.

Henry reached over taking Kate's hand, holding it for some time.

The couple arrived at Doc's home. Henry reached in the trunk and grabbed Kate's two suitcases and a carry-on bag.

"What's in this one bag," Henry said referring to the carry-on, "for its size it's a little heavy."

"Makeup," she replied.

"Kate, that's the last thing you need."

"Thank you, Honey. Well, I bought some at the store while we were on break, and some clothes."

"So that's where you disappeared to."

"Oh, and I don't even have to do any laundry," she exclaimed, "I did almost all of it at Melissa's parent's home yesterday."

"I wish I would have been that smart."

As the couple entered the house only the sound of Doc rocking in his leather recliner could be heard. He put a book down as Kate walked up to him. She bent down kissing him on the forehead.

"So how did your business project work out?" he inquired of them.

"Actually," Henry said nodding his head slowly, "it couldn't have worked out better for both of us."

"Grandpa, I'm glad you're sitting down, there are a few things you need to hear."

"Okay," Doc said as he customarily placed both hands on each side of the chair, sliding himself up in his chair to hear better.

Kate took a deep breath trying to get everything in proper order in her mind.

"Grandpa, Henry now knows his last name, where he was born, and the date that took place."

Henry stood nodding his head while his face reflected a broad smile.

"And how did that come about?" Doc asked.

"Kate and Melissa went and got it for me. I wasn't told how or when, but essentially that's what took place."

Doc shook his head back and forth.

"So what's your real name?" he inquired.

"It's Morgan, Henry Paul Morgan," declared Henry smiling.

"And, Grandpa, Emma's husband's name was Paul."

"I know, Honey," Doc responded. "I would imagine Emma is thrilled to hear that news."

"She was, Grandpa. She was very pleased and taken back by the news. We're going to see if we can get Henry's last name changed."

"That's a wonderful idea. I'll give my lawyer a call," Doc stated.

"Emma asked us to use her own lawyer, if that's okay."

"Good," Doc stated, "just so long as someone does something."

"We'll definitely do something," Henry said.

"Would either one of you like a cup of coffee, something cold to drink?" he inquired, as he got out of his chair.

"Grandpa, —"

"Yes."

"Grandpa, —"

"What is it, Honey?"

"I asked Henry to marry me."

"What!"

"I asked him to marry me."

"Thank God someone asked someone. I was beginning to worry about you two. Didn't have the backbone for it, huh, Henry?" Doc said as he slapped him on the back.

Doc reached over and took Henry's hand in his. Henry was amazed at how strong the grip of his hand was as they shook hands. It wasn't one of those handshakes where men sometimes shake each other's hand to try and see who has the strongest grip, however, it was firm, one demonstrating joy and love for the other as well as Kate.

"Wait a minute," Doc stated, "did you say, yes?"

"How could anyone say no to her?" he responded.

Doc reached over and hugged Kate. Yes, Doc was thrilled. He knew there was no better match for Kate to find than Henry, and her for Henry as well. That fact had always been very evident to him, and everyone else who met or knew the couple.

"So now you two pick out a ring, and plan a date."

"Well, Grandpa, we need to show you something."

Kate walked over to her purse, opening it she removed a small piece of tissue paper. As she unwrapped it Doc could see what appeared to be a ring. With the last section of paper removed he was astounded by what was presented to his eyes.

"What bank did you two rob while you were gone?"

"Grandpa, this was given to me by Emma. Apparently her husband Paul had bought it for her sometime ago. She wants me to have it as my wedding ring, to keep it in the family. What's your thoughts on that, Grandpa? I feel a little intimidated by it. Melissa and Henry both think I should keep it. What's your feelings on it, Grandpa, what do you think?"

"One of the hardest cases I've ever had to deal with concerned Emma's husband. The two of them were very much in love. Emma literally lived at the hospital when Paul was there in his final week or so. The nurses saw to it she was fed, and there was always a blanket to cover herself with at night when she sat in the chair. I think the only time she left his side was to refresh the clothes she wore. If Emma gave you the ring she got from Paul, don't dishonor her or Paul's memory by not wearing it. Someday you'll be glad in your heart you took that step for Emma and Paul."

"Then that's exactly what I'm going to do, Grandpa, honor both Emma and Paul."

Doc nodded his head.

"Thank you, Grandpa."

"Now, what do you say we have a cup of coffee before I give you some news," Doc stated.

"I'm not done, Grandpa, if you don't mind."

"Mine can wait," he said.

"Grandpa, Mr. and Mrs. Summers gave Henry and me a check for the work we did in their store."

"Good, so I can get a loan from you," Doc joked.

"Grandpa."

"Well, I've missed having you around to joke with. You know, Kate, I missed having you here with me. No one likes to come home to an empty house."

"I know, Grandpa. As I was saying, they paid us. Grandpa, they gave us more than double what Henry put down in his bill."

"That doesn't surprise me in the least. Anyone who has observed the work you two have done would be glad to get away that cheaply."

"We think we should put that extra money towards our wedding and start saving now."

"I don't think you should do that," Doc said.

"Why not?"

"Because I have a better place for you to put it."

"And what's that, in the bank?"

"Towards your honeymoon."

"We've talked about that already. We're going to skip it, and wait for a little while."

"You talked about honoring Emma and Paul by wearing the ring. Now it's time for you to honor me in the same way, by allowing me to pay for your wedding."

"Oh, Grandpa."

"It would be my honor to do that for both of you, and frankly I will not take no for an answer. Please Kate, let me do this for you and Henry, it would mean so much to me. You can use your money towards a honeymoon."

It was only a moment after those words were spoken to her by Doc that they found their way deep into Kate's heart. She hugged Doc, small tears forming in her eyes.

"I love you Honey, after all, you're my favorite granddaughter," Doc stated as he savored her embrace.

"And I love you, too, Grandpa," she said as Doc placed a kiss on her cheek. "You realize, of course, I'm your only granddaughter," Kate said with a smile.

"It was just another one of my little jokes but, Kate, I do love you."

"I know you do."

Henry thought to himself as he stood watching them hugging, this is something wonderful for one's eyes to behold. He always enjoyed the love each one demonstrated for the other, their deep family ties. It was something he had always wished for since he was a small child. Whenever Kate would yell or state strongly the words, "Grandpa" it made his heart sing within.

"Now, there's something I want to tell you two," Doc said. He looked at Kate and realized she had more to say, her face reflecting that to him. "Okay, it's obvious you have more to say. Go ahead."

"Maybe Henry should," Kate expressed to him.

"Well?" Doc stated, anxious to hear what he had to say.

"The Summers family, Kenneth and Susan, have given me their baby grand piano," Henry said smiling.

"That is quite a gift indeed."

"I was so thrilled I couldn't even speak to thank them. It was just so unexpected."

"I can hardly wait to hear you play it," Doc declared.

"And I can hardly wait to play it again," Henry said.

"Now, Grandpa, what's your news?"

"I've been seeing Jean for quite some time now. Actually I've grown quite fond of her, and I think she has feelings for me as well. We've been going places together, dinner, concerts, movies, walks."

"It sounds serious," Kate observed.

"Kate, I think it might be reaching that point. I just wanted you to know that."

"I'm very happy for you. You know, I ran into her at the store one day. I doubt if you could do any better than her. She's very nice, and I really like her a lot."

"Or she could do a lot better than me," Doc said.

"Grandpa, that's not true. Well, I think you two look cute together just the same."

"Oh here we go again with the looking cute together language," Henry said. "Doc, if you like her and she likes you, don't worry about it, things will take care of themselves before you know it. Just tell her and be done with it. I ought to know."

"And that bit of knowledge comes from a man who had to be asked to get married, really," Doc said in a chuckling voice. "Okay, let's see if I've got this all straight in my mind. Henry knows who he is, Kate got a big diamond from Emma, Henry said 'yes' to your proposal, and the two of you made some extra money. Oh, and Henry got a piano. Does that about do it?"

"And you've got a girlfriend, yup, I think that covers everything," Kate stated.

"Good. Now let's sit down and have some coffee together," he said.

Doc turned and walked over to the kitchen area. He started a pot of coffee as he snickered to himself once again.

The Words Guy

One morning Kenneth, much to Susan's surprise, asked if she would pack a lunch for both of them. Usually the two would go to one of the local restaurants they frequented.

"Sure. What would you like?"

"Oh, just a sandwich and some olives will be okay."

This was something she was not accustomed to doing for either one of them, still she did as he requested. Susan, however, had a little trouble finding small paper bags to place the sandwiches in, so she decided to put everything into a large one. Once at work Kenneth placed the bag into a small refrigerator he had in the corner of his office. When lunchtime arrived Kenneth asked Susan to accompany him so they could have lunch together. Rather than sitting in his office, Kenneth wanted to experience something new.

The two walked down the steps and headed for the employee's break room. When they entered, ten to twelve people were sitting together eating their lunches.

"Hello, Mr. and Mrs. Summers," a woman in the back stated.

"Hello," Kenneth responded. "Would any of you mind if Susan and I have lunch with you, we both would enjoy your company?"

The woman nodded her head. No one, of course, objected.

Kenneth took a seat. He looked around the room and realized he was unfamiliar with many of the faces he saw, let alone knowing their names.

"To tell you the truth," Kenneth said, "I really don't know most every person in here."

He stood up and began walking around the room taking their hands and shaking them. Susan could see the employees had a look of surprise on their faces. Kenneth greeted each and every one of them. She could, however, see they were definitely warming up to his gesture. Once he finished he turned and addressed them.

"When Susan and I found out how badly this room needed to be taken care of, we took steps to fix it. We should have known that much sooner, and for that we're sorry. The both of us appreciate every last one of you, and with that said, I'll just shut up and let you eat."

A couple employees laughed. Susan opened the bag and handed Kenneth a sandwich. He removed it from a plastic bag and began to eat.

"Is that all that you have in that big bag, a couple of sandwiches?" asked a man by the refrigerator.

Susan nodded her head.

The man shook his head back and forth.

"Say, anyone interested in a chocolate pudding?" a woman asked.

"I've got some black olives in a plastic bag I'd be willing to let go," Kenneth stated much to Susan's amazement.

"Oh," the woman remarked, "I love olives, especially black ones."

"Trade?" asked Kenneth.

"Trade," she responded.

The two passed their bartered items to the other, laughing as they did.

"Anyone interested in a week old donut?" laughed another person.

"Can you still bend it?" Susan asked.

"I could two days ago," came the response.

It was then and there that the Summers became a part of their employees' family or, perhaps it was vice versa. Susan and Kenneth made sure they ate at least twice a week with their employees. They even shifted their meal times so as to join with other groups in eating together. Kenneth, along with Susan, loved the time they spent with the people, the employees feeling much the same way. It wasn't simply because of a lunchroom makeover that changed the circumstances, it was the fact that the Summers treated the people as equals, and that was evident to all of them. Whenever they were going to join the employees for lunch, Kenneth made sure Susan packed a few extra items to trade with. It was a little highlight in his day, which he enjoyed participating in with their newfound friends.

Another day started carrying with it a new assignment for Greg to learn in the running of the business. He made his way up the steps and walked through a doorway leading into a hall. It was the first thing in the morning. Greg wanted to accomplish his task before work actually called him to his assigned duties. He walked a short distance down a hallway stopping at an old wooden oak door. A vintage frosted glass window with the words painted in black, "Store Security" stood before him. He reached down, taking an old brass doorknob in his hand. Turning it, he stepped through the door.

Behind his desk sat Ted Sheppard. He stood up and offered Greg his hand.

"It's nice to see you, Greg."

"As well as it is for me, Ted."

"Before we get into why you're here, I'd like to say something," Ted announced as he sat back down in his old leather chair.

"Go ahead," Greg said, "I'm all ears."

"I hear good things about you, Greg. People sometimes ask me why you're moving from job to job, they're not used to seeing that. I just tell them it's a new system Mr. and Mrs. Summers are trying out, and you're the guinea pig. That seems to answer any questions they have."

"I'm glad to hear that from you. To tell you the truth I didn't really know how long I could get away with this charade to begin with."

"I think I know why it's worked so well for you thus far," Ted offered. "It's your personality, people like you. How individuals react has a lot to do with their first impression of a person. That was even true for me with you in the beginning."

"Maybe so," he said, nodding his head.

"So what can I do for you, what is it you wanted to see me about?"

"First let me say that what I want you to do involves a little detective work."

"Good, I've missed that part of my old job."

"I don't know if this is something I should even have you do, or it's just something that's been bothering me for a long time and I want to resolve it one way or another. Either way, I need your help to do it."

"Does this have to do with an employee here?" Ted asked.

"Not in the least. Actually I wanted to get your guidance on a subject, get your opinion on my idea. The fact of the matter is, I would actually be going far beyond what Mr. and Mrs. Summers expect me to do, or have even authorized me to do in just talking to you about it. Still I don't want to step on any toes, that's not my intent."

"From what you've said so far, it sounds like you're going out onto the end of a limb and you can hear it cracking behind you already, that is, if I understand you correctly."

"Well, something like that, but I wouldn't put the final act into play without their permission."

"I see. Well, what do you need me to do?"

"And, Ted, before I tell you, can we keep this to ourselves?"

Ted chuckled.

"The last time I was asked to do that, it was Melissa who asked the same thing of me."

"Really?" Greg stated in a surprised voice.

"I guess that runs in the family, but yes, that's no problem at all."

"Thank you."

"Well, tell me what you want me to keep secret that's so important to you to begin with?"

Greg walked over and took a seat in front of the desk. He began outlining his thoughts to Ted.

"Hmmm..." Ted said.

He listened as Greg explained to him the where, when and why of his idea. Ted just shook his head, understanding now why Greg was doing what he was. It all made sense to him.

"Well, when I have some information for you, I'll let you know."

"Just let me know what you can," Greg said.

"Okay. Then I'll talk to you later."

"All right."

"Oh, Ted, do you have any idea on how long this is going to take?"

"It just depends," he answered.

"Okay, and thank you for your help."

"Well, Greg, don't be too premature on that thank you, I haven't done anything yet, and who knows if I can."

"Thanks just the same."

Greg opened the door, closing it behind him as he exited the room. He headed off to his next assigned job hoping to learn more about the operations of the business.

After Greg left the room Ted smiled as he thought to himself, I knew I'd like that kid.

It had now been about four weeks since Greg began working in the "Gold Mine" as he liked to refer to it, the jewelry department. He even surprised himself with how easily he could make the items fly off the shelf.

Greg bent over the jewelry counter admiring the various rings, bracelets and other gold items that adorned the shelves of the glass cases. High intensity lights made even the smallest items glimmer to prospective customers' eyes.

"Can I help you?" Greg asked an older gentleman as he walked up finally stopping before the case in front of Greg.

"I would like to talk with Mr. Wilson. Is he here?"

"That would be me, sir. What can I do for you?"

"I understand from people that I work with that you're the one to see when it comes to buying jewelry."

"Well, I'll be happy to help you, but what are they saying about me?" asked Greg.

"They referred to you as the words guy."

"Pardon me, did you say the worst guy?"

"No, no, the words guy, w-o-r-d-s guy."

"Oh, I misunderstood you, I'm sorry."

The man chuckled to himself. "That's okay. I work with a lot of different men and they keep saying you're the best one at making their gift to their girlfriends or wives come to life, so to speak, and that's why I'm here. I need some of your words to help me out."

"Now I see what you mean, sir. What can you tell me about the person your gift is going to be for?"

"It's for my wife. Through the years I've purchased her many items in gold, silver, and even platinum, but now I need something special for our 50th anniversary. What do you suggest? Money isn't really my concern."

"Money should never be the main concern when it comes to gifts, although the lack of it can hinder you at times. The right gift, no matter how cheap it is, will out shadow the wrong one no matter what it costs, even if that person spends bookoo bucks on the wrong one.

"I'm sure you're right on that one."

"Well, I have a couple of ideas to start with and then we'll go from there. If you don't like any of my suggestions, we'll take it to the next level."

"Sounds good to me."

"First, and there's two ways of going on this idea. You get a picture of yourself and place it into a gold locket."

"What's so unusual and special about that?" he asked.

"It's what you say that makes any gift unique to that person. You tell her that every time she opens the locket and gazes at your picture she'll see the image of the man who feels he's the luckiest person in the world to have the love of such a wonderful and precious woman."

"I really like that," the man said laughing as he nodded his head, "but it is kind of common; isn't it?"

"Yes. I'd even have to say so, but you'd be surprised how many people go with that, and that's why I mentioned it to you."

"I need something really special."

"I have another idea if you care to hear it."

"Please."

"It has to do with a locket also. On the inside of it we'll have a small diamond attached to the right-hand side, but not quite in the middle. We can take a very small piece of coal and do the same thing with it, just next to it."

"Why the coal?" the gentleman asked.

"You tell your wife that as long as it takes for the piece of coal to turn into the diamond next to it, that's how long your love for her will last."

"How can I ever thank you for such a good idea, Mr. Wilson?"

"By calling me Greg."

"Thank you, Greg."

"Listen, if you don't mind I do have one more suggestion for you."

"Please," he said again.

"Does your wife like flowers, any kind in particular?"

"She loves roses."

"So does my wife. Let's you and I try to find a gold locket that has a beautiful rose engraved on the front of it."

"Good idea." the gentleman said smiling. "Coming here and talking to you has really helped me out. The people at work were right, you do have a way with words."

Greg smiled as he helped the man look through the inventory of lockets for that certain special keepsake. Finally their hunt met with success.

"I'm curious to hear what you found out," Greg stated as he took a seat in front of Mr. Sheppard's desk. Ted reached down and pulled a drawer open. He retrieved a manila folder from inside and placed it on the desk.

"I think you'll be surprised by the information contained in this," Ted stated.

He reached over with his hand and slid it across the desk to Greg. Greg took it in his hands and opened it. He began reading it, shaking his head as he did.

"So what are your personal conclusions?" he asked Ted.

"In many ways I think he got a very raw deal, and his family ended up paying for it as well as him."

Greg nodded his head in agreement.

"So the question is, is there anything I can do about it? I know it's not my place, but just the same I have to talk to Mr. and Mrs. Summers about it. I'm hoping they'll feel the same way I do about this. Maybe we can help them out."

"It's in your blood, isn't it," Ted said, "you just hate to see people taken advantage of, especially when they have so much to lose."

"Well, I don't know if I'd quite say it that way, but maybe you're right."

"You know, Greg, Mrs. Summers is a lot like you, she's always got her nose into something, trying to help people out."

Greg nodded his head again as he took the folder and closed it.

"Can I take this with me?"

"Of course. Remember, you can't recall where you got this information from; understand?"

"You won't have to worry about that."

"That's good enough for me. I don't know what you may feel you can do about it, but just the same, good luck."

"Thank you."

"And, Greg, if there's anything I can do to help you, you know where I am."

Greg stood up and started for the door, stopping long enough to thank Ted for the information he now held in his hands. He nodded his head to Ted as he closed the door behind him.

Greg quickly returned to his assigned job training. He stopped long enough to place the folder in a drawer out of sight.

"Come in," Kenneth announced in reply to the knock on his office door.

An older gentleman wearing a suit walked into the room.

"I don't know if I'm in the proper place or not, but I was told by someone downstairs I could talk to the owners of the store up here."

"That would be me, sir," Kenneth stated, "and this is my wife, Susan, as well as our daughter, Melissa. Now, how can we help you?"

"I'm here about Mr. Wilson. Greg, I think his first name is."

"And what seems to be the problem?" came the hesitant voice from Kenneth.

"I was just downstairs looking for him, he's nowhere to be found. Have you fired him from the jewelry department?"

Now the women were both interested to see what the man had to say, Kenneth being very much interested himself.

"Should I?" Kenneth asked, not knowing what to say.

"Listen, I need to talk to him, and it's very important."

"I can have him paged." suggested Susan.

"Well, that would be a good start, thank you."

"Would you like to have a seat, sir?" Kenneth said.

"No, I'll just stand, if you don't mind."

"Of course."

"I'll page Greg now, sir," Susan stated, "he'll be here in a just a moment." Susan turned and left the room. Within a few seconds or so they could hear her voice over the sound system.

"Will Greg Wilson report to the main office immediately, immediately please?"

Susan hurried back to Kenneth's office, not wanting to miss anything that might take place. Within a few minutes Greg walked into Kenneth's office. Before he had the chance to say anything the man turned to Greg.

"Do you remember me, young man?" the gentleman said.

"You were the —"

"The diamond and coal man."

"Oh, yes, now I remember you."

The man held his hand out to Greg indicating he wanted to shake his. Now Kenneth, Susan, and Melissa were all dumbfounded. A handshake was the last thing anyone thought would happen at this juncture.

"So how did it go for you, sir?" Greg asked, curious to hear his answer.

"The party our family threw for my wife and me was an unexpected treat for the both of us. They had a cake and old pictures of our wedding on a table. There were a few gifts from our children. We have three girls, all married. We love each and every one of them dearly. They did a wonderful job setting everything up. All of our grandchildren were there also. There were lots of friends, relatives, and some other acquaintances of ours as well.

After cutting the cake, and opening some gifts I felt it was my turn. I handed my wife the locket in the small box you had decorated for me. I knew you did your best to prepare it with the diamond and coal, but still I was very nervous that she may not like it. Once she opened it I spoke to her the words you told me to say. I've never observed my wife and daughters weep as much as they did. It was a wonderful day, and in my family's eyes, I was a hero to all of them."

"So everything worked out well for you. I'm so happy for you both, and by the way, happy anniversary."

"Thank you so much."

"Oh, it's your anniversary?" Susan asked.

"They've been married 50 years," Greg declared.

"How wonderful," Susan said smiling.

Looking over towards Kenneth and Susan the man asked them a question that was on his mind for a few days now.

"I know this isn't my place to ask you, but would you care if I took your employee, Greg, out for lunch? There's a place called the Golden Rib Restaurant, and I understand they have very good food there. I've asked my wife to meet me there at noon, and I'd like Greg to accompany me, if it's okay."

"Kenneth, it's almost noon now," Susan stated.

"I'll tell you what, sir," Kenneth said, "he can go under a certain set of circumstances."

"And what would those be?" the gentleman asked.

"That we all meet your wife, and you allow us to pick up the meal as our anniversary gift to the both of you."

"Oh, I can't do that."

"You can and you will... please," Susan said.

"I get to go, too; right?" Melissa quickly vocalized, not wanting to miss out on any time with her husband and family.

"Of course, Honey," Susan said.

"Then it's set," Kenneth stated, "we'll all meet at noon at the Golden Rib Restaurant."

"You're very generous," the gentleman said as he looked at Kenneth.

"Not really, I'll just slip the bill to my wife when we're done and no one's looking at me," he joked.

As the four of them walked through the front door to the restaurant, the gentleman stood up and waved to them.

"They're over there," Melissa indicated.

"Oh, I see them," Susan said.

As they joined the man and his wife, Kenneth introduced himself along with his wife, Melissa, and Greg.

"This is my wife, Terry Caldwell, and my name is Robert. I neglected to introduce myself earlier, so I wanted to get that out of the way. Please have a seat and join us."

"Thank you," Kenneth said as the four of them sat down.

"I understand you've been married 50 years," inquired Susan.

"Yes, we have," Terry said smiling.

"That's something you don't hear very much about anymore concerning marriage, longevity."

"And I think the reason for that is because of the hard work that's involved," Terry said. There were days, I will say this, when Robert walked a thin line between the end of a frying pan swing, and being hugged to death," she joked.

"Did you hear that, Greg?" Melissa said laughing.

"Every happy marriage has its days, it's not all a bed of roses, but you just keep working on it." Terry continued. "You are a unique person, Greg. Robert told me how he wanted that very special gift for me on our anniversary and you helped him. Just having him beside me healthy was all I really wanted, but I knew that he would get me something anyway. He explained how people in his business told him to go check with the 'words guy', simply because you were so good at matching the right gift for the perfect occasion."

"Excuse me, the what?" asked Kenneth.

"The words guy," repeated Terry," that's our employee's nickname for Greg at Robert's place of business."

"If I may, Mrs. Caldwell, can I see what Robert gave you?" Susan inquired.

"Before you do that, Mrs. Caldwell," Greg said interrupting Susan.

The Promise

Greg knew the words spoken to Terry by her husband that evening may come up, and he wanted to make sure Robert's wife understood it wasn't just Greg's idea on the words alone, though that fact was evident to both Greg and Robert. In Greg's mind it was better to give Robert as much credit as possible.

"It's Terry," stated Mrs. Caldwell.

"Terry, thank you," Greg said. "Your husband put a lot of thought into your gift. You should know he was very concerned that your gift be one that represented the strong bond of love he feels for you in his heart each and every day."

Robert smiled with Greg's words being said.

Terry smiled as well as she reached behind her neck and undid the clasp. Taking the locket in her hand, she held it out.

"I love the rose on the front of it," exclaimed Melissa.

"As do I, it's my favorite flower."

"Just like me, Mom," smiled Melissa as she looked in her mother's direction.

"Now just look at this," Terry said as she opened the locket.

"What is that," Susan said. "I understand the diamond, but what is the small black piece sitting next to it?

"Coal," Terry proudly stated.

"Coal?" Susan said. "I'm sorry, I don't understand. I heard your husband mention something about coal in the office, but I didn't catch everything he was saying, in fact, I didn't get the coal part either."

"And neither did I, when I first got this from Robert," Terry said smiling, "that is, until Robert told me what it meant." Terry reached over taking Robert's hand is hers, squeezing it slightly.

"What does it mean?" Melissa asked.

Terry smiled as she once again gave Robert's hand a squeeze.

"He told me, and everyone at our party, that as long as it takes for the piece of coal to turn into the diamond next to it, that's how long his love for me will last."

"Oh, how sweet and wonderful is that," Susan said.

"It sure is," Melissa added.

"It's not everyone who can put into words, such precious words as my Robert did," Terry said smiling. "Our daughters and I haven't cried like that in years. The children were simply taken back by the words of their father to me."

"You did a great job, Mr. Caldwell," Greg said.

"I had some outstanding help," he answered with a wink.

Kenneth looked at the happy couple before him as he stated, "I don't know if your husband told you or not, but my wife and I would appreciate it if you would be kind enough to allow us to buy your lunch and celebrate your anniversary with you. We would be honored if you'd allow us to do that."

"He did, and we will," laughed Terry.

"Wonderful," exclaimed Susan.

It was like a festive meal, at times a party. All six people sat around the table laughing, joking, enjoying one another's company. Kenneth couldn't remember the last time he had sat with strangers and enjoyed their company so much.

As they sat eating dessert, Terry turned to Greg, "So how long have you worked for Mr. and Mrs. Summers?"

"I think four and a half months now," Greg said nodding his head.

"And all in the jewelry department?" asked Robert.

"I've been there about a month, maybe just a touch longer."

"That explains a lot," Susan said.

"What do you mean?" Kenneth asked.

"In the last month our jewelry sales went up 32.5 percent."

"And probably most of it from my employees," laughed Robert. He turned and looked at Greg as he asked him, "Greg, are you happy with your job there, and please don't get upset you two," Robert stated quickly looking at both Kenneth and Susan, "but I was wondering if he might want to do some odd jobs for us."

Susan and Kenneth did not expect this turn of events, the offer by Robert, and their faces were quick to reflect that to him.

"First of all, I'm not trying to steal your employee, though I wish he worked for me, but I was just wondering if Greg might like to pick up some extra money along the way. It would strictly be on a percentage basis."

Kenneth looked at Susan, her at him as well. Neither one said a word, each not knowing what to say. After all, it wasn't their decision to make in the first place. But still...

"I own an advertising company. My employees use words every day, it's our business to make people want to purchase merchandise. Unfortunately there are times when we get bogged down, our minds just don't work, they get stuck in neutral. I need that spontaneous spark, the creativity your mind has to offer, and I think you can do that for us. When I heard my own employees were going to you for help with ideas, that spoke volumes to me. Now, Greg, it would be a part-time job or whatever, and you could even work at home if you'd like. We'll accommodate you in any way we can. What do you think?"

"That's a very generous offer, sir," Greg said. "Really, I would have to think it over."

"I think you should take it, Greg, I think it would be fun for you," Melissa expressed.

"Fun, I wouldn't exactly call it that," Greg said.

"Let me give you an example of what you could be dealing with," Robert said, "maybe that will help you to make up your mind. Right now we're working on an advertisement for children's bicycle helmets. They are very much on the pricey side, very pricey. They are almost twice the price of their competitors, and so that seems to be somewhat of a problem for us to deal with. People simply like cheap."

"Why wouldn't you use that to your advantage?" Greg asked.

"I'm sorry, you lost me."

"The fact that they're so pricey. I think your ad should be simple, opposite in nature, and to the point. You could start out, 'At any price the wellbeing of your child should come first in your heart, we understand that, that's why we cost more. We use the finest materials etc., etc, you know what I mean."

Robert starting laughing. He then finished Greg's thoughts with his own words, "And would you trust your child's life to anything less, we hope not. Simplicity at its finest, and to the point. Who would have ever thought that, and then twist it to use it to your own advantage. Now that's the kind of input I need from you."

Now thoughts of losing Greg began to run seriously through both Susan and Kenneth's minds. Neither one of them wanted to look down that path, let alone walk it.

"Greg, when I go back to the office, I'm going to suggest this idea of yours to our people. I think we've been looking at it in the wrong way. If, by chance, we go with that proposal of yours, and I think there's a strong possibility of that, I'll see to it you get a check for your work from us."

"That's not necessary, sir."

"Well, it is for me."

"Mr. Caldwell, I think I'd like to do it, work on the side for you and your company. However, my first responsibility and loyalty is to Mr. and Mrs. Summers, they come first."

"I understand that, Greg, and I admire that in you. That will be no problem whatsoever."

Greg extended his hand out to Robert, they shook. Robert reached into his suit pocket and produced a business card.

"Give me a call at your earliest convenience, we'll talk some more."

"I will."

"This has been a very interesting luncheon," Kenneth declared.

"That it has," Susan added, "that it has."

"For all of us," Robert commented.

Melissa took Susan by the hand as they smiled at each other, Melissa being very proud of her husband, Susan of her son-in-law as well.

Sometime had passed now and all the plans had pretty much been put into place. A large section of the city park was reserved and paid for. Food had been ordered, soft drinks, buns, and even ice to keep things cool. The announcement in the form of Melissa and Susan's flier was back from the printers and was ready to be delivered to the employees. It was time for the picnic to be announced, and the Summers were excited to see the employees' reactions.

One can only imagine the looks exhibited on the employees faces as they studied over the flier included with their paychecks. Some thought it to be a joke at first, simply too good to be true. Others read the notice that was posted in the break room. It was soon the talk of everyone throughout the store. A day off with pay, games, free food, and their families were welcomed to attend, even encouraged by the words in the flier. What else could they ask for, some said.

As Greg walked around the store, he heard the people talking excitedly about the picnic. "Are you going?" "My kids will love this!" "I think my husband would love going!" were just a small sampling of the words he overheard that day. He made notes in his mind. It was his intent to let Kenneth and Susan, as well as his wife, know what people thought. After a short time he was able to make his way to the office area upstairs. Greg walked into Susan's office.

"Good morning, Mom," he stated to Susan.

"Hi, Greg."

"You should hear the people talking throughout the store, it would do you and Dad's heart good to hear them. Everyone is all excited about the picnic."

"That's good to hear. In fact, my phone has been ringing steadily. Mrs. Stefan down in clothing told me her mother and father would be visiting from out of town that day and wondered if they could come. I told her, if they're family, bring them. She was thrilled. To tell you the truth, I can hardly wait for that day to get here."

"Me, too. Say, where is dad and Melissa, I haven't seen them around?"

"They're around. Kenneth and Melissa told me they had a couple of things they wanted to get together. By the way, Greg, this is for you."

Susan reached over near the corner of her desk and retrieved an envelope addressed to him. He took it from her glancing at the corner to see the return address.

"Oh," was all he said.

"Well, aren't you going to open it?"

"I suppose."

"I couldn't help but notice it's from Caldwell Advertising."

"I see that. It's not like I get any mail delivered here at the store, in fact, I was kind of surprised you had this for me."

"Have you done any jobs for him lately?"

"Actually a couple. Did you know he has quite an impressive number of large accounts he deals with yearly? I couldn't believe some of the big-named clients on his list."

"He must be a good businessman."

"I'm sure he is."

"No, I mean because he hired you," Susan said smiling.

"Thanks, Mom. When Melissa told me it would be fun for me to do this, I thought she was really mistaken, but to tell you the truth, I'm really having fun doing it."

"It's always fun to work, when the work you do is fun," she answered.

"Now you're a philosopher, and a darn good one at that, I might add," he chuckled.

Greg reached into his pocket and took out a small pocketknife. He pulled the blade out and ran it across the back of the envelope causing an opening. Next he reached in and pulled a folded piece of paper out. As he unfolded the paper a check slid out and fell to the ground. He reached down and picked it up, looking at it as he did. He nodded his head as he read the sheet of paper that had once held the check. Greg placed the check back next to the sheet of paper and folded it back up. He placed it into the envelope.

"Good news?" Susan inquired.

"You could say that, Mom. Will you give this to Melissa when she comes in, she'll know what to do with it."

"I'll be glad to."

"Thank you. Well, I better get back to work before the owners fire me and I have to start looking for a new job."

He walked over to Susan giving her a kiss on her cheek as he handed her the envelope.

"See you later, Mom."

Susan nodded her head as he left the room. The urge to take a quick peek at the inside of the envelope started to consume her thoughts. No one would ever know, was her rationalization for the compulsion she felt. Still the craving to do so persisted. Finally she could take it no longer as she picked it up and held it up to the window attempting to see its contents. This act of hers was, of course, futile since the sheet of paper protected any prying eyes. She knew the simple solution was obvious, just open it up, pull the papers out, thus answering her question. Susan, however, understood it was wrong to do so and ended up laying the envelope down on the desk once again. As she sat working she felt as though the envelope had eyes within it, and were looking out between the flaps at her. She even surmised it was watching her every move. Finally she could take it no longer. She picked up the envelope and turned the open flap so it faced away from her.

With the opening of Susan's office door Melissa and Kenneth walked in together laughing.

"What's so funny?" she asked.

"It's a secret; right, Dad?" Melissa said in a chuckle.

"Oh, we were just out and about, huh, Melissa?"

"A secret over what?" inquired Susan.

"Oh," Kenneth said smiling, "you'll learn soon enough."

"Oh, there's an envelope Greg got in the mail. He said you'd know what to do with it," Susan said.

"Thank you, Mom," she answered. She turned to her dad laughing, "This is going to be so funny; isn't it, Dad?"

"It sure is," he answered.

"Aren't you going to open it," Susan said, a little frustration showing in her voice.

"In a minute, Mom."

"I think you should open it now, it might be important."

"Has Greg seen it?"

"Yes."

"Okay," she answered as she once again turned her attention to her dad.

"We could even put some —"

"Melissa, it could be important."

"Okay, Mom. Where is it?"

Susan handed it to her, having already retrieved it off of the desk. Susan knew there was a check inside the envelope, and she wanted her curiosity answered. It was driving her nuts.

Melissa went over and sat down in a chair. She opened the envelope and pulled a check from its interior. Susan observed Melissa as she bit down slightly on the lower part of her lip. Melissa next took the sheet of paper and read it. Susan watched as Melissa smiled, placing the check back into the envelope.

"Well?" Susan said.

"It's from Mr. Caldwell, his advertising business."

"I saw that from the envelope."

"He sent Greg a check for his work on the children's helmets."

"And?"

"Susan, that's none of our business," Kenneth said in a somewhat sharp tone of voice.

"It is if we lose our son-in-law to his business. You saw how much he liked Greg at the lunch we had together. He wants to steal him from us, and I won't have any of it."

"Susan, listen to yourself. Greg's not going to leave us over a few part-time hours. He couldn't possibly make that much working for him a few hours a week."

"Well," Melissa said, "I think Greg does all right. He's getting more and more stuff being farmed out to him. Whenever they're stuck on something and need a solution, Greg gets a call. Only last night someone from Mr. Caldwell's office dropped some stuff off to him."

Susan nodded her head as she looked in Kenneth's direction.

"See, what did I tell you," Susan declared.

"Greg isn't going anywhere," Kenneth said.

"Are you sure?"

."Mom, Dad, I'm sure he isn't, in fact, I know he isn't. Last night, after the man left, he told me how much it meant to him the day you told him you wanted to make him part of our family business. He loves you both, me the most, of course." Melissa chuckled slightly. "Greg wouldn't do anything to jeopardize that relationship with either one of you. He's too much of a man of his word to even consider doing that."

"Well, I would just hate to lose him from being a part of our business."

"I understand, Mom."

"Melissa, can I ask you about the check?"

"It's none of our business," Kenneth said loudly as he looked at Susan.

"My mind just needs to have that question answered," she said. "Please."

Melissa again opened the envelope and pulled out the check. She glanced at the check and then handed it to her mother. Susan looked at it for quite awhile and then handed it to Kenneth. He held it in his hand for sometime also.

"Unbelievable, simply unbelievable," he said.

"And you think we might not lose him over a part-time job," she exclaimed.

Kenneth then slowly read out loud the sum on the check, "Eighteen thousand five hundred dollars. And this he made in approximately a minute and a half over a lunch we paid for. It's simply unbelievable."

"Maybe it's for a couple of jobs he did?" offered Susan.

"The memo on the check reads, 'Children's helmets,'" Kenneth stated, "so I don't think that theory flies."

"Mom, Dad, we want you to use this money towards the picnic, we both do."

"So that's why Greg said you'd know what to do with it," her mother said smiling.

"He knew he was getting the check. Greg told me he still wants to help you out with your party. He explained to me how badly he felt that it's cost you nothing but money ever since he's started here. I think that really bothers him a lot on the inside."

"Honey," Kenneth said, "you put this towards a home along with the rest of the money you two have saved. I think the best part of this is that I know no matter what life presents you two with, Greg will be able to find a way to support you."

"Thanks, Daddy," Melissa said.

"Susan, let's you and I go out for dinner with Greg and Melissa tonight to celebrate, some place really nice and expensive, if that's okay with them."

"We'd love to, Dad."

"And just so there's no misunderstanding, you and Greg can pick up the tab."

Together the family members laughed.

The Yokes on Me

As Greg lay in bed he felt a small jab in his back.

"Good morning, Honey."

He turned over onto his back and looked at Melissa, her hair slightly disheveled. Greg gently moved some hair that covered a small portion of her eyes. He slid his arm under her shoulder as she cuddled next to him, placing her head upon his chest. Greg slowly rubbed his hand up and down her arm as she smiled at him. He smiled back. How beautiful she looks were his thoughts.

"Honey," Melissa declared, jumping up slightly, "we have to get going, it's going on seven o'clock, and there's so much to do. Come on, we've got to get moving."

"I'm going to need some energy with all the work we have to do today," Greg stated as he reached over pulling Melissa closer. She gave him a big kiss.

"There's your energy, now let's get moving. Today is going to be a big day for us," she stated with almost a childlike tone of excitement in her voice.

That was one more thing Greg loved about her, the emotions she exhibited with even the simplest of things. Her enthusiasm for projects, no matter how small, was always contagious.

"So what time are we supposed to meet your mom and dad at the park?" he asked.

"Eight o'clock. They want to have plenty of time to make sure everything goes smoothly and is completed before 10:30. The picnic starts at 11:00 a.m. sharp. Greg, I'm so excited. Dad and I went out shopping one day and got some surprise joke props. I can hardly wait to use them."

"When are you going to use them, and what are they?"

"At the baseball game, and you'll have to wait and see what dad and I do. We finally had to tell my mom because she was driving us nuts asking about it. She loves our ideas and wanted to join in."

"I can hardly wait to see that," he expressed as he got out of bed.

It didn't take long for the two of them to get ready. Greg could hear Melissa singing as she combed her hair in the bathroom, an occasional amount of "la, la, la's" in place of words she obviously had forgotten or didn't know. He walked to the bathroom stopping in the arch of the doorway. He leaned up against it and listened as Melissa continued her singing. Greg saw her reflection in the mirror. He looked at the t-shirt Melissa had on. He started to laugh.

"Where on earth did you get that?"

"Dad and I ordered them special. What do you think?"

"I love it."

"It really wasn't that hard to find or get made," she said as she turned and pulled the t-shirt slightly sideways to allow the words to be read easier. The t-shirt bore the words, "Summers' Summer Picnic" which were imprinted in black letters on the front of it.

"We got one for all of us except you, of course. Honey, when do you think you'll finally feel comfortable enough with learning the business?"

"I think you never stop learning."

"You're probably right. I was just wondering."

Once dressed, Greg and Melissa got into their car and headed for a local restaurant for breakfast. Instead the couple opted to use a drive thru restaurant to save time. Arriving at the park they met with Melissa's mother and father who were already waiting. Greg smiled as he looked at Kenneth and Susan dressed in their yellow t-shirts with the same words imprinted on them. The two women laughed as they admired the other's garb.

"You've been doing your clothes shopping at the same women's store that I have," joked Susan.

"Then how do you explain dad's outfit?" laughed Melissa.

Greg and Kenneth walked over to a group of large trees.

"So I was thinking of having them set up the — oh, what do they call it? I can never remember the name," Kenneth said shaking his head.

"Oh, you mean the air filled gym or big box the kids bounce in? What do they call it, I can't think of the name either."

"Well, anyway, Greg, what do you think about placing it here?"

"I think that's a good idea, plus the ground looks nice and level."

"You see the tables over there, we can put the food in that area. We'll have to pull the tables together and add a few more."

"We're going to need lots and lots of tables, Dad," Greg said.

"You really think so?"

"From what I heard at work, yes."

"Good, we want the party to be a success."

"I think it will be."

"Oh, they're here already," Kenneth announced with a smile.

Looking over in the parking area Greg recognized his mom and dad's car. After parking, four people exited the car, Edith, Frank, Kate, and Henry.

"I'm surprised to see you all here," Greg said.

"Well," Edith declared, "we do have a couple of family members who work for the Summers family; don't we?"

"We're here to help but, of course, I was bribed by free food," Frank said as he rubbed his stomach in a circular manner.

Melissa went up and hugged Kate, giving a quick hug to Henry as well.

"I'm so glad you two came," she said.

"Well, your mother called me and asked us to come," Kate said. "We wouldn't want to miss it."

Hearing a slight tap of a car horn, the group turned their attention once again to the parking area. Getting out of a car was Doc and Jean. They walked up to the group.

"I was instructed by this beautiful young lady beside me that I could get a free hotdog, bun included, and a drink if I was willing to help some people put on a party," joked Doc.

"Well, you're at the right place," smiled Kenneth.

"So where do we start?" asked Frank.

"How about the table area?" Greg said.

"Sounds good to me," Henry stated.

"Well, I'll be happy to lend a hand, " Doc said.

That's when the city park began to transform into a festive party area. A large banner was strung between two trees with the words, "Summers' Summer Picnic, Welcome Employees and Families." Over in one section four bales of straw were placed. The twine binding them together was cut and spread out, needing only coins to be hidden within them. Two 55 gallon barbeques stood ready. Several bags of charcoal were piled behind them waiting to be loaded and lit. Oversize coolers filled with hotdogs, hamburgers and buns sat over to the side. All the condiments for bringing them to life were soon placed on a table. Large coolers containing various sodas were filled with ice.

The men and women worked diligently preparing various areas. The air gym was filled and awaiting eager little kids to be tossed around as they bounced in it. Baseball equipment was put over by the diamond. A van with the words, "Animals Made Of Air," pulled into the parking lot soon finding an empty space to occupy.

"Who is that?" Frank asked Kenneth.

"He's a gentleman who makes animals out of balloons and hats as well."

"I've seen guys do that before," Frank said nodding his head. "I don't know how they can do that all day and still keep breathing. It takes a lot of work to blow up one balloon after another. The kids are going to love him."

"That's our hope," Kenneth smiled.

"Where do you want these burlap bags, Dad?" Greg asked.

"I don't know," answered Frank, as Kenneth said, "I'm not sure."

Both men looked at each other and laughed.

"Why don't you decide where we should start the three-legged race and put them there," Kenneth suggested.

"Okay," Greg said as he walked off.

"An old-fashioned three-legged race, huh." Frank said as he shook his head, "Boy does that bring back memories."

"It was Susan's idea. She said she wanted a little nostalgia included in the day's activities."

"I personally think it's a good idea."

"Well, then you're going to love the egg toss, and the carrying of the water in the spoon to fill the cups with water."

"We did that when I was a kid," smiled Frank.

"Susan wanted our party to reflect the days of yesteryear, and so that's our theme. Remember when people used to put a balloon under their chin and pass it onto the next person?"

"No, I think it was an orange."

"I think you're right," Kenneth said nodding his head.

"I'll be right back."

"Where are you going?"

"To get some oranges. I'll be right back."

Kenneth smiled as Frank headed in the direction of his car.

Susan looked at her watch as Edith and Melissa put the final touches on the tables. White paper had been rolled out covering the tables giving a fresh and clean appearance to their tops.

"It's really shaping up nicely, isn't it?" Edith expressed to the others.

"Mom, look over there, people are starting to come," pointed out Melissa.

"They sure are," Susan said.

Susan took a quick look over to where the barbecues sat. Smoke swirled from the drums, their wire grates getting hotter with every passing second. Henry and Greg appeared to be discussing the cooking jobs they both were looking forward to handling.

Susan looked past the snow fence and watched a woman with her two children flying a kite. What a beautiful day to do that, she thought. She could feel a soft breeze blow through her hair as she watched. The wind captured the kite raising it quickly into the air. It darted back and forth then made several slow and gentle movements through the air. A few large clouds acted as its backdrop. The kite's tail followed its partner's lead with each movement the breeze presented to it. Susan soon became mesmerized as she watched.

"Mom," Melissa said, her mother not replying to her. "Mom," she said once again.

"Oh, I'm sorry, I was just watching the children over there with their mother."

Melissa turned to see what had captivated her mother's attention so much. She soon found herself doing the same thing. Now both women stood watching as the kite meandered through the sky.

The day met with more success than anyone had anticipated, employer or employee. The weather cooperated putting its best face forward. When the baseball game commenced, Melissa, Susan, and Kenneth played the parts of umpires. As Kenneth stepped behind home plate Melissa yelled out loudly, "Dad, you can't do that without some protective face gear." She then ran to the dugout grabbing a big bag. She quickly went to her father's side. He reached into the bag pulling out a white goalie mask, akin to one found in a horror movie. The people laughed heartily, all enjoying his sense of humor. Melissa once again turned and ran to the dugout returning with a large black garbage bag. She retrieved a large old pillow from its interior. Melissa then took some rope out and tied it around him. Kenneth would clean the plate with a heavy-duty broom, much to everyone's delight.

It had been decided earlier that each team had to consist of half men and women. As Kenneth surveyed the field he chuckled to himself. Not only were there men, women and some older children on the field, each team appeared to consist of more than twenty five people. The score mattered to no one. Kenneth would stand in the way of the catcher as someone attempted to reach home, thus hampering their efforts. Sometimes the catcher would kick dirt onto Kenneth's shoes, complaining loudly. Kenneth then returned the favor.

Between innings Susan started yelling loudly that it was too hot out, the sun was simply baking her. Off again Melissa ran to the dugout retrieving another bag. Upon returning to her mother, she reached into it handing small Chinese fans to nearby players. She instructed them to fan her mother to cool her down. The players stood in a circle around Susan fanning her, some moving their hands quickly up and down. Spectators reflected their pleasure by applauding and laughing loudly.

Next Melissa took a giant red pair of sunglasses out which, of course, Susan put on her head. Once the game was over, Kenneth declared it a draw as players and fans booed him alike. Kenneth took a bow. He then went and joined Susan and Melissa heading to the food area.

"Oh, there's Doc and Jean sitting with Frank and Edith," Susan stated. "Melissa, we'll join you a little later, if that's okay."

Melissa nodded her head as she watched them walk towards the two couples seated at a picnic table.

As Melissa stood in a short line for food she noticed two kids standing on the other side of the snow fence. They were obviously taking a break from their kite flying. She watched the two girls, their eyes large as both of them explored everything taking place before them.

"You kids hungry?" she inquired.

Both children nodded their heads.

"Here, come over here to the open part of the fence, we'll get you both a little something to eat. It sure smells good to me, how about you?"

Once again the children nodded their heads.

"Kids, leave the nice lady alone."

It was the mother.

"I'm sorry if they're bothering you," she said.

"No, we're just visiting. Would it be okay if they came around the fence and had a burger or hotdog with me? I'd enjoy their company."

The children looked up to their mother, both hoping for the right response from her.

"Well, I don't know, it's really not our place to intrude."

"You wouldn't be... please. Do I know you?" asked Melissa as she studied the woman's face.

"I don't think so."

"Well, just the same, you kids come around the fence here with your mother and we can all get something to eat. Please," Melissa again stated. "I really would enjoy having someone to have a hotdog with. I'm by myself now."

"You're very kind, thank you."

"Thank you," both children said.

The four of them walked along the fence to an opening. Together the small group proceeded over to Henry and Greg's position. Greg, however, had left just before they got there as he took a plate full of burgers to a table of older women sitting together.

"What do you have to offer the four of us?" Melissa said.

Henry looked down at the two young girls and smiled, a big white chef's hat on his head.

"Only the best burgers and hotdogs in the universe. Now what's your choice?" he stated in an excited voice.

"Can I have one of each?" questioned one of the girls.

"Honey, no," the woman said.

"Oh, it's all right, ma'am," Henry stated nodding his head, "we're trying to get rid of them. She would be doing me a favor."

Henry then bent down to one knee making eye contact with her.

"And if you can eat those, I'll cook you some more, but don't forget to get a bag of chips and something to drink; okay?"

"Yes, sir," she responded.

"And do you see that table over there," Henry said as he pointed with his finger, "I understand they have some desserts there they need to get rid of, too."

The young girl smiled.

"Thank you," the woman said to Henry.

"Mister, what happened to your head?" one of the little girls asked.

Melissa could see the horror on the mother's face with that question being asked by her daughter.

"Do you see that burger over there on the corner of the grill?" Henry asked.

"Yes," said the little girl.

"Well, it came from a real tough cow, and I had to fight with it to get it onto the grill. He gave me quite a battle."

"Oh," she stated, "so that's what happened."

Henry nodded his head as he stood back up. The woman smiled at Henry, grateful to him for not getting upset with her child over her question. He turned a few burgers and then placed some onto the waiting buns. Henry was sure, however, not to give them the burger he had just referred to. After getting their plates made up, Melissa and the family went over and had a seat together.

"Thank you so much for sitting with me, Melissa said, "My family is visiting with some out of town friends and my husband is busy, so I'm happy to have your company."

"You're welcome. Thank you for the kid's food as well as mine. This is really nice what the Summers are doing today," she said as she looked around at the various people enjoying themselves.

"Yes, is it," Melissa answered.

"I love your t-shirt."

"It was a gift for today."

"Mr. and Mrs. Summers have such a wonderful reputation in the community."

Melissa nodded her head as she made a mental note to tell her mom and dad what she had just heard.

Greg walked over to a table of six older women to personally deliver their hamburger requests to them.

"I just don't get it," Greg said as he put the plate on the table, "why do I have to deliver these burgers to all of you personally? Let me see, could it be because I can never say no to beautiful women, or could it be I'm just a sucker for the smile of an attractive lady?"

"All of the above," one woman yelled out.

"You're probably right," Greg said smiling. "Now, if any of you don't find the burgers cooked to your liking, just let me know and I'll be happy to get you another one."

"Greg, when are you going to come out in the open with us?" asked a woman in a blue blouse.

"Pardon me?" he responded.

"Look, we all know you're married to Mr. and Mrs. Summers' daughter, we've known that for a few — for awhile, months now."

"I've known that for a long time," offered another woman.

Many at the table nodded their heads.

"Listen, can I confide in you?" he asked.

"By all means," one of the ladies said, the others nodding their heads in agreement. Two women actually bent forward to better hear him.

"Of course," another agreed.

Greg looked around for a moment as if to see who was nearby and maybe listening. The women followed his lead as they looked around also. He knew full well asking these women to keep a secret was like asking your pet dog to stop wagging its tail as it looked eagerly at the treat in your hand. Yes, he was certain anything he said would be common knowledge very fast. It just depended on which woman moved the quickest to her target, the next employee or person.

"Were you spying on us?" asked the woman in the blue blouse. "I was just wondering."

"No, no, and no. Mr. and Mrs. Summers offered me a job in the office."

"Why didn't you take it?" asked the same woman.

"Well, give me a chance to explain it to you.

"Okay," she said.

"I wanted to learn the retail business from the bottom up, the basement to the top floor."

Some of the women nodded their heads.

"It wasn't, nor has it ever been my intention to spy on anyone or anything along that line. I just wanted to learn everything I could about the business. Now, it seems my secret is out. I would like to say something to all of you.

While I haven't had the pleasure of working with any of you here, I have learned to love and respect the employees and their hard work. It truly has been an honor for me to experience that daily."

"Mr. and Mrs. Summers are wonderful people," stated a woman at the end of the table, "just look at this party they've thrown for us. And let's not forget the break room."

Some of the women nodded their heads in agreement.

"Let me say something about that," Greg was quick to say. "When they found out it wasn't up to their standards, or anyone of yours, they dealt with it immediately. I know it bothered them both that you had to deal with that day in and day out."

The woman next to Greg spoke up.

"Remember the day Grace had problems with her child at school, being sick so much? Mrs. Summers looked the other way and made sure she got paid every day, even when she had to stay home with her child."

A woman on Greg's right added, "And when Alice Farmer's husband almost died from that accident. Remember, he was bedridden at home for so long? Alice told me how Mrs. Summers brought in meals for her that she could take home. She even sent her home early quite often, while she would take her place behind the register."

Once again the woman at the end of the table interjected, "Greg, you're very fortunate to be a part of the Summers' family."

"I know I am."

"They're wonderful people, and we love them for how they treat us," another offered.

"Like equals," a woman stated.

"Yes, they do," the woman in blue, said.

"That's not it at all for me," conveyed a woman in a flowered blouse, "it's that they treat you like family."

Now the women all nodded in agreement with one another.

"Do you think we should do something for them?" asked one of the women.

"That sounds like a good idea," another said.

"Well, this looks like a good time for me to leave," Greg said. "If you do decide to do something, whatever it is, I know them well enough to understand they'll love anything you do. If by chance you decide to do nothing, they'll be just as happy. Well, have a good time, ladies. I'll see you later."

"Thanks for the burgers, Greg," he heard a couple of woman say as he walked away.

The games played by everyone, the adults as well as the small children were filled with fun. Whether it was digging into the straw pile with every single child finding coins of different denominations, or the baby race, there was loads of entertainment. All contestants who entered the baby race won a prize automatically, a twenty-five dollar gift certificate to the store. Every contest or game drew a large group of spectators.

As Susan and Kenneth participated in the egg toss something occurred to Kenneth. He thought he'd have a little fun for everyone at his own expense. When Susan tossed an egg high into the air, Kenneth put his hands behind his back, lined it up and let it smash into his head. Everyone applauded his efforts to make them laugh.

"I guess the yokes on me," he exclaimed as he wiped his face with a towel.

There were numerous gifts given out by the Summers to their employees, and the prizes people won were astounding to them. There were many store gift certificates, some in fairly large amounts. Ten gift certificates were handed out in drawings entitling the employee to a paid day off of their choice. The grand prize consisted of an individual winning a week off with pay. The day was amazing, one not to be forgotten by anyone.

As the day drifted to an end Susan announced that anyone who had not received a prize of any kind should take home a bag of hamburger or hotdog buns along with a package of uncooked meat to match. She also threw in eight packs of beverages along with a few bags of charcoal.

When it came to putting everything back together, the employees dug in with helping hands, although they weren't asked to. Tables were placed back to their original position. Parents instructed their children to pick up any papers they saw laying around. Henry and Greg removed the banner. When the straw was raked up and placed into bags for disposal, some children stood by watching for any undiscovered coin treasures. Some were actually found by them.

Two women watched their children running around looking for loose papers to capture and put in to the bins. As they stood talking one suggested they should get a thank you card and have it signed by everyone. A few other employees walked up to them. Soon that was the only topic of discussion among them. One woman offered her own idea of what to do. Smiles soon adorned each person's face as they thought over the suggestion. It was something that was clearly unusual, as well as thoughtful. The fact that it was a little costly didn't seem to deter any of them. Yes, that's what they would do. Now came the hard part, keeping it a secret until it took place.

It had now been almost a week since the picnic and Susan and Kenneth were still feeling the aches of that day. With the calling of the alarm clock, Susan got up and out of bed, her eyes only half open. She tied the two ends of her robe together as she made her way down the steps. Walking over to the coffee pot she yawned before removing the decanter from the maker. She poured herself a cup and sat down at the kitchen table for a few minutes. Oh, that tastes good, she thought. Thank goodness for coffee pots with timers. The coffee is always waiting for you when you get there. And what would I ever do without my daily caffeine to keep me going, she thought once again, probably walk around like a zombie sleepwalking. Now, wouldn't that be a sight to see. She smiled as she took another drink from the cup. Susan next placed the cup just under her nose as she took a deep breath of the aroma coming from it. Slowly she shook her head back and forth, blinking her eyes, trying to awaken from her tired slumber.

"You downstairs, Susan?" Kenneth yelled from the balcony.

"Yes, I am," she answered as another large yawn took control of her mouth, spreading her lips far apart as her voice gave out a tired sound.

Kenneth soon joined her as he poured himself a coffee.

"I think I'll get the morning paper, Honey," she declared as she stood up and walked to the front door. Stepping through the doorway she disappeared momentarily. Kenneth sat at the table, a yawn taking control of his mouth as well. Susan walked into the kitchen area, her eyes showing a slight dampness. The newspaper hung in her hand at her side.

"What is it, Susan?"

"You're not going to believe it, you're just never going to believe it," she repeated again.

"What is it?"

Susan turned the newspaper over to the last page and laid it on the table in front of Kenneth. He slowly looked it over, a large smile coming across his face as he did.

"You're right, I never would have believed this," he said.

The complete last page of the newspaper had been devoted to a message to the Summers family from their employees. Across the top it read in large letters, "Thank you Summers Family for the Employee Picnic." Below it in a smaller font were the words, "It's nice you consider us part of your family." In every space imaginable the signatures of their employees were signed.

"You know, Susan, I think each employee had to go down to the paper and sign their name so this could be printed. I think that's how it works, but I'm not sure."

Susan reached up to her eye and wiped a small tear from it.

"Kenneth, I'm going to have this framed and hung in your office, and I think I'll pick up another paper and do the same for mine."

"What a great idea," he replied. "Let's put one in my office here at home, too."

Susan nodded her head in approval.

"Kenneth, I'm so proud of you for going along with Greg's idea, and look at what it's accomplished for us. Our employees love and appreciate us."

"Yes, I guess you're right, in fact, I know you are."

As she stood behind her husband she nodded her head again.

"Just wait until next year," Kenneth said laughing slightly as he spoke.

Susan reached down and placed her hand on Kenneth's head. She rubbed her hand quickly back and forth like one would do with a young boy, as she laughed.

"I'm so excited," Susan exclaimed.

Susan's actions to Kenneth brought back to him memories of when Melissa was a very young child and would sneak up behind him and do the exact same thing.

"You and I have got to make a point of thanking Greg and Melissa for this, too," he said as he reached up trying to comb his hair back into place with his hand.

Susan bent over and kissed Kenneth on the top of his head. The sound of the phone calling out grabbed both of their attentions.

"It's awful early for a call," Susan stated, " I hope nothing is wrong."

"I'll get it, Susan."

"Okay, Honey."

"Hello. Yes, we did see it, Honey, your mom just pointed it out to me. Yes, it is wonderful. I know, and we both had lots of fun as well. Okay. Susan is going to have it framed for the office here and at work. Yes, I think it's a good idea, too. I'll have her frame one for you also. I'll tell her that. Well, we'll see you both later. I love you, too. Tell Greg we said hello. Good bye."

Kenneth walked over and retook his seat in front of Susan.

"Melissa?" Susan stated.

"Uh-huh."

"She saw it, too, I could overhear what you had to say to her."

"And do you want to know the best part of her call?"

"What's that?" she asked.

"She said they were both very proud of us."

"Well, it's not every day something like this happens."

"You can say that again," Kenneth agreed.

"When I finally wake up I think I'll get dressed, then we can head down to the store and my office. Kenneth, do you think I should make an announcement when we get there, I mean thank everyone?"

"I think that's entirely up to you, Honey, but I think the people know that already. Let's do this instead."

"What's that?"

"Why don't you and I go around to each department and thank them personally."

"That's a great idea."

"We'll do it together," he expressed. "I think it would mean more to everyone if we did it that way."

"And let's not forget to bring Melissa with us," Susan added.

"And Greg, too, after all, his secret is out now."

Susan smiled as she nodded her head. "I'm sure you're right."

"And Susan, don't forget to pack some trading materials in my lunch," Kenneth joked.

Susan bent over and kissed Kenneth on the top of his head. She then messed up his hair as she laughed again.

"You're really happy, aren't you," he expressed as he smiled up at her.

"We have so much to be thankful for, Kenneth."

"I know, Honey... I know."

The Singing Italian

"So why aren't you wearing the ring I gave you?" inquired Emma of Kate as she placed her favorite teacup back on the table.

"Emma, I love the ring, it's just that I don't want to wear it until Henry places it on my finger the day we get married."

"Ah, I see," Emma stated as she nodded her head now understanding why Kate was reluctant to wear the ring. "We've got to work on the wedding plans, get you two hooked up, as it were."

"Well, Henry and I haven't talked about a date yet, but still in all, I think you're right, we need to make plans."

Those were the words Emma longed to hear from Kate's mouth, or even Henry's, though she thought her chances were better by working on Kate.

"So what do you think? When would you like to get married, what month?" Emma asked.

"I would love an autumn wedding with the color of the trees changing, a touch of frost in the air, everything about it. That's my favorite time of year."

"It surely is a beautiful time of year, you'll hear no arguments from me. So we better get cracking, we only have a few months to work with."

"I didn't say this year," Kate was quick to state.

"Honey, sometimes waiting is not the way to go. You think, oh, I'll get back to it in a minute. It's like leaving ice cream on the counter too long, it melts away to nothing. We need to strike while the iron is hot."

Kate let out a deep breath as she shook her head.

"Emma, it's not how fast you make it to the finish line on something like this, as long as you're both in each other's hearts when you finish."

"Honey, I'm not saying you should rush it, —"

"Good," Kate stated.

"— but we still can do it in that timeframe."

"Emma, you know you're going to be a very important part of our wedding, and I want you to help us plan it. I just want to make the decisions that are meaningful to me."

"Of course. I think it goes without saying."

"It's nice to know we're on the same page so to speak," Kate added.

"Of course, and Melissa is your Matron of Honor," Emma said.

"That's right, and Kim is my bridesmaid. Greg is Henry's best man. Melissa didn't originally plan on having a large wedding party, and neither do I. She was satisfied with quality, not quantity, and that's my thinking as well.

Emma, did you call me here this morning just so we could plan my wedding?"

"Well," Emma said nodding her head, "that was my hope."

"Now that I'm here and we have that straight, let's kick a few ideas around and see what we can come up with."

"So where would you like to start?

How about where it's taking place," Kate said.

"And that's a good place to start," Emma replied as she nodded her head. "Now we're going to have to get in touch with a minister."

"That shouldn't be any problem for us since I think Pastor Phil would love to do our ceremony."

"That takes care of that then," Emma expressed.

As the two women worked together Kate kept track of everything on a pad of paper. Both were surprised at how much work even a simple wedding entailed.

"I think I want my wedding outside at Creek Side Park, if at all possible."

"Oh my, the weather could destroy that idea," Emma said shaking her head.

"Or it could be a beautiful backdrop."

Emma nodded her head once again. "I hear many weddings have taken place there. You could have a trailer or motor home brought there to get ready in," suggested Emma.

"That's a good idea. I'm sure Henry or Grandpa knows someone who will help us out."

"What would you think about putting a large tent up if the weather looks iffy. We can reserve it, and we'll have a good idea a week before if we'll need it or not."

"Great idea. Thanks, Emma," Kate said.

Emma smiled knowing Kate felt she was really helping her out, kind of like a motherly thing to accomplish. She loved being an important cog in the wheel to Kate's plans.

"So how about the reception?" Emma asked next.

"The church gym should work out fine or maybe just a restaurant."

"Henry won't really have anyone there other than me, me being his only real family, I'm sorry to say."

"Emma, I don't ever want to hear you talk like that again. You're the most important one in his life when he talks about family, and the fact that you're the only one doesn't matter. To me it demonstrates how much you mean to him. You're as much a part of his life and mine. Please don't belittle that fact. He loves you so very much, just as I do."

Emma didn't respond with any words, she just enjoyed the fact that she was considered an essential part of Henry's and Kate's life.

"Kate, I was wondering something. Do you think it would be alright if I invite Sid and his wife to the wedding?"

"Without a doubt. I also know there are some other neighbors you may want to include on that list. To tell you the truth, I was wondering whom you were going to invite. I know you have some lady friends and other neighbors who, I'm sure, would want to join us. You can invite anyone you wish, we'll just add them to our list. Obviously it's going to be a small wedding. I really don't have anyone around here to invite. Doc, I'm sure, will have some people from the hospital, but that's about it. Of course, Melissa's mom and dad will be there. Oh, and Dan and Kim's parents will be invited."

"Were you hoping for a large wedding when you were growing up? I know some girls dream about their wedding day being so filled with loved ones and lots of friends."

"Kind of. After my mother's death and father's disappearance, those thoughts didn't seem important to me anymore."

Emma reached over taking Kate's hand in hers as she nodded her head.

"No matter who is at your wedding, the size of it, whatever it turns out to be, in the end it won't matter. You'll have Henry's love, and just as importantly, he'll have yours. When Paul and I were married, you could have put our whole wedding party into a shoebox. The love you two share from that day on is what really matters. Keep that in mind, Kate."

"I will," she said as she put her other hand on Emma's.

Emma turned her head to the front door as she heard a knock.

"I'll get it," Kate stated as she got up from her chair. She made the quick walk to the front door opening it.

"Please, please come in. What an unexpected and pleasant surprise," Kate exclaimed.

"Thank you, Kate," stated Melissa as she entered the room.

The two women exchanged hugs.

"Melissa, I never expected to see you here."

"I got a call from Emma, she said you two were going to work on your wedding plans, and since I've had a little practice in that area, she thought you two could use my help."

"What a great idea, Emma. Thank you." Kate smiled. "It makes this a lot more fun."

The women sat together like three musketeers making plans to attack any unforeseen problems. Each enjoyed expressing their thoughts and ideas to one another. No suggestion was too trivial not to be given a complete and thorough discussion. Emma couldn't remember having as much fun around her kitchen table in quite some time. The time passed by incredibly fast. With a pad full of items written down, Melissa asked the women if it would be okay with them if she treated everyone to lunch.

"So where do you two want to go?" inquired Emma.

"Do you remember the restaurant you, Henry, and I went to after the trip to the cemetery," asked Kate.

"I sure do, Richard's Steak House," said Kate.

"Why don't we go there. I don't think Melissa has ever been there."

"Where we go makes no difference to me," Melissa said.

"Okay, it's settled, we'll go there," Kate said nodding her head.

The three women got into Kate's car and headed to the restaurant. The drive there only took a few minutes. Pulling into the parking lot, Kate found a parking spot not too far from the front door. She thought to herself, Emma won't have too far to walk.

As they entered the dining establishment, Emma nodded to Kate. Kate looked over into the direction Emma indicated with her nod and recognized a familiar face. It was the very same waitress that had served them the last time they were there. As they seated themselves, the waitress walked over to their table.

"I remember you two," stated the waitress, "you were here with the gentleman who sings so beautifully."

"He's my son," Emma said quickly.

"And you're his wife, I assume," the waitress said as she looked in Kate's direction.

"She isn't quite yet, but very soon we hope," Melissa said smiling.

"And your name is… Judy," Emma said.

"Oh, you remembered?" Judy stated somewhat surprised.

"No, I just read your nametag."

Judy smiled.

"Now, what can I get you three to drink?"

"I'll have a water," Melissa stated.

"Water with lemon, please," Kate said.

"A hot tea, please," Emma added.

"I'll be back with your drinks and give you a chance to look over the menu."

As Judy left the table she walked over to a gentleman standing behind the register. She stopped and spoke with him for a few seconds, and then started getting the drinks. The man stepped from behind the counter making his way over to the women.

"Hello, ladies," he stated.

"Hello," Emma said.

The other women nodded.

"The last time you ladies were here I understand there was quite a commotion that took place."

"Pardon me?" Kate said.

"I wasn't here that day, of course, but I sure heard about it. I've had people, my regulars, asking me when he's coming back. We have a small group of musicians that play here on weekends, but every once in a while we run into a problem getting them all here. Now, what do you think the possibility is of having him doing some part-time work for me, singing that is?"

The women looked startled with that question, all except for Emma. She had learned not to be too surprised when it came to matters dealing with Henry.

"So exactly what are we talking about, what's your thoughts on it?" Emma asked.

"The real problem is whether or not he's free in the evenings on short notice, otherwise there's nothing to worry about. The instruments stay here all of the time. He's more than welcome to make use of the electric piano if he wants."

"Well, he really sings mostly ballads, is that a problem for you?" Emma inquired.

"Take a quick look around the restaurant," suggested the man. "Our customers tend to be on the older side so to speak and, therefore, that wouldn't be a problem. Our crowd would prefer a good slow love song they can dance to. And just so he knows, our sound system also has a CD player attached if he wanted to make use of it. This is a card to my place, would you see to it he gets it and gives me a call?"

"I sure will," Emma said as she took the business card.

"Thank you. I'll expect to hear from him at his earliest convenience."

The man nodded to the women, then returned to his original position behind the register.

After having shared in a tasty meal, the woman went back to Emma's home. The subject of Henry's offer seemed to dominate their discussions.

"I think Henry could make some extra money to put towards our honeymoon," contemplated Kate, "or even toward another car for himself."

"You don't really expect him to get rid of his car," Emma declared, "it's one of the three loves of his life."

"Three?" inquired Melissa.

"Yes," Emma said. "There's Kate, myself, of course, and then the car."

"I'm glad you listed you and me before the car," chuckled Kate.

"So do you think he'll take the job?" Melissa asked.

"I'm going to work on talking him into it," Emma stated.

"Well, where did we leave off?" Melissa asked.

"I think with the announcements," Kate said.

As the afternoon wore on much progress had been made, more than Emma even expected. The only refreshments the women had were the hot tea Emma offered to them. However, when women plan such meaningful day in another's life, the thought of food is far afield from their minds. Their thoughts were much too cluttered with more important things to think about.

A gentle wrap on the door sent Kate to answer it. It was Henry.

"I just stopped by for a visit and you've got a parking lot full of cars out there," complained Henry with a smile.

"Just two, Henry," Kate said.

"Well, it seems like more," he responded as he placed a kiss on Kate's cheek.

Observing that Emma put her finger to her cheek gently tapping it, Henry walked over to her and did the same thing. Melissa thought to herself, Oh, why not. She then copied Emma's motion putting her finger to her cheek, tapping it slowly as well. Henry gave her a quick kiss on the cheek as the two women chuckled.

"You know these lips only have so many kisses left in them, and Kate's already reserved most of them," Henry joked. "Now, the reason why I'm here, it's almost supper time and I thought I'd take you out to eat, Mom."

Emma smiled as she looked at the two women sitting across the table from her.

"And I know just the place to eat," Emma said with a wink to the women.

"I've heard it has really good food, if you're thinking about the same place I am," smiled Melissa.

"Yes, I am. Henry, let's go there," Emma stated in a somewhat strong voice, "I never did get my chance to buy you the meal I promised you and Kate."

"Well, alright," Henry said nodding his head.

"I probably should head home," Melissa expressed, "By the time I get home and everything—"

"Spend the night with Doc and me, he'll be so happy to see you... please," implored Kate in earnest.

"I'll have to call Greg and let him know, but I know he wouldn't care."

"Good," Kate said.

"I always have a suitcase packed with extra clothes anyway, no matter where I go."

"Your mother really instilled that in you; didn't she?" laughed Kate.

Melissa nodded her head.

It wasn't very long before the party of four found themselves walking into the restaurant. Seeing the sign suggesting patrons to please be seated, they found their way to a table.

"Back already, I see," the waitress stated.

"The food is so good here," Kate responded.

"Judy, I'll have a cup of hot tea," Emma said.

"And let me see," Judy stated, "water with a lemon for you, and another hot tea for you, sir?"

"That's right," Henry expressed.

"And for you, Miss?" Judy asked.

"I'll have a cup of coffee, please," answered Melissa.

It was but a moment later when the owner of the restaurant came walking over.

"Hello, sir," he stated, as he reached out his hand to Henry. "You and I haven't met, but my name is Richard and I own this restaurant."

"It's nice to meet you, and my name is Henry."

"So I see you got my message and decided to come in person, great."

"Pardon?"

"We haven't had the chance to give him your card yet," Emma added quickly.

"I see. Henry, what would you think about coming here every once in a while and doing a little singing? I'm not talking a lot of work for you, but I hope you'd consider doing it. Of course, I'd want to hear you sing before any arrangements would be finalized."

"Well, —" Henry said, a facial expression of confusion written across it.

"My place obviously is a restaurant first, but in the evenings we have our dance floor available for patrons. Most of the people who come in here later just want a simple place to sit and enjoy one another's company and, perhaps, dance. We do have a bar, otherwise it's very low key. If you decide to we can make some type of monetary arrangements."

"Well, I —"

"Why not give it a try?" Kate suggested.

"Henry, you're here obviously, sing something so I can at least get an idea of what you have to offer me, if that's okay," Richard suggested. "I trust my help, and they told me you're very good, but still I need to hear for myself."

Henry nodded his head. He stood up and walked over to the sound system and instruments as Richard followed him.

"Here's the CD unit, this is the main —"

"Components to the sound system," Henry said nodding his head as he answered Richard's sentence. "Any song you want to hear in particular?"

"Don't you need some music?"

"It's already written in my head."

"Okay," Richard responded somewhat confused by Henry's statement, but then he wasn't a musician, so what did he know. Richard thought to himself, not only would he name one song, he'd name five and thus see if Henry could be tripped up. If he was good, great, but he felt it was better to know now than be embarrassed with a crowd of patrons sitting in his restaurant waiting for something that wasn't going to appear. Yes, better to know now if it's a mirage or an oasis.

Henry nodded his head with Richard's selections being named. He picked up the earphones, plugged them into the electric piano and began making adjustments to the piano's settings. He knew no one would be able to hear anything until he removed the earphones from being plugged in, since that's how he had set it up to begin with. Henry next turned on the speakers. Richard stepped back and then walked over by the cash register area and waited to hear if Henry was all that his employees had raved him to be. Henry slightly cleared his throat, his usual habit before singing. He placed his hands on the electric piano keys.

Over at the table the three women smiled at each other. They wanted to see the faces of the people once Henry would begin singing to them. The women knew what to expect from him, and they could hardly wait for him to start. Kate winked at Melissa, she returning the wink back. Emma smiled, being every bit the proud mother.

As the notes filled the air Henry's voice gently poured out the words to the first song. The music slowly built with a crescendo, and then gradually found its way down with every word he sang. Before anyone realized it, the music blended into another melody. The ease with which the songs were brought together was astounding, almost as if they were composed that way originally. And so it went, one song leading into another, all acting in complete harmony, all merging together as one. At one point Henry exchanged the English words with that of the Italian language. Many patrons smiled demonstrating their approval as they absorbed each and every song sung to them.

As was expected by Kate, Melissa, and Emma, the room became totally and utterly silent other than for Henry's voice and the music he played. When he finished people stood up applauding. The three women smiled. Henry nodded his head as he returned to the table. One gentleman actually patted Henry on the back as he walked by him.

"Can you start this Friday?" asked Richard.

"Well, I don't know. You know, I don't even have anything special I could wear," Henry stated.

"I don't care what you wear, bib overalls, shorts, a bathing suit, I just don't really care," indicated Richard. I wouldn't be paying you for how you look in your clothes; I just want your voice. Have you seen what some singers wear, unbelievable. Some even look like they're wearing rags. So do we have a deal, Henry?"

Henry nodded his head.

"Now as far as the pay goes," Richard said, "what I'll pay you —"

"I want to be fair with you, sir, I don't want to take advantage of you. So is it okay with you if we put it on the back burner for now, we can work it out later?"

Nodding his head, Richard said, "That sounds more than fair to me." In Richard's mind he thought, I've never dealt with anyone where money wasn't paramount in the discussions first. He liked that fact in Henry, an honest man.

"So Friday at?" asked Henry.

"How about seven-thirty, does that work for you?"

"That's okay."

"Fine, I'll see you then," Richard stated as he held his hand out to Henry. "Deal," Richard said.

"Deal," answered Henry.

The two men shook hands. Richard returned to the cash register area.

"What a night," commented Henry, as he returned to his seat.

"Oh, and Henry, my treat tonight on the meal," Emma exclaimed.

"Okay. Mom, in that case I think I'll have dessert."

Emma smiled at Henry.

"Wait a minute, did the three of you have lunch here today, you had to have," surmised Henry.

"We wanted to make sure the food met your standard for excellence," laughed Melissa.

"I'm going to see if Grandpa can come here with me Friday," Kate suggested.

"If he's not out with Jean Parker, or has plans with her," smiled Melissa.

"I think the two of them are seeing a lot of each other," Kate said as she nodded her head.

"Your grandfather is a wonderful man," Emma expressed, "and from what little I've seen of Jean, they would do well together."

"She's kind of taken control of his free time," Kate stated nodding her head back and forth.

"Wasn't it you who told Doc to ask her out in the first place?" Emma asked.

"Yes," Kate said with a somewhat sad face showing.

"You know what, I think you're getting a little jealous over her," Melissa said.

"It's just I kind of hate having to share him," Kate expressed.

"But you would be the first to want him happy; right?" Emma added.

"Of course," Kate said.

"Well, remember what they say," Emma said nodding her head.

"And what's that?" inquired Kate.

"Be careful what you wish for, after all, you asked Doc to take her out," Emma expressed nodding her head as she spoke once again.

"Like I said earlier, I just kind of hate to share him."

"I know what you mean, I hate to share Greg, too," Melissa said as she smiled.

"Does anyone want to share a dessert?" asked Henry.

"I will," Kate said.

"How about you, Melissa," asked Emma. "I wouldn't mind sharing something sweet."

"That sounds good to me, too."

With the end of their meal Emma signaled for Judy's attention.

"The bill, please," Emma stated.

"There is no bill for your meal," Judy said.

"Here we go again," joked Henry.

"Richard said the meal is on the restaurant this evening."

"Will sing for food," Kate laughed, "I've got to get that sign made."

"Well, just the same, we are leaving you a tip," Emma stated. She was a little frustrated at not being able to take her son and his fiancée out for dinner, as well as their special friend. She, however, thought it was wonderful they were treated to yet another scrumptious meal for the price of Henry's singing.

"You'll hear no argument from me," Judy said as Emma reached into her purse.

It was on that very day that another stepping stone was put into place for Henry to step onto and move forward in his life. Though he and Richard didn't realize it at the time, both of them began a journey together. As people learned of the "Singing Italian" as he was soon nicknamed, crowds quickly grew expeditiously in size. Singing in Italian on occasion, when requested, brought many people of Italian decent to the restaurant. Not only did the business fill up quickly, it became known as the place to take your loved one to. Richard, being the good businessman that he was, soon took advantage of that fact. He had the lights lowered a little more and bowl candles placed on each table. Richard also talked Henry into increasing the amount of days and time he sang.

Judy made more in tips, as did the other waitresses. She surmised Henry's songs made customers feel good and, perhaps more generous with their tip offerings. Either way, they were happy.

One day Richard, with the weather turning nasty, decided it was a good time to do some odd errands. Upon his return to the restaurant he was amazed to see people standing in line outside of the building. That fact alone was not what surprised him. People often did that to make sure they got a table for dinner and an opportunity to take in Henry's voice and, perhaps, even dance. However, what did astound him was that it was raining very heavily now. Umbrellas dotted the outside of his establishment. He thought to himself as he watched the people in line, I've got to pay Henry more, he deserves it. I think it's time to give John Steward a call, even if it hurts me in the end.

Handshake as Our Bond

Lifting his cup to his mouth, Henry took a quick sip of the hot tea. He placed the cup down and picked up his fork.

"Mom, I'm glad you invited me over for breakfast."

"It beats the breakfast you're used to making for yourself, and I know that for a fact."

"It sure does."

"Son, I talked to my lawyer yesterday, and that's what I wanted to talk to you about, to catch you up on the progress he's made."

"I hope it's good news."

"He thinks everything will come together in a month, maybe two, if things go as he plans."

"Now that is good news," he commented, "I'm frankly tired of people at the restaurant asking me my last name.

"So what do you say to them?" she inquired, knowing his strong position in that particular matter.

"I just tell them I simply go by Henry. I think some people think I'm a criminal on the run," he joked.

"And, Son, once you get your last name changed, you can change Kate's also."

"That would really be something, wouldn't it?"

"Yes, it would... Kate Morgan. I like that... Kate Morgan," she repeated.

"Mom, what would you think if Kate and I had just a small wedding? I know you've talked to Kate about it. She's talked to me, also."

"You two have actually talked about it?" questioned Emma, a surprised look on her face.

"Yes, we have."

"How wonderful it is to hear those words from you today, that you two could be thinking the same as me," she smiled.

"I should bite my tongue for saying this, Mom, but in the bottom of my heart I always liked the fact that you pestered the both of us about getting married. I knew I wanted to marry Kate, but —"

"It was the last name problem, I understand."

"But I also wanted to save money to pay for it, the wedding that is."

"I can help you out, Son."

"Never in a million years, you need to keep whatever money you have. I know you've got medical bills and such. In fact, I was going to ask you if it was okay with you if I contacted the doctors about your bills. Maybe I can help you out a little with them."

"Thank you but no thank you, Sweetheart. Doc and I have already taken care of that situation, talked it over I should say."

"I'm here if you need me."

"I understand."

"And so is my wallet."

"I know, Henry. Now, how about some more toast?"

"You wouldn't happen to have a little honey, would you?"

"Yes, I do."

"Great."

"So what are your plans for today?" asked Emma.

"Richard, the owner of the restaurant, has asked me to stop by this morning around nine o'clock."

"What does he need?"

"I don't know, he didn't say. I think it has something to do with my hours."

"You've been spending a lot of time down there."

"I know. The good thing about it is I've been making a few extra bucks," Henry said with a little nod of his head.

"Sid and Jackie stopped in and told me they went there for dinner a couple of days ago," Jackie said it was hard to get in and they had to wait. Did you happen to see them?"

"As a matter of fact I did. I even embarrassed Sid a little," Henry said smiling as he spoke.

"And how did you do that?" Emma asked.

"I sang a very romantic love song to Jackie that I told everyone was at Sid's request."

Emma laughed.

"Well, I better get going, Mom."

"Richard seems like a very nice individual," Emma said nodding her head as she reached for her cup of tea."

"I think he is."

"Oh, I forgot your honey."

"That's okay, it gives me and excuse to come back for another visit."

Henry stood up and bent over giving Emma a very light kiss on her cheek.

"Was that a feather that brushed my cheek, I didn't even feel it."

"Oh, Mom," smiled Henry as he put a bigger kiss on her cheek.

"Now that's better," she said smiling.

"Bye, Ma."

"See you later, Honey."

The door to the restaurant gently swung shut behind Henry as he walked over to the register area. Twenty or more customers sat around enjoying various selections of breakfast foods. Some waved to Henry as he walked by, he returning their wave.

"Good morning, Henry," Judy's cheerful voice stated.

"Hello. Is Richard here?"

"He's in his office. You know the way."

Henry nodded his head as he made his way to the hallway and then back to Richard's office. The door was open. Two men sat in the room, Richard behind his desk and an unknown individual in a wooden chair to his right in front of the desk.

"Henry, I want you to meet John Steward, a good friend of mine for many years."

"It's nice to meet you, sir."

"As it is for me."

"Now, Henry, the reason I asked you to be here today is two-fold," Richard started out, "and I'd like to take it one step at a time. Is that okay with you?"

"Whatever you say."

"Good." Richard got up and motioned Henry to follow him. Getting to the main part of the restaurant Richard walked right over to the dance floor section, only stopping after stepping behind the sound system.

"Henry, I know you're not working now, but would you please sing a song or two for me?"

"What would you like to hear?"

"How about something to make my patrons look forward to today," smiled Richard, not having any better idea than that to offer him.

"Can you sing a love song?" John asked.

"If you'd like," Henry said, various titles running through his mind. He thought for a moment or two trying to figure out what would best suit the two men's requests.

"John, let's you and I get out of the way."

Henry turned on the electric piano and microphone system.

"Ladies and gentlemen, if you don't mind I'd like to sing a couple of songs for you this morning."

The applause was loud for the amount of people in the restaurant. Women smiled at their husbands knowing how Henry would sing a lot of love songs. Yes, it was the females who lingered on each word Henry sang. He could see them taking their partner's hand in theirs when he vocalized soft and romantic words through his songs. Richard looked over at his friend, John, and smiled.

As Henry began playing the introduction to a song he winked at Richard as he thought to himself, a song to make his patrons look forward to the day. The words to the song, "Oh, what a beautiful morning" began to fill the restaurant. Everyone simply sat as they enjoyed what Henry's voice had to offer them. It was about a third of the way through the second song when a woman yelled out from a side table, "In Italian!" Henry smiled at her, his words immediately going into the Italian language. It was obvious to both Richard and John as they watched the women listening they were mesmerized by his singing in Italian. The faces on the men expressed their pleasure as well.

With Henry completing the song the patrons demonstrated their appreciation for his gift to them. He nodded his head as he walked over joining John and Richard. Together all three went back to Richard's office.

"Well, what do you think, John?" Richard asked.

"More than I ever dreamed," he answered.

"So it's a go?"

"Definitely, if the paperwork can be worked out."

Henry didn't know what was going on, so he did what he had observed Doc practice for many years. When you don't know what to do or say, keep your mouth shut.

"Henry," John stated, "I'm in the music business. What would you think about recording a few songs on a test basis?"

Henry looked over at Richard. Richard nodded his head slightly to one side as if indicating, "It's up to you."

"Gee, I don't know."

"If it works out, Henry," John went on, "we'll get your face on a CD, you'll make some good money, and besides that —"

"My face on a CD?"

"It's your scar, isn't it," John stated. "Do you think any of those people you just sang for looked at your scar?"

"Not really."

"Now, let's you and I take it one step at a time. First, we'll get you recorded, see how you sound in a studio."

"Can I bring my girlfriend?"

"Of course."

"Can my mom come?"

John looked over at Richard, Richard giving John a little nod of his head.

"Of course."

"Mr. Steward, I don't want you to feel I'm some mama's boy or baby, it's just that my mom doesn't get out very often and I thought it might be a chance for her to see an area other than just around here. Besides, I know she's never been in a recording studio."

"I see. I think that's a good idea, after all, I love my mother, too," John said with a smile. "Now, if things progress as I think they will, you'll need someone you trust to be your agent. So if I were you I'd find someone to handle that down the line."

"I already have someone who can do that for me."

"Oh, good. And when can I meet with him?"

Henry gestured in Richard's direction. Richard looked at Henry's hand.

"We've always done business with a handshake as our bond, and I see no reason to discontinue that now. Will you act as my agent?"

Richard smiled as he took Henry's hand.

"Thank you, Henry, this means a lot to me."

"And me, too."

The news of Henry making an audition at a recording studio spread faster than a hot flame in a parched forest. Kate called Melissa, Melissa called Kim, Kim called Dan, Dan called his parents, and so it went on, and on. Before long everyone in Creek Side knew what had happened. It was the highlight of conversations around the tables at Mom's Country Kitchen. There were, however, some who weren't so thrilled to hear the news. People who had Henry do work for them were very much concerned. Who would they find to replace him? How would they find someone as accomplished and honest, and as reasonably priced as he was? Still in their hearts they were happy he would be given this opportunity.

Within the week a number of songs were recorded. John was extremely happy with how things were proceeding, plus he got to deal with his long time friend, Richard.

"I've played some of your songs for different people in the music business, and they want me to have you go ahead and record a CD or two," John said looking at Henry.

"That's wonderful," Henry replied.

"We believe it would be advantageous for all concerned if we do a mixture of both English and Italian songs, it allows us to hit more than just one market."

Henry nodded his head.

"Now we need to talk about the cover of the CD, the title and so forth."

"What are your thoughts on it, Richard?" asked Henry.

"Well, I agree with what you said before, so I wouldn't use your face on the cover, with the scar and so forth."

"Can I make a suggestion?" John asked.

"Sure," Richard stated, as Henry nodded his head.

"Picture this in your mind," John said. "We have a picture of the state in outline form with the words, 'Country Songs with a taste of Italy.'"

"I don't know," Henry said. "I like the words, but not the picture part of it so much. And the more I think of it, it sounds like it's a country and western singer's album."

"I think he's right," Richard said.

"Oh, I think I've got it," Henry said with a little excitement. He took a deep breath, hoping his idea would be pleasing to both men. "On the front of the CD is a photograph of the Old Mill Restaurant with the words, 'Love songs with a little taste of Italy.'"

"I love it," John said, "it's like — it's like having dinner with someone you love in an Italian restaurant. The question is where do we get the photograph. I'll have to look into the stock archives."

"Actually I know someone who is in possession of the perfect picture," Henry exclaimed.

"Wonderful," smiled John.

"And I've seen that photograph, it's beautiful," Richard added.

"Would it be possible to have an e-mail address or something put on the back of the CD in case someone wanted to purchase the photograph?" Henry asked.

"I think that can be worked out," John said. "We'll have to get permission from the photographer, of course."

"I don't anticipate that being any problem at all," smiled Henry.

"Good," John stated. "So all we need to do is have you sign some papers and —"

"We don't just shake hands on this?" Henry asked.

"No, we don't, Henry," John said looking confused.

"Richard," Henry said as he turned his head in his direction.

"John, as you know Henry and I do everything with a handshake so —"

"I've never done that, but I trust you Richard, and I absolutely have no reason to distrust Henry, so —" John held his hand out to Richard shaking it, and then Henry. "Nobody would ever believe that a contract would be done in this way," laughed John.

"I've never done it any other way," Henry said.

"Well, we'll check on the photograph, see if there's any problems with using the Old Mill in the picture and then we'll take it from there," smiled Richard.

"Suggest to the people who own the Old Mill that we'll find someplace to put their name and address on the CD, that may entice them to go along with it," John said.

As the men left the room, Henry could hardly wait to tell Kate and Emma the results of his conversation with John and Richard. He wanted them to both know how their presence with him the day at the recording studio had brought him luck.

John, on the other hand, couldn't wait to express to colleagues he knew in the business about his, "Handshake Contract." He knew they would think he was nuts for doing business in that way, but he didn't care. He had faith in both Henry and Richard. John also knew they each trusted him, and he took that as a compliment. It was a trust he would not break.

Richard knew he was doing the right thing when it came to Henry, however, he felt it would cost his business in the end. Still, he could make some money being Henry's agent, though that thought didn't seem very important to him now.

Now Take a Deep Breath

It was the day Emma never thought her heart would ever see. Kate and Henry were being married, and she was more than overjoyed. The small wedding was held outdoors in Creek Side Park alongside a beautiful section of the stream. The sun was bright and warm with an occasional cloud drifting by taking in the wonders below. Colors on the trees surrounding the area presented themselves in a magnificent tribute to the day. Red, yellow, and golden leaves filled the park. A warm breeze blew through the tree leaves bringing them together as if they were applauding the couple.

Together Kate and Henry stood before friends, relatives, and Pastor Phil. Doc McDonald had just taken a seat next to Jean after walking Kate down a makeshift aisle between rows of chairs filled with well wishers. Pastor Phil thought to himself, what a beautiful autumn day, it's just glorious. After all their worry about the weather, I'm glad such a wonderful couple were rewarded with today's splendor. Pastor Phil looked up and silently said to himself, "Thank you for answering my prayers."

Henry smiled as he looked at Kate. She had never looked more beautiful. Kate's eyes, though slightly watery, sparkled from the sun as it shone down upon everyone present. The ceremony didn't take very long to conduct, perhaps a half an hour or less. Smiles were prevalent everywhere. As the wedding proceeded an occasional car horn being tapped could be heard acknowledging the event taking place. Kate and Henry would simply smile at each other when that occurred.

Susan looked at the wedding party. Melissa was the Matron of Honor with Kim standing next to her. Greg was the best man and Dan finished off the remainder of the group. As the rings were exchanged Emma sighed as she watched Henry place her "family heirloom", as she thought of it, onto Kate's finger. She envisioned how happy and proud Paul would be that Kate wore the ring as a part of their family now.

As the young couple stood in front of the people Pastor Phil felt compelled to speak to them quietly. He spoke in a voice only loud enough to be heard by the two of them.

"When I married Greg and Melissa, I told them how happy it made me inside, privileged if you will, to perform their ceremony. I wish to express those same thoughts to both of you. You honor me by allowing me to do this. Thank you both so very much."

Kate reached up slightly and kissed the pastor on his cheek. Henry extended his hand out to him as they shook.

"Thank you," the young couple said in unison.

With the wedding completed and after a short drive through town, Kate and Henry arrived at the church gym for their reception. The couple's plan was to enjoy a small wedding on a warm autumn day and then a quaint reception. Everything was falling nicely into place.

Emma waited outside the gym door for Kate and Henry's arrival. She wanted to be the first to stand in line and congratulate them. Doc and Jean stood next to her. The newlyweds were greeted by Emma, then Doc and Jean. Upon entering the gym, Kate and Henry were both astonished as they observed a complete corner wall full of gifts. They were piled high framing their wedding cake. The amount of gifts were staggering.

"Oh my, oh my," came Emma's usual comment when she first saw them.

Doc smiled along with Jean.

"Henry!" was all Kate could say, her eyes filled with the sight of ribbons, bows, and many colors of wedding wrapping paper.

"Well, I'm not cleaning all this mess up, and neither are my gals," Ruth said smiling as she walked over to Henry and Kate. "Bend down Henry so I can give you a kiss," she demanded. Ruth reached up slightly giving him a kiss on his cheek. "And you young lady are a very lucky woman to have married this man, but not nearly as fortunate as Henry is to have found you. Now, let me give you a little kiss and hug, too."

"Thank you, Ruth," Henry said, still shocked at the amount of gifts sitting before them.

"They just started coming and just wouldn't stop. I looked for a stick to beat the people off with but I couldn't find one," she laughed, "and so I gave up. Like I said, you're going to have to take them all home with you, we're not cleaning up after you."

Kate smiled at Ruth's humor. Pastor Phil walked up and placed his hand on Henry's shoulder.

"Apparently people wanted to be a part of your wedding. They knew it was going to be a small intimate one. I got many calls the last few weeks from people asking what they could do to show their love for both of you. I just simply told them to drop any gift off at the church. We've been getting them all week long, morning, noon and night. So we decided to leave a place for your wedding cake and started placing them here in the gym. It was a wonderful problem we had, where to place the next gift, the one after that, and so on. You know, I've never seen anything like this in my entire life."

Kate and Henry smiled.

"Congratulations you two," Pastor Phil's wife, Marsha, stated as she walked up. "I can see you're both stunned by all of this. You can't believe the amount of fun I had the last two weeks dealing with everyone who stopped by to drop off a gift for you two. It was unbelievable. And just so you know Kate, we were very careful how we placed each gift on top of or next to one another. Do you see that section over on the left-hand side, the package with the extra large bow?"

"Yes," Kate answered, "it's high."

"I couldn't help myself. I had Phil help me with my project since I was just so curious. I had him get up on a little ladder while I held a tape measure at the bottom. It's six feet tall there. Of course that's the highest point but still…"

Kate smiled.

"People are starting to come in, Kate. Maybe you and Henry ought to form a line or whatever you plan on doing," Marsha said.

"Thank you, we will," Kate said.

It may have been a small wedding reception, but Henry was sure the walls were swelling outward with all the love the room held for both of them. He looked around and observed Susan and Edith sitting at a table with their husbands. Edith, of course, held a box of tissue in one of her hands. Melissa and Greg visited among various tables. Dan and Kim sat with his parents. Kim's parents joined them at the table shortly afterwards.

At one point Emma approached the wedding table as Kate and Henry sat alone.

"I am at a loss for words, I just don't know what to say. My heart is filled with so much love for both of you. You have made an old lady very happy today. I know if Paul were here he'd feel the same way."

Kate reached over with her right hand as she began to roll her wedding ring around and around with her fingers.

"Emma," Kate said with a somewhat small smile, "I don't know if I would have ever been able to get Henry to be my husband if it wasn't for your interference, and your love for both of us. I owe you much more than you can ever imagine."

Tears began to form in Kate's eyes as well as Emma's.

"I love you, Emma, and I don't know if I've ever told you that. If I haven't, I'm sorry for that."

Kate stood up and walked around the table. She reached out and embraced Emma. Together the two women shared tears with one another. They held each other tightly for some time. Henry stood watching the two women in his life sharing a moment filled with love, tears, and happiness.

After Pastor Phil's blessing of the meal, it was served immediately. The six in the wedding party sat together at the head table joking, laughing, and enjoying each other's company. Emma sat visiting at a nearby table with Doc and

Jean. They sat quietly eating, an occasional conversation passing between the three of them.

"So when do we hear wedding bells for you two?" Emma inquired.

"Emma, please, not now," Doc said as he could feel the air escaping from his body in a deep exhaling breath. Doc knew every time Emma was around his emotions danced to and fro, his mind never in sync with her present. Today was no different.

"I don't know if you know this or not, Jean," Emma said, "but Kate actually asked Henry to marry him. She just got tired of waiting for him to do it."

"Really!" Jean said.

Doc just took another deep breath as he closed his eyes. Jean seeing the expression on his face silently chuckled within.

"Sometimes people wait too long," Emma stated, "they waste away opportunities to be together. They toss away chances for happiness, throw laughter to the side, miss out on lots of different things. I'm sure both of you understand how sad that can be."

"Emma, please!" came Doc's usual expression concerning her.

"Oh, come on, you know I'm right, Doc."

"Emma, please!" he repeated, his nerves starting to churn even more within his body.

"If your love is true, you'd want to be together every moment of every day; right, Doc?"

"Emma, please!"

"Yes, if it's true love, you let the other one know how you feel, your deepest inner feeling of love for them."

"Emma, please, not now!" his voice slightly elevated.

"You don't hide your true feelings, you free them."

"Now, that's enough!" Doc said sternly.

"Maybe being at a wedding will make that little spark within you —"

"Okay, that does it!" Doc said abruptly. "For many years I've listened to you state what's on your mind, you never once listening to anyone when they've asked you to stop. I know you haven't listened to me at all for many years now.

Well, now it's time to start a new strategy in dealing with you, Mrs. Emma Greene."

Jean and Emma were both taken back with his statement and brazen attitude.

"You mean I might have said something to upset you?" Emma said, acting as innocent as a child denying he ate some cookies with crumbs still lingering on his lips.

"So here's how it's going to go from now on between us. Emma, if you have something you want answered, ask it outright. I'll answer your question straight and to the point; got it? No more of this beating around the bush on my part, and especially yours. I'm tired of playing this silly game day after day. Do you understand me?"

"Good!" Emma stated firmly. "Now, about those church bells, when do I hear them for you two?"

Now was Doc's opportunity to show Emma how serious he was with her as he blurted his words out without thinking them over first.

"I have a tremendous amount of feelings for Jean. I've been falling in love with her for quite some time now. I'm going to ask her to marry me eventually, I just don't know when or how; got it?"

Emma merely shook her head up and down slowly confirming what she already knew about the couple. Doc could observe a small smile on Emma's face. Jean looked a little shocked. As he looked at Emma he began to realize what had just transpired through his words. In a moment of unyielding stubbornness with Emma, it cost him the battle. He put his head into his hands.

"Doc," Emma stated, "you haven't told Jean that yet, have you, your inner feelings for her?"

She smiled as she continued looking in Doc's direction, knowing full well Doc's approach with her had badly backfired on him. Doc, his head still in his hands merely shook it slowly back and forth.

"Well, Jean, what do you think now, are you going to cut him loose or keep him? I personally think you should keep him. For his age he's not too bad to look at, and he does make a halfway decent living."

"Emma, please," Doc said softly reverting back to his old ways.

"Well," Jean said, as she winked at Emma, "I think you're right on the looks part, but don't you think he should lose a couple of pounds?"

Emma smiled at Jean nodding her head.

"And he did say he was falling in love with me, although he didn't say he loved me for sure."

Doc now started to peek between his fingers at Jean as she continued evaluating the situation between the two of them.

"We do have fun when we're out together, and we also have a lot of things in common."

"And that's important," Emma stated nodding her head.

Doc's eyes moved in Emma's direction, although he kept his face hidden behind his fingers.

"You know, Emma, even though he only thinks he's falling in love with me, I've fallen in love with him already sometime ago."

"Are you certain?" Emma asked, "It could be a sour stomach or gas. I have heard people talking about their being more fish in the sea, if you know what I mean."

Now Doc's hands were off his face and onto the table. He still didn't say anything, continuing to keep his mouth shut, as was his custom.

"Yes, I'm in love with him," Jean said with a smile while nodding her head up and down.

"And maybe this will prove to you I do love you, too," Doc stated as he pulled Jean close to him and placed a big kiss on her lips. People sitting around them were shocked, yet getting a kick out of watching what had just occurred.

"Will you marry me?" Jean asked while laughing.

"Yes, I will," Doc said with a chuckle.

"Ah-hah, it does run in the family, the women have to do the asking," Emma expressed to them as she laughed.

Doc reached over and gave Jean another softer kiss. He then held his hand out to Emma and took one of her hands in his. Doc pulled it to him and kissed it as well.

Susan, Kenneth, Melissa, and Greg joined Emma, Jean, and Doc. Neither one of the four individuals possessed any knowledge of what had just taken place between Doc and Jean. Henry, spotting them all sitting at the table, walked over to say hello, too.

"Hello everyone," Henry stated.

"It's nice to see you, Henry," Jean said. "Your wedding was beautiful."

"Thank you," he said as he nodded his head.

"You know, I love you Emma," Doc said, "but you sure have a way of getting under my skin every once in a while."

"Only once in a while?" chuckled Henry.

"Emma really did something nice for me though," Doc said, "and I want everyone here to know that."

"And what was that?" asked Susan.

"She got Jean to ask me to marry her."

"I didn't know that," Melissa quickly stated with a surprised look on her face.

"I didn't either," Susan said.

"Wait a minute," Greg stated, "she asked you to marry her?"

"She sure did," Doc said smiling.

"I don't see a ring on her finger," Henry said as he lifted Jean's left hand with his and moved it slowly around showing everyone her finger.

Jean laughed as she went along with Henry's motion.

"Well, we haven't gotten one yet, it just happened a few minutes ago," Doc said.

"You know what this means; don't you?" Greg said with a smile.

"I sure do," Henry said.

"And what would that be?" Doc asked.

"She has to buy her own ring," Henry said. "When the girl asks the guy, she has to buy her own ring; right?"

"That's right," agreed Greg.

"Really!" Melissa said.

"So I have to buy my own ring, huh?" Jean said nodding her head back and forth.

"Let's get one at our store, Jean, that way you get an employee discount," suggested Susan. "In fact, if I go with you we can get a double discount."

"I'll tell you what," Doc said, "you buy it, and you can use my money, then we'll be covered both ways."

"That's not a bad idea," Melissa declared.

"Suppose I change my mind," Jean joked, "do I get to keep my own paid for ring with your money?"

"I would think so," Emma said.

"Now it's getting confusing," Doc said. "Let's just you and I go ring shopping Monday. I'm not on call at the hospital, if that's okay with you?"

"I have to work," Jean said.

"For something this important, you take Monday off," Susan stated.

"And who is going to cover for me?"

"How about you and me, Greg?" Susan said smiling.

"It would be fun, count me in."

"Well, thank you," Jean said.

"Do you need any help?" Emma asked.

"No, thank you. I think you've helped enough for one day," Doc said.

"Well, we better get back to the wedding table, Greg, Melissa," Henry stated.

"Yeah, you're probably right," Greg said as he stood up.

The sound of glasses clinking brought Kate and Henry's lips together. Greg stood up in what the people assembled thought to be a toast.

"Today a wonderful couple were united in marriage." He looked down at his wife and smiled. Melissa's face bore the hint of fear upon its surface. "They were both in our wedding, although in different capacities, of course. It is customary to offer a toast to the couple, but I'm not going to do that. Instead I'm going to ask someone here to do that for me, someone who loves them to no end. A person that really knows and understands both of them... Melissa."

"Oh no, Kenneth," Susan stated, "why would Greg do that to her?"

Kenneth merely shook his head from side to side slowly, fearing what would happen next to his daughter.

"Look at her face, Kenneth, she looks scared to death."

Melissa stood up next to Greg, a piece of paper in her hands.

"I made notes," she said.

A small amount of laughter was heard.

Greg sat down beside her. All Kenneth and Susan could do was to hold their breath. Together they knew what to expect from their daughter. She most likely would fall apart at any second. They understood she was terrified of speaking in public, and yet here she was attempting to do something she didn't have to do in the first place. They were proud of her, and scared to death at the same time. It was Greg now they began to have contempt for.

"Do something, Kenneth." Susan said in a demanding voice.

"And what should I do?" he answered.

On the table before Greg was a sheet of paper, an exact duplicate of what Melissa held in her hand. Greg placed his cupped hand over his mouth, his fingers slightly facing his chin so no one could see if he were to say anything. He leaned on his elbow. He spoke gently and firmly to Melissa as she stood next to him.

"Take a deep breath."

Melissa complied with his instructions.

"Now take a sip of water."

Once again she followed his directions.

"Slow and easy," were his next words to her.

"I have known Kate since we were little kids," Melissa read from her sheet. "I am so happy and honored to be here at her wedding." Melissa's eyes began to water. "The two best friends —" Melissa froze.

"Oh, Kenneth," Susan said.

"Deep breath," Greg said. "Now do one more. Good. Okay. Now start with the two best friends."

Melissa smiled half heartedly, then wiped her eyes.

"I just can't bear to watch this," Susan said as her eyes began to water. It was breaking her heart as she observed her daughter struggling. Kenneth didn't know what to say, let alone do. He reached over and took Susan's hand in his.

Greg softly repeated himself to her. "The two best friends."

Melissa continued on. "The two best friends I've ever had consisted of Kim and Kate. They were both in my wedding. We are both in Kate's wedding today." Melissa reached down for a tissue from a box that Greg had intentionally placed nearby earlier. She slowly wiped her eyes.

"How wonderful is that," Melissa said before stopping again. Her voice had a distinct quiver to it.

"Deep breath now, good. Let's count to three together... one, two, three. If we have to count again, Honey, don't count out loud; okay?"

The last sentence by Greg actually made Melissa smile a little.

Hearing Melissa counting out loud disturbed Susan immensely. "She has no idea what is going on," Susan said.

"Actually she's doing a pretty good job of it," Kenneth said.

It was Greg's firm and assuring voice to her that comforted Melissa's tightly wound emotions. He consoled her, and she felt stronger because of it.

"Take another drink, Honey, and then smile at everyone, you show them you're in control."

Once again she complied with his instructions and then continued with the toast.

"Henry, I have come to love you as a wonderful friend, even as a brother, not just as Kate's boyfriend... and now her husband. You are very precious to me."

Melissa's eyes began to water even more. She nervously reached down and picked up a napkin instead of a tissue. She wiped her eyes again.

"I keep a very special spot in my heart for you, Henry. I wish — I wish I had —"

"Take a drink of water. Do it slowly, there's lots of time. Good. Now, you left off at 'I wish I had —' "

Melissa continued as she looked down at the paper in her hand.

"I wish I had met you sooner... Henry. Kate and you are so wonderful together. When I look at the two of you I... I know there could never be more love shown between yourselves than what I've observed the last few years."

Melissa nervously started to crumple the paper in her hand as she began to tremble.

"Don't squeeze the paper too tightly or you won't be able to read it. Good. Take a deep breath again. You're doing a wonderful job, Honey."

The people in the audience could observe the difficulty Melissa was enduring with attempting to get her words out. They admired the job she was doing. Everyone understood the deep feelings she had for Henry and Kate, her words reflected that very fact, though her emotions demonstrated it even greater.

"I love both of you and want to express some thoughts concerning a few things some people may not know about you."
"You're doing a great job, Honey. We're almost done, keep it up."
"Henry takes care of his mother like... like no son I've ever heard of doing."
Melissa once again wiped her eyes.
"Wonderful, you're doing great."
Melissa looked down and observed Emma wipe her eyes as well.
"The way he shows his love to her is the same way he demonstrates it to Kate daily. It is warm, it is kind, it is —"
Melissa's voice abruptly stopped.
"Take a deep breath and let the air out slowly. Let's do it together. In... and now out. Beautiful. Don't crumple the paper anymore, it's starting to get ragged. You last said, 'It was warm, it was kind, it is —' Okay, now let's start over again."
Melissa began again, "It is warm, it is kind, it is a love we all should wish for."

Susan and Kenneth sat there stunned at Melissa's handling of the toast. Susan wiped her eyes. She felt that her daughter's emotions were being pulled too tightly together and were waiting to snap. Susan was very much concerned with the possibility of her daughter not only embarrassing herself, but more importantly falling completely apart. A distaste for Greg's actions began to fester for what he was doing by letting Melissa take his place in the toast.

"Kate, you have meant everything to me through the years. You have always been like an invisible guiding light when I needed you. When I would ask you questions, you always gave me your honest and thoughtful response. Thank you for that."

"Perfect, Honey," Greg stated reassuringly. He could see the strength building inside of her as she spoke. He was proud of her.

"I wish both of you the very best in your future together. May every day you spend together be filled with the warmth of sunshine… and each night abound with the wonderment of stars. And when those days are occasionally filled with raindrops, may a rainbow always announce your love for one another."

Melissa grabbed for the tissue box taking several in her hand as she did.

"That was so beautifully done," Greg stated. "I'm so very proud of you."

Greg removed his hand from his mouth as he looked up at Melissa, tears flowing heavily from her eyes. As she turned to Henry and Kate, she continued crying as Henry took her in his arms. Kate placed her arms around Melissa as well. Now Melissa started to sob strongly. The three of them embraced, the women sharing their tears with one another.

The audience showed their appreciation for Melissa's heartfelt toast with a showering of applause. None of them really heard the applause of the audience, being too consumed in the world of their personal surroundings to even notice.

As Greg stood up he realized Melissa had forgotten something.

"To Henry and Kate, God bless both of them," he said with a smile.

"You did a wonderful job, Melissa," Kate said.

"Yes, she did," Henry added.

"Thank you."

Melissa turned in Greg's direction and smiled. Greg nodded his head.

"Yes, and thank you, too, Greg," Kate stated.

"Pardon me?" he said.

"We could hear you both," Kate said smiling.

"He tried to be very quiet. I needed his help, I'm sorry," Melissa said.

Kate gave Melissa another big hug.

"Greg and I even practiced together. I didn't want to fall apart on your wedding day and spoil it. I asked Greg to help me because I wanted to do something special for both of you, each one of you meaning so much to Greg and me. I hope you don't mind."

"Mind... Melissa, I couldn't believe you would even attempt to do this after seeing what happened at your own wedding. For you to do this, attempt it even with Greg's help, —"

Kate's eyes began watering even more as she spoke. "— means so very much to me. Thank you. I think this is one of the most precious wedding gifts I'll ever have the pleasure of remembering when it comes to this day."

Melissa smiled.

"Melissa, can I please have your speech to put in my wedding album?"

"Of course you can."

Melissa reached over in front of Greg to retrieve his copy of the toast.

"Oh not that one, I want the one in your hand."

"But it's all crumpled up."

"I know," Kate said smiling, "and that's the one I want to keep."

Once again the women hugged.

"So Henry, where are you going on your honeymoon?" Greg asked with a little gleam in his eyes.

"We're staying home for a little while until I can raise some money. I want Kate to have something to remember and so we'll... we'll wait."

"So you're staying home on our honeymoon, Honey," Kate said, "while I'm off enjoying myself?"

Henry looked at Kate, her face reflecting one of her biggest smiles of the afternoon.

Melissa joined in her smile as well.

Henry just looked at her and Melissa, confusion written across his face.

"Well, I met with Greg and Melissa earlier and they showed me their pictures of Hawaii, all of their literature, what to do, what not to do."

"And..." Henry said.

"We're going to duplicate their trip."

"Huh?"

"I've saved enough money from your singing job, and Grandpa gave us some money for a wedding gift."

"No, he said the wedding was his gift to us, I remember him saying that," exclaimed Henry.

"But an outdoor wedding is a lot cheaper, at least that's what he told me."

Henry didn't know what to say, he was speechless.

"Well, your house or Hawaii? Buttered toast or a luau, it's entirely up to you, Honey. We can always throw the tickets away," Kate said jokingly.

"Do you think I would look good in one of those flowery shirts?" Henry inquired with a smile.

"I know you would," Kate replied. "Then it's settled, we'll go to Hawaii."

"Thank you, Honey," Henry said as he wrapped his arms around Kate and kissed her lightly.

Melissa and Greg simply smiled at each other.

Susan walked up to Greg and asked if she could speak to him alone for just a second or two. Together they walked over by the presents as if to be admiring them. Kenneth followed shortly behind them. This gave them some privacy.

"Greg," Susan stated, "I'm sorry to have to say this to you, but it needs to be said just the same. Melissa did not need to be put through that ordeal over the toast. You should have never made her do it, she's a fragile girl. You know how she was at your own wedding. She doesn't need any more of that emotional turmoil and stress in her life. I am so very disappointed in you."

"I understand," Greg stated, "but if I could explain why I —"

"I know she felt she had to give her vows and speak in front of the people at her wedding, and thank God for Kim, but there was absolutely no need for her to face these people today. I'm not very happy with you right now. What is wrong with you, what were you thinking?"

"I understand your feelings, and I am sorry you had to go through all the —"

"I don't know what to say, Greg," Kenneth expressed as he shook his head.

"I'm sorry," Greg uttered.

"This was not at all appropriate for you to do to her whatsoever," Susan stated in a very firm voice. "I never thought I'd say this to you, but Greg, I'm ashamed of you. Your wife should come first. Well, I think that's enough said on this subject for now."

Susan could see Melissa coming in their direction.

"Hi Mom, Dad," Melissa said as she walked up. "Aren't all of these presents so wonderful. I heard that —" Melissa stopped dead with her words. She looked at Greg, her mother, and then finally her father.

"What is going on?"

"Nothing, Honey," Greg said. "we were just admiring the presents is all."

"I said, what is going on?" she repeated in a demanding voice. "I've seen these looks before, I know my husband's face, what just happened?"

"Well, Honey," Susan stated, "I was just expressing to Greg that Kenneth and I thought he should have given the toast instead of you."

"Was I that horrible?"

"No, Melissa, you did very well under the circumstances, but Greg shouldn't have allowed you to be put under all of that unnecessary pressure. Your father and I could both see the trouble you were having speaking. We just wanted to let Greg know our feelings on it, that we were somewhat disappointed in him to say the least. We're simply not happy with the way he handled all of this. We just wanted him to know our feelings concerning it all."

"Greg," Melissa said, "will you please get me a glass of cold water, I think my throat is going to be dry in a few minutes."

"Melissa, —" Greg said.

"Please, Greg."

Greg turned and walked away without saying another word. Melissa took a very deep breath, trying to get her words in proper order.

"Did Greg tell you why he didn't give the toast?" Melissa asked.

"No," Susan responded.

Kenneth nodded his head back and forth.

"What did my husband say when you said you were disappointed in him?"

"He did say he was sorry," Kenneth said.

"He said he was sorry, that he was sorry," Melissa said as her eyes began to water.

"We didn't really give him a chance to speak on the subject," Kenneth added.

"He wasn't given an opportunity to defend himself then?"

"Well, no," Susan said.

"And why not?"

"I don't know, Melissa, your father and I never really gave him the chance to talk, but just the same, he shouldn't have done what he did to you."

"Has my husband ever done anything to either one of you, that has ever caused you to be mad at him, or disappointed in him?"

"Other than today, no," Susan stated.

"Do you think Greg would allow me to do anything that would make me feel embarrassed in front of people?"

"Melissa, your father and I actually are somewhat ashamed of him for what he did to you and I told him so. Say what you will, he just shouldn't have placed you in that predicament."

"Oh, Mother, no, you didn't say that to him, that you were ashamed of him?"

"Well, yes, kind of."

"We did," Kenneth stated.

Susan didn't respond any further as she looked at her daughter's face. Melissa's eyes were beginning to water heavier now, and then she began to cry. Susan had not seen her daughter cry like that since the evening when Melissa attempted to flee her father's grasp. Susan knew right then she must have done something terribly wrong, but still she felt upset with Greg's actions.

Melissa took another long breath as her parents looked at her, both wondering what her next words or actions would be to them.

"Mom, Dad, I love you both very much, but I love Greg also, and I want you to know why I'm so concerned with what you two just did to him today."

"Him, did to him?" Susan said in a somewhat angry response.

"You're the ones who should be ashamed of yourselves," Melissa stated nodding her head back and forth, "for how you both treated him. I'm so very upset with both of you right now. I just don't know what to say."

"Melissa, we thought —" Susan stated.

"Oh Mom... Dad, what you did to Greg is horrible, unforgiveable. Neither one of you really understand how much love he demonstrates to me every day in big and little ways, and today with the toast was one of those examples. You both owe him a tremendous amount of apologies." Melissa began to sob even more. "I hope he can forgive you both," Melissa stated in a strong voice tempered in tears.

Kenneth and Susan looked at each other somewhat shocked with her statements. Melissa reached up and wiped her eyes as she shook her head back and forth slowly once again.

"I wanted to give the toast for Kate and Henry at their reception, it was very important for me to do that for the two of them. I told Greg that. He didn't feel I should do it. Greg fought me all the way on it. He knew of my great fear of public speaking. He also understood I would have trouble putting words together to express my feelings for both Kate and Henry, and then do it without breaking down. When he realized he couldn't change my mind, that's when he threw his heart into helping me every day. Did either of you notice his hand in front of his mouth as I spoke?"

"I thought he was ashamed for having put you into that position," Susan uttered, now fearing what her daughter may further have to say.

"No, it wasn't that at all. When I started talking I began to tear up, my voice quivered strongly. Both of you had to have seen that. He would tell me from behind his fingers, ever so softly to take a deep breath, take a drink of water, where I had left off in my sentence. Greg encouraged me all the way through my toast, telling me how proud of me he was. He didn't just lead me through my toast, at times he literally pulled me through the rough spots I was facing. I never could have done it without him at my side."

Melissa's eyes continued watering, though her voice remained strong and clear. Susan could feel tears forming in her eyes as they made their way down her cheeks. She knew full well she had overstepped her bounds as a mother protecting her daughter, and had done a great injustice to Greg in doing so.

Susan reached out to her daughter with her arms, however, Melissa stepped back from her. This action alone by Melissa brought an incredible amount of fear into Susan's heart. She remembered her doing that same action to Kenneth, not wanting to be touched by him. Now she was doing that to her, and it scared Susan tremendously. The thought of losing her daughter now ran through her mind.

"Greg helped me with the words, though he was sure they still remained my thoughts. When I first read my little speech at home I couldn't even get a few words out before I would cry, and this with just Greg and me alone. He patiently sat with me for some time, actually working hard with me. We spent literally hours of work for me to speak five minutes in front of people who love Kate and Henry. At times Greg would stop whatever he was working on and tell me, 'It's time to practice.' He made me work hard on it.

Greg's the one who came up with the idea to put his hand up to his face so people wouldn't see him speaking to me. I don't know if Greg and I can ever forgive you for what you've done to my husband just now, but both of you had better —"

"Here's your water, Honey."

"Greg," Susan said, as she literally grabbed him around his neck and hugged him hard. The plastic glass of water fell to the floor as Greg put his arms around Susan. She began sobbing on his shoulder.

"I'm sorry Greg for what I said to you, please forgive me. I should have never said what I did. Please... will you please forgive me?"

"When will we ever learn to keep our mouths shut when it comes to you, Greg?" Kenneth declared as he shook his head back and forth. "I'm also sorry, Greg," he added, "I hope you can find it in your heart to forgive me once again."

"So is everything alright now?" Greg inquired as he looked at Melissa and her parents.

"You tell me," Melissa said, still very much put out with her parent's actions, especially her mother.

"Well, it is with me. Come here, Honey," Greg said as he stretched his free arm out to her. He then placed his arm around Melissa's shoulder as he pulled her close to her mother and him.

"Do either of you two have any problems, because I sure don't," he smiled.

Kenneth smiled at Greg.

"I love you," Melissa said.

"I know."

"And I love you, too, Greg, and I'm really, really sorry," Susan said as she wiped her eyes.

Greg nodded his head as he smiled at her. Kenneth reached over and patted Greg on the back lightly.

Greg looked down at the two women as he stated, "Honey, your parents did a wonderful thing for you just now. They showed just how much they love you and are willing to go to protect you at all cost. They love you so much that they're even willing to get mad at your husband. That's a pretty impressive love they've just demonstrated to you."

"You always look for the good side in things, don't you?" Melissa expressed through her damp eyes.

"Whenever I can."

"And thank God for that," Susan said softly. "I'm so sorry for what I said to you before."

"If you really are that sorry, and I'm sure you are, I could use a home cooked Italian meal one day as a peace offering. Remember the meal you cooked that tasted so good that my dad and I asked to take some of it home with us?"

Susan nodded her head.

"That's what I'd like, if it's okay with you." he smiled.

Greg could see Susan's face as she looked up at him and smiled slightly.

"You tell me when you want it," she said as she kissed his cheek. "And, Greg, thank you for being so understanding."

"Ah, I get that from my mom," he said, a small smile exhibited on his face.

What If

Sunday morning announced to Frank's stomach he was in for a treat, one of Susan's tasty meals and Edith's desserts. Getting up, the two of them got dressed and did some odd jobs around the house.

"What's on the dessert tray today?" inquired Frank.

"It's been some time since I've had the chance to make this," answered Edith, "but I made some apple strudel for a change."

"And are there any samples left, I hope?"

"Just a few."

"Good. You know Edith, I kid you all the time about your cooking, but you are very good... yes, impressive at it. I'm a very lucky man."

"I am, too," Edith expressed as she walked up to him and gave Frank a small kiss.

After attending church, they headed over to the Summers.

Arriving at the Summers's home they discovered Greg and Melissa were already there. The parents were welcomed into the house even before the doorbell's music drifted into silence. After the usual hugs and such, Frank and Edith stepped towards the kitchen. The smell of something tasty cooking emanated from the oven area.

"Oh," stated Frank as he lifted his arms up and pretended to walk in his sleep straight to the oven. "I can find a great meal even in my sleep," he joked.

"I'll have to try that," Kenneth said as he stood up, took a peek in the direction of the oven, closed his eyes and made his way over to it.

"To the left more, more to your left," Frank yelled out.

"You're just trying to confuse me so I don't get anything to eat."

"Caught me, huh," Frank laughed.

"I was smart enough to take a peek first, as if I really needed to," Kenneth said smiling.

"What is it that smells so good anyhow?" Frank stated as he took a deep breath in through his nose.

"It's one of Greg's favorites," Kenneth said. "Susan cooked it especially for him."

"Well, I hope I get some," Frank stated.

"I'll see you do, Dad," Greg said.

"Dad," Melissa said, "can we turn the television on?"

"We have company, Honey," answered Kenneth.

"I know, but they're supposed to be running one of the ads Greg came up with, and I want everyone to see it, me included."

"Well, I want to see it, too," her dad confessed.

Melissa turned on the television. Fortunately Greg knew the channel number along with the time it was to be aired. There was nothing left to do but wait. It wasn't very long when Greg quickly stated to everyone in an excited voice, "This is it!"

The television screen went completely black. A man's voice was all that came from the darkened TV screen. "Is this how you feel when you're lost... in the dark? What if you're late?" A quick picture of a clock's face flashed on to the screen. "What if your friend's out-of-town family is waiting to have dinner with you?" Yet another picture flashed on the screen, this time a turkey dinner set on a table. "What if you needed to find a hospital?" A picture of a man dressed as a doctor appeared. And so it went on and on, quicker and quicker pictures flashing on the screen with the same question being asked, "What if?" Finally all that filled the screen was a sea of smiling faces with the letters, "GPS" covering some of them, and then a brand name. The man's voice spoke the final sentences of the ad.

"Yes, what if. We're here for you... when you need to be there with them. And ladies, it's the perfect gift for the man who thinks he knows where he is, but is afraid to ask where that might be."

"Well, what do you think?" Greg asked.

"I thought it was cute," Susan said.

"It's different. I liked it," Frank stated, "especially the words."

"I should buy one of them for you Frank," Edith suggested.

"I've never seen an ad start out completely in the dark. That's really unusual," offered Kenneth.

"So you and Mr. Caldwell are doing okay, I gather?" asked Susan.

"He's doing better than just okay, Mom," smiled Melissa. "Greg, can we tell them now?" Melissa asked.

Greg nodded his head back and forth.

"Darn," Melissa said with a slight smile.

Susan and Edith placed the food on the table. As the families ate Edith wiped her mouth with her napkin placing it down beside her plate. She looked around the table and made the following comment.

"I thought Kate and Henry's wedding was just wonderful. The weather, it was perfect for an autumn day."

"And did you see the colors on the trees?" Susan asked.

"Oh," was Edith's response as she placed her hand over her heart and sighed slightly.

"Your meal is wonderful, Susan," Frank stated as he set his fork down, "tasty, scrumptious, mouthwatering, and delicious."

"I think she gets the idea, Mr. Food Connoisseur," Edith said.

"Did you consult a food dictionary before you came here today?" Kenneth inquired.

"Well, I was starting to run out of adjectives to describe her cooking," Frank confessed.

"No dessert for you today," Edith said.

"But, Edith, your desserts are so tasty, mouthwatering, delicious and —"

"I get the idea, Frank, I get it. You can be quiet now," chuckled Edith.

"Greg," Melissa said as she looked at him.

He nodded his head back and forth once again.

"Oh, Melissa, your toast at the wedding was so... it made me cry," Edith said. "I could tell it was from your heart, each and every word you spoke."

"Thank you, Mom," Melissa said as she smiled. "My husband helped me with it."

Melissa looked over at Greg and winked.

"Just the same, it was beautiful. I could hardly believe you could — and don't take this the wrong way, Sweetheart, but actually it amazed me that you could get through it after seeing you at your wedding."

"Greg and I practiced a lot... an awful lot."

Kenneth and Susan looked at each other, both feeling guilty for what they had done to Greg earlier.

"So let's clear the table and have some dessert," Susan suggested.

"Greg," Melissa once again said as she looked at him.

"I'll tell you what," Greg stated. "let's get the table cleared, get a fresh cup of coffee poured, and then Melissa and I want to talk to everyone about something."

Melissa jumped up, excited to get everything moving.

"Here Mom, you get those dishes over there. I'll help Mama Edith with these. Dad, and you, too, Dad, get moving, you can both help."

Susan and Edith never saw their husbands move so fast to remove items from the table, helping to put the food away as well. Melissa was the taskmaster and she wanted everything done now. Everyone got a kick out of Melissa and her no nonsense approach to getting it all put away. It was clear to all she was very excited, but why, that was the hidden mystery. Once the jobs were done, coffee in everyone's cup, Melissa instructed everyone to retake their seats.

"Greg?"

"You do it, Honey. I think you're too wound up not to be the one to do it."

"Thank you, Greg. Mom and Dad, Mama Edith, Dad Frank, many Sundays ago, before our wedding actually... in fact, we sat around this very table and discussed my grandmother and great grandmother's ability to attend our wedding. I was overwhelmed that they were here, it made me so happy." Melissa smiled as she reflected back on her words. "Anyway, Greg and I have something for all of you."

Confusion now abounded in every parent's facial expression as they waited to see what would occur next. Greg stepped from the room for a moment returning with a couple of small boxes in his hands. Both of them were wrapped in red paper, with a matching red bow. Greg walked over and placed a box in front of each couple.

"You do love the color red," chuckled Susan.

"She sure does," Edith said.

Melissa looked at the four parents as she stated, "If you would all like to open your gifts, then Greg and I can share them with you. Your surprise is within them."

As the parents looked at each other they opened the boxes. Inside each box was an envelope with a small red bow on the corner of it. As they looked at the envelope the front was addressed in handwriting to each set of the parents.

"Now, if you will open the envelopes we hope you'll find something all four of you can enjoy together," Melissa said, as she started to gently sway back and forth in excitement.

"Oh my goodness," Edith stated loudly.

"Are these real?" Susan asked.

"They better be," chuckled Greg.

As is typical when gifts are given to couples, the women are the ones who usually open them, thus leaving the man unaware at times what the gift really is. They are somewhat left in the dark. Both men wondered what the gift boxes possessed.

"What is it?" Kenneth said.

"Can I see it?" Frank asked.

"Frank, it's two round trip plane tickets to Italy," Edith exclaimed, "and they're first class."

"What, are you serious?" Frank stated in a louder than normal voice.

"Yes, it is, and we have two also," Susan said smiling.

"These are really a wonderful gift, kids, but I think you should have saved your money for a house," Kenneth was quick to say. "Don't take me wrong, these are marvelous gifts to receive, it's just that perhaps —"

"Kenneth is right," Edith stated. "It's a lovely thought, but just the same —"

"So you don't want the rest of your gift?" Melissa asked.

"There's actually more?" Susan's surprised voice asked.

"You're kidding me," Frank said shaking his head in disbelief.

"You know what," Melissa exclaimed, "I don't want to hear a single word out of any of you until Greg and I have finished with this. Does everyone understand me?" Melissa stated in a strong voice.

Greg loved it when Melissa asserted herself, seeing her coming out of her shell. As Melissa continued she looked directly at her parents.

"Sometimes family members are quick to jump to conclusions when it's best if they take a deep breath and wait and see what's really going on behind the scenes."

Susan looked over at Kenneth. They both knew who those remarks by her were aimed at, and they knew to keep their mouths shut. Better to only be burned once, Susan thought.

"Moving on," Melissa said, "If you will look in the bottom of each one of your boxes, please. It's hidden just under a flap of cardboard."

As the parents looked further into the box a check laying facedown was soon discovered. Picking it up both couples read the amount, $5000, made out to each set of parents.

"Melissa—" Kenneth began.

"I didn't say I was done. Greg, did you hear me say I was done?"

"No, I didn't, Melissa," Greg said with a chuckle.

"I'm sorry, my mistake," Kenneth quickly stated. He smiled at Melissa as she continued on with her thoughts.

"The package you have before you has a duplicate. There are actually three gift boxes all together which are the same. Each one is an exact copy of the other. The third box, however, will be delivered tomorrow to Grandma Cameo."

"Oh," was all Susan could say, her feelings very mixed at this point, as well as the other parents. None of the parents wanted to deprive their children of the opportunity to buy a home at the expense of their vacation, no matter where it may be to.

"You may have some questions," Melissa expressed, "but they'll have to wait for a few more minutes. Honey, do you want to take it from here?"

"Melissa and I have planned this for quite some time now. The tickets, of course, are self- explanatory. The money is for what money is meant for, spending. You can use it to pay for your lodging, but we do not want to hear you brought any of it back with you. You're to eat at the finest restaurants, purchase a souvenir or two, a remembrance, a keepsake, something of your choice, but it is to be used strictly for your enjoyment. Maybe you'll hear about a special tour you want to go on, either way, that's what we want you to use it for."

Edith reached up and wiped her eyes with her napkin. Once Susan observed Edith doing her customary reaction to any kind of news, good or bad, she followed her in kind as she wiped her eyes as well.

"Greg," Melissa asked, "are you going to tell them about the ad?"

"Melissa and I have put a fair amount of money away for a house, in fact, we're doing a very good job at it, thanks to my wife. The tickets and your spending money came from my working at the Caldwell Advertising Company. The fact of the matter is, we got a fairly decent check from them for our work on the ad you just watched.

When Melissa and I are at home and I'm working on a project, we spend our free time working on them together. It may surprise you to learn that Melissa came up with some great ideas on the wording you just heard in the ad. She's a very smart and clever woman, and I was very lucky to have her help on this ad campaign."

"Can I tell them about the preparations and stuff being made?" Melissa asked excitedly.

"Of course you can, Honey."

"All of you mean so much to both of us. I can't imagine — I can't fathom being without any one of you. Melissa reached up and wiped a small tear from her eye.

"Take a deep breath, you've got all day," Greg said in a soft voice to her.

Melissa not only smiled, she laughed a little out loud. She then walked the short distance over to Greg putting her arms around his neck pulling him slightly into her. She gave him a kiss. She smiled again at him before she went back to her original position.

"I can't image being without any one of you let alone all four of you, but Greg and I are willing to give it a try."

Melissa looked over at Greg as she walked over and got a box of tissue off of the counter. She then carried it over and handed the box to Edith, anticipating her need for them.

"Now," Melissa continued, "there's a couple of things you should all also know. We've contacted your brother Norm. He'll take care of your mail while you're gone and keep an eye on the house. Of course, we'll take care of yours here also."

The four parents looked at each other. They all knew this had been well planned out.

"Greg and I feel comfortable enough to take care of the store while you're gone and, besides, you'll only be a phone call away. Now does anyone have any questions?"

"I do," Edith said.

"What is it, Mom?" Greg asked.

"Why?"

"Honey, can I tell her, please?" Melissa said excitedly again.

Greg merely nodded his head in approval.

"Mom, do you remember saying how you'd love to go to Italy someday when we all sat here on a Sunday having dinner and making the wedding plans? You even mentioned needing a translator."

"Yes," Edith said nodding her head.

"Well, Greg and I thought we could kill two birds with one stone."

"I'm not following you, Melissa," Edith said as she shook her head in confusion.

"One, you and Frank get to see Italy with my parents on our dime."

Melissa really enjoyed using that phrase, "on our dime," since that was what Greg and her had heard from the parents about going to Hawaii for their honeymoon.

"Two, you'll have your own personal translators with you. Three, everyone gets to visit Great Grandma Maria. Four, my mom gets to visit with her own mother with all of you. Five, it's free. And six, — I guess there is no six. When I said two birds with one stone, I think I miscounted the birds," she chuckled.

"And the stones," Frank said laughing.

"Well, I think it was more like a flock of birds," Greg chuckled. "So does that meet with everyone's approval?"

"Can I ask you a question, Greg?" Kenneth said in a very serious tone as he placed his hand on Susan's.

"Of course."

Kenneth swallowed hard in his throat. He didn't like the possible answer his question may bring to him and Susan.

"Are Susan and I holding you back, I mean… Greg, would you be better off in your life with our daughter if we were to let you go from our deal at the store? You seem to have the world at your doorstep with the ad company. I mean if —"

"Dad," Melissa said sternly, "I told you before, Greg's not going anywhere, he's not going anywhere at all. He told me that he'd never —"

"Melissa, there's something I haven't told you yet. I just haven't found the right time to talk to you about it," came Greg's timid voice.

Melissa turned quickly to face her husband. "What is it?" she asked.

"Mr. Caldwell has requested me to handle even more work for him."

"Oh, Greg," Melissa said in a disappointing voice.

"I told him I would do more work, but my heart is with my family and yours, they come first, just as you do. So, Honey, if you don't mind spending more nights working with me… actually spending more of your free time with me—"

"What would you two say to this suggestion?" Kenneth asked. "Melissa has her own office at work. Since most of the time she gets her work done quickly you two could take advantage of that and work together on projects when you're both free at the store. Now, it's only a suggestion, but that would definitely open up your evening hours. I think Susan would go along with that idea; right, Honey?"

"What a wonderful idea, Kenneth," Susan said smiling.

"Will that work for you two, I mean, you can do two jobs at the same time and still have some time for yourselves in the evening."

"Thank you, boss," Greg stated as he put his hand out to Kenneth. The two men shook hands. "And thank you, too, boss," Greg said with a smile as he reached around and placed a kiss on Susan's cheek.

"I do have something I wanted to bring up to both of you concerning the store," Greg uttered softly. "You may not like my idea, but it's something I thought I'd like to try."

"Greg," Kenneth expressed, "I've made many mistakes in my life, some big, some small. I know some of those bad decisions involved you. I've learned to trust your judgment. So whatever it is, you do what you feel is right, and I'll live with your decisions... I trust you that much."

Frank reached over and laid his hand on Edith's shoulder. She looked at him and smiled. Greg looked over at Melissa, a smile adorning her face.

"You're not allowed to sell the store, you realize that?" Susan joked.

"Even if I can get a halfway decent price for it?" expressed Greg jokingly.

"Only a halfway decent price?" asked Kenneth.

"Well," Greg continued, "don't worry, it won't be that big of a deal, but still..."

"Now I am a little worried," Kenneth said.

"I'll tell you what, Dad, why don't I approach my idea while you're enjoying Italy, that way I won't feel like you're looking over my shoulder. Is that okay with you and mom?"

"You're in charge to do whatever you want, but Melissa is still the boss while we're gone," Kenneth stated.

Melissa smiled at that thought.

"Say Kenneth, what's the fishing like in Italy?" Frank asked.

"That's something we'll have to explore," he said.

"We'll be kind of like Lewis and Clark, only in Italy, but which one am I?"

"Take your choice," Edith stated.

"Can I say one more thing?" Greg asked.

"Of course," Edith said.

"Why yes," Susan added.

As was usual with Frank and Kenneth, they just nodded their heads.

Greg looked in Melissa's direction as he winked at her.

"What I wanted… what I wanted to say —"

"Take a deep breath, maybe a drink of water," Melissa said laughing as he spoke.

Greg smiled as he said, "avere un buon tempo."

"What does that mean?" exclaimed Edith loudly.

"Have a good time," Susan replied in a surprised voice.

Frank smiled at Edith as he exclaimed, "ti amo."

"And exactly what does that mean, Frank?" Edith declared again.

"I love you," Frank proudly stated.

"Now I have to learn Italian just to speak to my own family," Edith uttered as she shook her head back and forth. "I know Melissa taught Greg, but who taught you, Frank?"

"Kenneth has been giving me a few lessons on the side."

"Susan, I need some instructions also," Edith was quick to say.

"I'd be glad to."

"Susan, you and I definitely have to talk, and don't you even count on sitting with your husband on the plane, you'll be too busy teaching me the language as I sit right beside you," Edith stated.

"We can talk fishing," Kenneth suggested.

"Good idea," Frank said.

Much of the rest of the afternoon was taken up with discussions of what clothes to pack, where they would visit, tourist traps to avoid, etc.

"Kenneth, what would you think about staying with my grandmother for a few days?" inquired Susan.

"What a wonderful idea," he answered.

"Listen," Edith was quick to say, "I wouldn't want to put anybody out, and besides the kids gave us money for lodging."

"Edith," Susan said with a smile, "you know you can trust what I have to say, so please trust me on this. You'll love staying at my grandmother's home."

"Well, if you say so."

"Let me worry about that part, okay?"

"If you say so." Edith responded again.

"Good."

Sitting on the couch in the living room Melissa and Greg sat back holding hands as they listened to their parents batting back and forth different ideas. Greg gently massaged her hand with his thumb. Melissa released her hand from Greg's as she cuddled into his shoulder. He placed his arm over her shoulder. She lifted her hand taking his in hers.

"You really came up with a great idea, Honey," Greg said as he squeezed her hand.

"Thank you, Sweetheart."

Greg reached down and kissed the top of her head as he pulled her closer to him.

"I need to ask you something, Greg," Melissa said as she turned her head in his direction.

"What's that?"

"Yesterday at the reception when my parents literally attacked you, you didn't get mad. What were you thinking when this all went on, especially since they didn't give you a chance to explain or defend yourself?"

"Sometimes you need to look at why something is happening instead of just getting upset at what is happening to you. Do you follow me?"

"I think so. My mom and dad were mad at you, that was very evident to me."

"And the reason for that was?" Greg asked.

"Because they thought you were putting me through something I couldn't handle."

"That's right. And the reason for that was?"

"Because..."

Greg nodded his head at Melissa.

"Because they love me so much."

"Exactly."

Melissa reached up and kissed Greg.

"And when did you come up with all of this analysis anyway?"

"Actually I have you to thank for that."

"What!"

"When you told me to get you a glass of water it gave me the time to put two and two together, so to speak. Sometimes you need a few minutes to think things over, and you gave me that precious time."

"So I was pretty smart to do that," she laughed.

"You sure were."

"Honey, I love you."

"I know… and I love you, too. But do you want to know something else just as important?"

"What's that?"

"Everyone in the next room loves you and me an awful lot, too."

Melissa smiled with that thought as she once again cuddled into Greg's body.

Wrapped In Red

With the parents expressing to the kids in a phone call they had arrived safely in Italy and were having fun visiting with relatives, Greg took the first step in his plan. He went to see the new boss.

"Good morning, boss," he said with a smile as he walked into Melissa's office.

"Good morning, employee," she laughed.

Greg walked behind her desk and gave her a small kiss.

"Now, can I get a raise?"

"No, but if I were you I wouldn't give up trying to influence your new boss."

Greg reached down and gave her another quick peck on her cheek.

"Honey, I'd like to show you something when you've got some time."

"I've got time right now," she replied.

"Remember when I told your parents I wanted to do something concerning the business while they were gone?"

"How could I forget? I was going to ask you on the way home what it was all about, but I was actually just so tired I simply forgot."

"I think you were tired because of all of the excitement with the gifts and all."

"Probably so. I was just too tuckered out."

Greg handed Melissa a manila folder he had in his hand. Melissa opened it and began reading. Greg said nothing as he watched her perusing the interior of the folder. He understood the facial expressions she demonstrated on her face. He thought he probably exhibited the same ones when he first read the interior contents of it.

"This is so sad," she stated as she closed the folder and pulled it up against her chest, her arms wrapping around it. "What are you thinking? I know you have some thoughts on this otherwise you wouldn't have gone this far with it. You have his complete background, schooling, family, everything. It's just so sad."

It was obvious to Greg that Melissa was bothered by what she had read, and so he tried to brighten up the atmosphere just a bit.

"Well, I thought I'd ask the smartest and most beautiful woman in the world for her help," he said smiling. "Now do I get a raise?" he chuckled.

"No, but as I said before, don't quit trying."

"Melissa," Greg stated in a serious voice as he pulled out a chair and sat down, "do you have any ideas at all on how we can find a place in your family's business for him? I'm at a complete loss."

Melissa slowly nodded her head back and forth, clearly in deep thought.

"The problem as I see it is two-fold. First of all, he's very qualified to do a job, unfortunately that job belongs to my mother."

"Maybe we could replace her in part."

"Replace her!"

"Not literally, but make her wish she had more time to do other projects, give her a different job to love."

"Such as?" she inquired.

"Well, do you remember last winter how hard she worked on setting up the coat drive for the community?"

"Yes, and she even complained she needed more time to put some of her ideas into place."

"And don't forget last spring and fall, the food drives she initiated. Your mother did a wonderful job putting it all together."

"Well, we'll just have to convince her she could be the community charity person, or whatever, so to speak."

"Hmmm," Melissa said softly.

"You know what Honey, we're getting way ahead of ourselves. What if the guy doesn't want a job anyway? What if he's lazy, though the information in that folder wouldn't indicate that at all. Maybe we're wasting our time, but until we have a place for him, that he wants to take advantage of, we're just spinning our wheels."

"Well, Honey," Melissa said, as she reached across the desk taking Greg's hand in hers, "let's work on the job part first, that's the most important part to our puzzle. If we can accomplish that, and he's the person he appears to be, the rest will all fall into place."

"And that's why you're the boss," Greg said as he got up and placed a quick kiss on her cheek. Greg turned and walked out of the office, his mind beginning to whirl with different concepts on how to handle the problem at hand.

Never in her wildest dreams had Edith enjoyed a trip so much. Frank, on the other hand, not only loved the beauty the country had to offer, he savored every morsel of food. Italian was becoming one of his favorite foods. Of course with Frank, if he was in Germany or Ireland that, too, would quickly become one of his favorites.

"You can actually taste the love in the food," Frank once said at a meal, but was quick to add that it wasn't as good as Susan's. Susan, of course, smiled knowing Frank to be what he was around the dining table, one who just enjoyed good tasting food, whatever it may be.

When eating a couple of meals prepared by the three women, Maria, Cameo, and Susan, it was Frank who always was the first to loudly praise their cooking. Cameo and Maria soon fell in love with Frank's comments about their cooking. Yes, Frank had a smooth way with words when it came to food, and the women loved making sure his plate was always kept full.

One evening the group retired to the patio to soak in the remnants of another beautiful day.

"Susan," Edith said as she smiled in her direction, "your grandmother has such a beautiful home. I had some reservations about staying here, perhaps putting her out, but it's almost like I'm staying in a lavish hotel. And her garden is so gorgeous. I just loved walking around it with her. You know, when we took that stroll yesterday neither one of us needed an interpreter, the plants and flowers did all the talking for us. And when we went into town, the architecture of the city took my breath away."

"I think the thing that stuck me so much about this visit," Susan stated, "other than visiting with my family, was when Kenneth was able to get tickets to the opera. You could see my grandmother absolutely loved it. She even whispered in my ear she thought Henry was all as good, if not better than the performers that sang that night."

"Even I enjoyed it," offered Frank.

"The tickets were quite expensive," Kenneth said, "but that's what our kids wanted us to do with the spending money, spend it as Greg stated."

"If I may say this," Cameo said, "you've done a magnificent job raising your children, all four of you. You should all be very proud."

"We are," Frank said.

Susan and Kenneth nodded their heads as they smiled at Cameo.

"Thank you, Cameo," Edith said.

"I felt so honored when I received the gift of this trip from your children," Cameo expressed. "Actually I looked it over and over, it was too good to believe, and first class tickets nonetheless. To even receive spending money, I was so taken back by that. I called Melissa and Greg right away. Greg answered the phone. I asked him why they had done this for me. He basically said it was a subject that came up in their discussions. They had talked it over and he wanted to do something special for his new grandmothers. He said Melissa joined him in that desire also. He even told me it was Melissa's idea originally."

"Greg lost his grandparents at a fairly young age, I understand," Susan said, "and Melissa wanted to share both of hers with him."

Edith nodded her head with those words being spoken by Susan.

"That's so sweet of her," Cameo said with a smile. "You must be paying them very well at the store."

"Cameo," Kenneth stated, "none of the money they spent came from us for any wages they earned from their jobs at the store. Together the kids earned the money from a side job Greg has. He shares all the credit with Melissa. She loves working with him and spending as much time together with him as she can get."

"It must be some kind of a side job to do so well."

"Greg is a very intelligent young man," Kenneth said, "and as I said, the two of them work together at times. He's even mentioned to all of us how proud he is that the two of them have had the opportunity to join forces. Greg doesn't sit there and take any accolades without including her in them. I respect him for that. I wish I had seen that in him sooner. He deserved that much, if not a lot more from me."

Frank and Edith looked at each other as Kenneth spoke, very proud of their son, and their daughter-in-law as well.

Susan got up and went into the home for a short time. When she returned, she carried a large tray in her hands.

"And who would like a tasty treat?" asked Susan as she came forward with a tray consisting entirely of Italian desserts.

"Me," Frank said as he quickly jumped to his feet taking the tray from her.

Maria and Cameo laughed as they watched Frank. Yes, they loved having him around, especially at mealtime, or in this case, snack time. He was that spark that made sharing meals together fun.

"Do you realize, ladies, our vacation time is almost over?" Kenneth said shaking his head.

"Oh," Edith reflected sadly.

"I'm actually looking forward to seeing the kids," Susan expressed.

"So am I," confessed Edith.

"Me, too," Frank said.

"Oh, my gosh," Edith said in an excited voice, "I almost forgot the gift for your grandmother, Susan."

"What!" declared Susan in amazement.

"Greg and Melissa didn't know what they should do concerning your grandmother. They both wanted her to have something also. Wait here, I'll be right back."

Edith quickly rose from her seat and made her way into the house. She was gone a few minutes before returning with a small flat box in her hands. The gift was wrapped in red paper with a red bow on the front of it.

"Well, I know who wrapped the gift," laughed Susan.

"It's kind of a tell-tale thing with her; isn't it," smiled Kenneth.

"Actually Melissa gave me the gift unwrapped along with the bow and paper," declared Edith. "She was worried they'd open it at the airport if it was wrapped and maybe break it or something might happen to it, so she gave me everything I needed. I was put in charge of making sure this made it to Italy safely and that it be handed to Susan, so here you are. I was instructed, however, by our children that you were to say something nice to Maria, and tell her how much they love and miss her."

Susan took the gift and smiled as she turned to her grandmother.

"Grandma," she stated in Italian, "this gift is from Melissa and Greg. It is their wish for you to know that they hold you in their thoughts daily, and love you very much."

Susan handed the gift to her grandmother. Maria smiled as she took it in her hands. She held it for sometime as she rubbed her hand gently over the present. It was more than obvious to everyone she appreciated this treasure, whatever it may be. It was also evident for all to see that Susan's words to Maria about her great grandchildren, meant a great deal to her. And now for them to remember her with a gift, brought a smile to her heart. Maria took a look around at the happy faces as she began to unwrap the present. Her hands slightly trembled from her age as she took on her task. Pulling back the paper it revealed something in tight plastic wrap. Actually she noticed there were two items concealed in the wrapping paper. As she pulled them from the wrappings, her hands revealed two CD's.

"They are CD's from your American singer," she stated proudly in her Italian tongue.

"Yes, they're CD's from the singer at your great granddaughter's wedding," answered Susan in Italian.

Maria went on as she expressed herself in her Italian voice.

"Such a thoughtful thing they have given me. I can now show my friends how beautifully he sang at my great granddaughter's wedding. I can hardly wait for them to hear it. So wonderful is my precious gift from them," she smiled, her eyes having a slight haze to them.

Susan reached down and gave her grandmother a gentle hug. Cameo and Kenneth quickly joined them. Frank and Edith stood up from their chairs and walked over to them. They all joined together in a group hug.

"I'm going to miss her so much," Edith declared, as she wiped her eyes, and then blew her nose. "Tell her that for me, will you, Susan?"

"I think she already knows that, but I will just the same."

After a short time had passed the group decided to move indoors with the wind making a cool and abrupt change in direction. Kenneth took the CD's from Maria and opened them for her. Maria placed one of the CD's into her player and began listening to Henry's tenor voice. Once again it captivated her as she listened. Henry's songs were both English and Italian in nature.

Maria sat in her chair slowly rocking back and forth as she took in every note that was sung. At one point there was the usual brief silence between the two songs. Much to Maria's surprise her favorite song, "Nessun Dorma," had been placed on the CD. Susan watched as her grandmother placed her crossed arms over her chest, her eyes beginning to water as Henry's voice filled the room. Maria's mind was quickly drawn back to the night of Melissa's reception. It was as if she was reliving that evening, every second in all its glory. The song rekindled every precious emotion she had enjoyed so much that night. Tears began to freely escape the corners of her eyes as they slowly ran down her cheeks. Everyone in the room couldn't help but watch Maria, her face telling them of the wonderful feelings she was experiencing. They all had observed how happy Henry's singing of the song made her feel the evening of the reception. It was not just Maria who was soon feeling that same way. The memories of that night came flooding back to each and every one of them as well.

Maria stood up and walked over to the player once the song came to an end. She hit the button that allowed her to replay the song. Maria then turned the player up somewhat louder. Susan thought this was because she wanted the neighbors to hear his voice as well or, perhaps, expecting them to ask whose voice it was. And if they did, she could tell them once again about her beautiful great granddaughter's wedding, and of Henry singing for them at the reception. Either way, she would win.

Heads I Win Tails You Lose

Henry and Kate smiled as they walked towards the front doorway to their home. They had just returned from an exciting fun-packed two-week honeymoon. Henry had never had this much time away from his tools in his whole life. There were occasions when he felt guilty about it, but when he experienced the warm sand seeping between his toes, or looked at Kate in her blue bathing suit, those thoughts quickly disappeared. It was the most enjoyable time either one had ever experienced in their lives.

Kate had travelled extensively on vacations and on family trips, but with Henry, it was a different story altogether. He never had the time or enough of a fortune to do anything that extravagant. The world Kate introduced him to was at odds with anything he had experienced in his adult life, let alone in his childhood. In Hawaii, there was time to share quiet times together watching a sunset. It was a world strange and beautiful to him.

When they went somewhere and an occasional person looked at him funny, he never questioned it. He knew that perhaps it was his scar, but chose to believe that it was merely because he had such a beautiful woman on his arm and they were simply jealous of him.

The flight home was long and tiring. Henry's favorite part of it was when Kate would drift off to sleep and lay her head on his shoulder. He would gently lay his head on hers and occasionally drift off to join her in quiet slumber. Once the plane landed, their suitcases retrieved, they picked up Henry's car and were off to their home.

As they reached the front door, Henry set his suitcase down, grabbed Kate in his arms lifting her high. They were face-to-face smiling at each other as he held her tightly.

"I understand from old movies it's a tradition for the groom to carry the bride over the threshold," he smiled.

"And who are we not to carry on that tradition," laughed Kate.

Kate reached down and opened the door as Henry carried her into their home.

Once things were settled, Kate was biting at the bit to go and see her Grandfather. Henry, on the other hand, wanted to visit with Emma.

"So who do we visit first?" Henry inquired.

"Let's flip for it," Kate stated as she reached into her purse for a coin.

"Okay. Go ahead and flip it."

Kate took the coin and placed it into the flipping position on her hand.

"Heads I win, tails you lose," she laughed.

Henry smiled as she flipped the coin into the air.

"What is it?" he asked with a small smile on his face.

"Tails."

"Well, I guess it's off to see Doc first."

Kate smiled at Henry. Every time there was a dispute on where to go, what restaurant to eat at, Kate would retrieve a coin and end up flipping it through the air making the same declaration, "Heads I win, tails you lose."

Kate knew Henry was smarter than to fall for that every time, and the fact she got away with it reminded her that he'd let her win no matter what. It really didn't matter to Henry, he knew he could never say no to her anyway.

"Well, let's get over there and surprise him," Kate exclaimed.

Henry just smiled.

There were numerous things that Kate loved about Henry, things he never knew about. One such item was that Kate felt protected just by his presence, and she loved that. Henry always treated her like a princess, another small but precious reason she carried him in her heart so tightly. Her wellbeing and happiness were all he really cared about, other than Emma's, of course. How he worried and looked after Emma was another reason to love him. A simple coin toss, she thought, just another item in a long list of why she adored him so much.

A soft knock on the front door revealed the presence of someone stopping by. Opening the door Henry was happy to see Sid and Jackie on the porch.

"Come in, please," Henry was quick to state to them.

"Thank you," Sid said, as they entered the home.

"Henry, Kate, do you have a minute?" Jackie inquired in a somber tone.

"Sure," Kate responded with a questioning look upon her face.

The two couples moved into the living room section of the house.

"We're glad to see you're back safely. How was your trip?" Sid asked.

"Sid," Henry said as he looked at Sid's expression, "you're not here to talk about our trip, I can see that on your face. What is it?"

"It's about Emma," Jackie uttered.

"Is she okay?" Henry was quick to ask.

"She's fine. While you were gone, Emma had a small relapse with her heart."

"I've got to go and see her," Henry frantically stated as he began to look for his keys. "Where are my keys, Kate, I can't find them."

"Henry, stop it!" Jackie said loudly as she grabbed him by the arm. "Stop it right now, please. Henry, Emma is safe at home and actually doing pretty well. She spent a couple of days in the hospital and now she's at home resting."

"I shouldn't have left her and gone on the honeymoon," Henry uttered.

"That's silly, very senseless to say, and I know that's what Emma would say about that. Now don't you go and make this any worse than it already is, do you understand me?" Jackie said as she pulled Henry to her with his arm. "I've gotten to know Emma very well. She is a proud woman. If she heard you say that, it would break her heart, and she's had enough trouble with it as it is."

Henry looked at Jackie not knowing now what to say. Kate walked up to him and put her hand between his arm and body.

"Sid and I watched over her like a hawk. We were never far away from her," Jackie expressed to them.

"Thank you," Henry softly uttered. He reached up with his hand and wiped a few tears away.

"Now here's what you're going to do. You and Kate wait until tomorrow and then you go and visit her. Act as if nothing's gone on, and remember she's a smart woman, you can't just fool her with simple words. She reads people's faces like a roadmap."

Henry and Kate nodded their heads knowing how truthful that statement was.

"I know I can't get away with anything with her," Sid said. "Remember when you were in the hospital and I wasn't supposed to let her know about it and — nope, she could read me like a gas meter."

"It's like an open book, Sid," Jackie was quick to say. "It's not that I want you to hide the fact that you found out she was in the hospital while you were gone, I just don't want you to say anything about you shouldn't have gone, that's all. I think it would be better for her not to hear that from you at all. Henry, am I making sense?" Jackie inquired.

Henry nodded his head.

"Jackie, I don't know how we can ever thank you and Sid," Kate said as she walked over and gave Jackie a half hug.

"Now that we've explained why we're here, I wouldn't mind something to drink," Jackie stated with a small smile.

Together the couples sat down. They talked about the honeymoon and the fact that Henry watched out for sharks per Greg's suggestion. Jackie and Kate tried to keep Henry's mind off of Emma, but both knew that was like trying to pick fruit from a fruitless tree. After about an hour or so Jackie and Sid bid the newlyweds good-bye.

"I think we should go and visit Doc," suggested Henry.

"Are you sure, Honey?"

"Yes. It will be good for you to see him, and tomorrow we'll go and visit Emma, just like Jackie suggested."

"Are you alright, Henry?"

"Yes. I learned today that people are out there to watch over Emma like me, and that makes me feel so good inside. Actually I'm comforted with what I heard this afternoon from them."

Kate walked over to where Henry was sitting on the couch and sat beside him. She leaned down into his waiting arm as she cuddled into him.

"Let's wait a couple of minutes and then we'll go."

Henry nodded his head as he kissed the top of Kate's head. She reached over with her free hand and took his in hers. She gave it a gentle squeeze.

Upon arriving at Doc's home, the first words out of Henry's mouth concerned Emma's wellbeing. Doc's words were right to the point, not wanting to hide anything from him. His appraisal of the situation comforted Henry greatly. To his surprise, he was much more relieved than he ever would have anticipated being.

Fortunately for Henry, their visit at Doc's home was upbeat. Kate worked hard making sure the conversations moved along with no lag time or spaces between the subjects. She knew Henry's mind would be elsewhere, and her intent was to keep him as distracted as much as possible. Her plan seemed to be working quite well as she noticed Henry smiling more and more with every sentence that was exchanged between the three of them. The fact that they had just returned from their honeymoon opened a door wide open to a room filled with a large assortment of subject matter.

The next day the couple drove over to Emma's home. Walking up the steps they were greeted by her at the front door. Henry could see she looked tired and not her usual self. He thought her gait was slower as she walked to the kitchen area.

"So Mom, did you miss us?"

"With every breath I took," she smiled.

Henry looked at her face. To his eyes she didn't look quite right, not sharp in appearance. Sitting down at the kitchen table, Emma turned to both of them as they joined her.

"So how was your honeymoon, beautiful I imagine."

"It was so wonderful," Kate said. "Emma, both of us missed you so much." She smiled at Kate.

Kate could see the difference in her appearance also, a slight thing here, another small item there. Her fingers showed a slight trembling to them that she hadn't noticed before.

"Paul's ring looks beautiful on your finger," Emma expressed.

Kate reached over and took Emma's hands in hers.

"I've gotten to love it more with each passing day. I don't know how I can ever thank you and Paul for it." Kate wanted Emma to know she felt Paul had played as an important part in giving of the gift to her as Emma did.

"Kate and I have some things that can't wait to be done until later," Henry said. "We're going to leave you now, but we'll be back again shortly." Henry could see that Emma had her bathrobe on and was either just getting up or perhaps was preparing to lay down. Either way, he thought she needed some peace and quiet.

"Well, you just got here."

"I know, Mom, but we'll be back real soon."

"Well, in that case I think I'll take a little nap."

"You do that. Like I said, we'll be back real soon."

Henry bent down to one knee as he reached over and kissed Emma on her cheek.

"So can I give you one of those, too, Mom?" Kate stated as she reached over and placed a small kiss on Emma's other cheek.

"You called me, 'Mom,' Kate."

"Did I?"

"You certainly did," Emma said as she nodded her head.

"Well, good," smiled Kate. "I'll see you later... Mom."

Emma smiled once again.

Henry and Kate turned and waved slightly before going through the door. Once in the car neither one of them spoke. They just tried to comprehend what they had just observed concerning Emma's condition.

With the phone ringing Pastor Phil's wife, Marsha, was quick to answer it.

"Hello," she stated.

"Is this Pastor Phil's wife?"

"Yes, it is."

"Good. This is Greg Wilson."

"Nice to talk to you, Greg."

"The same here. I was wondering if it is possible for you and your husband to have lunch with my wife and me this afternoon. I know this is very short notice but I wanted to talk to you both about something, pick your brains so to speak."

"You mean today?"

"Yes, if it's at all possible. However, if that's out of the question —"

"No, today is good," she replied as she looked at the date book sitting in front of her. "Where do you want to meet?"

"Well," Greg said thinking for a second, "how about Richard's Steak House? I haven't been there yet and I hear it's got very good food."

"That's fine. It's now ten forty-five, how about eleven-thirty or eleven forty-five?"

"Great. Oh, and just so you know, it's our treat."

"That isn't necessary."

"Just the same, our treat."

"My husband and I never turn down a free meal," Marsha joked. "We'll see you then."

"Good-bye."

"Good-bye."

Melissa and Greg sat at a restaurant table awaiting Pastor Phil and his wife to arrive.

"Hello, Melissa," came Judy's voice.

"Hello," she answered. "You remember my name, that surprises me."

"Well, any friend of our Henry's I try to keep their names close to my mind and lips," she chuckled. "Let's see, coffee for you, Melissa."

Melissa smiled at Judy's good memory as she nodded her head.

"You remembered?"

Judy nodded her head once again.

"Just coffee for right now, please," Greg added. By the way, we have a couple that will be joining us. Please put their food on my bill if you don't mind."

"I'll be glad to."

"Thank you."

"Oh, they're here," Melissa said, as she waved to the pastor and his wife as they stood by the door.

Once seated, Pastor Phil asked Greg what he could do for him.

"Let's wait until dessert, we can talk it over then, if that's okay with you?" Greg said.

After the ordered meals were placed in front of each customer Pastor Phil said, "Shall we pray."

Greg had prayed at home on numerous occasions, but Melissa was not as accustomed to it, especially out in public. Edith and Frank usually handled that when at Melissa's home or theirs. She felt a little uncomfortable which Pastor Phil could readily see. He made his prayer short and to the point.

The four sat eating their meals while enjoying the company the others had to offer. They talked about the Christmas Program of a few years ago and how much it had impacted different people's lives. Pastor Phil believed his sermon from just that night alone was the best he had ever given in his life. His wife readily agreed with him.

Melissa disclosed how Greg and she had met that night, how they fell in love over that very weekend. Marsha was taken by every word she heard, having a soft spot in her heart when it came to the subject of love. Marsha had very strong feelings for her own husband along that very line as well.

Once dessert had been placed upon the table, Greg started out by getting right to the heart of his thoughts.

"Why I wanted to talk to you is really quite simple and hard at the same time. My mother-in-law is a very generous and thoughtful woman. She reaches out to people who are in need, whether at work or in the community.

What I want to do is take her full-time job and convert it into a part-time one. Then I hope to channel her energy into some type of charity work, you might say. I guess what I'm trying to say is, what do I say to her to convince her to do that without making her think I'm trying to get rid of her? It's not my intent to hurt her feelings in any way."

"And the reason for that is what?" Pastor Phil asked.

"I know somebody who needs a job badly, and the job he's qualified for the most is my mother-in-law's. I want to get him hired part-time, if possible, but not hurt Susan's feelings in anyway."

"That's an interesting dilemma you have there."

"Yes, it is," Marsha agreed.

"First of all, I commend you for your feelings for this other person." Pastor Phil thought the problem over for a moment. "I'll tell you what I do when I'm faced with something I don't know how to handle, and it usually works for me."

"And what's that, Pastor?"

"It's like you're driving down the road and you realize you're going a little too fast. You look ahead and see a police car timing off to the side. I've found it best not to worry about it, just approach your problem head on. If he's got you, he's got you. Most times they're looking for someone going faster than you are anyway. So don't worry about the officer, just go on and let what happens happen. Don't beat around the bush with Susan, so to speak, just move ahead. Be frank with her, tell her exactly what's in your heart, what you want to do and why. The truth can be an awfully strong tool to use when dealing with people. Individuals basically want the truth to be told to them, whatever that may be. Besides, you may be surprised with some wondrous results. Just make sure you do it with a tender tongue."

"So you got stopped by a police officer?" joked Greg, "otherwise I don't think you would have used that analogy or comparison."

"Well, I simply told him I was on the way to a funeral and was running late. He let me go."

"That's a pretty good excuse to use," Greg smiled.

"But the thing is, Greg, it was the truth. Do you see what I mean?"

"I sure do. Thank you, Pastor."

"Take your predicament and face it head on."

"Kind of like grabbing the bull by the horns?"

"Exactly. A lot of times it's the best way to approach any problem."

"Thank you."

"You're welcome, and good luck."

Greg nodded his head.

"Say, Greg, can you let me know how you make out with this in the end?"

"Sure."

Marsha looked at her husband and smiled. "You're working on another sermon, aren't you?"

Pastor Phil never answered his wife, but his smile told Marsha tons. After finishing their desserts, Pastor Phil and Marsha excused themselves and left. Melissa and Greg remained seated at the table. Judy brought over their bill.

"I'm going to do exactly what he suggested," Greg said nodding his head.

" I wonder what my mom's reaction is going to be?" Melissa stated.

"We'll find out, won't we?"

"We sure will. So what's your contingency plan, if any?"

"I don't have one. I guess it will be what it's meant to be."

Greg picked up their bill, placed a tip on the table, and the two of them walked up to the cashier's area.

"Honey, this is where I got the two CD's for my great grandmother."

Greg handed the bill along with his money to the gentleman behind the register.

"Hi, Melissa," he stated.

"Hello," a somewhat confused Melissa answered him. Then she recognized him.

"You know just about everyone here, don't you?" joked Greg, as he looked over at his wife.

Melissa nodded her head.

"Oh, any friend of Henry's is a friend of mine," came the man's reply, "and we all know Melissa.

"I don't see any CD's, aren't you carrying them anymore?" she asked.

"We ran out last night. By the way, I'm Richard, the owner here and Henry's agent. And you are?"

"Greg, Melissa's husband."

"Nice to meet you."

"Nice to meet you, too."

"We have an order coming in later today. You know, this is a small town as I'm sure you're both aware. So far I've sold 350 of them. I can't keep them on the shelf. People are buying them as gifts or for themselves. They just disappear like hotcakes.

"Richard, what would you say to unloading some of them to me?" Greg asked.

"What a great idea," Melissa stated excitedly. "we'll put them in our store."

"Can I make a little suggestion to you?" Richard asked.

"Of course."

"Have one of Henry's CD's playing almost all of the time. I'm sure you'll be amazed at how fast they'll go. People seem to gravitate towards them."

"Thank you," Melissa said.

"You're welcome. I got a call from a guy yesterday who was wondering about making reservations for one of those secret whatever trips. I don't know what you call them. You know, a bus trip or something where people don't know where they're going and —"

"Oh, I know what you mean, where a bus full of people go on a Mystery Trip," she said.

"Yeah, that's it," Richard stated. "Anyway, he was inquiring about having one of them come here to the restaurant and having Henry put on a show or program for them. Apparently the guy was passing through town, stopped to eat dinner, and now he wants to bring a tour group in. Unbelievable."

"That's exciting," Melissa stated.

"Well, I haven't talked it over with Henry yet, he's still on his honeymoon, but I expect him back shortly. And as far as the CD's go, I can let you have a hundred or so, but I need the rest myself."

"Thank you, sir," Melissa said. "Let's get them on the shelves before my mom and dad get back to the store."

"Whatever you say, Honey."

"And if you want to stop back later today, I'll put everything together for you," Richard suggested.

"Thank you, so much," Melissa said.

I Want to Fire Her

Once the world travelers' plane landed and everyone got seated into Kenneth's car, Susan turned to the group. "Let's go right to our house first," Susan suggested. "after all, your car is there. I'll throw something together to eat quickly, and then you can decide if you want to spend the night or go on home. What do you think?"

"I think I'd like to dive into my own bed," Frank stated, "but I'm awfully tired from all of the travel."

"Me, too," Edith added.

"Then it's settled, a quick meal and some relaxation," Susan confirmed.

"You know what I'd like to do?" Edith said.

"What's that?" Kenneth asked as he pulled onto the roadway.

"Start reliving our trip in my mind. It was just wonderful. I miss your mom and grandmother so much, I can't believe it."

"I know what you mean," expressed Susan.

"I'll tell you what we're going to do when we get home," Kenneth said.

"And what's that, Honey?"

"We're going to get on the phone and call your mother and grandmother. You know your mother isn't supposed to leave for another two or three days."

"Oh, I would like that," Edith stated, "but how am I going to talk to your grandmother without my interpreter?"

"We have more than one phone," Kenneth said, "in fact, I think we've got four. Problem solved. Everyone can have their own telephone."

Kenneth pulled the car into the driveway. Melissa's car sat to one side in the driveway. As he did he noticed some lights on in the back portion of the house.

Before Susan or Kenneth could open the doors to the car, Melissa and Greg came running out to them. The parents quickly undid their seatbelts and went to be with their children. Edith grabbed Greg and hugged him tightly, Susan doing the same to Melissa. Once she let go of her mother, Kenneth took Melissa in his arms and held her just as tightly. Greg gave each father an embrace as well.

"It's so nice to hug my test dummy," he laughed.

Melissa remembered those words so well, "test dummy." She recalled how her mother told her dad to practice hugging, and that the two of them were to be the "test dummies" he was to use to practice on. Melissa loved hearing her dad use that phrase.

"Come on, Mom and Dad," Melissa said laughing "we have a surprise for you."

"I'm too tried for another trip right now," Frank chuckled.

As everyone entered the house the smell of something cooking was evident in the air. Looking at the table in the dining room, it was set with candles burning. In the middle of the table sat a large bouquet of red roses with a white ribbon containing the words, "Welcome Home."

"Oh, these are beautiful," Susan stated.

"Yes, they are," Edith added.

"Mom, when you get home," Greg smiled, "you'll find the same thing awaiting you. We wanted to make sure both of our mothers were covered."

"Thank you, Honey," Edith said, "Now I have something to look forward to when I get there."

"And we have something for the men as well," Melissa said excitedly.

"And what would that be?" Kenneth asked.

"Come here, guys," she said.

"Follow her, gentlemen," Greg instructed.

Going into the office the men found two packages wrapped in red paper along with large red bows. Just off to the side were two more red paper wrapped gifts.

"Those look like fishing rods to me," Frank guessed out loud.

"They are! Oops… I should have waited until you opened them," Melissa said with a smile.

"I don't get it," Kenneth stated.

"Well, Dad," Melissa said, "Greg had to do an ad for a fishing rod company. He asked them what the very best fly fishing rods were they made or carried. He wanted to buy you each one. They liked his work so well, they gave him one."

"And then when I offered to buy another one from them," Greg said, "they gave me another one free. These didn't cost me a dime. I think the fact that I told them who I was giving them to, two world-renowned fishermen," he chuckled, "that impressed them. Boy, did I enjoy working with those people. It was lots of fun."

"Look at this," exclaimed Kenneth as he opened a somewhat large square looking box. "It's unbelievable, Frank. I assume he got one, too."

"He did," Melissa nodded.

"They're just beautiful," Frank said.

In Frank's hand he held a matching vintage looking split-willow fly fishing basket. Its edges and top were made of tooled leather along with the carrying harness. The gold buckle on the strap shone slightly. Each strap had the father's name etched on them.

"Thank you, kids," Frank expressed.

"Yes, thank you both," Kenneth said.

"I got the idea of your names engraved in the leather from Kate's tool belt," Melissa said. "Henry had her name put on his gift to her sometime ago."

"It really looks nice," Frank said.

"It sure does," smiled Kenneth.

After opening the gifts the men simply played with their new toys.

"These are top notch rods," Frank said.

"They sure are and very expensive," joined in Kenneth. "Now the fish really don't have a chance at all."

"Thank you both again," Frank said.

"Well, it was really all Greg on this," Melissa said.

"Thanks, Greg," Kenneth said as he swung a portion of the rod back and forth like a knight testing his sword.

"Remember, we're partners, Melissa. They're from both of us," Greg said.

The smell of food cooking began to fill the home even more as the couples took their seats.

"Oh, it smells so good," Susan stated.

"You can say that again," Edith agreed.

"I had expert teachers," Melissa said.

Both women smiled at her.

"We figured you would all be tired from travelling and so Greg and I decided to cook you dinner," declared Melissa.

"Honey, it's simply wonderful," Susan expressed. She then looked over at Greg and made the same statement to him, however, using different words in her comment.

"So Greg, do Susan and I still have a store to go back to work at?" joked Kenneth.

"I wanted to talk to you about that, or really you, Mom, but now is probably not the time to do that."

"Greg always seems to have bad timing when it comes to bringing up subjects," laughed Melissa.

"Well, with those words of yours, I guess I need to find out what you mean," Kenneth said.

"It really has to do with Mom's position at the store."

Now Edith's ears perked up. She had been down this path before and loved it when it occurred. Yes, it was soap opera time again, one of those infrequent moments when she could sit, observe, and watch every facet unfold before her eyes. She adored these discussions, miniature battles where no one was hurt and much was learned about the other side. It was exciting to see who captured whose flag in the end.

"Okay. Mom," Greg said, "Let me ask you a few questions, if you don't mind, and then we'll go from there. Is that okay with you?"

"Of course, Greg," Susan said as different thoughts began running through her head.

"Last year you worked on the coat drive for needy children, I know you remember that."

Susan nodded her head.

"I also know you've worked very hard on several food drives for the community."

Once again Susan nodded her head.

"And then there was the time the high school band needed new uniforms; remember that?"

She nodded her head once again.

"You love helping people in need; don't you?"

"I'm beginning to feel somewhat like a bobble head by all the nodding I'm doing, but yes, Greg, I do."

"And what about Alice Farmer, and Grace with the sick kid."

"Alice Farmer, isn't she one of our employees?" Kenneth asked.

Susan once again nodded her head slowly but said nothing.

"What about her?" Kenneth inquired.

"It's not important, Dear," Susan replied.

"The heck it isn't," Greg said in a strong voice. "Your wife brought meals in for her when her husband was bedridden just so she could take care of him, and didn't have to prepare meals when she got home. And let's not forget that you ran the register so she could leave early to be with him on more than one occasion. Not important, indeed!"

Susan, as well as Kenneth, was surprised by Greg's emotions. She had never seen him that upset before in such a good way, or anyway for that matter. Actually, she thought, I've never seen him upset in a bad way, come to think of it.

"I didn't know that," Kenneth stated as he shook his head. "So what exactly are you looking to do, Greg?"

"I want to fire her."

"What!" both Kenneth and Susan said at the same time.

Edith thought to herself, oh, here we go, this is great. I wonder what's going to happen next. Yes, I love these discussions. She knew, however, in the end everything would be worked out in a loving way, at least that's what she thought would happen.

"Should I go on?"

"Please do, Greg," Susan declared, "I want to find out if I have to get dressed for work tomorrow."

Kenneth put his hand on his forehead and closed his eyes as he nodded his head back and forth. He wanted to hunt out a spot in his subconscious that would act as a sanctuary to the headache he was beginning to feel. As he contemplated Greg's words, he remembered how many times he had been burned by his quick emotions over Greg's ideas, and how many, if not all, were actually beneficial for him in the end. He knew what to do immediately. Kenneth took a deep breath.

"Tell me what your idea is, I'm all ears," Kenneth said as he looked at Greg.

"Honey, will you get the folder, please?" Greg said.

Melissa stood up and walked towards the living room.

"Here's my idea," Greg said. "Susan moves from full-time to part-time. If she wants to go back to full-time, that's her decision to make alone. That way there's no pressure on her. We hire a part-time individual to fill in for her. This will leave mom with the freedom to do the things she loves the most, helping people." Greg turned and looked at Susan. "Mom, I know you well enough now to believe in my heart you'll never regret your decision if you decide to do this. I just hope you'll consider it."

"Here you go, Honey," Melissa said as she handed Greg a manila folder.

"Thank you."

"Are you in on this, too?" Kenneth asked.

"I'm afraid so, Dad."

"Hmmm," was all he said.

"Dad, just take a minute to look this over," Melissa said.

"Okay, Sweetheart."

Greg then handed the folder to Kenneth. Susan got up from her spot and walked behind Kenneth to see what he was looking at. Edith and Frank couldn't help themselves as they joined her.

"According to this, he lost his job from the company he was at, they closed down. He suffered a horrific injury from a hit and run driver," Kenneth said as he slightly nodded his head. "He lost his car, his leg and almost everything he owns."

"Oh no," Susan said as she put her hand to her mouth. "This isn't the husband of the woman that tried to buy some shoes that Christmas, is it?"

"One and the same," Greg said. "It's a small world we live in; isn't it?"

"It sure is, Greg."

Greg looked over at Kenneth, trying to size up what his thoughts were on the subject.

"If you look deeper into the file," Greg said, "you'll see that he's an honest man who has simply run into a buzz saw of problems. He's an accountant who really could use a job. Apparently nobody wants to hire him because of his disability. They're concerned about him being at work every day, getting around, everything. Some places don't have an elevator. It's his left leg that he lost so he can still drive, but he doesn't own a car anymore, and besides, he couldn't afford the insurance on one to begin with."

Kenneth shut the folder and placed it onto the table.

"Susan, my office, please."

Kenneth and Susan got up and walked the short distance to Kenneth's office. He closed the door behind them.

Kenneth walked around his desk and sat down. Susan took a chair in front of the desk.

He sat slowly rocking back and forth in his chair, occasionally moving it sideways as the chair gave off a squeak every so often.

"I really have mixed emotions on this," he stated. "What are your feelings?"

"Every time we try to outguess Greg we've been proven wrong, and I don't want that to happen again... never," she stated in a firm voice.

Kenneth laughed slightly as he nodded his head back and forth.

"I'll tell you what," Kenneth said as he got up from his chair, "Greg said you could go back to full-time anytime you wanted to. If it's okay with you I say we give his idea a chance, but it's your decision to make solely."

"Say Kenneth," Susan said with a small laugh in her voice, "I thought we owned the store."

"I thought so, too," Kenneth said, "now our kids do."

"I hope they don't think about firing you, too," Susan said as she got up. Kenneth shook his head as he chuckled also.

"Susan, ever since the day Greg came into our lives it's been a roller coaster ride. Between him, Melissa, everything we've gone through, it's just been unbelievable."

"But what a wonderful journey it's been," she said with a smile.

"I have to agree with you on that, Susan."

"Kenneth, if you had it all to do over again with everything that's gone on, would you want to?"

"With all my heart, but I definitely would have tempered my words concerning Greg. We have a much stronger family, two wonderful kids, and great friends in Frank and Edith. To tell you the truth, Susan, I've never been happier."

Kenneth walked up to her as he took Susan in his arms. They kissed. Kenneth looked down at Susan, she smiled at him again. He kissed her once more.

"I love you, Susan."

"I know you do," Susan said nodding her head, "and I love you, too."

Kenneth knew in his heart her reply was strong and true, just as his had been to her.

Susan and Kenneth returned to the dining room and retook their seats.

"Is there anything else we need to know about your proposal?" inquired Kenneth.

"Actually there is," Greg replied. "I haven't brought up the subject with the man, I wanted to wait to talk to the both of you first. After all, you two have the final say."

"Well, tomorrow is just as good a day as any other. You go and talk to him and see what he has to say. You can let us know what you find out when you get back."

"Can I go with him?" Melissa asked.

"If you want to," Kenneth said.
"Thanks, Dad."

The next day appeared as any other except for the fact that Greg and Melissa knew they had quite a bit waiting on their plate to do. As they got dressed the couple discussed their options. Should they go in the morning, afternoon, try to call the man. They were simple questions with hard answers. Greg thought the reason for that was because he had so much invested in what he was attempting to accomplish with the gentleman. He didn't want to disappoint Melissa's parents, but still, he had no idea how the man would react or feel about his offer.

Greg pulled the car up in front of a well-kept house. He looked at Melissa sitting at his side.

"This is it, Honey," she stated.

"Well, good luck to both of us," he said as he started to get out of the car.

"I'll go in with you, Greg."

"I knew you would. I don't think anything I would say could keep you from going with me."

Walking up to the front door Greg reached over in front of Melissa and knocked on the door. He knocked again. The inside door was opened by a young girl. Melissa's jaw dropped.

"I know you," the little girl said with a smile. "Mama, the hamburger lady is here."

Within a matter of seconds a woman appeared at the front door, the very same lady who had flown the kite with her children at the park the day of the Summers' Summer Picnic.

"Oh my goodness, I know you," she stated as she began to open the door.

"It's nice to see you again," Melissa said smiling.

"Please come in," she implored them.

"You know this woman?" Greg said, surprised by what had just transpired.

"Oh, we go way back, at least to the picnic," laughed Melissa.

"Yes, and thank you again. My kids really enjoyed the burgers and hotdogs."

"And I appreciated you sitting with me."

"Wait a minute," the woman said once again, "don't I know you, too? You were the young man who helped me in the store that one Christmas when I bought shoes with the gift certificate I won."

"It was your lucky day, I guess," Greg said with a smile.

"It certainly was. Well, what brings you to our home?"

"Is it possible for me to speak with your husband?" Greg said.

"He's out in the back, I'll take you to him."

"I can do that, Mommy," the child suggested.

"That's fine," Greg said.

"He's right this way, Mister." The little girl reached up with her hand to Greg, something he wasn't expecting. He reached over and took her hand in his as they turned and walked to the back of the house.

"Here, have a seat, please," the woman suggested.

"You know something," Melissa said, "I don't think we ever took the time to actually introduce ourselves. My name is Melissa."

"And mine is Robin, nice to meet you," she laughed.

The women took a seat on the couch and began visiting.

Greg followed the little girl as she led him to the back door. She reached up pushing it open.

"He's out in the back," she said.

"Okay."

Together they walked hand-in-hand to a small building near the back of the lot.

"Daddy is in there."

"Thank you."

The child turned and headed back to the house. Greg knocked on the door not knowing really what to expect.

"Come in," came a reply from within.

Greg opened the door and walked into the room. A gentleman was sitting in a chair in front of a metal desk. A pair of crutches were leaning up against a cabinet nearby.

"If you're here for money, you're a few years too late."

"I'm not looking for money, but I am looking for a good honest man. Do you know where I can find someone like that?"

"A whole man?"

"Whole, half, as long as the parts I need aren't missing. That's all I need to know, and the rest makes no difference."

"And what parts would those be?" he inquired.

"A smart brain, hands to work with, a hard worker, honest, not afraid to get up in the morning and show up to work every day. Those are the parts I'm looking for. Do you know anybody like that?"

"I only have one leg, fellow, you can see that; can't you?"

"You know what, let me tell you what I want and then we'll talk. What do you have to lose in listening to me."

"Nothing, I guess."

"Good. My name is Greg Wilson, and you are?" Greg already knew everything he needed to know about him, he just wanted to soften up the situation.

"I'm Frederick Carpenter, but you probably already know that," he said as he reached up with his right hand and shook Greg's.

"Nice to meet you."

Frederick nodded his head.

"Summers' Department Store is in need of a part-time bookkeeper, someone to handle payroll, accounts payable, keep the books, perform general accounting duties. I heard from somebody you might be interested in a job like that. Now, I'm not sure exactly what the pay will start at, but I can tell you this. The Summers are very fair, and I know that from my own personal experiences."

"And how would I get to work, I only have one leg?"

"I see three options available. First, there's the bus system. You're not that far away from their store. Two, there are car pools, once you get to know the people who live close by. Three, I have been authorized to work out a deal with you where we'll see to it you get a vehicle, a company car so to speak. The insurance would be covered by the store. You have your right leg; you can drive. You'd be working in an office of your own. You would be on the fourth floor. Fortunately, the building is equipped with an elevator. The next question is obvious, do you want to take advantage of this opportunity or not; it's your decision to make."

"I don't have a suit."

"Who cares, you're not auditioning for a clothing store ad. A couple pair of pants, a few shirts, what else do you need?"

"Some money to buy some clothes with, mine are really old. I have a little money, some, but not too much."

"What do you say I come by and pick you up about eight o'clock in the morning the day after tomorrow. We can head down to the store and get those things for you. I get a store discount and we can worry about the funds later. In fact, let's do it tomorrow. I'll pick you up at eight o'clock. Like I said, we'll go to the store and pick out some clothes for you there."

"And why me? What brought you here to help us out, my family... and me?"

"That's a good question, but unfortunately I have a commitment I have to get to. We can discuss it tomorrow or some other time."

"So tomorrow at eight o'clock?"

"Yes."

"I'll be ready."

"Good. I'll see you then."

"Thank you."

Greg just nodded his head as he left the building. Opening the back door he walked into the house.

"Are you ready, Melissa?" he asked.

"Yes."

"I would like you to meet my two daughters," Robin stated. "This one you met, her name is Betty. The other one here with the chocolate smile on her face is Annie."

"It's nice to meet you kids."

"So how did it go?" asked Melissa.

"Very well," he said with a nod of his head.

"Good."

"I'll see you tomorrow morning," Greg said to Mrs. Carpenter."

"You will?"

"Talk to your husband, he'll explain everything to you."

Greg and Melissa turned and made their way to the front door and then out to their car.

"So everything worked out well?" Melissa said as she opened the passenger door to the car.

"Sort of. I may have bitten off more than I can chew."

"So what's new about that?" she said with a smile.

"Well, I may have to buy the man a car, though that thought ran through my mind before we even got here."

"Oh," she said.

"And pay for the insurance on it as well, which I thought might happen, too."

"Boy, when you bite off more than you can chew, you really mean it."

"I'm sorry."

"Why?" she laughed, "You know I'm behind you one hundred percent, and besides, living with you is always an adventure. That's what makes our lives so much fun together."

Returning to the store Melissa and Greg went immediately to the office area. Going into Susan's office they realized she wasn't there. They then went to Kenneth's office. As they entered through the door they found Kenneth sitting at the desk, Susan standing behind him looking over some paperwork.

"So how did it go this morning?" inquired Kenneth as he looked up at them.

"I'm picking him up tomorrow morning and I'm going to purchase him some clothes for work."

"Mom," Melissa said, "do you remember the woman and the kids flying the kite at the park when we were putting on the picnic?"

"I sure do," Susan replied with a smile as thoughts of that day quickly ran through her mind. "The kite almost hypnotized me as I watched it dart back and forth in the wind. I remember that part well."

"And what do you think the odds are if I told you her husband is the one Greg wants to hire in your place?"

"You're kidding me?"

"Nope."

Susan nodded her head back and forth.

"Do you know anybody who wants to sell a used car cheap?" Melissa said with a chuckle in her voice as she looked over in Greg's direction.

"I'll find something, Melissa, don't worry about it," Greg said.

"I know you will," Melissa stated.

"So what's wrong with your car?" Susan asked.

"Oh, nothing," Greg said.

"My husband wants to buy Mr. Carpenter a car to get to work with and also pay the insurance premiums on it. Doesn't that beat all?"

"Why would you do that, Greg?" Kenneth asked.

"Because he needs one. I told him the store would pay for it and the insurance, that way he can get started. That was the first thing that came to my mind when I started thinking of him getting to work to begin with. He needs transportation to get to work. It's my responsibility and I'll live with the consequences of my statements. Sometimes you just need to help people out."

Susan nodded her head in agreement.

"Don't worry, Mom and Dad, I'll see to it that the insurance bills are paid for, but first I've got to buy a used car. I told him the car was a store vehicle, so don't anyone say anything to him, he doesn't need to know that information."

"Well, I was planning on buying Susan a new car," smiled Kenneth.

"You were?" Susan said in a surprised voice.

"Of course, I was. Don't you remember us talking about it?" Kenneth stated as he winked at Susan.

"Oh, yeah, we talked about it," Susan replied. She figured she wasn't really lying about it since they were discussing it now.

"Greg, you give the man Susan's old car to use if we hire him, and we'll put it in the store's name. That way the store can eat the insurance bill as well."

"Dad, you don't have to do this, I said I would pay for it."

"Well, a wise young man once told me not so long ago that sometimes you just need to help people out."

"Thanks, Dad," Melissa said.

"You're welcome, Honey."

"Yes, thanks, Dad," Greg added.

"So when do we meet this gentleman?" Susan inquired.

"How about tomorrow morning?" Greg said.

"I'm looking forward to it," Kenneth said.

"Thanks again, Dad," Greg stated. "Well, I better get back to work, I've got to earn my keep."

"Mom, can I go with you when you start looking for a new car," Melissa said with a smile, "and something in red might be nice for you, too."

Do You Like Ice Cream

Greg pulled up to the Carpenter's residence the following day at precisely eight o'clock. He watched as Frederick made his way out to the car. Greg was surprised to see how well he accomplished his movements on the crutches. After Frederick pulled the door shut to the car Greg pulled out onto the roadway.

"Well, Frederick, you ready to start a new day in your life?"

"Why don't you call me Fred for short, if that's okay with you?"

"It is with me if it's alright with you," Greg said. "Fred, I hope this works out for you and your family, but I want you to realize there's no promises being made here."

"So do I… and I understand what you're saying."

"Good."

"You know what they say, Greg, hope for the best, plan for the worst. I've had the worst part, I can only hope for the best."

Greg nodded his head slightly.

"And, Greg, I owe you an apology."

"For what?"

"My attitude yesterday, it was on the short side, and I'm sorry for that. Here you are trying to help me and I'm returning your help with bitterness in my words. I want to apologize for that."

"Ah, forget it."

"Thank you. You should have seen my wife this morning, she was so happy. Robin was up easily by five-thirty this morning pacing the floor. She made me a big breakfast, and I think that was because she didn't know what else to do with her time. I think her nerves were getting the best of her." Fred said. "You know, I realize my family has suffered a great deal over the past few years, but we're very lucky in some respects. My wife and I love each other, the kids are great, and when I find my missing leg I'll buy a little glue and everything will be back together like it was before," chuckled Fred.

Greg laughed. "Have you checked into getting an artificial leg? You still have your knee, if that makes a difference."

"Money," Fred stated.

"I'm sure there are programs out there."

"I don't know. There might be, but when you're trying to put food on the table and keep a roof over your family's head, that becomes your first priority."

Greg nodded his head. He began to really feel for Fred and his family, more than he ever anticipated. He wondered how everything would end up for the Carpenter family, how the Summers would feel about him, and more importantly, if he could really handle the job. Yes, today was the beginning of a new pathway for them to follow. Greg hoped it would be a smooth and straight journey for them to undertake together.

Entering Susan's office, all three members of the Summers family were in attendance. The first thing Greg did was to introduce Fred to them. Susan and Kenneth shook his hand, then Melissa.

"Oh, I see you had the back page of the paper framed from your family picnic?" smiled Fred.

"Why yes, we did," Susan said. "I was so proud they did that for us. I just wanted to find a place in my office where I could look at it every day."

"And you, young lady," Fred stated as he turned in Melissa's direction, "made that day very memorable for my two girls. They talked about the free food they got and the real mean burger, whatever that means, that attacked some man. They also spoke about the scar he got from it."

Melissa laughed as she thought of Henry's description of the burger and him fighting with it.

"Well, Mr. Carpenter, —" Susan began.

"Would you mind calling me, Fred?"

"That's fine," Susan said. "I've been working on some figures here. I was wondering what you can tell me about them?"

It was obvious to both Susan and Fred that she was getting a feel for how well he would be able to handle the job. It was just a small test, but a test nonetheless.

"May I?"

"Of course," she replied.

Fred took a quick short hop to the chair and sat down. He leaned his crutches up against the desk as he looked down at the figures on the sheet.

"Would you like to use my calculator? It's just to your right."

Fred didn't respond as he studied the figures over, running them through his mind.

"I would say you're about… eight hundred and fifty… two dollars short, if I'm not mistaken."

"Eight hundred fifty-two dollars and three cents to be exact," Susan stated in amazement.

"Can I show you something, Mrs. Summers?"

"Only if you call me Susan."

Fred smiled at Susan and then turned his attention back to the sheet. He picked up a pencil to point out different columns of figures as he spoke.

"If you were to take this column of numbers here, and I'll call them column one, move it over to this section and then drop this into place here, I think you'd find things are much easier to keep track of. When figures are being used in conjunction it's easier to keep them close, that way your eyes aren't jumping back and forth so much trying to keep track of the figures or find additional ones. They're hooked together so to speak. Of course, everyone has their own personal way of doing things and that may not work for you. It's just a suggestion."

Susan looked over to Kenneth. Kenneth nodded his head, she nodded back to him.

"Mr. Carpenter… Fred," Susan said as she held her hand out to him, "welcome to the Summers' Family Store."

Greg immediately held his hand out to Fred, who was quick to take it.

"Thank you everyone."

"Melissa is going to need some information for our records, so Kenneth and I will leave you in her capable hands," Susan said as she and Kenneth headed towards the door. "Oh, Fred, I hope you like your new office. Melissa, see me when you're through."

"I will, Mom."

"And Greg, I need to talk to Fred about his wages before he leaves. I'll see you then, Fred."

"You can count on it, Mrs. Summers," Fred answered.

Once the paperwork was completed, Greg suggested that he and Fred should go to the men's department to get some pants and shirts.

Getting off the elevator they made a short turn and started down the aisle. Every employee they passed was sure to wish Greg a good morning.

"The people here really like you; don't they?" Fred said in more of a statement than a question.

"It's not just me, they love the whole Summers family. You'd have to go a long way to find anyone better to work for."

Entering the clothing department, Greg and Fred were immediately approached by a young gentleman.

"Good morning, Mr. Wilson," the gentleman by the name of Patrick stated.

"Haven't you and I talked about this before?" Greg asked him.

"Yes, sir."

"Well, try it again," joked Greg.

"Good morning, Greg," came his reply.

"Now, that's better. We want to get this gentleman about ten pairs of slacks, and maybe twelve or so shirts ought to do it."

"Greg, I don't really have that much money. I was thinking about a shirt, maybe two at the most."

"Well, in sports they have signing bonuses, and that's what we'll consider this. Patrick, this goes on my store account."

"Yes, sir... Greg."

"And, Patrick, is Mrs. White here today? Is this one of her scheduled days to be here?"

"Yes, it is."

"Perfect."

Once the pants and shirts were selected, Greg took the heavy bags in hand and headed to the back of the men's department with Fred.

"Good morning, Greg," came the voice from a older woman sitting behind a sewing machine.

"And how are you, Mrs. White?"

"Didn't we talk about this before?" she said with a smile.

"Yes, we have, June, and I love playing this game with you."

"So what can I do for you?"

"June, I'm stepping over the bounds here, but is there any way in the world you can shorten ten pairs of pants this morning? I know our customers come first, so keep that in mind."

"Well, I've been known to be bribed on occasion."

"I understand completely," Greg stated with a smile. "Fred, I'm going to leave you here with this beautiful young gray haired lady who appears to be about..."

"Careful."

"... just under 29 years of age, maybe 28."

"Thank you, Greg."

"You're welcome. I'll be back in just a few minutes, that way you can get everything figured out."

"Thank you, Greg," Fred said.

Greg nodded his head as he walked away.

Waiting until he was sure Greg was out of earshot, Fred asked, "June, may I ask you a question?"

"Of course," she replied as she opened the bag of pants and began sorting through them.

"What's it like working here?"

"Do you like ice cream?"

"Who doesn't."

"How about sundaes with lots of whipping cream and a cherry or two on the top?"

Fred laughed. "Now you're making me hungry."

"Working here is like when you go and buy a sundae and they forget themselves, they put extra cherries on the top along with a little too much whipping cream. It's just the way you would make it for yourself at home if you had all of the ingredients. Do you understand what I'm trying to say?"

"Yes, I do."

"So are you taking a job here?"

"I'm going to be their part-time bookkeeper."

"So you'll be up in the office area with them."

"I guess I will."

"You're a lucky man. Now, let's take these measurements and get started. Would you like to step behind the curtain for a second?"

"Of course."

June handed Fred a pair of pants. "Let me know when you've got them on."

"I will."

When Fred stepped back to June's position she inquired as to how he wanted her to handle the shortening of the pants for his one leg. Once that was decided June, being the professional she was, made quick work preparing her latest project. She lined the pants up, made the appropriate marks on them, then picked up a pair of scissors to start.

Greg walked up carrying a bottle of orange flavored soda along with a candy bar.

"Are you still holding the pants hostage?" he asked.

"Until I get my payment," June answered, a slight smile reflected across her face.

"Here you go."

"Thanks, Greg. I'll begin working on them now."

"Fred and I are going upstairs to the break room and then I'll stop by later to pick them up. I'll just leave the shirts here, if that's okay."

"Fine. Don't be in too much of a hurry though," June warned.

Greg nodded his head.

"Say, Greg," she said, "did you know Mr. and Mrs. Summers have been eating lunch with the employees every once in a while in the break room?"

"I didn't know that."

"Why don't you and Melissa come with them one day, we'd love to have you join us there, too."

"That sounds like fun."

"But you've got to watch out for Kenneth, he's a shrewd food trader."

"Food trader?"

"Yep. Ask him about it, he'll tell you. And remember what I said, don't be in too much of a hurry."

"I won't. I don't want to stand here like I'm looking over your shoulder, nobody likes that."

"Especially young 22 year old gray haired women," laughed June.

"So your age is going the other way even more now?"

"It always does with attractive women such as myself."

"See you later, June," Greg said with a chuckle as he and Fred walked away.

Entering the break room Fred was very much impressed.

"This is the break room?" Fred said in amazement.

"Actually a friend of mine did the work refurbishing it together with his girlfriend, and now wife."

"They do wonderful work."

"Yes, they do," Greg said as he looked around.

"Boy, this is really nice."

"Fred, the reason I bought you here is because I knew it would be quiet in here at this time of the morning. I wanted to ask you if there was anything you needed to know further, if you had any questions you felt uncomfortable asking in front of the Summers. You can ask me anything at all."

"I'm actually overwhelmed to tell you the truth, Greg. When my wife hears everything that's happened today she'll be so excited. I hope she doesn't do what she did yesterday."

"What's that?"

"After I explained everything to her, when you and Melissa were gone, she told me she was tired and wanted to lay down for a little while. She closed the bedroom door behind her. I could hear her crying in the bedroom. This ordeal over the last few years has taken a tremendous toll on her. It's been a very difficult time for her."

"And for you as well, I imagine?"

"Yes, it has."

"Maybe someday you'll look back on this morning and remember it as the day things turned around for you and your family."

Fred nodded his head.

"Greg, on the pants and shirts —"

"Forget it."

"I just can't. Would you mind if I gave you so much money a pay period or whatever until I've paid you back?"

"Let's do this, we'll take it one step at a time. If you still feel the need to pay me back later, we'll cross that bridge when we get to it. Don't forget, I said it was a signing bonus."

"Sounds good."

"Another thing you should know, when it comes to being an employee. When your wife starts looking for school clothes for your daughters, or she needs anything, remember to tell her the Summers give a fairly descent store discount to their employees."

"I will."

Getting off of the elevator Greg and Fred went to Melissa's office. As they walked in Fred couldn't help but notice something.

"You have the same framed page of the newspaper hanging here as in your mother's office," Fred declared.

"Not only does my mom and I have it, so does my dad," chuckled Melissa. "Our family is very proud of what our employees have done for us.

Now, I think I have everything in order for you. You will have to sign a few documents so we can get you on the payroll, which you'll be handling shortly, I assume. Take your time and read them over and then just sign where I've marked the red "X" on the sheets."

"I don't have to read them," Fred said.

"Well, you might want to, though I will see to it you get a copy of each one."

"I'll just sign them. From what I've seen of this place and the people who run it, the last thing I need to worry about is something going wrong. To tell you the truth, I think you'd address any of my concerns immediately if anything did happen to come up."

"Okay," Melissa stated with a small smile. Once he signed them she handed Fred his part of the documents.

"I'll be back in just a minute."

Melissa left the room.

Kenneth and Susan accompanied Melissa as she returned to her office.

"I understand from our daughter congratulations are in order." Kenneth held out his hand to Fred who took it immediately.

"I want to thank everyone here for this opportunity. I'll do the very best job I can for your family and the business. Thank you."

Kenneth held his hand out once again in Fred's direction. Fred reached over and attempted to shake it, however, there was something in Kenneth's hand.

"Oh, I'm sorry," Fred said, "I thought you wanted to shake hands again."

"No, but these are for you."

Fred reached out with his hand once again as he received a set of keys from Kenneth.

"Now, these keys are to a vehicle you can use to go back and forth from work. If on occasion you need to run to the store for something, food, doctor, whatever, Susan has seen to it that the car is fully insured by our store. I would hope you would use good judgment when it comes to that."

"Thank you, Mr. and Mrs. Summers. I wish you could understand how much this means to me and my family."

Melissa's heart felt as if it wanted to explode with happiness. She had met Fred's family on more than one occasion. She adored his wife and their two little girls. Not only was she thrilled with how everything was turning out for them, the help her parents extended to them, she was also very proud of the man she had married.

"Mr. and Mrs. Summers —" Fred said.

"It's Susan and Kenneth," stated Susan.

"Is it okay if I take a little time in calling you that?"

Kenneth and Susan smiled

"Of course," Susan expressed.

"When I go home I was wondering if you would care if tonight I took my family for a car ride down to the park to celebrate?"

"Let's see," Kenneth stated, "food, doctor, and park. I think I forgot to mention that one. Of course, you can."

"Thank you."

"So is anyone hungry?" inquired Susan.

"I know I am," Greg stated.

"Fred," Susan said, "would you join our family and some of our employees in the break room for lunch? Oh, and just so you know, I packed an extra lunch just in case you decided to accompany us. This will give us a chance to introduce you to some of our employees."

"I would be honored."

"Good."

"So how many meals did you pack, Mom?" Melissa inquired.

"Don't worry, Honey, I took you and Greg into consideration."

"And what about my trading items?" Kenneth asked.

"And a bag full of trading items, too," Susan said laughingly.

"Trading items?" Fred said.

"Oh, you'll love the trading part," Kenneth stated, "it's my favorite part of lunch with the people."

"I heard something about you and trading food," Greg said.

"And what was that?" Kenneth asked.

"They say you're very shrewd."

"Good, I'm getting a reputation," Kenneth stated.

"Oh, my goodness," Susan declared, "I forgot to go over your wages with you."

"Let's do that tomorrow morning," Fred suggested. "Greg told me you were very fair people, and I trust Greg completely."

"So do I," smiled Melissa.

"I guess we all do," Kenneth said.

"What time should I be here tomorrow?" Fred asked.

"How about eight-thirty tomorrow," suggested Susan.

"I'll be here, and on time."

With lunch over, and Kenneth having made what he considered to be some great food trades, the Summers family went back to their offices. Greg and Fred stopped to see Mrs. White to pick up the completed tailoring. Greg carried the three large bags of clothes as he showed Fred where the car was parked.

"This car is very nice," commented Fred as he looked around the interior. "It's so clean, almost like brand new."

Greg nodded his head. He knew how well groomed Susan was at all times in appearance, he would expect nothing less in her car. Greg noticed an envelope on the seat next to Fred.

"What's that?"

"I don't know," Fred responded. Fred picked up the plain envelope. As he turned it over his name was handwritten on the front of it. He opened it and found a card inside. As he pulled it out, three twenty-dollar bills fell from its interior. He read the note as he shook his head.

"What's the deal?" Greg asked.

"The card is from Mrs. Summers. She wrote a note in here asking me to treat my family to a nice dinner tonight to celebrate my new job after we go to the park."

"I'll be."

"That's so thoughtful of her to do."

"She's that kind of a woman. Listen, I'm going to put your clothes in the backseat for you."

"Thanks, Greg… thanks for everything." Fred reached his arm out of the open window and shook Greg's hand.

"I'll see you tomorrow."

"You can count on it."

Fred put the key in the ignition and started the car. The sound of a man's tenor voice began playing from the CD in the car.

"I better get this CD back to her."

"Why not listen to it on your way home; tomorrow is soon enough," Greg said.

Fred glanced at the instrument panel. They thought of everything. He smiled as he looked at the gauge for the gas tank, which read full.

Greg waved to Fred as he drove from the parking area.

"You did well, Greg. Actually I'm very proud of you."

Greg turned around to see Ted Sheppard standing behind him.

"Thank you, but I'm just one piece of the puzzle. There's Kenneth and Susan, they had a lot to do with this, along with Melissa."

"But you played a very important part in this whole thing coming together."

"Thank you for all of your help. I couldn't have done it without you."

"Maybe so, but you threw the first pitch in the game, and just now the last one."

Greg nodded his head slightly.

"What would you say to a nice cold bottle of soda?"

"You buying?" Ted asked.

"Yes, I am."

"In that case, I don't mind if I do," he chuckled.

As they turned and walked towards the door, Ted placed his hand on Greg's shoulder.

"I'm very proud of you, Greg," he said nodding his head.

"We both should be proud," answered Greg.

Both men smiled.

As Susan came into the house carrying the mail Kenneth chuckled to himself. What made him laugh within was the large smile on her face. He expected to see this very reaction emanating from her even before she retrieved the mail. After all, it was Melissa's birthday, and that was the key to everything. Like a bird's quest to see its birdhouse in the spring, this new custom was an eagerly welcomed sight as well. Susan held an envelope high in her hand, which she waved back and forth as she approached Kenneth sitting at the kitchen table.

"So he didn't forget," smiled Kenneth, "I mean he did it again. Well, we thought he would."

"I don't think he will ever not do it or forget," she responded, her smile still wide upon her face.

While Sunday meals were shared together with both families, it having become quite the ritual now, this was completely different in nature. After the marriage of Melissa to Greg, and with their daughter's birthday the following spring, a series of events started to fall into place. This was now the fourth year of Melissa's birthday being celebrated as a married woman. It was something Kenneth and Susan looked forward to as a family event. It started simply enough with a very similar envelope to the one Susan now held in her hand. This one act by Greg became something the couple treasured. Both wondered if Greg would continue on with what he started the previous years, or if he had anything new up his sleeve on this occasion.

Susan laid the envelope down on the table in front of Kenneth. After taking a seat next to him, she took a sip from her coffee cup. She looked over at Kenneth and smiled again. On the table sat the handwritten envelope, which was addressed to both of them. It didn't read "Mr. and Mrs.," but rather to Mom and Dad Summers. The return address simply read, "Greg," and the appropriate address where he and Melissa lived.

"So are you going to open it?" he asked.

"Why don't you do it this year?"

"No, this is something you should do, Susan, you're the one who gave birth to her," he said with a smile.

"Thank you."

Kenneth nodded his head as he watched Susan take the envelope into her hands. She picked up a knife from the table and slid it across the back of the envelope. Reaching in, Susan took out a card from its interior. On the front of the card were the words, "Thank you" with a beautiful bouquet of red roses on its front.

"He even thought of red roses again this year," she smiled. "I'll bet he hunts for the right card throughout the year, just to get one with red roses on it."

"I'm sure you're right, Susan."

Susan opened the card. The card was blank on the inside other than a handwritten note addressed to both of them. She began reading it out loud to Kenneth. It reflected a small poem written by Greg.

"Mom and Dad. The gift you've given me, shall forever always be, one that I will cherish, throughout eternity." It was signed, "Thank you for my wonderful wife. With all my love, Greg."

"Isn't it something," Kenneth stated, "that on Melissa's birthday we get a thank you card from Greg for having our daughter. Unbelievable."

"I think it's absolutely wonderful," she replied nodding her head.

"Oh, so do I," he was quick to reply, "so do I."

"I'm going to put it in the china cabinet in place of the one we got last year. I think I'll take the one from last year and put it in the drawer for safe keeping with the others."

"So you want to keep them?"

"Without a doubt. As long as Greg sends them, I'll hang onto each one of them. The fact that he'd even do this means so much to me."

"Me, too."

"Kenneth, we're so fortunate to have Greg as our son-in-law."

"And Melissa to have him as her husband," he agreed.

While the couple sat enjoying a very late weekend breakfast, the doorbell rang.

"I'll get it," Kenneth announced.

Getting up he walked over to the front door. Opening the door he was greeted by a man who stood before him with his hands full. The gentleman carried a very large bouquet of red roses shielded in decorative cellophane protecting the flowers in a glass vase.

"Susan, it's for you," Kenneth said as he stepped aside.

Susan walked over to the front door smiling as she did. She took the flowers from his hands and thanked him. Kenneth reached for his wallet.

"Just a minute, sir," the deliveryman said as he turned and walked back to his vehicle. Opening the vehicle's door he retrieved a small box with a red bow on its top. He then returned to the front door and handed it to Kenneth. The couple looked at each other as they smiled once again.

"Greg did it to us again," Kenneth laughed.

"Yes, he sure did," chuckled Susan.

Kenneth quickly reached into his wallet and tipped the gentleman.

"These are just beautiful," Susan said as she turned and walked over to the table. She set them down and began unwrapping the protective covering over them.

"So what's in the box, Kenneth?"

"Well, I think it has something to do with fishing since the wrapping paper has pictures of fly rods and fishing items on it. Actually it looks a little funny with the red bow on top."

Kenneth sat down again at the table as he observed his wife fussing over the flowers. He smiled as he watched her adjusting each one of them into place. Once they were arranged, she bent over them and took a deep breath.

"They smell just wonderful."

"Susan, the only thing more beautiful in this room is you."

"Thank you."

"Those roses remind me of the day our daughter married Greg. Just before I walked her down the aisle I told her how much she looked like you on the day we were married. She was every bit as beautiful and stunning as you on our wedding day, and just as you are today. Maybe it's the flowers that remind me so much of those two wonderful days in my life."

"Well, Kenneth, if that's true then I should have flowers delivered here every day."

"But none could compare with your beauty... and, Susan, I'm a very lucky man... just like Greg."

Susan reached over and kissed her husband. As she pulled back from him she looked into his eyes and the large smile he exhibited across his face. She then repeated the same gesture to him, but with a little more passion.

"So open your present, I want to see what it is."

Kenneth opened the gift carefully. It contained a cloth pouch with a zipper running along three sides of it. Inside was a variety of fishing flies.

"These are perfect," he said.

Susan nodded her head as she smiled once again.

Melissa's birthday was celebrated that evening after dinner. It was filled with an abundance of usual items, family members, friends, and a tasty meal. There was, of course, cake and ice cream, gifts, and a large amount of laughter sprinkled here and there. After finishing up with the dessert and opening of presents, everyone sat down to visit and enjoy each other's company.

With the young people busy in the kitchen along with Susan, Edith took a seat in the living room with Frank and Kenneth. At one point as the two men visited Edith noticed something. She stood up and walked over to the china cabinet and peered in. As Susan walked up to her, Edith inquired about the thank you card that sat on a shelf behind glass doors to the case.

"That's something we got from Greg today," Susan expressed with a smile as she spoke.

"Oh."

"Each year, as well as this year we receive a card from Greg, a thank you card. I guess he wanted to thank us for having Melissa."

"Oh," Edith once again said.

Susan began to feel uncomfortable, as if Edith might be feeling badly since she and her husband hadn't received a card. She didn't know quite what to say.

"You want to know something funny?" Edith said.

"What's that, Edith?"

"I didn't get anything today on Melissa's birthday, no thank you, nothing."

Now Susan began to feel somewhat hurt inside over Edith's feelings of being left out, crushed somewhat. As she looked at Edith she contemplated what to say to her on the subject, but couldn't think of anything. Her mind drew a blank.

"No, nothing at all," she continued. "Susan, what do you get on Greg's birthday?"

"Nothing."

"Interesting," she smiled. "On Greg's birthday from Melissa I got a thank you card, I received a dozen red roses and Frank…"

Susan started laughing as she reached over and hugged Edith. Now she understood what Edith meant about the names, Greg's card for her, Melissa's card to Edith.

"We've got some pretty special children," Edith said with a smile.

"We sure do," she replied as they hugged each other again.

"Say, Susan, have you got any tissue?" Edith laughed.

"Right this way, Edith, we can share the box together," Susan chuckled.

"And then we can both give our kids a big hug."

"That sounds like a wonderful idea," agreed Susan.

The two women turned and headed in their children's direction. As per their conversation, each mother gave their child a large hug.

Grand Opening

Henry walked through the front door of Richard's Steak House and headed immediately to Richard's office in the back. Seeing him sitting behind the desk, Henry took a chair in front of him.

"It's good to see you, Henry."

"The same here. I got a message that you wanted to see me, so I came right over. What can I do for you?"

"I think we're at a point in our relationship where we need to make some important decisions."

"Such as?"

"Henry, I don't want to do anything to hinder your career, but I have to keep an eye on my own business interests as well. Let me explain to you what I'm contemplating. I know I can fill this place with your voice, that's not a problem with this size of a building. What I'm thinking I'd like to do, with your help, is to add an additional section to the restaurant and expand it by two-thirds. Now, that would be a costly venture on my part, but economically it could be a small treasure chest waiting to be tapped."

"That sounds interesting, Richard."

"I've been contacted by various people wanting to book your services, have you perform a singing program for different groups that would come here to the restaurant. I guess before I do anything, I need to know what your thoughts are along that line. I would hate to make a huge outlay of money and then have you decide to leave."

"I wouldn't do that to you."

"I know, but I'm sure you can understand my concerns."

Henry nodded his head. "I have an idea, Richard."

"I'm all ears."

"Though you and I haven't really known each other all that long, we can both agree on one thing."

"And what's that, Henry?"

"We trust each other."

"I think that goes without saying."

"What do you think about this proposal? I'll build the addition, that way there's a big savings. You'll get it done for the cost of the materials. I'll sing evenings, weekends, whatever we decide on. You don't pay me a dime. The money you would have paid me would go towards the materials. When everything is all said and done, you can give me a portion of your business."

"And how much of a share would that be?"

Henry thought for a minute. "How about a quarter? Does that sound like too much?"

"Well, my seating would go up quite a bit, then the shows and bus people will add up. Deal."

Richard held his hand out to Henry. Together the men shook hands.

"And, Richard, if it turns out that's not a fair deal for you, we can renegotiate it."

"Either way," Richard said with a smile.

"Good. I'll start drawing up some plans for you to look over."

"I'm looking forward to seeing them."

"Great, and then we can look them over together."

Richard nodded his head.

"Richard, I want to talk to you for a minute about —"

"Is there something wrong with our deal?"

"No, it's not that at all. I just wanted to tell you something." Henry sat quietly for a short time. Richard simply waited for Henry to continue.

"When I was a young man I met a man by the name of Sam Allenby. He was someone who I trusted, someone who I got to know very well. I considered him to be a true friend of mine. You're obviously a few years younger than he was, but I wanted you to know how much you remind me of him."

"Thank you, Henry, that means a lot to me. I feel very honored to be placed on the same level as him."

Henry said no more on the subject, he just nodded his head.

Within a matter of a few weeks the framework stood in place. Henry had to subcontract some of the work, but he figured it was well worth doing. Kate joined in the construction project and was very helpful. Henry let everyone know Kate was entirely in charge, and if there were any questions they should address them with her. She loved being called boss. Kate knew any questions that she needed answered were only the distance from her lips to Henry's ear away. She also was available to keep an eye on the workmen to make sure a piece of bad lumber wasn't used and then hidden from view by other wood.

Periodically Richard would take a walk around the construction site and view the headway that was being made. He was happy with what was being accomplished. When Henry would see him meandering around the construction area, he always stopped to discuss any ideas he had or asked for Richard's input. Each man seemed more concerned about the other man's opinion than his own. At last the project was completed, other than seats and carpeting being put into place. Although the job was considerable, it took much less time than anticipated.

Seeing Henry walk into the restaurant one day Richard waved to him, trying to get his attention.

"What's up?" Richard.

"In one week we're going to have three or four bus loads of people coming in. Will we be ready? To tell you the truth, Henry, I'm a little nervous over all this money outlay."

"Let's do a little math," Henry suggested. "How many people are coming in total?"

"I'd say 130, 135 people more or less."

"And that's for one show?"

"Yes."

"And you're charging them how much a piece?"

"Eighteen dollars."

"Let's take the lower figure of 130, times $18.00. It comes out to roughly... Oh, two thousand three hundred dollars. Now, that's one night, Richard. There are, of course, other things you'll be making money on such as drinks, food, CD's and a like. If you're concerned things aren't going well, I'll spend another half an hour behind the microphone so the people feel they're really getting their money's worth. I told you I'm behind you one hundred percent, and I am. If everything goes south, I'll still be here for you."

"Thanks, Henry. I think it's just nerves. By the way, I've got a check here for the CD's I sold for you. I have another order coming in a few days."

"Put it towards the bills."

"That wasn't our agreement, this money is yours alone."

"Richard, we're partners, and we're partners in everything."

"Thanks, Henry."

"By the way, how much do I owe you for being my agent?"

"Well, I haven't charged you anything."

"Aren't we a couple of funny business partners?"

"Well, at least we're honest enough to admit it," he laughed.

Henry held his right hand out in front of him. "Look at this, this hand represents the best contract I've never signed."

Richard laughed.

The opening night of the expansion had arrived. As planned, the construction was all completed. Though they didn't say anything, both men were excited to see how everything would work itself out. As Henry drove towards Richard's Steak House he couldn't help but notice lights being reflected off of clouds in the sky ahead of him. The closer he got to the restaurant the brighter the lights were. Henry pulled into a parking spot that was reserved for him, his name printed neatly on a sign designating that fact. Henry smiled as he looked off to the right and observed four searchlights on a rotating stand. Their lights acted like a beacon in the night calling attention to the business. Off to the back of the parking lot sat four charter buses. Most of the rest of the lot was filled as well. Henry got out of his vehicle anxious for the evening to start, yet feeling a little apprehension in his gut.

As Henry entered through the front door, he was immediately greeted by Richard. The two men looked at each other and smiled.

"I love the lights, Richard."

"I heard about them and just couldn't resist myself."

"And weren't you the one worried about money?" chuckled Henry.

"I know," Richard said.

"Can I get a cold glass of water, Judy?" Henry asked.

"I have it ready for you, lots of ice just the way you like it, and it's really cold now."

"How did you know I wanted one?"

"Every night you sing you ask me for one, I'm just getting used to it. I think your mind is somewhere else and you do it without realizing it."

"Thank you, Judy."

Henry walked over and sat down on a stool. He looked over at the closed doors that led to the addition. Music playing from the sound system filtered through the air from the other room.

"You've got about five minutes," Richard stated.

"Okay."

"I'll introduce you and you can take it from there."

"That sounds good."

Henry could see Richard was a little nervous just by his actions.

"It's just like any other night, Richard, only a few more people."

"I suppose so. Well, are you ready?"

"Whenever you are," Henry answered as he followed Richard to the double doors. He stood just outside of them as Richard walked up onto the stage. Stacked keyboards, and a sound system were to his left. He welcomed the people and then made a short introduction about Henry. The people applauded as Henry walked toward the stage. He smiled as he took his place on the platform beside a microphone.

"Tonight I am gratified to see all of you here, though with these lights shining in my face it's difficult to see your faces. It makes me feel like I'm in a lineup at a police station."

Some of the people chucked.

"I usually start out singing one of my favorites, but tonight is special for me and my business partner, Richard, who you just met and introduced me. So let's see if I can make it special for you also. Now, since you're our guests this evening I thought it might be fun to play, stump the singer. You name a song, one that everyone has heard of. High school fight songs from your alma mater don't count, but songs we've all heard of. If I can't play it for you or sing it, I'll give you a free CD. Now, how does that sound to everyone, fun I hope."

The audience applauded. Soon numerous names of songs rang out as Henry took on their challenge behind the piano. Not only did the people love listening to his voice, they enjoyed playing the game. At one point Henry stepped from the stage as he sang without any musical accompaniment. He began walking among the people as he continued to sing. As he reached the back part of the room he smiled. Emma and Kate sat together listening to him. As the song came to an end, the people applauded once again.

"I would like to take this opportunity to introduce everyone to my mother Emma, and wife Kate who, unbeknownst to me, have come to join us on this very special evening."

Once again the audience showed their approval with their hands.

"Mom, would you stand up, and Kate."

The two women stood and then nodded their heads, Emma even waving slightly. After a few moments they both sat down.

"I almost feel like a celebrity," Emma whispered.

"I know what you mean," Kate answered softly.

"I would like to dedicate the next song to my mother, if I may."

Henry returned to his position on the stage. Emma smiled as she looked at Kate, Kate returning her smile. Making a few adjustments to the settings on the electronic pianos Henry then placed his fingers upon the keys. The music softly spoke their notes through the speaker system as the score to the song "Mother" began playing. Henry once again filled the room with the magnificence of his voice. This time, however, it was a little different. Each word seemed sweeter, more tenderly sung than usual. Now the audience almost looked spellbound with the words he sang. People were mesmerized. As Henry continued to sing, he could observe a man sitting in the third row reach up and slightly wipe his eyes.

Once the program was over Henry stood outside the doors as the people began to file out. The group around him was considerable. Emma stopped by long enough to give Henry a kiss on his cheek and to thank him before Kate took her home.

A woman put her hand on his arm.

"Sir, I so wanted to have you sing a song I love, but my mind went blank, and I just couldn't think of the title."

"It was probably the excitement of the evening. So how does it go?" he asked.

"Well, something like La, La, La, La, La,... La, La, La, La, La."

"Oh, I think I know which song you're referring to."

Henry began to sing a few words to a song.

"That's it, that's it!" the woman said excitedly.

"Well, why don't you join in with me and we'll sing it together?"

"Oh, I don't know if I could."

Henry looked at the people assembled around the two of them.

"Say," he said loudly, "how about helping out this young lady and me. I'll start singing her song and every one of you can join in."

As Henry began singing the song the whole group of people began joining in. With the ending of the song the people applauded.

"Thank you so much, sir," the woman said with a smile.

"It's Henry, and you're welcome."

It was the little things Henry did that endeared him to his audiences so much. Arriving at work very early one evening, Henry took a seat at a table.

"Can I get you something to drink?" Judy asked.

"Just coffee, please."

"What are you doing here so early?"

"Kate has a headache and was going to take a nap to see if it would go away, so I decided to come in early and give her a little quiet time."

"I wonder how much quiet time the bus driver out back is getting?"

"What do you mean?"

"Apparently the charter service messed up, or someone did, and the bus driver is catching it from the people. They're an hour and forty-five minutes early now, and they've been out there fifteen minutes already. It's one of those mystery trip deals, and what they're doing here this early is obviously a mystery to all of them."

"Make that coffee to go, will you?"

"Anything you say."

"Thanks."

Henry immediately walked out the door to be with the people waiting on the bus. Stepping through the bus door Henry smiled and waved to everyone. They knew who he was immediately. Henry saw the name, "Bob" on the bus driver's nametag. Though he was a complete stranger to Henry, that didn't deter him from attempting to take a bad situation and make it better for all concerned.

Turning to the bus driver he winked and then stated loudly, "I'm glad to see that Bob came through for me, and I apologize to you, and especially to him for being late. Ladies and gentlemen, your bus driver, Bob, and I set this up some time ago. He asked me if he brought a busload of people here, kept it a secret from all of you, and I'm sure he did, if I would give you a little pre-show. I've known Bob for a little while, and he's quite the guy." Henry figured he hadn't lied to anyone since a little while could be a matter of a second or two. "I'm very pleased to visit with you as part of your mystery trip." The individuals loudly applauded the driver as well as Henry. They were thrilled with this unexpected turn of events.

"And one thing you all should know before I start, Bob will accept any large tips you may want to offer him. And ladies and gentlemen, he deserves it for coming up with this idea in the first place."

Again the people applauded. Henry thought mentioning the tip was the only fair thing to do. He wanted to remind them the driver had suffered some abuse at their hands for something he had nothing to do with. Henry figured the people needed to realize things aren't always as they seem. Of course, nobody knew that better than Henry and the bus driver.

Henry would select someone from the passengers, a person he thought was very outgoing and ask them to sing a duet with him. A small group of ladies were put together as a makeshift singing ensemble. The laughter they experienced made the time fly quickly.

One of the female passengers asked Henry to tell her a little bit about himself. She explained she didn't really know anything about him other than hearing his voice on a CD. At this point Henry began sharing with the group little things he had experienced recently in his life.

He conveyed the episode with Melissa's wedding vows being read by Kim. How he sang the song for Greg and what his vows meant. He alluded to the grandmothers making it to the wedding. Henry told how he had received the gift of a baby grand piano, and why he got it. It was apparent to him the stories touched many of the women's hearts on the bus. With pride, he declared that Kate asked him to marry her. The group of individuals not only laughed loudly, some applauded hardily, especially the women.

When one person inquired about his scar, he was frank and to the point about it. Henry told them the whole background behind his scar. People appreciated his candor, the openness he expressed.

One of the last stories Henry shared with the group was concerning the little girl, Mary, and what she meant to him. He explained his part in playing Santa Claus and of her question to him that broke his heart. Henry actually wiped his eyes at one time as he spoke about her. He relayed to them how he felt the little girl had caressed his heart with her words, how she literally changed his life and made it better.

When Henry expressed to them he had to leave and get ready for the show, many begged him to stay. As he walked near the front door of the bus to leave Henry felt a hand on his arm. He turned and saw it was the bus driver.

"Thank you," Bob said with a smile.
"It was my pleasure."

Eventually the busload of people made it to their seats. Almost immediately they began to share with others what had happened to them in the parking lot. Some of the people expressed the fact they were actually jealous of them. It was on this night that Henry received the largest round of applause he had ever been awarded when the program was completed.

The parking lot soon grew too small with every busload that appeared outside of Richard's Steak House. Many people returned to hear his voice again. Every show was different. Even in Henry's mind he didn't know what to expect, or exactly what would occur when he stepped onto the stage. Many times he played to the desires and whims of the audience, which seemed to come natural to him. No matter what he did, he could do no wrong in the eyes of the audiences. Henry loved performing, and the people cherished his performances.

Together the two partners started making more money. Though they weren't getting rich by any means, they were making a very decent living. Richard found it necessary to hire someone to handle mail orders for the CD's and take care of bookings and such. As the months passed by, Richard's hidden fear over money concerns not only diminished; they vanished completely.

One day Henry and Richard were sitting in his office area to the business.
"Richard, I want to thank you."
"For what?"
"Ever since you and I became partners my life has improved, and I know I have you to thank for that."
"Really?"
Henry nodded his head.
"I have more time to be with my wife, I'm back to working on my hobby, and our bills are being paid."
"You and I have a good thing going for us, Henry."
"Yes, we do, and I'm very thankful for that."

"Just so you know, this week I'm paying off all of our business loans."

"All?"

"All. And another thing, our place is paid off in full."

"I thought you were going to say just my quarter share was paid off," Henry said.

"You mean your half."

"Pardon me?"

"I want you and me to be partners, half and half in everything. Is that okay with you, Henry?" Richard said as he smiled.

"Only a fool would say, 'no,' and I'm not a fool."

"Now we can start to save a little money, both of us."

"Thanks, Richard."

"And thank you, Henry."

Henry laughed as he stood up and put his hand out to Richard. Richard stood as they both smiled and shook hands.

As they began to sit down the phone rang. Reaching across the desk Richard picked up the phone and answered it.

"I'll tell him immediately."

"What is it?"

"Emma has just been taken to the hospital. Your wife drove her there. Apparently she wasn't feeling very well and Kate didn't want to take any chances."

"I'll talk to you later," Henry said as he left the room.

Richard just nodded his head, hoping everything would be okay for him.

It wasn't very long at all before Henry was standing over the hospital bed of Emma. Kate stood at his side.

"I didn't want to take any chances with her, I just brought her here immediately."

"Thank you, Kate."

"Oh, stop fussing," Emma stated. "Get a little heartburn and the world goes crazy."

"Well, we'll see what the doctors have to say, Mom."

The Promise

The wait wasn't terribly long when the doctor on duty walked into the room. He reached out and shook Henry's hand. It was obvious Emma wanted out of the hospital as soon as possible. Both men could see that by her facial expressions, and hear it in her words as well.

Henry remembered Emma once telling him, the only good thing about hospitals is if you want to die, visit one. He thought her feelings along that line stemmed from her spending so much time with her late husband Paul in one, this very one. Yes, she did not like being held captive, especially here.

"So when do you unlock this cage and let me go?"

"Well, we would like to keep you overnight for observation," the doctor stated.

"You want observation, stand by the back door and watch me leave."

The doctor could see by the monitor that Emma's heart beats were rising.

"Mom," Henry said in a forceful voice, "here's what's going to happen, like it or not. You're going to spend the night here. Kate and I will pick you up in the morning, only when and after they say you can go. Understand?"

"Yes, Henry," she answered as she lowered her head. She was smart enough to know when to give up when it came to Henry. Emma also understood certain battles weren't worth fighting, and she had already lost this one to her son.

As she lay in the bed Emma observed Kate rolling her wedding ring around and around her finger. She knew this only happened when Kate was extremely concerned or worried about something.

"What is, Kate?" she asked.

"What?"

"It's obvious you're concerned about something. Is it because of me or is there something else?"

"I don't know, I just —"

"For years I've done that very same movement with my own wedding band. Whenever I'm concerned about anything big, Paul being in the hospital, unexpected bad news, various things, I'd roll my wedding ring around and around on my finger. Tell me, Honey, what is it?"

"I don't think this is the time or place to do that."

Henry's attention immediately focused on Kate.

"What is it, Honey?" Henry said as he placed his hand on Kate's shoulder, "You know I'm here for you."

"And so am I," Emma was quick to say.

"Well, I just found out a few days ago... I'm pregnant."

Henry let out a yell as well as Emma, though hers was not quite as loud. Emma's blood pressure rose on the monitor. Nurses came running.

"It's okay, it's okay," the doctor informed them. An older gray haired nurse looked from behind the edge of a curtain she had pulled back to observe what had just happened.

"Kate just told everyone she's pregnant," the doctor announced.

Some of the nurses began to clap. Kate just stood in place wearing a large smile. Then came the bombardment of questions. When are you due, is it a boy or girl, what are you hoping for? Of course, there was the inevitable one, have you thought about a name?

The older nurse turned around and began walking back down the hallway to the nurses' station. She shook her head as she thought to herself, boy, I'm sure glad it's not me again. Seven times is enough for anyone to go through that.

The nurses returned once again to their duties. The doctor left the three to discuss the news they had just received.

"Why didn't you tell me sooner?" Henry asked.

"It just didn't seem like the right time."

"And now is?" he said.

"I was thinking to myself that I'd be in here one day and, I don't know, my mind just —"

"You've made me a very happy man," he said as he kissed her gently on her lips.

"I'm going to be a grandmother."

"Yes you are, Mom, yes you are," he repeated.

"Now, you've got to get me out of here so we can go shopping together," Emma said, as she reached over and took Kate's hand.

"There will be plenty of time for that, Mom, and just so you know, I'm looking forward to your help."

"Now you come over here and let me give you a kiss," Emma said as she pulled on Kate's hand.

Kate moved the foot or so over to Emma's position and bent down. She received a customary kiss on her cheek, as well as a smile from her. Emma then pulled Kate closer to her for a hug. Emma whispered in her ear "You've made me so happy, Kate. I'm just so overwhelmed with love for the both of you. Thank you."

For whatever reason, Kate felt a closeness expanding within her heart with Emma's actions. She had on many different occasions received a hug or a small kiss on her cheek from her. It was something that was not out of the ordinary. However, this time it seemed uniquely heartfelt. With her own mother gone, and the circumstances as they were, Kate felt a true unity building between the two of them. Kate looked down at Emma and smiled, a love for her growing steadily stronger with each passing moment.

Fortunately Emma was released from the hospital after only a couple of days. That having occurred, Henry was sure to keep a keen eye on her daily. Each day, when possible, he would stop and visit Emma in her home. In the back of his mind he wanted to spend as much time as he could with his mother. While Emma's health concerns seemed to dominate Henry's thoughts almost completely, it was like a two-edged sword. If he wasn't worried about Emma, it was Kate who absorbed his attention.

As months passed, Henry could observe Emma almost daily deteriorating in different ways. It was evident to him she was becoming progressively worse. When he expressed his thoughts to Kate, she would agree with him, though she tried to temper her feelings when talking to him about Emma. She didn't want to unduly alarm Henry, but she didn't want to make light of it either. Kate could observe signs in Emma's physical appearance that she didn't like seeing either. When she had an occasion to talk to Doc, she would express her thoughts to him about Emma's condition. Doc was very guarded with his words concerning Emma, not wanting to upset Kate, not wanting to give her false hope either. Doc knew very well he had the physician/patient relationship foremost to deal with. How Doc handled Kate's questions was very much along the same line as he did with Henry.

Field of White

When Melissa and Greg arrived at her parent's home she was surprised to see that the dining room table was already set. What intrigued her the most were the additional four plates that had been set into position.

"Are you having guests other than Greg's parents, it's usually just the six of us on Sunday?"

"Well, you'll just have to wait and see," Susan said with a smile.

With Edith and Frank walking through the front door Kenneth was quick to check out Edith's dessert offering.

"You brought two of them?" Kenneth said somewhat surprised.

"And both pies are different," she replied. "Well, Susan said she was having company today and wanted me to make sure there was enough to go around."

"Who is she having?" Melissa asked Edith quickly, trying to do an end run approach to her mother's non-answering of her question.

"She didn't say."

Susan smiled as she looked over at Melissa.

The front doorbell rang. Melissa quickly went to answer it, wanting to see who was hidden behind the door.

"Oh, it's so nice to see you two kids, and Mr. and Mrs. Carpenter," Melissa stated. "Now, let me see if I can get your names right. You are Betty and your name is — "

"Annie."

"That was my next guess," laughed Melissa.

"Welcome to our home. Come in," Susan said.

"It's nice to see you both," Kenneth added. "Let me take a second and introduce you to everyone."

After the appropriate introductions the people all moved to the dining room. Having once seated themselves, Susan and Edith put the food onto the table.

"I understand you work for the Summers' family, from what was said earlier," Frank stated.

"It's been about six months now," answered Fred.

As the people ate Melissa noticed her mother looking over at Kenneth, he returning her glance every so often. Once the table was cleared, and desserts enjoyed, Kenneth looked at Fred and his wife, Robin. Kenneth started speaking about Fred's job at the store. He looked at Robin as he spoke.

"Your husband, Mrs. Carpenter —"

"You can call me Robin if you like."

"Robin, your husband has done more than just a credible job for us. We're very, very, happy with his performance. He has not only allowed Susan the freedom to work on her charity interests, we're proud of the work he's done for us. You should be, too."

"We are."

Edith's ears began perking up. She never wanted to miss any words that would be exchanged around the table. This time it didn't involve her son or Melissa, it was a new set of characters in the old soap opera, she thought.

"Now, let's cut to the core of why you're all here." Kenneth turned his head to look at Fred.

"Fred, we have talked this over, Susan and I, and we want to make your job a full-time position."

Robin placed her hand to her face, completely surprised by this turn of events.

"Well, what do you think?"

"Thank you," was all Fred could say.

"Good," Kenneth said with a nod. "You're up, Honey."

"Fred, my husband and I have discussed this and we're both in agreement, in fact, we won't take no for an answer. We feel you have done more than your share at work since joining us. There were days when we know you stayed longer than you had to and we both appreciated that. Every day you beat us into work. I have yet to find a single mistake in any of your calculations. You impress me... us, to no end."

Susan got up and went to the kitchen cabinet. She opened a drawer and removed an envelope from its interior. Walking back to the table she handed it to Fred.

"Now, this is for you and your family. You can open it now," suggested Susan.

As Fred opened the envelope his wife watched along with the two children. He pulled out a check from its interior. He let out a deep breath.

"Fred, my husband and I want to give your family the pay you would have received from both of us had you been working full-time since the very beginning."

Robin looked from her husband's side. She began to cry softly.

"Are you okay, Mama?" little Annie asked.

"Very much so, Honey, very much."

"Thank you again," Fred said. "This is very generous on the part of both of you. Thank you is hardly enough to say how I feel."

"Fred," Susan said as she turned her head to him, "the only figures we found a mistake in were our own calculations. We should have done this sooner. Oh... and Greg, you were right."

"What's that?"

"When you said I'd love having the time to work on my various charity projects, you were right."

Greg smiled.

Everyone sat visiting at the table as the little girls enjoyed a smaller second helping of dessert.

"More coffee?" Susan asked.

"Oh, I'm fine," Frank said.

"Anyone else?"

Not hearing any responses Susan walked over and returned the coffee decanter to its position.

"Mom," Melisa said, "Kate is starting to get real close to her delivery date. We need to pick out a baby gift, but what I don't know. I wanted her gift to be very special in nature."

"I understand, Honey, but we may have a little problem with that. I can't think of anything at the store that falls into that category, and something homemade is out of the question."

"Not necessarily so," came Robin's voice.

"Excuse me."

"I'll make a baby blanket for you, if you like. I crochet."

"Oh, Robin, would you do that for us?" Melissa said in her usual excited voice.

"I'd be happy to."

"And I want to pay you for your work," Susan declared.

"Really, not on your life," Robin said with a smile.

"I think she's due within a week or two," Susan said, "maybe three. Will that be a problem?"

"Then I'll start as soon as I get the yarn tomorrow."

"Thank you so much," Susan said.

"It will be my pleasure. Is there anything special you want in the design?"

"How about something with different animals on it, can you do that?" Melissa asked.

"Of course," Robin smiled.

"Thank you, Robin."

"And ladies," Fred said, "she does beautiful work."

"I can hardly wait to see it," Melissa declared.

Within a week as Susan stood talking to Kenneth in his office one morning. There was a small rap on the office door.

"Come in," Susan said.

The door opened slowly as Fred walked in, a large bag in his hand. Kenneth could see he was having some difficulty with his crutches as well as handling the large bag at the same time.

"Here, let me give you a hand," he said.

"No, no, it's okay, I've almost got it."

Kenneth had learned one important thing about Fred during their relationship. He knew Fred was a proud man, one who never asked for help if at all possible. Kenneth admired that about him.

"So what do you have in the bag?" Susan asked.

"It's your baby blanket. Robin wanted me to bring it in for you."

"Oh, I have to get Melissa, she'll want to see it. I'll be right back."

With Melissa returning with her mother, both women waited for the other to make the first move towards the bag.

"You open it, Melissa."

"No, Mom, you do it."

"Then I'll do it," Kenneth said.

"No, you won't," Susan was quick to state, "and besides, I don't know if your hands are clean. After all, this is for a baby. You do it, Honey, Kate's your best friend."

Fred stood watching as Melissa took the bag from him and opened it. He hoped his wife's work was two-fold. One, it met with what they desired the gift to look like and, number two, the quality of workmanship met their standards. However, Fred had no real worries when it came to the quality of his wife's skills. As Melissa pulled the blanket from the bag she couldn't help herself as she exclaimed loudly, "Oh, Mother!"

Fred smiled to himself with the two words having been spoken. He knew his wife had exceeded their wildest dreams in a gift. The white blanket was soft and warm looking. Along its edge were eight six inch squares depicting various animals in different colors. There was an elephant, lion, hippo, tiger, zebra, giraffe, rhino, and monkey.

"This is so adorable. It's almost as if the animals are on a field of snow," Melissa said. In her excitement she reached over and kissed Fred on the cheek.

"I love it. Will you tell Robin I'm so happy with it? I wanted something special for my friend and you two delivered it. Thank you again."

"Fred, do you think your wife would be interested in making a few baby blankets for us?"

"I'll ask her."

"Say Fred, are your kids in school today?" asked Melissa.

"Yes, they are."

"Mom, Dad, is it okay if I take Robin out for lunch to thank her?"

"That's a wonderful idea," Susan said. "Would you mind if I tagged along?"

"I'd love it. I'll call her and see if she's free."

"I think she will be," Fred said, "She never mentioned that she had any plans for today."

"Fred, will you have a seat for a minute, Susan and I want to discuss something with you," Kenneth said in a somewhat serious voice.

"Mom, I'll go and call her right now."

"Good idea, Honey."

Melissa left the three in the room as she went back to her own office to make the call. She wanted to be the first one to thank Robin personally.

"Fred, as I said, Susan and I wanted to talk something over with you."

"What is it?"

"Susan has checked into... we'd like to ask you if you would think about... I know there are places..."

"Oh, Kenneth, really," Susan said loudly. "Fred, Kenneth and I want to help you to get an artificial leg. Now, I've done some checking and you'll have to make an appointment, you'll be evaluated and so forth. What do you think?"

"I would probably miss some days of work with appointments and such. I don't know."

"Fred, I had your job before you took it, I can fill in for you if necessary. So what do you think?" Susan said with an obvious smile across her face.

"I think I'd like to try for it."

"Great. Now, I have something I want to ask you since you've agreed to check into getting a leg." Susan walked over to be beside Fred. "Fred, if things work out along that line, do you think we can keep it a secret from your family, your kids if at all possible? You can go to appointments, fittings, whatever needs to be done. I don't know that much about it, still we'll back you all the way. And don't you worry about your pay, that should be the least of your concerns. What I want you to do, and it's your decision entirely, of course, but I would love to see the look on the faces of your children when you walk without your crutches to help you. Obviously your wife would have to know what's going on and so forth."

"Oh God, wouldn't that be something," Fred said.

"Let's all work together on this," Susan expressed.

"All of us," Kenneth stated.

"Thank you both."

Kenneth and Susan merely nodded their heads.

Melissa walked into the office, a smile on her face.

"She's free and I offered to pick her up."

"Oh, she'll love going out for lunch with you two," Fred said.

"And, Melissa, it's my treat," Susan said.

"Not on this one, Mom, I'm picking up the lunch. After all, like you said, Kate's my best friend. What would you think about going to Kate's home and giving her our gift afterwards?"

"You're just filled with great ideas today."

"I'm going to take the blanket downstairs and have it gift wrapped."

"Okay. Then we'll head over to Fred's house, have lunch, and then it's off to Kate's."

"I'll be back in a minute," Melissa said as she picked up the bag and headed towards the office door. "Thank you so much, Fred," Melissa said as she turned and left the room.

The two women having lunch with Robin was an unexpected treat for both of them as well as Robin. Fred's wife was fun to be around. Her sense of humor was expressive and funny. She would convey little stories about her children and various acts of mischief they had been involved in. Robin alluded to how the girls wanted her to keep a pet worm and other items of interest they would bring home to her. Susan shared with her some of Melissa's acts along the same lines throughout her childhood.

At one point during the meal Robin confided with them how difficult it was for their family during Fred's period of unemployment. She explained that flying the kite on the day of the Summers' Summer Picnic was simply a free way of having family fun time together.

"We've seen to it the girls never went hungry, of course, but that day at the park their eyes were as big as saucers when they saw the people, the food, and everything. I just didn't have it in my heart to tell them no when you offered them the hotdogs. I know it was a simple thing for you to do, but it meant the world to my girls. They talked about it all the way home. Thank you, Melissa, it meant a lot to us."

"I guess you never know what a simple act can mean to someone if you don't know what's going on in their lives," Susan expressed.

"And look how everything ended up," Melissa smiled, "I've got a blanket, Fred's got a job, and the kids got hotdogs and burgers." She laughed as she looked at the women.

"And you and I got a free meal," Susan said.

"We sure did," Robin said smiling, "and thank you for the meal also."

Melissa just smiled as she looked at Robin.

After having shared in the lunch with Robin, Susan and Melissa headed over to Kate's home. The drive was consumed with talk of Kate's baby blanket and how she would appreciate getting it. They both agreed she would love it. Upon reaching Kate's home, Melissa carried the gift into the house. A baby rattle was tucked into the bow. After the usual greetings, the women sat on the couch. Melissa handed the gift to Kate. She smiled as she opened it. Kate was thrilled with her gift, not only a useful blanket, it was a keepsake to be handed down at an appropriate time.

The remainder of the afternoon was spent discussing how Kate was holding up. Emma's condition was also a topic of discussion, however, Kate didn't offer her opinion as to how she was doing. Doc confided in her that Emma's condition was worsening daily. He expected to see the doctors at the hospital dealing with her problem in the near future. Neither one mentioned that fact to Henry. Let Emma and him enjoy their time together, Doc suggested to her, not cluttered with thoughts of what hasn't taken place yet. As the women spoke to each other Kate grabbed for her stomach.

"Are you alright, Kate?" Melissa asked.

"I don't know, I just felt a little funny."

"Here, Kate, let me get you something to drink."

"I don't think that's the water I've got to worry about."

"You mean —" Susan stated.

"I think my water broke."

"Well, you may need this," Melissa said as she grabbed the gift. "I'll bring it along just so you have it."

Within minutes the women saw to it that Kate was on the way to the hospital. A quick call to Henry and he was on his way as well.

As the women sat with Kate in a room, Henry walked in.

"How are you doing, Honey?" he said as he took her by the hand.

"I guess we're going to have a baby," she joked.

Henry smiled.

"Thank goodness you were visiting her when this happened."

"I guess it was meant to be," Melissa said.

"We're so happy for both of you," Susan said with a slight smile.

Doc walked into the room.

"Henry, can I see you now for a minute?"

"Sure, Doc."

"This way."

"Go on Henry, we'll both keep her company for now," Susan said.

Henry followed Doc down the hall for a short distance and then into a room. Sitting on a couple of chairs were Jackie and Sid. Sid was bent over, his head in his hands. He appeared to have been crying. Jackie didn't appear much better. Her eyes were red and swollen.

"Jackie," Doc said.

"Henry, I'm so sorry," was all Jackie could mutter.

"Is Emma dead?"

"No," she replied.

"Oh, thank God."

"We were sitting at the table visiting and the next thing I know she's falling to the floor. Sid grabbed her just in time. We had her rushed here as quickly as we could. It just happened a few minutes ago. Well, maybe twenty minutes. We tried to call you but there was no answer."

Henry began to shake his head back and forth, not knowing what to say or do. Tears came rushing to his eyes. Sid got up from his position and walked over to Henry. Together the two men hugged, trying to console each other.

"So Doc, how does it— how does it look to you?" Henry asked in a broken voice. "Don't play around with your words, just tell me like it is."

"Well, Henry, to be frank with you, I don't give her very long."

Sid began sobbing as Jackie put her arms around him.

"We'll do everything to make her as comfortable as we can, but her heart is very fragile. It's simply wearing out."

Henry took a deep breath, his eyes filling rapidly with tears.

"I feel like a man on a tightrope, Doc, Which way do I step, forward or backward?"

"What do you mean, Henry?" Jackie asked.

Henry didn't answer her.

"Kate's in here having a baby now and Emma, of course, is dying," Doc said.

"Don't say that!" Henry said angrily.

"Henry!" Jackie said.

"You said to tell it like it is," Doc stated firmly. "I'm not going to sugarcoat it, but if you would rather I not say what it is then —"

"I'm sorry, Doc, you're right."

"I understand how difficult all of this is to handle right now. Here's my suggestion. You visit with Kate for a while and let her see you're here for her. I'll check on Emma. Later I'll come and get you, then we'll go see Emma."

"Thank you, Doc. I'm sorry for how I —"

"That's okay, I understand."

"Henry, Sid and I will keep an eye on Emma for you, you know that," Jackie said in an assuring voice.

"Thank you both for everything," Henry replied.

"If anything — if there should be any change from what there is now, we'll immediately find you and let you know," Doc said.

"Thank you."

"Now," Doc went on, "you go back to be with Kate, and I'll check into Emma. Is that a plan?"

The parties all nodded their heads in agreement.

Henry walked back to Kate's room. As he did his thoughts were of the two most important women in his life, both of them needing his immediate attention. Henry wished he could cut his heart in half, sending one piece to be with Emma, the other half to be with Kate. His mind wrestled back and forth between the women he loved so much. Henry's emotions were sitting on both ends of a teeter-totter at the same time. One end held Emma, the other Kate. Which end carried the most weight, he didn't know. Henry knew they both bore the same amount of emotional anxiety for him. There was only one thing to do, let everything unfold before him. Henry knew he could only control what he was allowed to, the rest would take care of itself. He took a deep breath as he entered the room.

"Melissa and her mother went to get something to eat at the cafeteria," Kate said as Henry walked up to the bed. "They said they wouldn't be too long."

"So how are you feeling?" inquired Henry.

"Oh, I've had better days."

Within minutes Kate was showing the effects of preparing for childbirth. The contractions were very much present and closely spaced. One of the nurses timed them as Kate gave out an unfamiliar yell to Henry's ears. Things were moving according to schedule, but whose schedule was being followed, Kate's or the little baby within. Only time would tell. Susan and Melissa soon returned. They could see the stress Kate was going through.

"I'm sorry, you ladies will have to leave," a nurse stated.

"We understand," Susan said nodding her head.

Melissa walked over to be by Kate's side. She reached over the railing and gave her a kiss on her forehead.

"Why don't you go home, and I'll call you when I have some news for you," Henry stated.

"Thank you, Henry," Melissa said. She then took a couple of steps toward Henry and put her arms around him. "If there is anything, anything at all you need —"

Henry shook his head and smiled slightly.

As both women began to leave the room Melissa stopped momentarily and looked back at the couple as she stated, "We love you both."

Kate smiled as she lifted her hand slightly giving a wave to them as they walked out of the room.

The rest of the evening went as expected for the maternity nurses on duty. At the chosen time, according to the baby's timetable, Kate presented Henry with a beautiful baby girl. Henry sat beside Kate stroking her hand with his for some time as he looked at the baby cradled in his wife's arms.

"I love you so much, Kate," Henry said softly.

"I know."

Henry kissed her hand gently.

"So today was a day of gifts, a blanket for me and a baby for you," she smiled.

Henry smiled back, however, there was a hint of dampness in his eyes which Kate caught immediately.

"Honey, is there something wrong, something I don't know about. What's going on?"

Now Henry's cheeks had tears running down them. He reached up and wiped his eyes.

"What's wrong, Henry?" Kate said in a demanding voice. She definitely knew something was awry, and she needed to know what.

"Emma is in the hospital right now, too. Doc has conferred with other doctors and they agree with him. Emma doesn't have much time. I'm sorry, you didn't need to know all about this, especially in your condition with having just given birth."

"I didn't need to know all about Emma? Henry, this is when we need to hang onto each other the tightest. Honey, don't you ever feel you have to keep something from me like this, we're a team, remember that."

As Henry looked at her, Kate could see his love for her in his facial expressions, and the turmoil he experienced as well.

"You better go and see her, and now. Let me know what you find out, how she's doing. Will you do that for me?"

Henry nodded his head, and then placed a kiss on her forehead. He then reached over slightly and put a gentle kiss on the baby beside her.

"I won't be very long, I promise you."

"Don't you just make an appearance because of me, you visit with her. You take all the time you need for both of you."

Once again Henry nodded his head as he walked from the room.

Henry stood outside the Critical Care Unit for some time. He could observe Emma laying in a bed with various medical devices attached to her. Henry felt a hand on his shoulder.

"Go in and see her," Doc stated.

"Doc, is she awake?"

"She's in and out."

"Should I tell her about Kate and the baby?"

"Why don't we wait on that, give her time to rest. Besides, knowing her she'll want to run right down there and see the baby, maybe even offer her a piece of fruitcake."

Henry smiled through his damp eyes.

"She really doesn't need any more excitement tonight. Just try to comfort her as best you can. And by the way, congratulations to you and Kate on the arrival of your baby girl."

"Thanks, Doc."

Henry opened the door and walked in stopping beside Emma's bed. He stood there for a little while.

"Mom, it's me, Henry."

"Henry," came a very soft reply.

"Yes, Mom, it's me."

Emma's hand gently began tapping the blanket on the bed that covered her. Henry took her hand in his. He turned his head not wanting her to see that he had a face filled with tears. Emma seemed to drift off, not moving much at all, if any. Shortly thereafter her eyes opened slightly.

"Henry, you still here?"

"Yes, I am, Mom."

"Son, if I should die, you remember what you promised me."

"I do, Mom."

"I want you to sing Danny Boy at my funeral."

"I know, Mom, but please don't talk that way."

"Well, just the same."

"Mom, what would you say if I were to sing that for you now?"

"Oh, Henry, that would be so special. Please do that."

"I will, Mom."

"I never told you this, but I've got a little Irish blood running through this old lady's pipes. Maybe that's why I've lasted so long."

"Mom, you need to rest."

Emma didn't reply. Henry began to sing the words to the song Danny Boy. Though he sang it softly his words reached out the doorway into the hallway. Nurses and visitors stopped and listened as he sang to Emma.

"Mom, I'm going to let you rest now. Doc said you could use some quiet time. I'll be back a little later to check on you."

"Okay," came Emma's soft response. Within seconds she once again drifted off into a world of unconsciousness. Henry stood up and wiped his eyes. He then quietly left the room, his mind filled with numerous questions.

Upon his return to Kate, Henry tried his best to answer her questions concerning Emma. Henry explained the situation. He told her about singing to

Emma; that Doc thought it best to wait a little while before telling Emma about the baby.

"Henry, do you think Grandpa is right on that?"

"Well, he's been around ill people most of his life."

"I understand that, but what if she doesn't make it, she will have died without knowing she has a granddaughter. That would be a tragedy."

"Okay. Honey, here's what we're going to do, if it's okay with you, of course. First of all, I need to know you're physically strong enough to go and see Emma. Secondly, we'll see how Emma feels."

"You know, Henry, they always talk about women working in the rice fields, picking rice or whatever, they have a baby, and then they're right back to work. I'll be okay."

"So where's the rice field, I didn't see one. You need to take care of yourself first. We'll deal with this in the morning."

"It's almost morning now, just a couple more hours is all."

"We'll wait and see how those few more hours play themselves out; okay?"

"Okay, Honey."

For the Love of Mothers

Henry stood beside the hospital bed, his right hand reaching over the silver bedrails on the side of it. He held Emma's hand in his. Seated in a wheelchair, Kate was brought into the room by a nurse. In her arms was a newborn wrapped in a homemade baby blanket, the gift from Melissa and Susan.

Because of Emma's position in the bed it was difficult for her to see. Henry smiled gently as he looked at her. He reached over and picked up the baby from Kate's arms. Henry held the little one high enough so Emma could see the infant.

"Mother, I'd like you to meet our beautiful little baby girl, Miss Emma Elizabeth Morgan."

The words, Emma Elizabeth, brought tears to Emma's eyes instantly.

"Oh my, oh my," were her only faint words. She placed her hand onto the blanket beside her. She gently tapped it up and down. Henry knew immediately what she wanted. He delicately placed the baby next to Emma in the bed. Emma's arm cradled the baby girl as she looked at Henry. Emma's eyes now had a few tears running down the side of her face. Henry reached over to a small table next to the bed and retrieved a couple of tissue. He gently wiped Emma's eyes.

"I'm so proud," her weak voice declared.

Henry carefully lifted the baby up and turned her head down slightly towards Emma. She placed a tiny kiss on the child's forehead.

"Thank you, Kate… Son," she said, her words barely audible.

Kate smiled, her eyes damp with moisture. Henry returned the baby once again to be next to Emma. After a few minutes Henry carefully lifted the baby up and returned her to Kate's waiting arms. He could tell Emma wanted to say something to him, but her voice was very muted. He bent down over the bedrails to get closer to her.

"It's been a wonderful day for me," her raspy voice whispered, "and now I can talk to my Paul and tell him all about it."

"Emma," Henry said softly, "Paul's not here."

Emma gave him a small smile as she reached up and took Henry's hand in hers once again.

"But he is," she said.

Henry squeezed Emma's hand gently as he bent slightly closer to hear her last words to him.

"I love you, Son," she said as an alarm's monotone voice began to fill the room. Henry could feel Emma's hand go slack in his. More tears immediately formed in his eyes, his body feeling weak.

Kate was quickly wheeled out into the hallway. Henry turned and slowly followed her, not looking back as nurses began working on Emma. He knew in his heart she was gone from her earthly body. Henry also understood his memories of her would forever be captured in his own heart, just as much as Sam's were to him daily. He slowly walked out into the hallway placing his hand upon Kate's shoulder. Kate reached up and put her hand over his.

"She'll always be with us, Henry," Kate expressed to him, weeping as she spoke.

"I know... I know she will," he repeated to her as he reached up wiping his eyes with his hand.

Hearing what had just happened Doc quickly made his way to where Henry and Kate were in the hallway.

"There isn't much I can say to comfort either one of you," Doc stated, "but I want both of you to remember and understand this. Emma had a full and wonderful life. She had people who loved her and watched over her, and they were beside her at the very end when she needed them the most."

Henry nodded his head, tears still heavy in his eyes. Kate gently rocked the baby in her arms as she nodded her agreement.

"Henry, I'll take care of things at this end for you. You give me a call when you feel up to it and we'll go from there."

"Thank you, Doc."

Doc placed his hand upon Henry's shoulder and simply nodded his head as he spoke.

"There is one thing I want both of you to take from this day. Emma's heart was always strong enough to share her love with the both of you. Cherish that thought about her forever."

Henry stepped behind the wheelchair as he took a handle in each one of his hands. He began to push the wheelchair slowly down the hallway in the direction of the elevator and Kate's room. As she looked up over her shoulder at Henry, her heart was in agony for him. Kate knew she had never seen his face so filled with such sadness and sorrow. Henry's head hung down. He wept loudly as they moved away from the room. Kate bit down on her lower lip trying to keep herself from crying anymore than she had been. She didn't want Henry to feel any more heartache and anguish than he was already experiencing. She thought he had enough to struggle with in dealing with his own emotions, without trying to console her. Kate attempted to hide her flush face and eyes from him, though it was a useless gesture.

When Henry finally left the hospital, he went straight home. His first stop was to his bedroom dresser where he retrieved the envelope containing the letter from Emma that she had given him a few years earlier. While Henry's memories of events were impeccable, it still comforted him at times to hold an item such as this in his grasp. He stared at it in his hands, not opening it, just simply holding it as the memory of that day was relived in his mind. Henry took the letter from inside the envelope and unfolded it. He looked down at the list of items he was requested to do by Emma. Henry remembered the day she had given the envelope to him, instructing him to please adhere to her every wish. Yes, he told her then, all that she desired would be fulfilled. He began reading the letter for the second time, once the day he received it, and then now.

"Dear Henry, in case anything happens to me, will you be kind enough to take care of my funeral arrangements. Number one, notify my attorney."

"Number two, make my funeral arrangements with Marcus/Smith Funeral Home. Order a coffin in the moderate price range. Arrange for many beautiful flowers.

Number three, make arrangements with the church. I want a church funeral and pay the church well for the service. I wish to be buried next to my husband, Paul. The plot in the cemetery has already been arranged for. Please see to it that my name and date are engraved next to Paul's on our headstone.

Number four, I have a safety deposit box in the National Bank, where I have a copy of my will and some other papers. There you will also find time certificates, stocks, and bonds.

I have chosen you, Henry, because you are the most reliable, dependable, honest, and trustworthy of anybody I know.

Please take care of my grave and pray a little for Paul and me."

Once Henry had completed reading the letter he reached for the phone and called Emma's attorney. His next call was to Pastor Phil. After receiving a few preliminary instructions from both of them he got up and went into the front room. Henry sat back in his easy chair and allowed himself the opportunity to take a deep breath or two. He felt simply exhausted, his body even aching as he sat there. A slight headache began forming in the upper portion of his head. He closed his eyes attempting to picture Emma's smile in his mind, but his thoughts were fruitless. Maybe, he contemplated, a cup of coffee will help to clear my mind. He walked in a slightly staggering manner to the stove, his legs weak. Next he reached over and turned the burner on below the pot he used to heat hot water in. The phone rang behind him. He debated on whether to answer it, but then reached his hand out taking the receiver in it.

"Hello," his voice said in a trembling fashion.

"Henry, this is Melissa, I called to see how Kate and the baby are doing. She has had the baby, right?"

Henry stood in silence not saying a word, tears beginning to fill his eyes again. He sniffed his nose as he swallowed.

"Henry, did you hear me? How is Kate, I figured she must have had the baby by now. Is Kate okay?" her worried voice asked.

"Melissa," his voice choking heavily as he spoke, "Emma's dead," his voice trailing off almost to a whisper. "Emma's dead," he repeated as he began weeping loudly.

Melissa couldn't even imagine the pain Henry was now dealing with. With his words to her, her own heart began to break inside as well. Melissa began to cry. She knew, however, she had to get to him and Kate as quickly as possible.

"Henry, I'm so, so, sorry," her voice sobbing now as she spoke. "Henry, Greg and I will be there as soon as we can."

"It's not necessary," his voice said shaking with each word he spoke.

"Yes it is, and we'll get there as soon as we can. Henry, I want you to know how much people loved Emma, and how much they love you and Kate as well. Give all of us a chance to help you with whatever it is you need. And remember, Kate is going to need support in this as well."

"I understand," he said.

"As I said, we'll be there as soon as we can."

"Thank you. I have to go now," Henry said in an almost silent voice.

"Henry, I'll go to the hospital first, check on Kate and then we'll try to meet up with you as soon as we can."

"Okay," he stated as he reached over and hung the phone up.

Melissa, realizing Henry had hung up the phone, immediately phoned her mother. Susan answered it on the second ring. Once the situation had been conveyed to her, she told Melissa to meet them at her home as soon as possible.

"I'll see to it Greg comes with us," Susan informed Melissa.

"Thanks, Mom."

"Listen, Honey, I'm going to call Frank and Edith, they can inform Norm and Marylou we're going to be needing some flowers made up right away."

"That's a good idea. And Mom —"

"Yes?"

"— tell them to make them very special."

"I think that goes without saying, but I will mention it to them just the same."

Henry sat at the kitchen table staring at his cup of coffee. Numerous memories of Emma played out in his head. He smiled as he recalled how upset she was with him for not allowing her to take care of him when he was injured. The day she pointed out the workmanship of Jack Frost on the windowpane. There was the day on the porch when he sang Danny Boy to her. She expressed how she wanted him to sing that very song at her funeral. Henry knew it would be a heart wrenching promise for him to keep. He remembered the fruitcake gift for Ruth and the churchwomen; how Emma wanted him to deliver it for her and the ladies in the kitchen. The many cups of hot tea they shared together. Yes, there was always the warmth of a cup of tea to enjoy along with their conversations. Every thought of Emma opened a door or window to yet another wonderful memory of her. What would he do… a large void now encompassed his life.

A knock on his front door brought him quickly back to earth. He got up and walked to the door. Putting his hand on the handle he opened the door. It was Sid and Jackie.

"Can we come in?" asked Jackie.

Henry nodded his head. Sid's eyes were red and bloodshot, his face flush. As Sid stepped through the door each man looked at the other, both recognizing quickly the pain they each were suffering from. Sid reached his arms up taking Henry in them; Henry responding likewise. They held each other tightly sobbing, trying to offer the other comfort, but finding it for themselves in the embrace of the other. Jackie stood watching with watery eyes. She knew this was the best medicine for both of them.

"I'm going to miss her… her so much," Sid stated in a broken sentence.

"I know," Henry responded, "we both are."

"It feels like the day I lost my grandmother, she was the most precious person I ever — it's like I'm living that day all over again," Sid uttered.

"There were many times when we were having tea together when Emma spoke so highly of you and Jackie."

"She knew both of you loved her very much," Jackie offered.

As both men stepped back from each other they wiped their eyes.

"Henry," Jackie said, "we came here because we know Emma would want us to be with you. Now, I think — I know Sid needs to feel comforted as well as you. Perhaps we can all do that for each other."

Henry and Sid both nodded their heads as they stepped further into the house.

"Now, is there anything that needs attention at Emma's house, get the paper, check the furnace, bring in the mail, anything?"

Henry thought for a minute, running everything through his mind.

"Oh, Sophia, Emma's cat," he stated.

"What are your thoughts on her, Henry?" inquired Jackie.

"I don't know what to do with her. She would be Emma's first concern, I do know that."

"Well, Henry, why don't you let Sid and me take her to our home for now, that will give you time to tie up any loose ends, and she'll be well taken care of there. Sid and I love Sophia. Please let us help you in any way we can."

"I will, and thank you both," Henry mumbled.

"Henry, how is Kate handling everything, it has to be hard on her, having a baby and dealing with Emma's death as well."

"Kate's a strong and wonderful woman. I don't know how I could have handled any of this without her."

"If there is anything at all, just let us know. We'll go to the house now and see what needs to be done," Jackie said.

"We'll be back in touch with you," Sid stated as the two turned and left Henry's home.

Henry closed the door. He then walked over to the kitchen table. Taking the cup in his hand he thought to himself, what's next on this list?

Upon arriving at the hospital Melissa led the way to the front desk, moving quickly with every step she took. The others did their best to keep up with her.

"Is Doctor McDonald here?" she asked.

"I believe he still is."

"Good. Would you page him for me, please?"

"Of course," she answered. The woman working the desk remembered Melissa from when Henry had been hurt. She understood Doc and Kate had a very family like relationship with Melissa, as well as the rest of them.

As Doc walked through the folding doors, he immediately approached the group. The heaviness Melissa felt with the loss of Emma was evident to him in her face as he reached out to her, she being the closest one to him.

"Oh, Doc," Melissa said as she grabbed onto him tightly burying her head into his shoulder.

Doc held her snuggly in his arms as Melissa began sobbing. The rest of the group wiped their eyes, each one feeling the pain Melissa was dealing with. Even Doc's eyes showed a watering to them as he held onto her. Eventually, Melissa released her grip on Doc, stepping back from him slightly. She wiped her eyes.

"Thank you, Doc," Melissa stated, "I just needed to do that."

"We all need to be comforted at difficult times."

The members of the group all nodded their agreement as some wiped their eyes once again.

"Let me just take a moment or two to tell you a few things I think all of you should know. Kate gave birth to a lovely little girl very early this morning. She and the baby are doing fine. Henry, of course, was beside her for that.

We had a suspicion, a very strong one, that Emma wasn't going to make it much longer. I informed Henry of our wariness on that subject. After talking it over with him, we felt if Kate was strong enough, if she could at all handle it, we would take her to Emma's room to allow her to see the baby. I felt we had a very limited window to accomplish that. Kate, of course, asked Henry what he thought about it. Henry informed her that only she could answer that question, it depended entirely on how she felt. I admired Henry for that, not pushing Kate into doing something she just wasn't up to, especially under the circumstances. Anyway, Kate said she wanted to try."

"That sounds like Kate," Melissa said, nodding her head as she spoke.

"So Emma was able to see the child and hold her for a very short time in her arms. She was also able to place a small kiss on the child's head, from what I was told. She was even able to hear the child's name, Emma Elizabeth, just before she died."

"Oh, Mom, they named the child after her and Kate's mother. Isn't that just wonderful?"

"Yes it is, Honey."

Doc nodded his head agreeing with Melissa. He then looked at them all as he stated, "They named her for the love they possessed for Emma, and Kate's mother as well."

Susan, Edith, and Melissa all wiped tears from their eyes. Greg turned his head away as he reached up putting his hand to his face. Frank and Kenneth wiped their eyes.

"This may sound unusual because I'm going to use the word, 'happiest' in my next sentence. I think the one thing that makes me the happiest of all is that their child is named after two women I've known personally for many years... and that anyone would be proud to call their own mother."

The group of six people gathered together in a small circle and embraced. Melissa reached over taking Doc by his hand and pulled him into their group. A woman at the desk nodded her head at another worker standing nearby indicating for her to look in that direction. The two women exchanged smiles as they observed the support each person offered the other.

Arrangements for Emma's funeral were hard for Henry to handle in some ways, easier in others. He needed to pick out a casket, one in a moderate price range. He didn't like that request by Emma. Henry felt Emma deserved the very best, but followed her instructions as he had promised to do. With the help of Kate things did, however, go smoothly.

When it came to selecting a dress for Emma to be buried in, Henry's mind was at a complete and utter loss. He mentioned that fact to Melissa.

She spoke to her mother concerning that problem. Susan asked Melissa if she would talk to Henry about letting Edith and Susan handle that task.

"We can find something appropriate at our store," Susan suggested.

"I'll be more than happy to help you with that," Edith said.

"Good."

Henry, of course, was very thankful for their help. He had no idea what he would have done otherwise. With Kate just getting out of the hospital he found everyone very helpful. He was smart enough to make use of their help, as if he really had any choice in the matter. It seemed as though the two most frequent words in his vocabulary was the phrase, "Thank you."

Whenever a babysitter was needed the list of volunteers was long and eager to help. There were times when even two women offered to handle the chore, Susan and Melissa, Edith and Jackie. Kim's mother, along with Dan's mother stood ready, even begging for the opportunity to sit with the baby.

The church funeral preparations with Pastor Phil turned out to be the easiest of all the chores to complete.

"Henry, I'll contact the funeral home and we'll see to it that everything is taken care of." Pastor Phil slowly took Henry and Kate through everything they had to know step by step.

"I'll need a list of the pallbearers, of course. When can you furnish that for me?" he inquired.

"Well, let's see," Henry said as he looked to Kate for help.

"Henry, how about Sid?" she asked.

"Without a doubt," he said nodding his head.

"Sid?" asked Pastor Phil.

"A good friend of Emma and neighbor," Kate expressed to him.

"I see."

"What about Doc, do you think he would?" Henry asked.

"I know it would be an honor for him. Please put his name down, Pastor," she said.

"And I know two others we can ask," Henry said, "and I know Emma would like them," a small smile indicated on his face.

"Who would they be?" she asked.

"Joe and Jake Watson. We've shared Thanksgiving with them the last few years. She told me how much they both meant to her, especially Jake. She loved hearing about his schooling, just lots of different things going on in his life."

"Those two would be a very good choice if I do say so myself, " Pastor Phil commented.

"And for the last two, would you care if we asked Greg and his good friend Dan?" Henry asked Kate.

Kate nodded her head in approval.

"So that should just about do it," Pastor Phil stated nodding his head.

"I think those people would do Emma's heart good if she heard that list of individuals," she said.

"Pastor Phil," Henry asked, "can I please name a couple of honorary pallbearers also?"

"We can do whatever your wishes are."

"Would you please list Jackie, Sid's wife and Ruth as honorary pallbearers?"

"You mean Ruth from our church here?" he asked, somewhat surprised by Henry's request.

"Yes, that's her. Emma was quite taken by her at the Christmas Program a few years ago and I think Emma would like her name mentioned in an honorary way. Every year since Emma attended her first Christmas Program, she's requested me to take a large package of fruitcake to Ruth. She shares it with the women that work with her in the kitchen when they're needed. Is that okay with you?"

"I would be more than happy to add those two names to your list. I know they both will be honored."

"Good," Henry said.

"Is there anything special you would like me to mention about her, anything you feel you want expressed?"

"I'm in the process of writing some ideas down for you, Pastor, and I'll get them to you very shortly."

"Okay. Now is there anything else you can think of, either one of you?"

Kate watched as Henry took a deep breath, knowing what was coming. She also knew in her heart what Henry wanted to do was probably out of his grasp to accomplish.

"Pastor, sometime ago Emma requested me to do something for her, and frankly I don't know if I can do it."

"What was her request of you?" he asked.

"She asked me to sing the song, 'Danny Boy' at her funeral, but I just don't know if I can handle the pressure of doing it... if I'm even strong enough to attempt it."

"I see. Why don't you let me worry about that part. I know it sounds at odds with what you've been asked to do, but just simply let me worry about it. You have enough to keep your mind occupied with."

"I don't understand, Pastor."

"Well, we'll cross that bridge when we come to it; okay?"

"Whatever you say. I have the background music to the song, at least that part is taken care of. I'll see that you get it right away."

"Good. Now, I'll give you a call when and if I have any more questions of either of you. Perhaps you can give me a call tomorrow; okay, Kate?"

" I will," she said.

"I'll wait for your call. Now, I'll see you both tomorrow."

"Thank you, Pastor."

"By the way, where is your new little one?"

"Being watched for by a lot of wonderful and helpful women," Kate said smiling slightly.

"And I'll bet I know most of them," Pastor Phil said.

"You're probably right," Kate said nodding her head.

Henry was amazed with how much help everyone was for him and Kate. The women saw to almost everything from hot meals from the oven, changing diapers, putting the baby down for her nap, everything that is except for feeding the baby. That was accomplished by Kate behind a closed door.

"Kate," inquired Jackie, "would you have any objection to Edith and me taking care of the baby while you're with Henry at the funeral home?"

"I was wondering what I was going to do during that time. I don't want the baby out anymore than I have to."

"So it's settled," Edith said.

"And I'm just across the street if I'm needed for anything else," Jackie added.

"Thank you both," Kate replied.

As Kate and Henry sat together eating dinner, it was apparent to both of them that their hardest task was still before them. That burden alone was one neither of them felt comfortable doing, their time at the funeral home. Henry dreaded the fact of having to look at Emma in a casket. In his thoughts Henry could hear the voices of people saying how wonderful she looked under the circumstances, how natural she appears, almost as if she was sleeping. He shook his head as those thoughts played back and forth in his mind.

Miracle in Song

The morning sunrise beckoned to be answered to all who lay in their beds desiring a few more seconds of darkness to enjoy. However, the light was strong and intrusive to their eyelids. People began to stir to the calls of another day.

Henry lay in bed on his back with Kate nestled closely to him. He placed his free arm across his face attempting to hide the light from his eyes.

"Are you awake, Honey?" she asked him as she began to move slightly.

"Yes," he stated. "I know we're supposed to be at the funeral home a few minutes before one o'clock, but I just wish we didn't have to go."

Kate moved a little closer to Henry giving him an assuring kiss on his cheek. Henry smiled as he turned his face towards her.

"In my life there really hasn't been many good days to remember, to cherish. I can count them all on one hand."

"Oh, there's more than just that I'm sure," Kate argued.

"Well, the day I met Sam and Emma, that's two. Of course, the day I met and fell in love with you, that's another one."

"Well, you're up to three, keep going."

"The day I learned who I was, that was a very special one for me as well."

"That's four."

Now Henry was at a loss, he couldn't mention any more. His silence grew as he attempted to come up with more suggestions. Finally it was Kate who could no longer deal with the silence that surrounded them.

"What about the day you and I started doing our bathroom project together, I hold that day close to my heart. And getting the baby grand, doesn't that count? Henry, let's not forget the times you spent enjoying Emma's hot tea and her company. I can go on and on, and I think I will, you need to hear them, especially now. You have a lot of wonderful memories in your life, you just have to recognize them. Remember telling me about how you sang to Emma on the porch, how much she cherished that. Kate's voice became a little louder with each thought. What about the day you sang to me in the restaurant, I loved that day, it meant everything to me. You have a lot to be happy about in your life, and don't you forget it."

"And that's what I love so much about you, Honey," he said as he pulled her closer to him. "Kate I don't know how I would have ever dealt with all of this without you. I love you so much."

Kate smiled as she gently squeezed his hand.

"And Honey," Kate continued, "neither one of us mentioned the most important thing of all, Emma Elizabeth."

"I think we were too busy looking for things that weren't obvious to us, that's why we didn't mention her."

The sound of a small baby fussing alerted both of them to her presence. Kate reached up to Henry and kissed him on the lips.

"I better take care of number one in our lives now," she said to Henry who was already in the process of getting out of bed and going over to the crib.

"Let me take care of her, Kate," a small smile reflected on his lips.

Kate smiled as she watched Henry reach into the crib and pick the baby up. He slowly swayed back and forth as he began to softly sing a lullaby to little Emma Elizabeth. Within seconds the baby was back sleeping. Henry gave the baby a gentle kiss and placed her back into the crib.

The morning flew by as if it was in a rush to go somewhere. Edith and Jackie arrived early, wanting to be sure everything that needed to be done was taken care of. As the two women entered the home Kate smiled at the fact that both of them carried cooked meals that were ready to eat.

"If it's okay with you, Kate and I will eat a little early since we have to get to the funeral home, and still get dressed," Henry said.

"We can all eat together, I'm a little hungry anyway," Edith said.

"So which meal would you like?" Jackie asked.

"I don't know. Kate, do you have a preference?" Henry said.

"I'll tell you what, let's flip a coin," Kate suggested, "heads I win, tails you lose."

"Funny," Jackie stated.

Once the decision was made, the four of them sat down and enjoyed the home cooked meal together. Kate took a quick shower, then Henry. After getting dressed they both returned to the living room.

"You two look very nice," Edith expressed. "I don't believe I've ever seen you in a suit, Henry, other than at your wedding, of course."

Henry didn't respond, he just nodded his head.

This being the only suit he owned, it had always been tucked in the back corner of the closet wrapped in a plastic bag from the last cleaning. It was always ready, but seldom used. That was the way Henry preferred it to be.

"Your outfit is lovely," Jackie stated as she looked over at Kate.

"Yes, you do look very nice," Edith chimed in.

"Henry, Kate, you know both of you are in our prayers today," Edith stated.

"Thank you," Kate and Henry said in unison.

Together the couple exited the house and walked slowly out to where the car was parked. Henry opened the door for Kate. As he walked around the back of the automobile, he took a deep breath, his eyes slightly showing a watery glaze. Henry knew he would not be able to control them whatsoever on this day. After starting the car, the couple headed towards the funeral home.

Neither one spoke during the short trip, both having many thoughts running through their minds as they rode together. Henry pulled into a parking spot. After he turned the car off, Kate reached over and took his hand in hers. She gently squeezed it and then let it go. They looked at each other, but said nothing. Even though their voices were silent, much was said to the other.

They walked up the sidewalk to the funeral home. Henry took the handle to the front door in his hand. He took in a deep breath as he pulled it open and entered with Kate's hand holding his tightly in hers.

The funeral director was waiting just inside the door, expecting their arrival.

"This way, Mr. and Mrs. Morgan."

Henry and Kate were led down a hallway lit by brass light fixtures on the walls. Just outside of the door leading to Emma's viewing room the funeral director stopped.

"We have a guest book placed here on the podium for anyone who wishes to sign their names. We will also keep track of any memorial funds that are received. Who would you like those to go to?"

"The church," was all Henry said.

The director nodded his head.

"Right this way."

Stepping through an open doorway Henry and Kate saw Emma, the shell of her body lying in the casket they had selected for her. Henry froze just inside the doorway, unable to make his body take the next step into the room. After some time, he finally stepped forward. The director stood back as the couple went further into the room. Henry could feel himself whelming up inside. The pressure behind his eyes grew stronger with each step he took. Kate was experiencing the very same reaction.

On top of the lower half of the casket a huge red rose blanket with greenery spaced between the flowers had been placed. Its beauty draped over the edge of the casket. A long white ribbon was fed through the flowers. In gold lettering on the ribbon was the word, "Mother." Henry turned his head away momentarily, his eyes very watery.

It was then that Henry realized the fragrance of fresh flowers encompassed the room. The sweet nectar seemed to emanate from all around him. Henry felt as though he were standing in the middle of a garden. The floral scents were rich and full. As he lifted his head he slowly looked around. He was amazed to see the room completely filled with various floral arrangements. He hadn't noticed that fact at all, his mind so distracted from seeing Emma. Some of the bouquets were enormous in size, others simple and delightful to view. There were plants and flowers of various descriptions placed throughout the room.

On each side of the casket stood large matching red roses, and white carnation bouquets. Even they were something Henry had not noticed. Both were simply beautiful. He walked over to one of them. The card read, "Our deepest sympathy to both of you. Love, Susan and Kenneth." Henry wiped his eyes as he next stepped over to the duplicate bouquet to read its card as well. "Our thoughts and prayers are with you both. With all our Love for Emma, Greg and Melissa."

"Aren't they just beautiful?" Kate said in a soft voice as she placed her hand under his arm. Henry nodded his head as he bit down somewhat on his lower lip.

To its immediate side, perhaps two dozen red roses showed themselves well in both beauty and aroma. The card was simply signed, "We will miss her so much, Jackie and Mr. Fruitcake." Henry smiled to himself as he read Emma's nickname for Sid on the card. A large floral arrangement by a wall was from Frank and Edith, it's beauty holding its own among the others. It was made of pink carnations and pink roses with a sprinkling of baby's breath tying it all together. Henry and Kate slowly walked around looking at the different flowers, reading the cards as they did. The two would look at each other and smile slightly to the other.

Dan and Kim sent an arrangement along with both sets of their parents. A large stunning array of pastel flowers was the next bouquet that caught the couple's eyes. It was truly unique. The card read, "Your Loving Neighbors." Both were astounded at the number of people that sent flowers in Emma's honor. Even Pastor Phil and Marsha were represented by a fragrant bouquet on an end table. A six inch silver cross was part and parcel of it. It was elegant, to say the least.

A very large free standing floral heart arrangement in lavender and white roses, along with numerous carnations filled a corner area. On the side of it a card was attached. It read, "We share in your tears." Below that was written, "Emma, please! Say hello to Paul for us. Love, Doc and Jean."

Over on a small table a single rose with baby's breath sat doing what it could to stand out among the rest. Henry bent over slightly and looked at the card. Its words were simple and to the point. Its message, "I will miss you greatly, Love, Ruth" Henry reached up wiping his eyes once again. Kate put her arm on his shoulder, indicating she was there for him, that she felt his sorrow as well. She gave him a half-hearted smile as tears ran down her cheeks. He looked at her through his heavy damp eyes, glad she was there, needing her to be there with him. Together they simply shared in each other's grief.

As if acting as one, they walked over to a couch at the side of the room. Henry sat down. He placed his head in his hands as he began to weep softly. Kate sat down beside him, putting her arm over her husband's shoulder. Kate sat quietly as she gave him the time he needed to embrace the loss of his mother, to comprehend the emptiness his heart held for her.

After a short period of time the funeral director walked up to them.

"Is there anything that you need adjusted, anything you wish changed or moved, flowers, anything at all? I can give you more time if you wish it."

There was a small pause. The director watched as Kate took her wedding ring and began to roll it around her finger.

"Kate, can you please see to Emma?" Henry asked.

Kate nodded her head knowing it would be easier on her than for Henry to accomplish this task, even though her heart wasn't in it.

"I will," she replied.

Kate stood up and walked over to the casket and looked down at Emma. She wanted to see if any hair was out of place, anything that should be adjusted. Kate looked at the dress that had been selected for Emma to wear. Their selection was very appropriate and tasteful in style.

"Of course," the director stated, "the pearl necklace, the broach, her watch and wedding band will be removed and held for the family."

Kate simply nodded.

"I think everything is satisfactory," she said as she gently nodded her head again.

"Okay. If there's anything at all in addition you need, please feel free to ask us."

"Thank you," Kate replied as she turned and looked over at Henry. She returned to her husband's side to comfort him, to be comforted by him as well.

It wasn't very long after that when people began showing up to pay their respects. It came as no surprise at all to Kate or Henry when the first people in attendance were Susan, Kenneth, Greg and Melissa. That fact alone helped them both to make it through the rest of the afternoon, let alone the evening visitation. Kate and Melissa held each other for a long time, no words being spoken. The voice of their shared tears spoke everything that needed to be said between them.

During the course of the evening, as the couple sat visiting with the numerous people attending, Henry turned to see Sid standing at the doorway of the room. He stood there for quite some time, as if an invisible curtain prevented his movement into the room. Henry knew that feeling well, he had experienced it not so very long ago.

"Kate," was all Henry said as she looked up and saw Sid still standing at the doorway.

Together they walked over to him. Henry and Sid hugged, holding one another tightly as they shared in silent tears running down both of their cheeks. Kate stepped closer to the men as they placed their arms around her. Sid sobbed heavily as Kate and Henry attempted to comfort him. Henry knew deep in his soul that Sid loved Emma dearly, but still was surprised at the amount of heartache he openly demonstrated to them over Emma's death.

With the funeral visiting hours at last completed, the next step being the funeral the following day, Kate and Henry felt somewhat relieved. Now that everyone was gone, Henry walked over to the casket with Kate. She took his hand in hers as he gazed down at his mother. Henry placed his other hand on Emma's hand.

"I love you, Mom, and I always will," he uttered as he reached over and placed a kiss on her forehead. A single tear fell from the corner of his eye, landing on Emma's cheek. Henry reached over and delicately rubbed it slowly away with his thumb. "I'll miss you so very much, Mom," he said.

"She knows that," Kate said to him as she softly squeezed his hand.

Henry nodded his head, his eyes filled once again with tear-filled memories he held deeply for her.

The next day was the funeral. It was a beautiful day for a funeral, if any day for a funeral can be called beautiful.

As people were being seated in the church a folded card was handed to each one of the people in attendance. The front of the card had a drawing of lilies depicted on it. On the inside was a separate unattached sheet of paper. The card's inside listed Emma's name, date of birth, and the words, "In Loving Memory." A small scripture phrase was quoted on one side of the card.

Pastor Phil stepped behind the podium as Emma's casket was wheeled down the center aisle of the church. Following immediately behind the pallbearers and casket were two additional members, Jackie and Ruth. Henry and Kate, who had followed behind them took their seats in a pew. The pallbearers then turned the casket sideways, their escort completed for now. They took their seats in the front row.

Pastor Phil cleared his throat slightly as he placed a sheet of paper on the podium in front of him.

"For everyone of us life is a roadway, some very short in distance, others well traveled with many years of memories. There are, of course, days that are good, and some that are not so well appreciated. What we choose to do with those days is what makes us what we are. Emma chose to share with others.

It was during the Christmas season last year when I had an occasion to meet with Emma in her home. She had called the church and asked if I could stop by with my wife for a few moments during the day, which we did... per her request. She welcomed us into her home offering us some hot tea, and a piece of fruitcake. I will say the fruitcake was wonderful, in fact, the best I've ever tasted."

Sid nodded his head as well as others in attendance.

"I asked her what I could do for her. She stood up and indicated for me to go with her. We walked a few steps over to a Christmas tree in her front room. Emma reached up and took down an ornament in the shape of a silver cross and handed it to me. Without saying anything to either one of us she next reached over on the other side of the tree and removed another ornament, this one in the shape and colors of a rainbow. Emma then handed it to me also. Both of these ornaments were glass blown and very much antique in nature. I didn't say anything, just looked over in my wife's direction. I could tell by her expression she was wondering what was going on as well.

Lastly Emma retrieved another hand blown ornament with her hand, a red one, though at that time I couldn't tell what it was. She requested my wife to go over to the counter and take a few pieces of tissue from the top of it.

I remember so well that day as she explained her motives, and why she did what she had done. She expressed to us that the cross represented the life my wife and I chose to pursue together. The rainbow, however, was to represent what we were trying to help people achieve, heaven. It was obvious to both of us Emma had thoroughly thought this over. It was not something done on a whim or the spur of the moment.

Lastly, she presented my wife with the remaining ornament. It was then that I could see what it was. It was two hearts melted together as one. My wife, Marsha, smiled as she took it in her hand from Emma. We both knew what it meant, that our love should always be as one, together forever.

I've had many stories conveyed to me about different Christmas ornaments being given to them by Emma. They speak of how much each and every one of these decorations have become a part of their lives. It is the stories they tell that is important. We will forever cherish Emma's gifts to us. Every year when we decorate our own tree, just as others do, Emma's hand will have reached out and touched every one of us again.

At this point I would like to read to you something which Henry has written about his mother. I should preface this by saying that Henry and Emma are not related whatsoever."

Many of the people sitting there were shocked to hear those words. They had either assumed they were mother and son, or just took it for granted. No one had ever questioned that fact after seeing the two of them interact together. They had never heard Henry refer to her by any other name than Emma or mother. Emma, of course, followed suit as she called him son on numerous occasions.

> "Emma, no son could ever be prouder than I am to have someone as wonderful as you to love and be loved by. I once told you, thank you for allowing me to be your son, and now under these very difficult and sad circumstances for me, I want everyone to know how much you've meant to me. You were the gift I received from heaven when I lost the most precious person in my life, Sam. You took the place of that missing person and gave me your love. You filled that void when I needed it the very most. You are, and will always be in my heart... my mother. Thank you for everything you've done for me. I will forever treasure the many happy times we spent together. I shall miss you with every passing day, and keep you in my thoughts always. Your loving son... Henry."

Pastor Phil placed the sheet of paper back onto the podium. He took a second to look at the people sitting before him.

"Emma has requested Henry... her son, to sing a certain song she loved at her funeral today. Henry."

Henry stood up and walked the few steps to the front of the church. As the background music began to play the introduction Henry felt a tightness growing in his throat. Tears ran down his cheeks. He began to sing the song, yet only three words were able to find their way from his vocal cords to his lips, "Oh, Danny Boy." His voice seemed to completely collapse, the words gone from his vocal cords. Tears rushed down his cheeks even more, he began to sob. He couldn't stop. Henry was unable to continue at all. Kate stood up quickly going to her husband's side. She placed her arms around him, attempting to comfort him. Both of them held each other tightly. Perhaps it was because Henry had such a strong singing voice to begin with, but the anguish in his tears could be heard by all as he wept loudly.

Melissa turned her head away from the scene before her, unable to watch as she sat there. She looked over at her mother and dad, at a woman sitting close to them. Their eyes were filled with dampness as well. Kenneth simply moved his head back and forth slowly as if sharing in the torment Kate and Henry were suffering through. She looked down at the paper before her, the words to the song reflected on the sheet that was given to everyone. It was from deep within her very soul she found the courage to do what she felt needed to be done. Melissa began to softly sing the words as she followed them from the paper in her hands. Greg quickly joined in with her as they began singing together. Within seconds other voices joined them as they followed the couples' lead. The singing of the audience grew louder and louder within the span of but a few bars of music being played. As Kate held onto Henry, they seemed to find the fortitude within themselves as they joined in softy singing the words through their tears. Once the song was completed Henry and Kate, hand-in-hand slowly returned to their seats.

"Henry," Pastor Phil stated, "Emma's request of you has been fulfilled. She wanted you to sing that song today, though she didn't say you had to do it alone."

Henry smiled slightly as he looked up at the pastor. He thought to himself, now I understand why the pastor told me not to worry about the song being sung. Pastor Phil knew of the difficulty I would face in having to accomplish that task, and he took safeguards to see to it that everything worked out for both Emma and me. Putting the words to the song in the cards was just simply, "an in case insurance policy" for my benefit.

With the funeral service completed and Emma's casket safely placed next to her husband, Paul, the people returned to the gymnasium of the church to share in a meal together. It was, of course, an opportunity to express their thoughts and memories of Emma with one another.

As Kate and Melissa sat together at a table with their husbands, Edith walked in carrying Emma Elizabeth in her arms. Jackie was by her side. She handed the child to Kate.

"She's so beautiful," Melissa stated.

Hearing what Melissa had just said, Henry smiled as he said, "That's because she doesn't carry her father's scar."

"Oh, Henry, really," Kate said smiling as she began to rock the baby in her arms.

With the infant's arrival the women in the room clustered around her, drawn like a piece of matter to a black hole in outer space, unable to resist the child's magnetic pull.

Melissa and Greg got up and walked over to another table and sat down. Pastor Phil walked up to them with a cup of coffee in his hand.

"I'm so glad you started singing, Melissa," Pastor Phil stated, "otherwise I would have had to, and you know what my singing voice is like."

"That's why I started singing," Melissa jokingly said, "I've heard your voice before."

Together they laughed.

"You know, the fact you put that sheet of paper in the cards was a thing of genius on your part," Greg commented.

"I sometimes have those moments, but not nearly enough unfortunately," Pastor Phil declared with a smile.

"Just the same, it was a good idea."

"I knew what Henry would be going through, and even if he would have gotten every word out, the people could still follow the words along with him. I will say this, Melissa, you were the last person there that I thought would have done what you did. When you started singing, I thought it was a miracle. I know how hard that had to be for you, and under the circumstances. Thank you, Melissa."

Melissa smiled as well as Greg. He was very proud of his wife for what she had done, what she had accomplished for her close friends.

"Well, Pastor, my husband has helped me tremendously along that line lately, of me coming out of my shell so to speak."

"And I think he found a pearl within that shell," Pastor Phil said with a smile.

"Hello, Pastor," vocalized Joe.

"Hello."

"Pastor," Joe's son, Jake, stated with a nod of the head as he walked up behind his father.

"Well," Joe said, "I don't know how you do it, Pastor, week after week, funerals, weddings, hospital visits."

"And what about me?" questioned Pastor Phil's wife, Marsha. "Who do you think does all the background work?"

"Oh, doesn't that just happen by itself?" Joe joked.

"No, and even I'm smart enough not to joke about that," Pastor Phil acknowledged.

"You do a wonderful job of it," Joe said nodding his head. "Well, I better get over to see Henry. I saw Stella over with him by the food table."

"Stella brought some food for today's offering to the family?" Pastor Phil quickly inquired.

Joe nodded his head.

"Honey, you can stay here and visit, that's fine with me, but I'm not going to miss out on one of Stella's delicious offerings." Pastor Phil turned and quickly walked over in the direction of the food.

"Now there's a smart man," Joe said smiling as he watched the pastor heading to the food table.

"Hello," Richard stated as he walked up.

"I've seen you at your restaurant," Joe said, "but I haven't been formally introduced to you. My name is Joe Watson, this is my son, Jake, and this lovely lady is Pastor Phil's wife, Marsha."

"How do you do. I'm Richard, Henry's partner so to speak. He sings at my — our restaurant quite a bit, as you probably all know."

"So how is it going for you two?" Joe asked.

"Better than I could have ever imagined. We've got a large group of patrons who come in from out of town to sit and enjoy Henry's singing. It's all coming together for us. I think the thing I find somewhat humorous is when Henry is singing, and I don't mean when he's performing a show, but younger people are coming in to see him. I think they just enjoy the different music he has to offer them, and being able to dance to slow easy music."

"Well, good for you and Henry," Joe stated.

"You want to know something you'll find hard to believe?" Richard stated.

"And what would that be?" Joe inquired.

"Henry and I work strictly on a handshake, there's no paperwork between us. Can you believe that?"

Joe started laughing.

"I don't understand, why do you find that so funny?"

"Because that's how Henry's has always done business. A handshake with Henry is better than any paperwork that's signed, he's that honest."

The sound of a baby fussing, beginning to cry loudly could be heard over by where Susan, Edith, Jackie and Kate were sitting at a table.

"Would you like to see what I refer to as a little miracle in love?" smiled Kate.

The women looked at Kate, all confused with her statement.

Henry left his position by the food table and immediately walked over to Kate. He didn't say a word as he picked up Emma Elizabeth. He gently rocked her back and forth as he began softly singing a lullaby. Everyone stopped what they were doing and watched. Within a short moment his soothing voice placed the child asleep. When he finished the song it was one of the rare times Henry's singing did not bring forth the sound of applause to his ears. He bent down and gently returned the baby to Kate. He smiled at the two and then walked back to the table he had just left.

"If I hadn't seen that for myself with my own eyes I wouldn't have believed it," Edith said.

"Did you see how fast your baby fell asleep?" Susan asked.

"I think that's about the fifth time Henry's done that," Kate expressed as she nodded her head. "She always falls right to sleep, and sleeps for quite a while. These two have definitely forged a bond already. Every time Henry does it I call it, 'Emma Elizabeth's Miracle.' I know that's kind of silly to say, but I like saying it just the same."

The women's faces reflected their agreement with Kate's words.

"Emma Elizabeth?" a woman standing nearby said. "I understand the Emma part, but who is Elizabeth if I may ask?"

"Elizabeth was my mother. Henry and I named our little girl after our mothers."

"How wonderful," the woman said.

"Henry," Richard said as he walked up to him.

"Thanks for coming, Richard, we both appreciate you being here for us."

"I wouldn't feel right if I had missed the opportunity to let you both know how... how..."

"Thank you, Richard, I know what you mean."

Richard nodded his head.

"I know this isn't the time or place to bring this up, but I'm going to anyway. When I get back to the restaurant I want to make a few calls, but before I do that I need your input. You see, I saw what just happened with you and the baby. I want to set up a meeting with my friend at the recording studio and do a CD of baby lullabies."

"Great, I love it!"

"Boy, you're excited," Richard said, somewhat taken back by Henry's immediate enthusiasm for his idea.

"Stop and think about it, Richard. If I'm not home Kate can simply play a CD of my singing for Emma Elizabeth. She'll fall right to sleep. I love it."

"Deal," smiled Richard as he held his hand out to Henry.

"Deal," Henry said as he took his hand and shook it.

"I guess that's another contract we've just signed," laughed Richard.

Henry nodded his head as he smiled.

The Bouquet

Melissa opened the door to her parent's home as she welcomed Frank and Edith in with a hug and kiss. She took their coats and hung them in the closet along with Greg's help.

"Another Sunday dinner, and I'm as hungry as usual," announced Frank as he made his way into the kitchen. "What smells so good?" came his next usual comment.

"Well," Susan stated, always enjoying Frank's comments about her cooking, "it's pork tenderloin, garlic mashed potatoes topped with mushrooms, and your favorite, green beans."

"Is that all," he laughed, "Is there anything else?"

"Frank!" Edith stated loudly.

"How about some homemade soup and rolls?" Susan answered.

"Hmmm, that sounds wonderful," Frank said.

"Edith, did you make a pie, I'm hoping?" Kenneth asked.

"Coconut Cream," she replied.

"Kenneth, you and I are very lucky men," Frank suggested.

"Because our wives are such great cooks and bakers?" Kenneth said.

"Not just that, they're both beautiful as well."

"Well, so is mine," Greg was quick to interject.

Everyone laughed.

As the families sat around the table visiting, Melissa would occasionally glance at the dining room clock. Greg found himself following her lead, looking at it as well. As everyone was finishing up with their desserts, the doorbell rang.

"I'll get it, I'll get it," Melissa said as she pushed her chair backwards. She then went to the front door quickly. Everyone thought this a bit odd, except for Greg. He sat there with an obvious smile on his face.

"Thank you, thank you so much," they heard her say.

Melissa didn't return for a couple of minutes. She stayed in the living room appearing to be doing something.

"Do you need some help with something?" inquired Susan.

"No, everything is alright," she answered from the other room. "Just stay there and visit."

Melissa shortly returned to the dining room carrying six boxes, each one 2x2 inches by about 14 inches long. A red ribbon was tied around each one of them. She placed them down on the dining room table.

"Greg," she stated.

Greg stood up from his seat and walked over to the kitchen counter. Reaching up over it he opened a kitchen cupboard door and took out a tall crystal vase. Susan knew he had to have hidden it there earlier since it was not in its customary position.

"You found my favorite hiding spot," Susan joked to Greg.

Greg walked over to the sink and filled it halfway with water. None of the parents said a word, they just watched as the mystery went on. They could see this was well thought out ahead of time, and they enjoyed watching each act play itself out. It's soap opera time, thought Edith with a smile.

Turning to her parents, Melissa spoke slowly.

"Mom, Dad," she stated, then turning to Frank and Edith, "Mom, Dad," she said once again, "Greg and I have something for each one of you."

"We're not going on a trip or something?" inquired Frank.

"No, Dad, not this time," Greg answered with a smile.

Melissa handed Greg a couple of the boxes as they both placed one in front of each parent.

"Please open them," she stated.

As the ribbons were untied and the boxes opened, the parents smiled. Each box contained a long stem red rose. Greg placed the vase in the middle of the table.

"Now, if you would each place your rose into the vase," Melissa instructed.

Each parent followed her instructions, smiling as they did; still wondering what this was all about. Once again Melissa looked at Greg, a large smile still lingering on his face.

"Each one of these roses represents the people in our lives we both love so very much." Melissa smiling, turned to her husband.

"Greg," she once again said.

Greg reached down and took the last two remaining boxes and handed one to Melissa while keeping one for himself.

Together they opened their boxes. Each box contained a single red rose. Once opened the couple placed their roses into the vase as well.

"And these two final roses represent us, both of us."

Melissa turned and went into the living room for just a moment. She returned carrying another white box, however, this one much larger in size. She placed it on the table between herself and Greg. Together they opened it. The young couple removed a large group of small white flowers. They carefully placed them into the vase, tucking them in and around the roses.

"And now our bouquet is complete," Melissa said with a smile.

Kenneth and Frank looked at each other in confusion.

"That's a pretty bouquet," Frank said nodding his head.

"It sure is," Kenneth agreed.

The women looked at each other. Nothing was said between the individuals for quite some time. Greg and Melissa simply smiled at each other, neither one offering any explanation for what they had just done.

"Susan!" exclaimed Edith.

"Oh, Melissa, can it be what we think?" Susan stated loudly.

Melissa nodded her head, yes.

Both women jumped to their feet, each mother excitedly grabbing one of the children in their arms and began laughing. They held them tightly, then switched and began embracing the other one.

The men looked at each other, their faces showing confusion as usual.

"I don't get it," Frank said.

"Oh, Frank!" was all Edith could say.

"Well, I don't get it either," Kenneth stated.

"It's the flowers, Frank," Edith said loudly.

"They're baby's breath," Susan said with watery eyes, "the flowers are baby's breath. Melissa is pregnant."

Now the men understood, and were thrilled. They were quickly to their feet, hugging and kissing their children. Frank placed a kiss on Greg's cheek as he hugged him even harder.

"Now that's a beautiful way to tell us such wonderful news, " Edith said.

"Yes," Susan added, "it was very thoughtful. I just didn't get it right away."

"And neither did I," Edith said smiling.

"In my day they simply said there was a bun in the oven," Frank observed.

"Oh, Frank, really!" Edith said.

"I think he's right," Kenneth said, "but I think Frank and I would much prefer to hear the news this way; right, Frank?"

"You're right, Grandpa," Frank said laughing.

"Grandpa," Kenneth said, "it has a nice sound to it."

Facing the Bills

It had been a short time since Henry had been contacted by Emma's lawyer to set up an appointment to go over the will. The last time he was at the attorney's office, he had dropped off the sealed will. He wasn't in any hurry to see the bills he knew were facing him, but just the same it had to be done. In his mind he tried to put the amount of the bills together for a total. He just couldn't seem to get the amounts to adhere together and form an answer. There were just too many unanswerable items, too many variables to reach a final conclusion.

Henry parked his old faithful vehicle in front of the lawyer's building. Together he and Kate made their way into the office.

"We have an appointment with Mr. Eddington for eleven o'clock."

"Yes, Mr. and Mrs. Morgan," the secretary stated. "It's nice to see both of you. Mr. Morgan, my mom and dad enjoy listening to you so much."

"Thank you."

"Mr. Morgan, I was sorry to hear about your mother."

Henry nodded his head.

"Come in, Henry, Kate," Mr. Eddington stated as he stood in the doorway to his private office.

"It's nice to see you, Eric," Henry responded, "I just wish it was under different circumstances."

"Me, too, Henry. I was so sorry to hear about Emma, please accept my condolences."

"Thank you."

"I've got everything ready for you. Why don't you both come in and have a seat."

As the lawyer closed the door behind him, Henry looked over at Kate, she at him. Eric walked around his desk taking his seat. The couple took a couple of seats in front of his desk.

Both Henry and Kate took a deep breath as they watched him pick up some paperwork and begin looking it over. His glasses rested on the top of his brow at his hairline. Reaching up he pulled them down into position.

"First off, Emma left some bills, medical bills, and those are the first things that need to be addressed in her estate."

"I understand," Henry stated, as he took another deep breath and then swallowed.

The sight of Kate's hand moving slowly caught his attention, though he didn't really look to see what she was doing. He turned his attention back to Eric.

"Emma has instructed that any bills be taken out of your share in her estate. As far as any other bills, I don't really see anything of consequence other than the funeral."

Henry nodded his head.

"Can you tell me how much those medical bills are?" Henry inquired.

"From what I can see, they're somewhere in the amount of eighty-five hundred dollars. Emma apparently chose to make payments to the hospital on them, and was currently doing that from what I see. However, there will be additional ones with her last hospital stay."

"I understand."

Once again Henry could see Kate fidgeting with her hand nervously. He watched as she rolled her wedding ring around and around with her other hand.

"Emma's house has been left to a Mr. and Mrs. Sidney Jackson along with the contents. You are, however, allowed to take anything from it before it is finally turned over to them.

She has asked that Sid, however, be given the old Christmas bulbs under the condition that he continue helping them to find good homes filled with memories. Will that be a problem in anyway?"

"No, they're wonderful people," Henry answered in a whisper.

Kate nodded her head in agreement.

"Oh, I forgot, there is the funeral bill. No, I mentioned that already. That, of course, will be added together with the medical bills. To help offset the bills, you will receive a certain sum for acting as the administrator of her will."

Kate looked over at Henry who appeared to be completely dazed by what was transpiring before him. He was there, but with an absent mind in attendance. Kate began to cry softly.

"I'll, of course, take care of any of Emma's bills, medical, funeral, anything," Henry stated, as he looked down at the floor.

"No, you won't," Kate stated, "we will together."

Kate then reached down to her wedding ring and rolled it around on her finger. She thought to herself, maybe it's time to sell this ring and get that gold band from Henry.

"Mr. Eddington," Kate said with her voice very much shaky, "will you take this… please?" She held out her hand to him. He reached across the desk to her as she placed her wedding ring in his hand. "Would you sell this and put it towards the bills? I love it so much now, the memories it holds for me, but still there are priorities in life, just as there are in death."

"Oh, Kate" was all Eric could utter.

"Please."

Henry slowly shook his head back and forth, his eyes very watery. Kate's unselfish act meant the world to him, and he would be sure to express his thanks to Kate when they were finished.

Mr. Eddington placed the ring on the top of his desk. He turned his chair to a table behind him and retrieved a box of tissue. Kate reached out and took a few from the box as he offered it to her.

"Henry, Kate, it's customary to let me finish reading the will."

Kate and Henry both nodded their heads.

"As to my precious baby, Sophia, who has brought me so much joy, I leave her to Mr. and Mrs. Sidney Jackson. They have demonstrated a great love for her, and have cared for her when I needed that done."

Henry smiled slightly knowing how much his gift of Sophia had meant to Emma. He was happy she would be in a home filled with love for her.

"Emma left some money to Pastor Phil and his church as well, and also to Ruth and her ladies to be used as they see fit. You'll get a copy of the will and you can look that portion over if you wish. I just want now to get to the part that concerns you. As to the remainder of my estate, I leave it entirely to my son, Henry, and his wonderful wife, Kate."

"What does that mean exactly?" Henry inquired with a confused look on his face.

"Well, first things first." Eric reached over slightly and picked the ring up off of his desk where it rested. "Henry, will you take this ring and replace it on your wife's finger?"

Henry followed his instructions.

"Now that that's back where it belongs we can continue. Henry, in answer to your question, here's what it means. Any savings, bonds, time certificates, stocks, life insurance policies, that all reverts to you and Kate. You should understand that her husband, Paul, had a substantial paid up insurance policy on her, you being named the beneficiary. He also had a policy on himself that Emma received earlier. Emma placed his insurance money in the bank after Paul's death.

Not long after Emma had a short stay in the hospital, she came to visit me immediately after that. She requested me to put everything moneywise jointly between the two of you. Emma said she wanted her son and his wife to have something to remember her and Paul by. She loved both of you very much. I can still hear her voice from that day, 'And get it done right away. You don't want to hurt an old lady's feelings, do you?' I told her, 'no, I didn't.' 'Good,' she said. 'I'll check with you in a couple of days.' And she kept her word. Within a few days I received a phone call from her checking on my progress."

Eric chuckled slightly as well as Kate and Henry, his words bringing fond memories back to both of them.

"You know, I don't think I've ever moved so fast getting paperwork done or changed. She had quite a way of doing things. Emma surely was a wonderful woman."

Henry and Kate nodded their heads.

"Why wouldn't Emma just use the money to pay her bills off?" Henry asked.

"With older people, sometimes they want to make sure they have enough money to live on, and so they do payments, try to make it last. They'll look at weekly bills, monthly bills, not always the whole picture."

"Exactly what does this all mean?"

"Simply put, Henry, you and Kate, to the best of my judgment are worth approximately four million eight hundred and some odd dollars. I haven't been able to get it completely totaled up yet. I very well might be on the low side with some of these figures, but you and your wife are wealthy people as of now. Emma's husband, Paul, was a very wise and shrewd investor throughout the years. I wish I had purchased some of the stock at the prices he did. He bought stocks in companies that were just starting out, companies we've all heard about, and then he held onto the stock. His stocks split, and split, and split again. He took pennies and grew them into hundreds of thousands of dollars. I can only dream to have some of the stocks in my own portfolio for the prices he paid. Together they lived a happy and simple life. I don't think money was the main concern in their relationship. They were very happy together."

Henry looked at his wife and gave her a half-hearted smile. She reached over and took his hand in hers. They sat looking at each other, not saying a word. Yes, they understood what the money meant to them. There now was an opportunity to reach out and help certain needy individuals, some friends, get a few things they needed, too. It allowed them to obtain a larger home, one that would accommodate two pianos, perhaps one in the living room, another in an office or study. As far as getting a new car, Henry's heart wouldn't allow him to think along that line.

"Henry, we now have the money to fulfill our dream," Kate said as she squeezed his hand smiling.

"You two can pretty well do whatever you wish," Eric said.

"I suppose that's true," Henry answered with a broad smile.

"Both of you simply amaze me. I just don't understand how you can react this way, just sit there," Eric said as he looked at them shaking his head. "If someone told me I came into this much money, I'd be doing cartwheels down the street. Kate, you were even willing to give up your wedding ring a few minutes ago. I just don't understand it at all."

"Henry," Kate said as she looked over at him, "we both know we would have done it anyway, money or not, but this gives us the opportunity to make it easier to do. We've talked so much about doing it, let's do it for her... let's do it for all of us."

"And what would that be?" Eric asked.

"We want you to find someone for us, if at all possible, a little girl we love and make her a part of our family.

"But you just gave birth," Eric said nodding his head back and forth.

"Some families aren't complete until every piece is in place," Kate said. "We need to find the missing part in our lives."

"Where is she, who is she?"

"We don't know."

"This could be almost impossible. Do you know her last name?"

"That's where you come in," she continued. "You hire whoever you need to find her, and we need to start as soon as possible... please. We know her first name is Mary. She also has a burn mark on her cheek. Unfortunately both of her parents tragically died in a house fire."

"I'll be glad to do whatever I can for you two, but I'll need more than just Mary as a starting point. You've got to give me something to work with. I'll get on it as soon as I can but still..."

"You may want to start with my friend, Joe, over at the Second Chance store," Henry suggested. "He'll be able to give you some guidance or direction along that line."

"I'll be glad to do that for you two."

"Eric," Kate said, "just so you understand, we didn't know how much the medical bills and funeral bills would add up to. As far as the house going to Sid and his wife, we are both happy for them. They're wonderful people as I said. You see, before we came in here today we were simply hoping to break even, pay Emma's bills and leave without owing anymore than that. I thought we wouldn't have enough money to do that, that's why I gave you my wedding ring.

Our desire was for us to keep our status quo. We wanted our lives to stay as they are now, happy in everything we have and hold dear to each other. Henry enjoys singing, and with Richard as his partner, we're doing all right. That will not change at all. None of that is going to change, we'll both see to that.

Eric tilted his chair back as he placed his glasses back on to his forehead. He reached up and massaged his eyes.

"You know, Henry… Kate… I still can't get over the investments Paul pulled off. It's just… it's simply unbelievable, even mindboggling."

Henry took Kate's hand in his again as he looked in Eric's direction.

"I think I know what the best investment either one of them ever made was," Henry said, as he nodded his head slowly.

"And which one was that, Henry?" Eric asked.

"In each other."

Now everyone nodded their heads in agreement.

The End

In the second book of the series, the lives of Melissa and Greg are challenged. The young couple contemplate going down a road that offers them both enrichment, and a world opposite in nature to what they are accustomed to, It is a dilemma that faces not only them, but her parents as well.

Melissa and Kate learn first-hand what Henry had endured throughout his youth. Kate discovers why Henry won't ask for her hand in marriage, thus bringing Emma's dream to an end of a union between the two.

Many surprises are faced by both sets of parents which bring hidden treasures into their lives. Edith experiences something beyond her fondest dreams while Doc shares the greatest loss he ever suffered.

Made in the USA
Lexington, KY
16 August 2017